W9-AUD-094

THE
VOID

A WITCHING SAVANNAH NOVEL

J.D. HORN

47NORTH

The characters and events portrayed in this book are fictitious. Any similarity to real persons, living or dead, is coincidental and not intended by the author.

Text copyright © 2014 by J.D. Horn

All rights reserved.

Printed in the United States of America.

No part of this book may be reproduced, or stored in a retrieval system, or transmitted in any form or by any means, electronic, mechanical, photocopying, recording, or otherwise, without express written permission of the publisher.

Published by 47North, Seattle

www.apub.com

Amazon, the Amazon logo, and 47North are trademarks of Amazon.com, Inc., or its affiliates.

Cover illustration by Patrick Arrasmith

ISBN-13: 9781477825747
ISBN-10: 1477825746

Library of Congress Control Number: 2014908567

THE
VOID

A WITCHING SAVANNAH NOVEL

By J.D. Horn

Witching Savannah

The Line
The Source
The Void

To beautiful Savannah and the people who love her

THE
VOID

A WITCHING SAVANNAH NOVEL

ONE

"Newspaper says a road crew found another part of that poor woman out on Hutchinson Island." Claire grabbed a towel and a spray bottle from the bar and moved from one table to another, misting each with a cleaner that smelled of mint before wiping them like she meant to purge them of original sin. Magh Meall, the bar she owned along with Peter's father, Colin, would be opening soon for the evening. Claire's petite frame buzzed from one task to the next. Her tight dark curls bounced as she sped through her pre-opening routine. I noticed a few stands of silver had worked their way into those curls of late. I felt certain that the graying was due to the stress of losing Peadar, her true son, and the threat of losing Peter, the changeling she had raised as her own—the changeling I had married.

"I wish you'd let me help," I offered.

She responded by shaking her towel at me. "Sit." It was a command. "I got this." I had known Claire half my life, and I loved her with all my heart. I was proud to call her my mother-in-law. "They found a hand," she said, returning to the macabre report. "Didn't say which, but they are sure it's from the same body." Luckily I was past the stage of my pregnancy that would make the wholesome smell of the mint seem noxious. The image of a dismembered body was nearly enough to send me running to the ladies' room; two weeks ago the scent of the cleaner would have tipped the scales.

Claire didn't seem to take note of my discomfort. "Detective Cook and associates don't seem to be making much headway." She stopped mid-swipe and looked over her shoulder at me. "He hasn't shared any interesting tidbits with you?"

No, Adam hadn't shared anything with me. At least not intentionally. I had—without wanting to—picked up some images. Another wave of nausea threatened to whelm my resolve not to lose my lunch, and I fought to push it away. Outside of his screamingly nebulous impression of the woman's description—probably middle-aged, definitely Caucasian—a few of his stray thoughts had also registered, the most horrible one being even though parts of the body had been showing up over the Savannah area for nearly two weeks, each part was still absolutely fresh when found. That the parts showed no decay or evidence of refrigeration hadn't been made public knowledge. Still, it meant one of two things. Either the parts were being removed from a living woman. Or, whoever was behind the dismemberment knew a thing or two about magic. Regardless of which, Adam had been working surreptitiously with both Oliver and Iris to find this woman, another fact that had not found its way into Claire's paper, and I wasn't about to mention it.

Claire's voice went a half octave higher, coming out a bit softer. "Or maybe he's shared something with your uncle that's filtered through to you."

"Good lord, woman," Colin said, giving his wife a playful swat on the behind as he passed her. His short but wiry body danced away from the swat of her towel. She glared at him, but her mock anger quickly melted into a different kind of heat as she fixed her gaze on her husband. A smile passed between them.

"I tell you, Mercy, I don't understand this morbid fascination Claire has developed around this murder," Colin said to me. "It's the Celt in her, I'm sure of that." His black eyes sparkled.

"Oh, that's a fine thing coming from a Paddy such as yourself," she said taking another swipe at him with her towel. This one connected with a sharp thwack. "I have no fascination, morose or otherwise. I simply want to know that the nutter behind all this will be put safely away," she said, turning back to her work. "My heart goes out to this poor woman. No one deserves such a thing. I shudder to think that the choices she made, innocent or perilous, could lead to such a despicable end. Although I suppose even the little decisions you make can lead to disaster."

"September questions every choice, till October chills the air." Colin sang the words to a melody I did not recognize. "November swears the days grow not short, till dark December her lie lays bare."

"Don't make light of my feelings by quoting your maudlin poet."

"Ah, my love." The words came out in a warm timbre. "I'm not making light of your feelings, I'm trying to make your feelings light. Besides Mac an Fhailghigh is a fine poet," he said with a wink at me. "Although admittedly he does suffer somewhat in translation."

I could see the aura around Claire growing darker as she turned away and began cleaning another table. She had so many feelings, a knotted ball of hopes and fears, disappointments and angers, love and regret. I didn't read her thoughts as much as I read frustration at failing to find a way to express them. I could almost see her suppressing the emotions that had started to surface. "Which choices do you question?" I asked.

"I'm sorry, dear?" She looked up at me, pretending she hadn't understood my question as a way to buy herself more time.

"Which choices do you question?"

3

Her forehead creased and her jaw tightened, but only for a moment. She cast a guilty look at her husband.

"Go on, then," he said to her. "I'd be interested in hearing your answer too."

Claire licked her lips. "I have no regrets over choosing you, Mr. Tierney," she said trying to adopt a playful tone, but then she shook her head. "I wouldn't trade you for any other man, my love." An earnestness now filled her voice. "It's only sometimes I ask myself how our life might be different if we hadn't come to America."

"Coming to America was our dream," Colin said and raised his hands gesturing around the tavern as he turned. "*This* was our dream."

"Of course. And I feel blessed every day to be here with you. Sharing the life we have. I just worry. I worry about the forces that have found us, that have taken root in our lives." She turned quickly toward me. "I don't mean you, my girl. I mean . . . the others. I fear for all they can take from us." I knew when she said "us," I had been included in the pronoun.

My hand fell protectively to my stomach. I wasn't exactly sure who she meant by "the others." There were so many "others" now, so many who wanted to do my family and me harm. The worst of all of them was my own mother, Emily Rose Taylor. Every time I thought of her name, I saw it as it appeared engraved on the tombstone at Bonaventure. The marker still stood there, the name and dates unchanged, but now I knew the grave lay empty.

Claire was right. Emily had nearly taken Peter from us, and it remained still very much in her power to do so. She knew he wasn't human, that he was a Fae changeling. She also knew all it would take to steal him from us was to reveal this truth to him.

Unlike the child growing in me, Peter had no true footing in this world. The human child for whom he'd been exchanged had been returned to us. Sadly that return had come too late for a joyful reunion. Time moved at too great a differential between the world of the Fae and our own. The baby returned an elderly man; Claire and Colin's true son now lay buried in Laurel Grove Cemetery.

I didn't understand the reason for the exchange, but Claire and Colin's biological son had taken Peter's place in the world of the Fae, and Peter had taken that of the human child. The Fae who made the deal with Claire and Colin had warned them, the spell that bound him to our world was easily broken. Like waking from a dream, should Peter learn his true nature, the Fae spell would be undone. He'd have no choice but to return to his place of origin. Staying here would only drive him mad or kill him. And that was all the information she'd offered. Just a vague and useless warning. Not a single bit of advice we could use to protect him from learning the truth or fix the situation should the worst come to happen.

"The happiness we've built is so fragile," Claire said. "I love you, my girl, and you know I love the baby you are carrying, but I wonder. I wonder if we had stayed in Dublin . . . or if we'd left Savannah while Peter was still small." She looked at me. "Or if I hadn't been such a fool and invited that foul magician and his entourage into our lives—"

"No." I held up my hand to stop her. "I am convinced Emily knew long before you contacted Ryder. You were somehow led, maybe even spelled into doing so." It was Emily who had turned Ryder into a collector, a person who could steal someone's life force and convert it into magical energy. Emily's consort, Josef, who also happened to be my own half brother through my father, had followed Ryder into this very bar, looking for all the world like Ryder's devoted puppy. Later, Josef cut his master's throat, offering him and the demon Ryder had drawn into himself in order to power Emily's dark spell. At his end, Ryder was so high on drugs, I cannot say if he ever registered that he had been marked as a sacrifice all along.

Claire had asked me to take Peter's secret to my grave, but that cat was already long out of the bag by the time she'd asked. And I was certain the line's other anchors had also put two and two together, so Claire agreed it was best to bring my aunts and uncle into the know also. Aunt Iris had been researching tirelessly, trying to discover a loophole, a way to anchor my husband in this world, but witches had very little knowledge concerning Fae magic, and due to the recent conflict with the line's other anchors, sources that might have once been forthcoming to her veiled inquiries had dried up. The best solution we'd been able to improvise was Ellen's idea, so Uncle Oliver compelled Peter neither to hear nor see anything that might lead him to ascertain the truth about his link to the Fae. Still, we never spoke openly about the Fae.

Tucker Perry had financed Peter's dream of starting his own construction firm, but Peter's fledgling company hadn't stood a chance without Tucker's backing and connections, especially since Peter's pride made him incapable of accepting financial or magical aid from me. I still had trouble processing that my mother had arranged Tucker's murder for the sole purpose of bringing my Aunt Ellen pain. Another life Emily had ended, wasted, in the sole aim of stealing one more chance of happiness from her big sister.

And since Peter's old boss was not one to forgive Peter's attempt to become a competitor, there was no place for him on his old crew. So with our baby on the way, Peter had returned to working at Magh Meall, his parents' bar, full-time. Even after his dream died on the vine, Peter carried on, his warm and wonderful smile always on his lips. He remained optimistic, sure now that we were together everything else in life would sort itself out, provided he maintained a positive attitude and backed his outlook with enough sweat.

The mere thought of his smile brought one to my own face. "Somehow . . . and I don't know how," I said sliding myself off the barstool and crossing to Claire, "it will be okay. I promise."

I kissed her cheek, and she dropped the cloth she had been using on the table. She pulled me into her arms. "I'm holding you to that, my girl." Her lips arched up into a tremulous smile.

"I should be going," I said. I had dropped by the tavern hoping to see Peter before opening, but Claire had sent him out on errands, and I was due home. "Y'all need to finish getting ready to open, and I promised Aunt Iris I'd help her and Ellen do the shopping for Thanksgiving. This year we're pulling out all the stops, since Iris has someone *special* to impress."

"She still seeing that young lad of hers, then?" Colin called out from behind the bar.

I laughed. "She sure is, and I think it's turning serious." Sam was not a witch, and he was twenty years younger than my aunt. All the same, he was sincere and sweet and doted on her. He had been at her side practically since the night of Peadar's wake, when Oliver had spun Iris into his arms. Iris was totally besotted with her black-haired, blue-eyed, square-jawed beau. After she had wasted so many years married to Connor, I was thrilled to see her experience this exciting, new, and very much requited love with Sam.

"You're not worried about her?" Claire asked. "I mean, he isn't *like* you. These things usually don't last long between a normal person and a witch, do they?"

"Ah, my dear, don't be the dark cloud to one of our few silver linings." Colin leaned against the bar.

"A *regular* person and a witch," I corrected her, flashing back to a similar conversation I'd had with my Aunt Ellen a few months, no, a lifetime ago. I smiled at Claire to let her know I wasn't really offended. "And you are right. Things like this usually don't even get started between a regular person and a witch. When they do, they don't usually endure." Something about a witch's otherworldliness usually prevented a regular person from forming a lasting liaison with her. Adam and Oliver were one of the few exceptions I knew of, and the only reason their relationship didn't suffer was because Oliver had long ago compelled Adam not to sense the oddness that might have otherwise driven the two apart. "Sam had a motorcycle accident a few years back. He was wearing a helmet, but his head still got smacked pretty hard. He lost his sense of smell, and it looks like the aversion most folk have to magic too."

"Keep Ellen away from him then. We don't want her patching up his snoot and breaking his heart at the same time," Colin said and chuckled. He'd meant it as a joke, but Ellen and I had already had a very serious conversation about that very possibility.

"I'll make sure she keeps clear of him," I said. "I'll see you all later."

Claire reached out to give my hand a slight squeeze. "I wish you'd wait till Peter gets back to drive you home. I don't like the idea of you traipsing around out there by yourself these days."

I smiled and held my hand up before her eyes, letting blue sparks of magic dance along my fingertips. "I can take care of myself."

"Yes, I guess you can at that." Her shoulders relaxed. I knew she saw my magic as a mixed blessing. A very large part of Claire wished she could have had a *normal* son who would have married a *normal* girl. Then there was the side of her that didn't give a damn about normal. "We love you. We really do," she said, and her eyes crinkled.

"And I really love you two too." I rubbed my stomach and winked at her. "We both do." Her fingers wiggled in the air as a true smile returned to her lips. She grasped my bulging stomach gently. "Good-bye, my little love." She leaned in and pecked my cheek then released me.

I went to the door and pushed back the deadbolt. I turned back, my eyes suddenly hungry for one more look at them. I raised my hand and gave them a slight wave.

"Our best to Iris," Colin called out as I let the door close behind me.

- — -

Savannah was enjoying an unseasonably warm stretch this autumn; the thermometer had even hit eighty degrees. The air from the river was cooling things off a bit now. Still, the late afternoon was beautiful. Even though I was enjoying the walk, I realized how much I missed my faithful bike, the same beat-up old thing I'd been riding since I'd turned twelve. I missed the woven basket and the jammed and worthless warning bell. I'd stored the bike away a couple months ago, once I had grown too ponderous to ride.

I was only now coming to the end of my second trimester, but I was as big as if the pregnancy had already reached full term. I patted my precocious bump. "Mama's gonna buy you a bike trailer, little man," I said to my baby, my little Colin, dreaming of taking him on long rides, giving him his first views of his hometown, beautiful Savannah.

It worried me when I first began to balloon that there might be something wrong, but Ellen assured me that she sensed the baby's development was coming along fine, if a tad more quickly than anyone might have expected. "Little Colin seems to be perfectly healthy, but he is part witch and part fairy," Ellen had reminded me. "We have no reason to believe the pregnancy will unfold along a human timeline."

Thinking of Ellen, I realized it was nearing time for her to close up Taylor's, her new, albeit unimaginatively named, flower shop, so I decided to drop by and see if she'd like to walk home together. It was true I could take care of myself. My newfound magic was strong, and I was mastering it. Quickly. All the same, the reminder in the news that there was a person out there capable of dismembering a woman creeped me out. I wanted the company. I was a bit surprised to see the lights had already been turned off and the closed sign placed in the window. Another handwritten sign—"Yes, We Have Mistletoe"—caught my eye. The announcement struck me as less of a commercial message and more an admission of defeat. My aunt detested the parasitic plant whose pagan roots were deep enough to allow it to bloom into the Christmas season.

With a little reflection, I recollected why this would be so. When the Norse sun god Baldur's mother, Frigg, dreamed of his death, she extracted a vow from every hurtful thing in the world not to harm her son. She overlooked the seemingly innocent mistletoe. I guess it struck too close to home for Ellen. A woman who had all the magic in the world at her command, but who still failed to protect her son. "You do your best to protect the ones you love," I'd once heard her say to Aunt Iris. "You weave spells to ward off the supernatural and dress them against the weather, but still there is always the one event you couldn't have anticipated, the one person you never suspected would or even could do harm." I knew the thought of having to peddle the detested plant for a full month sent Ellen into a total funk and led her to close shop early. I touched the glass and hoped she'd have a better day tomorrow.

A movement near my reflection caught my eye. A child's laugh. High. Crystalline. I spun around to find an impossible sight, an all-too-familiar little boy with deep-blue eyes and blond curls. Wren, the demonic being who had made itself at home with my family for decades, hovered in the air mere feet before me. Wren, the creature my sister had fed with her magic, until he had grown capable of projecting a second and more complex identity. I'd known this version of the entity as Jackson, and I had very nearly given him my heart. The last time I had seen him, he had

10

held a knife to that heart, ready to destroy me so that he could free his brethren from their world of eternal shadow. I had believed him to be gone, blasted from our world by the power of the line. But here the little bastard was.

"Ellen's going to die, you know." He laughed again, the sound of icicles shattering as they fell to earth. "They all will. Ellen and Iris and Oliver and Peter and everyone you have ever loved. Then, when you are all alone, we will take you apart, piece by piece." My mind flashed on the dismembered body, as Wren glided within an arm's length of me.

"The line destroyed you. I saw it." I felt an iciness creep into my fingers as my pulse pounded in my neck. I raised a hand to ward him off.

"The line took much from me." His boyish tenor should have been incapable of carrying the pointed hatred that punctuated his words. A child's eyes should never be able to hold the rage this false child carried in him. "*You* have taken much from me, but I have friends who will help me get it all back and more."

The world began to spiral around us, images blending and blurring, spinning then slowing. We now stood in Troup Square, nearly a mile from where we'd started. The last glints of sunlight touched the armillary and set fire to the golden astrological symbols that adorn it. The sun's glow provided the demon child with an unmerited halo. I used my hand to block the excess light from my eyes. "Why did you bring me here?"

"Because we want you to remember. It's time for you to remember."

"Remember what?"

Wren's rosebud lips curved up into a wicked smile, then stained to an inky black. Within seconds, all color deserted his features. The demon's form stretched beyond the measure of its childlike disguise and lost all semblance of solidity. This demon was what the people of the low country call a "boo hag," and a boo hag was by nature a hungry shadow.

"The future," it said as it crawled up the armillary, looping the length of its elastic body around the base of tiny turtles and twining around the solstitial colure. I had once witnessed an encompassing darkness woven from these living shadows, but en masse they were indistinguishable one from another. I realized this amorphous shade was the manifestation of the entity's truest form, and I shuddered at the thought of my sister, Maisie, lying with it in its guise as Jackson, her limbs entwined with this vaporous abomination. Even worse, the impassioned kiss I myself had once shared with it.

The creature's nebulous form began convulsing; then what I reckoned to be its jaw came unhinged. Something like a watch fob spilled from its mouth and fell tangled among the points of the armillary's Polaris star. My stomach clenched as I recognized it as Connor's missing pendulum.

"Perhaps this will help your detective solve his puzzle," Wren's ever deepening and darkening voice rasped. Then the demon evaporated, leaving behind the flaccid chain.

TWO

Detective Adam Cook was not a happy man. He sat at our kitchen table without saying a word, tapping the bottom of his phone against the table's top. Finally he looked directly into my eyes. "I'm really starting to miss the days when you used to lie to me."

"You were given fair warning," I said as what remained of Abby's latest pie winked up seductively at me from its plate. As different as Abby, my self-proclaimed "white trash" cousin, was from my Aunt Ellen, their powers proved complementary. As Ellen could heal the body, Abby could aid the spirit, helping lead those who had lost themselves emotionally back to the light. Abby had given up everything, put her entire life on hold to come and help Maisie through her own homespun brand of magical cognitive behavioral therapy.

Food, especially baked goods, was to Abby as flowers were to Ellen. Abby's creations were the epitome of comfort food, indulgent and truly magical. The way my maternity jeans were pinching me told me I might have become a tad too reliant on Abby's form of comfort. I tugged at the elastic band and squirmed in my seat.

"You're beautiful," Peter had been telling me several times each day, somehow intuiting that my self-esteem had developed an inverse relationship to my weight. This morning I had rolled my eyes, and he pulled me into his clutches, tickling me. "Say 'I am beautiful.' Say it or I'll keep going." Laughing and nearly breathless, I finally gave in and said it. "That's right," he said and planted a wet kiss on my lips. I found myself smiling at the memory.

Adam was not smiling. He used his index finger gingerly to prod Connor's pendulum. "So this Wren demon, he said this was the key to solving my investigation?"

"He's a demon. Demons lie." Even as Iris spoke to Adam, she couldn't take her eyes off the fob and chain that had been her husband's constant companion, nearly an extension of his very personality. The mere mention of Connor's name could cause the joyous vigor to drain from Iris's face. Now the sight of his pendulum had caused her to look a decade older, despite the youthful new styling of her honey-blonde hair and her recent habit of borrowing my non-maternity clothes without asking first. Truth was, I enjoyed her enjoying them as much as I enjoyed her relationship with Sam. It was like she was catching up on all the years she had squandered on her departed husband.

She sat next to me, her arms pulled tightly around her sides. "I thought he was gone."

"I know. I thought Wren was gone too," I said.

"I meant Connor." Iris began to tremble. "I thought he was gone. Gone for good. I should have known it was too good to be true."

Oliver and I shared a guilty glance. I sighed and nodded.

Oliver leaned back in his chair and ran his fingers through his thick blond curls. "Listen, sis." Oliver paused as he screwed up his courage. He raised his eyebrows, and his lips puckered and shifted almost comically from side to side. His features relaxed, and he faced his sister. "Connor is gone. Very gone."

"What exactly do you mean by that?"

"The night of the wake at Magh Meall," I jumped in. "I decided to charge the atmosphere of the house, like you all wanted me to," I added as a quick defense, "to see if I could shake loose any of the house's memories about Emily and her activities. Connor's spirit had been trapped here." I didn't want to finish, because I knew she wasn't going to like that I had remained silent on that point.

"Yes?" she prompted as her eyes pulled away from the pendulum and flashed at me.

"Well," Oliver took over. "He took advantage of Mercy's own magic to launch another attack against her."

Iris's features softened. "I am so sorry. I have been such a fool. I thought we were finally safe."

Her tone prompted Oliver to repeat the rest of the story with relish. "Oh, Mercy was safe all right. When Connor came out to play, Mercy shoved his sorry phantom ass into a spirit trap the old buzzard—I mean Mother Jilo," he corrected himself as I glared at him, "taught her to make."

"A spirit trap?" The way she looked at me with a twinkle in her eye told me she wasn't really asking a question, merely expressing surprise. "Jilo did have such a flair for the classics." She drew a deep breath and shrugged, like she was trying to shake off Connor's taint. "What have you done with this trap? Where is it now?"

I lowered my eyes, not sure how she would react. I didn't need to worry, as Oliver barreled on, still in full raconteur mode. "I had it sealed in a cement block then compelled the captain of a freight ship bound to Guangzhou to drop it overboard as they passed over the Mariana Trench." He winked at me, oblivious to the unsettledness of Iris's mood. "With the cutbacks at NASA, it was the best I could do."

Iris stiffened in her seat. She turned away from her brother's grin and looked at me. "When were you going to tell me this?"

I bit my lip. "I meant to tell you the morning after the wake, but you remember, I caught you doing your walk of shame? You'd just connected with Sam."

Oliver snorted. "'Connected.'"

"Shut up, Oliver," Adam and I said at the same time.

"You've blossomed since Connor's been gone," I said. "You've been so happy. I'm sorry." I reached out for her, and she patted my hand. "I just didn't want to risk that."

"Not to worry. Doing the wrong thing for the right reason is a family tradition."

"Good. That's taken care of." Oliver whisked the pie that had been tempting me from the table and found a fork to dig in. A silent conversation passed between Adam and Oliver. "What?" Oliver asked in response to the unspoken challenge. "I have a fast metabolism. A taste of pie won't hurt."

"I was actually wondering how you could stand there eating after learning the demon who seduced one of your nieces and attempted to murder the other has returned and has been practicing some form of vivisection on an innocent woman."

"Don't jump to conclusions, Detective." Oliver took another defiant bite then pointed at Adam with his fork. "How can you be so sure the two things are connected?"

Adam slid back in his seat and put his forearm on the table. "Well, you and Iris agree magic has likely played a role in the preservation of the body parts we have found, and that this same magic is preventing Iris from doing her touchy-knowy thing." Until about six months ago, I had believed psychometry, the ability to touch a person or object and know their history, to be Iris's greatest power. Of course, six months ago I didn't know she was hiding her abilities in order to protect her husband's fragile ego. The woman, she could also fly, let the wind lift her to the skies. How she could have lived without that for so long astounded me. I had always assumed that Ellen was the most powerful of my mother's siblings. Lately, I had begun to question that and wonder what other tricks Iris might have up her sleeve.

Still, that Iris had been unable to pick up any impressions from the body parts was news to me. "Nothing?" I asked her.

"Nothing. It's like the hand and foot I touched were blank. Like they had been wiped clean of any possible impression."

Adam raised his eyebrows and angled his eyes at Oliver to deliver an "I told you so" look. Still focused on my uncle, Adam nodded toward Connor's pendulum. "We know that thing is magic. And we know your crazy evil sister, Emily—" He turned to me. "No offense."

"None taken." Our feelings regarding Emily Rose Taylor were much the same, even if my cocktail of emotions was a bit more emotionally complex than his. Emily and Josef had kidnapped Adam, beaten him to a bloody pulp, and then left him to fall to his death from the lighthouse at Hunting Beach. And they had done all this merely to get my attention.

"We know she is still out there," he continued, "and without a doubt still hell-bent on destruction. So, yeah, my Magic Eight Ball's sources point to yes. Your demon is connected to this murder." His hand shot out and clutched the pendulum, letting the fob fall to the end of its chain and swing. He looked at Iris. "Connor used this thing to answer questions and find things, right? Show me how it works."

"Sorry, but I could never bear to touch the thing, so it's going to have to be either Mercy or Oli." Iris's chair scraped the floor as she pushed back from the table. "But for the record, I think the demon showing up with Connor's pendulum is either a play for attention if he is, as I suspect, working on his own, or a trap if he does indeed have accomplices." She crossed the room to our kitchen's extraordinarily orderly junk drawer and riffled through its contents. "The minor demons, they love to brag, to make themselves seem much more formidable than they are. Most likely Wren collected the pendulum the night Ginny's house burned."

"He sure didn't seem very minor when he was holding a knife to my heart," I said. "Besides, Wren escaped the line. If he hasn't found access to some major mojo, he must have some connections with power. He said he had friends." Even as I made the point, I wanted more than anything for her to offer me an acceptable alternative as an explanation.

"Did he escape by his own means or with the help of these alleged allies? Maybe he did, but maybe the line simply shifted him unharmed, as it did with Maisie, and maybe when you brought Maisie back to us—"

"You got two for one," Oliver finished Iris's thought for her. "Little bastard has probably been hanging out, licking his wounds until he was strong enough to try to get a rise out of you."

Iris pulled a paper rectangle from the drawer. As she began to unfold it, I recognized it as a more-than-decade-old tourist map of Savannah and its environs. I had spent many childhood hours poring over it as I plotted the best routes for my then-nascent Liar's Tour, on which I trotted inebriated tourists around Savannah and made up the most lurid lies I could come up with on the spot about the landmarks we encountered. No harm done, as the fun lay in the fact that everybody knew I was lying. Still, a few of my fibs had over time worked their way into the fabric of Savannah's folklore.

Iris lost patience with the folds and shook the chart angrily open to its full size. "I know what you're hoping for, Adam," she said as she covered the tabletop with the map. "That Connor's tiny bauble will magically point to the location where our still-living, if much diminished, victim is to be found." She leaned toward him and patted his back. "I don't have the gift of prognostication, but I am fairly certain what you are hoping for will not be our actual outcome."

"We have to try."

"Of course we do," she said. "Still, I feel the need to remind you of two things before we do."

"I'm listening." Adam let the pendulum slide from his fingers and fall to the map.

"My first point is that the pendulum itself is not magic. It was never the source of Connor's tracking abilities. It was a focus for Connor's powers. In our hands, it will probably be nothing more than a brass sinker on a chain."

Adam nodded. "Understood."

"The second thing I want you to consider is that if this is a trap, the damned thing might well carry a curse. Mercy, how many pieces of jewelry have you been given in the past year?"

I knew where she was going with this. "Three."

"How many of those had been enchanted with harmful magic?"

I looked down at my wedding ring. "Only two, I hope."

Iris's eyes glimmered at my little joke. "That one, my dear, is blessed with good magic." Then the moment was over. Her smile faded and her warm gaze turned stern. Iris was back to being all business. She looked at Adam. "So whose well-being should we risk? Oliver's or Mercy's?"

Oliver rolled his eyes. "Really, enough drama. I'll yank the chain, and if anything happens, you two will shoot the winged monkeys." He reached for the pendulum only to have Adam slap his hand away with a loud thwack. "Ouch. Damn. What's wrong with you?"

"I believe Adam has decided the risk doesn't merit the anticipated return," Iris said.

Anyone else might have crumbled, but Adam had a stubborn streak almost as wide as my own. He grasped the chain and held the pendulum over the map. To our common surprise, it began swinging counterclockwise in a small precise circle.

"Drop it, buster," Oliver commanded. I knew he would have compelled Adam to obey if he still had that ace up his sleeve, but Oliver had surrendered the option of compelling Adam years ago. Adam had been none too pleased learning Oliver had compelled him to disregard the apprehension a non-witch usually suffered when encountering true magic. To placate Adam, Oliver performed a mini self-binding to prevent himself from being able to influence Adam with magic again. At least Oliver claimed this was the reason behind his action. I believed the truth was that he wanted to be certain that if and when he won Adam's heart, he would know he hadn't unconsciously compelled Adam to return his feelings.

Adam jutted his jaw forward and shook his head. "You're right, Iris. I can think of no good motive the demon could have for dropping this thing off and tempting me to have y'all use it." For a moment his eyes softened. "But y'all have to appreciate that I have an unsolved murder or three hanging over my head." I mentally tabulated the body count: Tucker, of course; then there was Ryder, whose corpse my mother had dumped in the Tillandsia house. Had Oliver told him about Ryder's woman, Birdy? "If I blow this investigation too, my career is going to be over."

"Oh," Oliver said, his eyes open wide. "I thought this was about finding justice for the poor woman Wren and associates have been hacking up."

Adam's head jerked back. He blinked. "That's unfair—"

"Damn right it's unfair." The words were out of my mouth before I even realized I was going to say them. I might as well finish the thought. "Adam has bent over backward to protect our family." My index finger was up, and it was pointing. "You reel that smart mouth of yours back in, or I will smack it for you myself."

"There will be no smacking anybody." Iris did some finger pointing of her own, this time in my direction.

"I didn't mean it," I said, feeling like a chastised six-year-old. "I just mean we owe it to Adam to deal with this in a way that doesn't leave him hanging."

"Damn," Oliver said, his chest puffed out and a lopsided grin on his face, delighted I had stood up for Adam, even if it meant standing up to him. "I'm really starting to miss the days when Mercy didn't like you so much."

We were all struck silent when the pendulum stopped dead and pulled toward the map like it had been magnetized. With his free hand Adam patted the pocket of his suit coat and retrieved a ballpoint pen. He clicked it and made an X on the map at a point near Columbia Square. He'd evidently been satisfied with the preliminary result of his experiment. He looked up at us. "It's a hit."

He lifted the pendulum and it instantly began swinging again. It fell with a thump on a second point. Adam had no sooner inked a mark near the cartoonish representation of Christ Church than the pendulum's weight bounced back into the air. It landed again on East Bay Street, near the point where it crosses Whitaker. Before Adam could mark the map, the pendulum bounced across the river and landed on Hutchison Island, right where the Talmadge Bridge crosses over the parkway. Adam seemed shocked by his own success, so much so that he didn't even bother trying to mark the spot.

The weight jumped back up and began to spin again, but this time instead of widdershins it moved clockwise. It dove again with such force the weight punched a hole through the caricature of a spitting lion that marked the location of the Cotton Exchange fountain. We'd find a permanent divot in the tabletop once the map was moved, of that much I was sure.

"Dang!" Adam exclaimed and dropped the chain. He hopped up and ran to the sink, turning on the cold-water tap and putting his hand under the stream. "The damned thing burned me."

"Let me see." Iris rose and joined him at the sink. "Just a burn. Magical in origin, but natural in effect. Let me get some ice for that."

Adam shook his hand once, twice. "No. That's okay. It'll be fine."

"Tough guy," Oliver said as he took hold of Adam's pen and marked the locations Adam had missed. Adam and Iris returned and studied the defaced map. "All right, does anyone see a pattern?"

"Four of the five are hits for where we've found body parts." Adam swiped the pen from Oliver's grasp and drew somewhat shaky lines between the points. He tapped at the map with his finger, pointing to the scrawls he had made. "There. Is that witch writing? What does that symbol mean to y'all?"

"It means you are grasping at straws," Iris answered shaking her head. "I'm sorry, Adam, I can discern no pattern in the markings."

I leaned in and picked up the pendulum. It still felt warm to the touch. "I don't see any pattern in the markings, but the pendulum spun left when it hit on places where you *have* found remains. It spun right before hitting on the fountain. I suspect that's where the next part is gonna turn up."

I no sooner got the words out than Adam's cell rang. He swiped it off the table and looked at the caller ID. "Cook," he answered before it had the chance to ring a third time. His eyes locked on to mine. "Yes. I understand. Cordon it off. Keep the tourists back. I'll be right there." He hung up and dropped his phone into his pocket.

"Her torso—headless—has turned up at the fountain." His face fell. He looked suddenly older, defeated. I realized he really had been holding out hope he'd somehow save this woman. I didn't know whether to think of it as optimism or denial, but I liked him even more for it. "I gotta get back to work." He focused on me.

"You keep close to your family for now, okay? No more sauntering around on your own."

"Okay."

He looked at Oliver. "Walk me out?"

"Yeah." Oliver went to the sink and rinsed out the dirty pie tin. "I should get going too," he said and turned to give Iris a kiss on the cheek.

"Thanksgiving. Two p.m. Thursday, you two," she called out after the men. "Don't be late."

"I'll do my best." Adam opened the door to the garden.

"Which means keep a plate in the oven, but don't wait up." Oliver pushed Adam out the door.

Iris turned to me. "I should have let you smack him."

"Yes, ma'am, you should have."

THREE

"I just caught the menfolk smooching in the driveway." Ellen came in and sat her purse on the table next to the map. "Adam informed me that we delicate ladies are no longer to be wandering the streets of the wicked city of Savannah by ourselves."

"The poor man's ego has suffered enough." Iris went to the cupboard and pulled down three mugs. "Let him believe he is protecting us, rather than the other way around. I'm not sure how he'd react if he knew we three fainting flowers have woven a cage of protective magic around him."

After the abuse Emily and Josef had dealt Adam, we made a pact to ensure he could never be snatched from us again. Oliver knew only enough about our spell to allow him both a case for plausible deniability and the ability to sleep at night.

"How was your 'meeting'?" Iris asked.

"Well, let's see, I sit down and say 'Hi, I'm Ellen. I'm an alcoholic. And a witch.' There's a moment of dead silence, then someone inevitably says, 'Keep coming back.'" In spite of her sarcasm, I could tell she was doing better. She glowed with health, and a bit of her old spark had returned to her lovely blue eyes. She brushed aside her blonde bangs and smiled at me.

"You discuss magic?" Iris asked with muted horror in her voice.

"'You're only as sick as your secrets,'" she quoted brightly, but then her tone fell flat. "At first I tried speaking in veiled terms, but it was too exhausting. Then I realized most everyone there was caught up in their own thoughts anyway. The ones who do listen are convinced I am crazier than . . . well, than I don't know what."

"But it's helping you?" Iris pressed.

"Yeah." Ellen nodded. "I think it is."

"Then you share whatever you want." Iris fetched the teakettle from the stove and filled it at the sink. "I think it will do some of these folk around here good to know the types of difficulties we Taylors face daily. Might even change a few people's opinions about us." She lit the burner and set the kettle on the flame.

"I think I'm beyond caring what anyone thinks about us. I am tired of being judged. I am tired of watching our neighbors grab their children and scurry away like frightened mice every time I say good morning."

"Now, Ellen, you know you are exaggerating. They don't behave that poorly toward us." Iris folded her arms and smiled. I agreed with Iris that our neighbors were never impolite, but there were many subtle bits of evidence that Ellen's feelings were not unfounded. Her new flower shop was doing well, but most of her orders were destined for hospital delivery, not weddings. Was it actual talk of Ellen's power to heal or merely intuition that led people to send her bouquets to the broken and ill, but not to mark an anniversary? People had always found witches to be useful, as long as we maintained a comfortable distance. Since I had gained my powers, I myself had noticed a remarkable change in the way the non-witches treated me. Even those with whom I had been closest had begun to draw back.

"Well, no, but if I yelled 'boo'—" Ellen stopped as her focus fell onto the pendulum I still held. "Where in the hell did that come from?" She took note of the map. "What is going on?"

"Have a seat," Iris said. I laid the pendulum down on the map, feeling somehow guilty for having been caught with it in hand.

Ellen shrugged and sighed. "This day just will not stop." She pulled out a chair across the table from me and sat. "What is it now?"

Iris and I looked at each other, silently debating which of us would update Ellen. "The map," I said, taking the coward's approach to the problem. After Paul's death, Ellen had used Wren almost as a surrogate, wasting the fruit of her maternal instincts on the false child. I'd start with the latest news about the murder and figure out a graceful way to bring up Wren in the seconds that bought me, at least I hoped.

"Wow, it must be bad if you are trying to start there." Ellen pointed at the pendulum. "Let's hear about that first. I thought it disappeared during the fire at Ginny's."

I shifted, trying to find a more comfortable position. My life had become far too sedentary for my liking. Especially at the current moment. Ellen continued staring at me, so I dove in. "Wren's back."

Ellen closed her eyes and drew a deep breath. "Then I haven't been hallucinating." She opened her eyes. "I thought I saw the little bastard lurking. I caught glances of him a few times out of the corner of my eye. I set fire to a ficus trying to hit him." She folded her hands on the table. "You got the pendulum off him?"

I nodded. "He passed it on to me with the message that Adam should use it."

Her hair fell at an angle as she tilted her head. She smiled. "Was that the bad part? The part I needed to sit down for?"

"Well, yes, kind of . . ."

"We have reason to believe he is involved in the murder Adam has been investigating."

Ellen turned her face toward her sister. "It is officially a murder, then?" The kettle chose that very instant to cry out, and I jumped a little.

Iris turned off the burner. "We don't know the details. Adam was just heading to the scene when you arrived, but a headless torso was left at the Cotton Exchange fountain."

"Lovely," Ellen said and turned to me. "That image will about ruin Old Rex for me forever." When Maisie and I were kids, we had dubbed the fountain's lion "Old Rex." I knew what she meant. Yet another happy memory tainted.

I watched as Iris scalded the teapot and started the brew. Ellen caught my attention by tapping on the map with her nail. "These marks. They're where the parts have been discovered?" I nodded. "What about the lines drawn between them?"

"Adam was looking for some kind of pattern in their placement," Iris responded for me. "He thought he'd discovered an occult symbol or something."

"Bless his heart," Ellen said reflexively. "I suspect he's correct in thinking there is a hidden meaning in this, even if he's naïve about what the message should look like."

"What do you mean?" I leaned back over the map, taking another look at the points where marks had been made.

"You're the tour guide in the family." Ellen pointed at the X Adam had put on Hutchinson Island. "Let's start there. A foot was found there, right?" she asked Iris, and Iris nodded her response. "What is significant about Hutchinson?"

I brushed past the untruths I myself had made up about the island to arrive at the accepted canon of stories, factual or no, that make up Hutchinson's official history. "It's where Alice Riley killed William Wise." This murder led to Alice being hanged. The first time in the history of Georgia that a woman died at the gallows.

I shuddered as a connection formed in my mind. "Alice was accused of practicing witchcraft."

Iris had spent years volunteering for the historical society. "In her day, any woman worth her salt was accused of it," Iris said as she carried a tray with the teapot and three mugs to the table. Ellen slid the map over so Iris could find room for the tray. "Still, she was tried for murder not witchcraft. She was a killer, but by no means a witch."

"Wasn't Alice pregnant at the time of the trial?" Ellen asked. I didn't like the next station where this train of thought was bound to stop.

"Yes, the court stayed her execution until she gave birth." Iris turned to me. "Listen, we could easily jump to conclusions and draw connections between you, a pregnant witch, and the unfortunate Miss Riley. But let's don't for now." She placed a cup of hot chamomile before me. "Drink that."

A look passed between my aunts. "The other foot. They found it near Columbia Square," Iris said as she handed Ellen a steaming mug. "In the middle of the street right in front of the Kehoe Mansion."

"Kehoe." Ellen took a sip of tea. "Savannah's king of cast iron. What could that signify?"

I shrugged. Nothing jumped to mind.

Iris took the seat next to Ellen. "What was that horrible lie you used to tell about the Kehoe family?" She looked at me through narrowed eyes. "The one that almost got me kicked out of the historical society."

"You mean the first time she almost got you kicked out."

"Yes." Iris snapped her fingers as my story came back to her. "You claimed Kehoe's wife, Anne, had an affair with a worker from the foundry, and Kehoe killed him and burned him in the furnace."

"Then added the ashes to the cast iron he used to build the Kehoe Mansion," Ellen finished for her. They both stared at me.

Ellen shook her head. "How did you come up with those horrid stories of yours?"

"It was just a fib." I had actually forgotten the part about the ashes until Ellen reminded me.

"A fib?" Iris looked at Ellen then turned back to me. "More of a calumny." I surmised she had forgiven me due to the smile on her lips. "I could never decide whether I should feel mortified by these fables you were spinning or proud of them. Every day I stood helplessly by, watching as you twisted the essence of your heritage to the benefit of your own unscrupulous purposes." She laughed, but from the way she squinted at me, she had remembered another tale to take me to task over. In the next instant her laughter dried up, and her eyes fell to the map. "What if we are looking at this whole situation wrong?" Iris wrapped her arms around herself as if she were fighting off a sudden chill. "What if instead of viewing the killer's actions as a message, we look on it as a spell?"

Ellen leaned in toward Iris. "You mean rather than looking for a logical connection between the places the killer has chosen, we try to uncover any magical correspondences?"

The use of magical correspondences helped to focus a spell by drawing like to like or substituting an item with similar attributes for another. In the most vulgar of its forms, the power of magical correspondences showed up as tourist shop Voodoo dolls. At its most refined it served as the basis of spiritual alchemy. Real witches rarely relied on it, using it only when the magic they were attempting fell outside their innate abilities or called for a higher level of precision than they could muster without habiliments.

"That makes it less likely we are looking for one of us then, right?" I asked. "A witch, I mean."

Iris was about to answer when her cell rang. Her hand pounced on it before it could ring a second time. The rise in color to her cheeks announced her caller was Sam. Her face glowed as a mischievous smile rose to her lips. She paused before answering, trying to come across a little less excited than she was. "Hello," she nearly purred. Ellen leaned toward her, trying to eavesdrop, but Iris gave her a playful push back. "Oh," she said, the shine leaving her eyes. "No, I understand, I do. Tomorrow—" she began, but her eyebrows fell. I knew that Sam had hung up.

"Everything all right?" I asked.

"Yes, of course." Iris forced a new smile on her face. "Sam was supposed to swing by this evening, but he's run into some difficulty with work. He's under quite a bit of pressure right now," she offered as apology for him when in truth none was owed. I knew she was merely repeating his own words. I had to wonder if things were cooling off, at least on his side.

Ellen flashed me a look that told me she was wondering the same thing. Iris caught on to our silent conversation. "Oh, for heaven's sake," she said, "he's got a project to finish before the holiday. Don't go reading anything into it."

"Reading nothing into anything," I said throwing up my hands. "Still, I will shrink his head to the size of a grape if he hurts you."

"And I," Ellen said, "will shrink the part he thinks with."

Iris placed her hands on her hips. "No one is shrinking anything. Please remember, I am quite fond of his 'thought' process." I was glad to see she had shaken off the gloom that had descended on her, her false smile making way for a true one. "Everything is wonderful. He's a bit stressed out. That's all." The smile faded as she fixed us with a steely glare. "Now, put that map away, and prepare yourself to face a true horror. Grocery shopping two days before Thanksgiving."

FOUR

Abigail pushed through the swinging door into the kitchen. "Actually, if you can spare Mercy, I'd like to borrow her for a bit." She focused on me. "We appear to be at the point of a breakthrough. I think Maisie is ready to discuss . . . that day."

That day. There was no need for Abby to be more specific; she was speaking of the day of the investment, when Maisie was to be installed as an anchor of the line, but instead caused all hell to break loose. Rather than accepting the role everyone believed Maisie had been born to play, she rebelled against the united witch families and handed me over to Jackson to sacrifice. With my death, she had planned to wrest control of the line from the other anchors and secure its magic for herself. I cringed at the memory, doing my best to push it down, set it aside, not let the true weight of what Maisie had put me through touch my heart. In order to welcome Maisie back into my life, I'd been forced to suppress my pain over her grievous betrayals, but seeing it all spread back out before me reminded me I had a lot to forgive Maisie for.

Jackson had harbored his own ideas, intending to double-cross Maisie and steal the line's magic for his own purposes. He planned to use it to free his boo hag buddies from the dimension where they had been trapped since the line's creation. Things didn't work out the way either of them had expected, though. For some reason, Maisie faltered at the last moment, and rather than harming her, the line had shown her clemency, moving her away from our reality to a place where she could work no harm.

Jilo had warned me against bringing the sister who had tried to kill me back into this world, and the other anchors had forbidden any attempt to locate Maisie, let alone rescue her. My family's insistence on doing just that was now viewed as the opening volley in what many were calling the "Taylor Rebellion." Still, the line had protected Maisie rather than punished her. And the line had helped me bring my sister home. I told myself that these points should stand as proof positive that in spite of everything, I was right to believe in her, right to try to find a way to move past the harm she'd caused that day.

That day seemed a million years ago, although in truth it had taken place in July, a mere four months ago. And a month before that, I had been an entirely different person. It seemed that an enormous gulf stood between the girl I'd been and the person I now knew myself to be. I felt proud of the woman I had become, or was at least in the process of becoming. Still, a part of me missed the girl I had been. Sure, I had led a privileged and sheltered life, and maybe I was a lot less mature than I ought to have been. But there had been something magical about that girl, her innocence and open heart, even if I had failed to see it at the time.

The thought of all that had occurred since the solstice morning I stumbled onto Ginny's corpse nearly made my head spin. I could barely wrap my mind around it. How could it have only been this last summer that I doubted my feelings for Peter and believed myself to be in love with Jackson? That this counterfeit emotion could have seemed real enough to me to send me out to Jilo's crossroads to seek a conjure to turn my heart away from

Jackson and back to Peter? Now I knew it had all been part of an elaborate lie, and the love I felt was not for Jackson, but for the magic that had been denied me. Maisie had fed Wren on my magic, helping him to grow and evolve until he could take on a new guise, that of Jackson. I had sensed my connection to this misappropriated magic and interpreted it as love for the man.

Even though the line had helped me bring Maisie home, she had not returned in good shape. Physically she was fine, but still she had spent several days in a coma following her return. Abigail had advised caution, since we had no idea what state of mind she would be in upon waking. So in much the same way that Ginny had diverted my power away from me, we—my aunts, my uncle, Abby, and myself—siphoned away Maisie's magic until we could determine the lay of the land.

Even after Maisie awoke, she remained still and unspeaking. Abby spent a few more days alone with her, commencing a course of treatment that we all hoped would provide a lasting cure. Abby started by leading Maisie in guided mediations, then moved on to good old talking once Maisie found her voice. It was only in the last few days that Abby felt comfortable allowing Maisie to reconnect to her powers, so we unkinked the hose a tiny bit, allowing Maisie's magic to begin to return to her in a slow and controlled flow.

None of us even knew how much of her own power Maisie actually had. Even before the two of us were born, Ginny had begun stealing magic from me and feeding it to my sister. My gut told me that my great-aunt's goal hadn't been to strengthen Maisie, but rather to weaken me; Ginny only intended to use Maisie to prime the pump, until she could manage to pull away my magic. Her goal was to feed it into the neighboring plane and ground it there.

There was evidence that Ginny realized the process didn't work entirely as planned, that even though the bulk of my power did pass harmlessly through Maisie and into the realm where Ginny grounded it, a good portion of it fed directly into Maisie. The rest of us had believed Maisie had been born a magical wunderkind with a dud for a sister. The truth was the energy was overwhelming her, destroying her from the inside. Ginny evidently realized she couldn't undo the attachment to Maisie without breaking the flow and returning my power to me. Whatever Ginny believed about me, she believed it strongly enough to risk destroying my sister.

Perhaps it was poetic justice that Wren killed Ginny. Ginny stole from me and damaged Maisie. Regardless of the source of Maisie's problems, she used the stolen magic to feed the monster that killed Ginny. God help me, I hated the old woman. Perhaps even more than Emily. I couldn't help but wonder if Ginny's evil had somehow infected my mother as well. Still, I had no idea why my great-aunt had hated me so, had feared me enough that she would attempt to strip me entirely of magic, and risk Maisie's well-being by force-feeding it to her.

The line itself put an end to all that. *That day.* The line claimed me as an anchor and returned my own magic to me. Now, the only power Maisie had was what naturally belonged to her. Yet even running on partial steam, it seemed, that magic was formidable. In just these few days, under Abby's guidance, Maisie progressed from zero to creating temporary miniature worlds where she could begin to work through her issues. The same issues that had driven her to offer me up as a sacrifice in an attempt to take over the full power of the line. It was intensive magical therapy, and frankly, when Abigail was through helping my sister, I intended to ask her to help me work on some issues of my own. God knows lately I'd been racking up issues like an overeager Girl Scout collects insignia badges.

"I think I'd like to stay also," Ellen said, pulling me from my thoughts. I noticed that she looked neither at Abigail nor myself, but to Iris for permission.

"We should perhaps have this conversation as a family—" Iris began.

"No." Abigail shook her head. "Maisie isn't ready to talk to the entire family all at once. It's Mercy she's done the most harm. Let the girls have a chance to talk things through first, and then we'll take it from there. You two go on to the store." Iris and Ellen hesitated, a silent conversation seeming to go on between them.

"I'm sorry," Ellen said, "but Maisie tried to kill Mercy. You're talking like they've squabbled over a stained blouse." If anyone could understand the complexity of my feelings for Maisie, it would be Ellen. Emily, her sister and my mother, had faked her own death largely so she could invent new and creative ways to turn Ellen's world into a living hell. I knew Ellen would never forgive Emily the harm she'd done. I didn't blame her. I had come to realize that it is possible for someone to go too far to be forgiven. The best you could do was walk away and pray they didn't try to follow you. I knew beyond a shadow of a doubt my mother had stepped too far over the line.

Now that Maisie was back, cogent and willing to talk, I had to learn if the same was true of my sister. I had to know for sure that she felt true contrition. That she knew she had done wrong. That she would never hurt me that deeply again. "It's okay. If she's ready to talk about what she did, I'm ready to listen."

Iris looked to me. "Are you sure you're up to facing this alone?"

"Really," Abigail said, "things will be just fine here. Go on, get—"

A thought hit me and sapped my reserve. "Wait," I said, my voice breaking. I felt guilty even bringing it up. I wanted to believe my sister was getting better; I wanted to believe in her. But I had been wrong before. "The timing of this breakthrough . . ."

Iris nodded and saved me from finishing my thought. "It gives one pause that it follows on the heels of her accomplice's return."

Abigail's face fell. "Her accomplice?"

"Wren showed back up today," I said.

Abigail's face pulled into a tight-lipped grimace. "That puts a different complexion on things." She tilted her head toward Iris. "It never occurred to you that perhaps y'all might want to share this tidbit with me?" Her face grew flushed. "Either I'm one of you, or I'm not."

"No." Iris stepped forward, attempting to draw Abby into an embrace, but Abigail pulled back. "It isn't like that. Not at all. We would have told you—it's only that it all just happened."

"And you figured you'd catch me up right after you found the right turkey?"

"Really, Abby." I crossed to her and embraced her. She accepted my show of affection. "Please don't think we do not appreciate you." For good or bad, my hormones decided to choose this moment to kick in, and hot tears fell from my eyes. "I am so, so grateful to you for all you have done to help Maisie. To help all of us, really." I gave her a squeeze. "We're all just treading water here. We had no intention of excluding you, we just hadn't gotten around to including you."

Her eyes narrowed and she pursed her lips, but I could feel her sense of affront begin to fall away. "Fine, fine." She patted my back and pulled a tissue from her pocket. "It's clean," she said as she dabbed at my cheeks. She stepped away from me, taking my aunts and myself into her gaze. Her expression had mellowed, but I could tell, although she may have forgiven me for the oversight, Iris and Ellen had not yet been cleared of culpability.

"Maybe," Ellen said, "we should put this talk off until we have a better handle on what is happening around here."

"No," I said. "If Maisie needs me to help heal, I will be there for her." I felt a thud in my chest. "But if she is still connected to Wren, I need to know it, so that I can deal with her." I turned my focus to Abigail. "I want to do this. I want to talk to Maisie about *that day.*"

"Then there is no way you are doing this without us," Iris said, emphasizing the "no." Her tone left no room for debate.

Abby acquiesced with a nod. "All right then. She's waiting for us upstairs. Let's get this done."

- — -

We found her in her room, sitting on the floor, cross-legged in the lotus position. Here was the sister who tried to murder me. The sister I had risked everything to give another chance.

Her silky blonde hair had been plaited into a French braid. Her eyes remained closed, her heart-shaped face smooth and composed. She seemed bathed in what I knew to be a hard-fought-for serenity. *It'll be quite a while before I'm able to pull that pose off again.* The thought hit me from nowhere, but in the name of all that is holy, I could not understand why it would be the first thing to come to mind. Well, that wasn't quite true. I knew it had already begun again. My insidious compulsion to compare myself with my sister. It was a lifelong habit, one I thought I'd kicked. I thought I'd grown up a bit over the last several months, but darned if I wasn't standing there ticking off all the ways she managed to outshine me without even trying.

I resented her for her serenity when my insides raged like a swirling ocean of fear, anger, and, yes, jealousy. A dark fragment of my soul, the part of me that wanted to strike out and hurt her as she had hurt me, took over. "Wren is back."

Her eyes flashed open, and she looked up at me. I quivered when I saw the heat that burned in her lovely blue eyes. What was it I saw there? Shame? Grief? Anger? An odd blend of all three? I had achieved my goal of shaking her, and I hated myself for it.

"I know. He's been calling out to me. Trying to get me to join him. Telling me to find a way to finish what I started."

Abby gasped. "Sugar, you should have told me."

Maisie's eyes flicked to Abigail. "I'm telling you now. I'm telling you all, because I want you to know what you're up against. You've been leading me to create these safe little worlds for myself, realities where I can work through my madness. But in the real world, none of us are safe," she said, unfolding her lithe limbs without ever taking her eyes off me. She rocked up to her knees and stood. "And I am not crazy. I'm not." She took a step toward me, almost as if she were challenging me to flee, as if she were testing me to see if I could move past my fear of her. I felt a bead of cold sweat break free and trace down my spine. I wanted to love her, but I wanted to run at the same time.

I held my ground, not so much from bravery, but as the intensity of her expression pinned me to the spot. "I know you aren't *crazy*, but . . ."

"What then? Loony? Don't try to lie to me." She looked at me with one raised eyebrow. "You were a crap liar as a kid, and anchor or no, you still are."

Iris moved past us and pretended to examine the books spread out on Maisie's desk. I read the cautious look lurking in her eyes, and realized that she was putting herself into a better position to strike, should it be necessary to contain Maisie. Ellen, too, seemed to take note of Iris's intention. She slid around behind me and mirrored her sister's station on the opposite side of the room. She wasn't capable of matching Iris's nonchalance. She stood stock-still, small lines forming around her eyes, and she prepared herself to intervene at the first sign of trouble. Abby did not seem worried; she remained at my side, a calming force for all of us.

"No. I'm not lying to you. I don't think you're crazy. To me that word means a permanent state. I would say 'unsettled' rather than 'crazy.' Listen, I'm sorry. You may be ready for this, but I'm not. I thought I was, but . . ."

Maisie willed my eyes to meet hers, and a sly smile crossed her lips. "I tried to kill you, Mercy. If the shoe were on the other foot, I wouldn't come near you again unless you were strapped tightly into a straightjacket and wearing one of those Hannibal faceplates. As a matter of fact, if one of us is crazy, it's probably you."

"I'm not crazy. Just hopeful."

"Pretty much the same thing in this world," Maisie said. "All the same, I need you to listen to me. I've been waiting for you to ask me how I could do what I did to you. Why I would even dream of letting a demon harm my little sister. You're afraid to ask, but I need to tell you why, and you need to hear it."

"I know why," I said, the words coming out wrapped in razor-sharp barbs. My impulse to flee having been thwarted, the need to fight brought fire to my heart. "You wanted power, and you would do anything, *anything* to get it." I heard the anger in my voice, and damn it, I wanted to make sure Maisie heard it too. "You wanted Peter." I nearly spat my husband's name at her. "And you weren't going to let anyone stand in your way. Even me, your own sister."

She went nearly limp, looking like a puppet on a slack string. She stepped back as tears fell from her eyes. "No. You're wrong. At the time, I thought it was true, but I was split. There was the part of me that covered up Ginny's murder. The part of me that plotted against you, but then there was another part. One that watched on in horror. That part did things to try to warn you. She . . . I tried to tell you in a thousand little ways. Tried to warn you not to trust me, but you never caught on."

"Because I trusted you more than anyone else. You were my center." I couldn't bear to look at her; I had to look away.

"And I betrayed you in the most heinous way." She stepped forward again, but this time I knew it was not a challenge. It was a plea for forgiveness. She took my hand, causing me to focus again on her face. I felt Iris tense on the periphery.

I drew a deep breath. "At the end. When you tried to stop. Was it because you realized you couldn't kill me, or because you learned I was carrying Peter's child?"

"That's what I'm trying to tell you. It wasn't for either of those reasons, even though"—her words rushed ahead—"it was for both." She released me and pressed both hands against her temples. She gritted her teeth and whined as if she were in pain. She stopped and took a few breaths, lowering her hands. "It gets so confusing." She tilted her head, a crease forming between her brows. "Hear me, Mercy. I'm not trying to excuse myself. I am not trying to rationalize my actions. I know what I did was monstrous." I watched her face wash over with horror, her eyes widening and her lips trembling. I knew she was reliving the event in her mind. "When they got to the point where the anchor energy was to settle on me, I heard a voice." Her eyes focused back on mine. "I couldn't say if it was a man's or a woman's."

"What did it say?" I leaned in and clasped both her hands in mine.

"That I'd done enough. I'd done everything it needed me to do. Then I was gone."

"You believe there was a force compelling you to act as you did?"

She pulled her hands back and crossed her arms over her chest, hugging herself. "No. It wasn't like with Uncle Oliver. I hadn't been forced to behave as I did. I did everything, *everything*"—she emphasized the word—"willingly. Just not for the reasons everyone, including myself, thought I had. It was like I had been playing the role of the villain until that moment. Somehow doing wrong had been the right thing to do, like I was acting out a necessary part. When the line took me, it freed me. The real me was free." Her eyes bored into me. "I can't explain it, but I know." Her hand balled into a fist and she pounded on her heart. "I know in here I

40

never would have harmed you. I would never have gone all the way through with it. Never."

Abby stepped between us and put her arms around Maisie. "I think that's enough for tonight."

"Yes," Iris said. "I concur." She took my arm and escorted me to the door. She began to speak, but then gave a curt nod toward Abby. Abby's eyes closed, and she nodded in kind. I didn't understand the silent conversation that had passed between them, but I struggled to stop Iris from dragging me through the door.

There had been forces working against my sister and me, trying to pull us apart even before we had been born. I freed myself from Iris's grasp and rushed back to Maisie. I pulled her from Abby's arms and into mine. She looked up at me in total surprise. "I believe you," I said and placed a kiss on her cheek. "I don't forgive you. Not really. Not yet. But I do believe you." A sigh escaped her, and she leaned her head on my shoulder. "We'll get to the bottom of this. Find a way to work through it."

She lifted her head and looked at me with the first smile I'd seen on her in forever. Perhaps the first genuine smile of her life. "Yes," she said. "I do believe we will."

FIVE

I startled awake. In my nightmare, Old Rex had come to life and was chasing a woman as if she were a gazelle in the African savannah. Then that woman was me. He wore me down, circled me until he was ready to pounce. Ready to rip me limb from limb. It was just a dream, and a silly one at that, but I would have liked to find my husband by my side when I awoke. No such luck.

Enough, I thought to myself. Enough of being a selfish little girl. Peter was up and out early for good reason. He had met a commercial real estate agent at the bar last night and had come home with a new scheme of opening up another Magh Meall over near the beach on Tybee. He and George, the agent, had an early appointment to scout out available properties. He hadn't sprung his idea on his parents yet, but honestly, the way he explained it, it didn't sound like the worst idea in the world. If he was willing to go into business with his parents, maybe he would extend the same courtesy to his wife and let me become an investor. Of course, Colin and Claire might have other ideas about it, but part of me really enjoyed the thought of Peter and me having a dream we could build together, just as his parents had.

The radio had nothing new to say about the torso found near the Cotton Exchange, but it did tell me our warm streak was going to continue. We were in for another hot one. I should have settled on one of Peter's T-shirts and elastic-waisted shorts as I was bound to spend the day as Iris's sous-chef, or scullery maid, depending on her mood and how well preparations for tomorrow were coming along. Yes, my good sense told me to dress casually, but for some reason I felt more of a need to feel pretty than I had for a while. Thumbing my nose at good sense, I chose another of Ellen's purchases, a pretty blue floral V-neck cotton dress with a fitted empire line. I sat before my mirror and made a bit more of an effort this morning than I had of late with my hair. "There, you look nice," I said to my plump-faced reflection. I nodded at myself to confirm the compliment. I was debating if I was really going to go all out and put on makeup when the doorbell rang.

I figured Iris would grab it, as she would probably be up and around early, especially since Sam hadn't slept over last night. I found my favorite training shoes and laced them up. They didn't really add to the outfit, but I had to balance pretty with practical. The bell sounded again. And again.

"I'll get it," I said to myself and hoisted myself from my chair, not an easy feat of late. I shuffled down the hall, and made my way cautiously down the stairs. The bell rang again. *I'm coming. The pregnant lady is moving as fast as she can.* I opened the door, and the sight of two well-dressed strangers led me to think I was about to be offered a copy of *The Watchtower*.

"Mercy." The voice was familiar, but I was completely taken aback by the sight of Martell Burke, Jilo's great-grandson.

Martell's typical teenage swagger and dress had been replaced, at least for the moment, by a neat black suit and tie and a sense of duty. I think I surprised him when I pulled him over the threshold and into a tight embrace. "You clean up pretty nice, there. I didn't even recognize you at first." He flashed me a smile, the first I'd ever seen on his normally too-cool-to-care face. I took a step back to take him in. The light in his eyes as he smiled reminded me of Jilo, and I reached out again to squeeze his hand.

"Who is it?" Iris asked, and I turned to see her approaching, drying her hands on a kitchen towel. "Martell," Iris squealed in obvious delight. "Look at how handsome you are." Martell smiled as Iris fawned over him. Iris planted a kiss on his cheek.

Someone cleared their throat, and only then did I remember Martell's companion. The smile slid from Martell's lips. "This is my cousin, Jessamine," he said and stepped aside. She waited just beyond the threshold. The tilt of her head, the illumination of the morning sun, and the way the doorway framed her colluded to make me think of an Andrew Wyeth painting. She was exquisite, breathtaking, a beauty so great it could only inspire devotion or the darkest of envy. Café au lait skin and cerulean eyes, auburn hair a shade nearly as vibrant as my own. She stood before me, her stance regal, her elegant neck bent so that her head rested at an inquisitive angle.

"Please come in," Iris said. "Please."

Jessamine entered our home like she was stepping into a carnival haunted house. She looked side to side, surveying the entry, the sitting room on its left, and the library that lay to its right as if she were expecting someone to jump out at her from the shadows at any moment.

She said nothing, and the situation grew awkward. "Pleased to meet you." I held out my hand. She did not take it.

She remained silent, merely standing before me and looking me over. Finally she felt moved to speak. "So you're the one Auntie Jilo was so mad for?" She watched me coolly for my reaction.

"The feeling was more than mutual. I was pretty crazy about her too." I smiled, hoping to see a bit of warmth creep into her lovely eyes. Nothing. "I loved her, actually."

"Make yourself comfortable," Iris said and motioned toward the sitting room we really only used when we had guests. Guests Iris was not sure she wanted to welcome any farther into the house, that is. I wasn't even sure Iris herself was aware she used the sitting room as a buffer. Jessamine took no notice of Iris's directions, turning instead to the right and heading into the library. Martell shrugged and went to the sitting room, leaving my aunt and me to follow Jessamine.

We found her standing before my grandmother's portrait that hung over the mantel. She examined it minutely, reaching up and holding her fingers a mere hair from the canvas.

"Adeline Taylor, my mother," Iris said proudly.

Jessamine pulled her hand back quickly as if she'd touched a flame. "She was a beauty." She glanced back over her shoulder at Iris. "You resemble her."

"Thank you," Iris said and smiled. "I'd like to think so, but she had a certain grace I fear I lack."

Jessamine turned fully toward us. "Your father must have loved her very much." She cast a look back at the portrait. "That face could cause a man to lose himself."

Something in her words riled me, but Iris's eyes crinkled in pleasure. "Well, I don't think Daddy lost himself, but he did lose his heart."

"Perhaps we should join Martell?" I found Jessamine's overt fascination with my grandmother's portrait a bit disconcerting.

"This was your father's desk?" Jessamine disregarded me and swept her index finger over the desktop, as if she were checking for dust.

"Yes, and his father's before that. It has very little value as an antique, but it holds a lot of sentimental value for his children."

"His children," Jessamine echoed.

It wasn't quite a question, but Iris felt compelled to respond anyway. "Yes, of course. Ellen and myself. And our brother, Oliver, of course." She hadn't included my mother. I understood.

"Were you close to your grandparents?" she asked, addressing me.

"Close?" I considered her question. I didn't like her demeanor, and she was getting a little too personal, a little too quickly. Still, she benefited in my sight from being related to Jilo, so I answered. "They seem so blurry to me. I do remember one time when I was playing outside on the porch, watching Grandma work in the flowerbeds, then turning and pressing my nose up against the window. Grandpa was smoking his pipe and reading a paper." I could see my grandfather's kind face looking out at me and smell the faint scent of cherry pipe tobacco.

"Darling, what are you talking about?" Iris looked at me like I was a natural born fool. "Your grandparents passed before you were even thought of."

A wave of confusion washed over me. "Of course they did." I knew that. I did. So how could I have been imprinted with such a clear memory?

"You must have heard our stories about them and imagined one as your own recollection." That, or maybe as a child I'd somehow managed to shake loose memories of them that had been imprinted on our surroundings. But no, that type of experience felt more like watching a movie, a three-dimensional movie, but a movie all the same. My "memory" of my grandparents felt as real to me as anything else from my childhood.

I struggled with the odd sensation of recollecting something I couldn't possibly have experienced, but Jessamine had already moved on. She crossed the room, her determined footsteps muffled by the same Persian rug where my grandmother had once stood. She picked up a photo of my grandfather, fishing pole in one hand, the other resting on an eight-year-old Oliver's shoulder. Grandpa hadn't faced the camera in this shot. Instead, he focused, his eyes full of pride and love, on his only son. I didn't know who took the picture. I assumed my grandmother had. Probably, as Oliver was beaming, his eyes turned up at the photographer rather than the lens. The picture had captured a truly magical moment, and I had always adored it.

Jessamine scrutinized it, holding it out at arm's length. The corners of her mouth turned down, and she looked down her nose at the picture, like she was viewing something distasteful. "They passed together, didn't they?" She set the picture down carelessly, letting it fall over face-forward.

Iris smiled nervously at me and rushed over to right the photo. "Yes." Iris angled the photo into its previous position. Jessamine watched her with an expectant expression. "An auto accident."

Jessamine's eyes widened and the corner of her mouth turned up. "Your family seems to be especially susceptible to auto *accidents*." She trailed the back of her hand across the headrest of a wingback chair. She blinked slowly and turned her gaze to me. "Perhaps you should invest in a defensive driving course."

"Perhaps you should tell us why you've come?" Ellen said, having entered the room with Martell in tow. Ellen's face was flushed. She regarded our guest through partially closed lids. Everything on my grandfather's desk shook and rattled. The table next to Jessamine began to vibrate and lurched an inch toward her. Jessamine cast a nervous glance at the table and stepped back. She had picked the wrong topic to make light of.

Ellen strode up to Jessamine, but Martell made a huffing sound and quickly insinuated himself between his cousin and my aunt. "Someone was messing around Gramma's grave last night," Martell said. The shaking stopped, and the room fell silent.

"What do you mean 'messing around'?" Iris asked, her face blanching.

"Doing magic," Martell responded. To him, I'm sure it seemed a complete answer, but he had no idea how imprecise a statement he had made. In response to our blank stares, he reached into his jacket and pulled out his cell. "Here, look," he said and pulled up a photo of Jilo's grave. I took it from his hand and expanded the picture, taking in the deserted talismans and sigils drawn on her stone and the surrounding plots. I held the phone out to my aunt, and Iris swiped it from me.

Jessamine pushed around Martell, even though she hadn't fully regained her composure. Her shoulders slumped forward and a bead of sweat rode her upper lip. "Someone—" Her voice broke. "Someone has been attempting a resurrection spell."

"Don't be absurd," Ellen said, and I turned to face her. "Jilo's been gone too long." She shook her head. "Resurrections are difficult enough, and by that I mean close to impossible, even when the body is young and healthy." Her forehead creased. "And fresh. I'm sorry"—she looked to Martell and Jessamine—"but Jilo was too old, and she had taken on too much." Ellen paused. I knew she was thinking about the toxic magic of blood and sex my mother had collected in Tillandsia. The poison Jilo had willingly taken into herself to save the people of the city she had loved. Ellen stopped just short of sharing this bit of information with Jilo's family. "More than a matter of minutes is too long. The brain, the internal organs, they shut down," she continued quickly, trying to cover the lost beat. "The body might be reanimated, but you could never achieve a true resurrection. Let me see that." Iris handed the phone to her sister. Ellen moved her hand around the screen, examining the remnants of magic. "No. This is not any kind of resurrection spell."

"No, it isn't," Iris concurred and crossed to the shelves that lined the room's western wall. "But I've seen one of the sigils, the big one, before. Could you forward the pictures to me?" she asked Martell, but never waited for a reply. Instead she crossed the room and pulled a heavy leather-bound book from a shelf. Its weight caused her to struggle a bit as she carried it to the desk. She opened the book and held her left hand over the pages. "Show me," she said, and the pages flipped forward. When they stopped, Iris reached out to Ellen, who placed Martell's phone onto her upturned palm. "Come," she said to Jessamine. "Look at this. It's used as part of a possession spell."

Jessamine went to the desk and bent over the dusty volume. "A possession spell?"

Iris nodded without looking away from the page. "Also known as a 'berserker' spell. It used to be fairly common, at least in connection with battles. Soldiers would use it to invite the spirits of the great warriors or even animal totems to possess them. The other signs, they don't fit in, but I'm sure whoever disturbed Jilo's grave was not trying to molest her." Iris handed the phone to Jessamine, then pulled her hand quickly back like she'd been shocked. The women's eyes locked—Iris's widened while Jessamine's flashed at first in surprise, then glinted with a trace of malice. Something had passed between the two women. Iris's psychometry had betrayed something I didn't think Jessamine had planned to divulge, but somehow this revelation had changed the balance of power between the two. Jessamine shook off any sign of insecurity, while Iris looked wounded.

"Then why are they messing with Gramma's grave?" Martell asked, breaking the moment that had passed between Jessamine and my aunt.

Iris cleared her throat and closed the book. "I suspect they were trying to tap into any residual power that might have been lingering. Could you put this away for me?" she asked, and Martell returned the book to its place on the shelf. "Your great-grandmother was a very brave woman."

"Perhaps a bit too brave," Jessamine said, crossing to Martell and dropping his phone back into his jacket pocket.

"Perhaps." Iris nodded sadly. "In the days before her passing, she opened herself up to some very dark magic." Jessamine bristled, but Iris held up her hand to fend off Jessamine's reigniting anger. "If she had not done so, we would not be standing here today. She saved my life. She saved all our lives. Hell"—Iris allowed herself a profanity—"she saved the whole city."

"And still you witches desecrate her resting place," Jessamine said. Her voice remained steely, but her eyes had softened. She seemed to be torn between her need to be angry and the realization of how important Jilo had been to us.

Iris did not make an attempt to defend witch-kind, even though I surmised she had already chalked the desecration up to magic workers rather than true witches. "I assure you we will deal with whomever committed this abomination, and we will deal with them harshly." She reached out and pulled Martell into an embrace. "I promise you this," she said in a near whisper.

Jessamine seemed to be satisfied with Iris's vow. She stood tall and, after casting another look at Martell, said, "We'll see ourselves out." She moved elegantly, her head held high as if she'd just won some great victory. I got the sense this entire encounter had meant something more to her than making sure Jilo's rest remain undisturbed. Iris released Martell and walked over to my grandfather's desk.

"Ladies," Martell said with a bob of his head, then followed his cousin out of the room.

"Martell," Ellen replied, as we both turned our attention to Iris.

Iris stood stock-still with her back toward us and her arms drawn around herself. She stared up at my grandmother's portrait. I sensed she was waiting, waiting for the clack of the front door. When that sound reached us, she turned back toward us. Her face had flushed, and the pulse in her temple betrayed a black anger. Tears welled up and rolled freely down her cheeks.

"Good heavens," Ellen said, then rushed to her sister's side. "We will deal with this." She pulled Iris into her arms and stroked her hair. "We will."

Iris struggled and freed herself from Ellen's embrace. "It isn't that," Iris said, a quiver in her voice. "That woman. Jessamine. She is one of us."

"A witch?" I asked incredulously.

"No." Iris clenched her fists. "She's a Taylor."

SIX

"Our families got history, my girl. Real history." Jilo's words spoken last July had come back to haunt me in November.

"What I read from Jessamine—" Iris shook her head. An anger like I'd only seen once before, the night she learned Connor had left me to burn in Ginny's house, descended on her like a cloud of flame. What bit of hidden history had she accidently uncovered? Her chin jutted forward. "I have to learn if what she believes to be true is indeed the truth. I have to learn if Daddy really did what she believes he did." Her voice dropped to a whisper. "And if he did, I will make him answer for it." I knew Iris had adored Granddad. She cherished his memory, and worked to keep it alive for the rest of us. I could see what she learned from Jessamine's touch bore witness that her adored father's feet were made of clay, and Iris was not taking this revelation well. She stood as stiff as a soldier at attention. The fists she held out before us were clenched so tightly that her knuckles turned white. Angry tears streamed down her face.

"How do you intend to do that?" Ellen crossed to put a sheltering arm around my shoulders. It was only then I realized I'd been trembling.

"I aim to ask the randy old goat himself. We are going to summon Daddy."

"No. It is too dangerous," Ellen said. "What if his spirit gets trapped here?"

We all knew Savannah acted as a kind of geological spirit trap. Something about this place could reach out and hold on to a spirit, keep it from moving on to wherever it was intended to go. I knew a man who swore the only way to make sure you wouldn't be caught in the trap was to be at least seventy miles out of Savannah when you passed. I wasn't sure about that, but I did know summoning Grandpa could be risky. Grandpa had passed through the trap cleanly the first time. If we called him down to our plane, his return trip to the great beyond might not turn out so well.

"Go upstairs and get Abigail," Ellen commanded me. "Tell her we need her."

I hurried from the library and found the foot of the steps in the quickest waddle I could manage. "Abigail," I called. I started up the steps. "Abby, we need you."

I heard a door creak open, and then Abby shushed me. "Maisie's sleeping. Last night took a lot out of her." Abigail's words reached me like a stage whisper. "What is it?"

"I don't really know, but, well, please come to the library."

I caught a glimpse of Abby over the bend of the railing. She wore a quilted robe, and had her hair bound up in pink curlers. She nodded. "I'll come right down."

I turned and headed back down the stairs I had climbed, taking them slowly. I'd hoped the storm would have passed, that Ellen would have managed to calm Iris before I found myself back in the library, but no such luck. "Yes, I'm sure," Iris snapped at Aunt Ellen as I came through the door. "I felt it in her."

Ellen turned to face me. "Where is Abigail?" I knew she was hoping Abby could help use her magic to calm Iris.

"She's coming," I said to Ellen. Then softly to Iris, "It's okay." I reached out toward her to put my arm around Iris, but she stepped away. She nearly vibrated with rage.

Abby entered the library, her hands still busy tying the belt of her robe. "Iris, what is wrong? Why are you so angry?"

Ellen's head tilted to the side and she spoke softly. "When Iris touched Jessamine, she sensed a connection between us."

"Connection?" Iris glared at Ellen. "Connection?" Her voice rose an octave over its normal pitch. "That young woman is our niece." She turned and stared at me with wide-open eyes. "Yes, your cousin. Jilo's great-niece is your cousin."

"Even if it's true," Abby said, "would it be that terrible? I mean, I know you girls think your daddy hung the moon, but he was only a man. Your daddy, well, he always had his bit on the side." Coming from anyone else, the statement might have pushed Iris completely over the edge, but I sensed Abby was sending out waves of comfort to Iris, trying to calm her and make her think rationally rather than act out of anger. It didn't appear to be working all that well. "We all knew it. Even your mama did." My eyes shot up again to my grandmother's portrait. "I'm sorry . . ."

Iris took a deep breath. She closed her eyes and took another. "It isn't only that our father was a philanderer."

Abby folded her hands as if she were in prayer. "Whatever you've seen, it's in the past. Let it lie between him and his maker."

"No." She shook her head. "God may prove too forgiving. That bastard is going to answer to me for his sins." Static electricity began to build around us, dancing on our skins. Abby patted her curlers, and as I felt my own unfettered hair begin to rise I understood why. Our house's power failed with a loud and final-sounding pop. A whitish-blue ball of lightning shot from Iris's fingertips into the center of our circle. It began a slow spin, dimming and taking on the color and sheen of mercury.

"Edwin Wallace Taylor, I call to you. Rise, return," Iris shouted. The orb at our center pulsed as convex images formed on its surface. Some dark, twisted, undoubtedly demonic. Others, anguished or fearful.

"Is that—" I began.

"Yes, it's Gehenna." Iris answered me before I could complete my thought. "The plane of existence reserved for those of us who have committed the gravest sins."

"Then it is real," Ellen said. "The place of eternal suffering." She leaned in to look more closely at the window that had formed between us and hell.

"It's as real as anything else," Abigail said shaking her head. "But like everything bad, I believe it is of our own making. God would never create such a place."

"How could you have known Granddad was there?" I asked, watching the individual faces that rose to the surface of the sphere, pressing against its skin, trying to break free from their place of bondage.

"I didn't know he would be there," Iris said, sounding defeated by the realization. "But it may be exactly where he belongs."

"You don't mean that," Abigail started, but the gravity emanating from this bulging window into hell grew strong, harder to resist. We each took a step inward.

This is not a good idea, I thought to myself.

"This is not a good idea." Ellen echoed my thoughts aloud. "It's some kind of trick. Daddy would never be . . . there."

"If what I read from Jessamine is true, Gehenna is exactly where he should be." Iris raised her arms so that her wrists bent in toward the light. Angry gashes formed there, letting her blood shoot forward to feed the spinning quicksilver globe. It swallowed the blood hungrily. "Blood calls to blood. Spirit calls to soul. Return." Her eyes flashed at us. "Say it. Chant it. Repeat after me. Blood calls to blood. Spirit calls to soul. Return."

I was afraid of what might happen if I obeyed Iris, but more afraid of what might happen to her if I didn't. I joined in. "Blood calls to blood. Spirit calls to soul. Return."

I glanced nervously at Ellen. She nodded and began the chant. "Blood calls to blood. Spirit calls to soul. Return."

"This is wrong," I heard Abby protest weakly, but a stern look from Iris squelched her dissent. Soon she added her voice, her magic to the spell Iris was weaving. "Blood calls to blood. Spirit calls to soul. Return."

"Edwin Wallace Taylor," Iris called out over our chanting, "I command you by this blood . . ." Iris focused all her power on the sphere in the circle's center as another spurt of blood left her and rushed into the orb. Without warning we were pulled in another step closer. The orb contracted, becoming smaller but remaining at the exact center of our constricting circle. For a short time it remained a perfect sphere, but in the next instant that sphere began to elongate, forming a recognizably human shape. A mannequin-like head with only the suggestion of features hung in the air between us.

"Show yourself, you cowardly bastard." Iris spat out the words, but the shape began to grow smoother, nothing more than a furrowed oval. The spirit fought the summons, evidently preferring damnation to facing its angry daughter. Another rush, another pull of gravity tugged at us, bringing us all within arm's length of each other. Without willing it, my hands reached out, one clasping Abby's hand, the other Iris's. We fell silent as a shock of energy shot through us.

"I said show yourself." Iris's words came out almost like a growl, and my heart jumped at the sight of her face. Her lovely clear eyes glowed with a red light. The pupil and iris had been erased, leaving only two shining rubies. "Return."

The gravity that had been centered on the shape at the middle of our circle suddenly reversed, repulsing us, knocking Ellen and Abby on their backsides. I was able to keep to my feet, but the wind had been knocked out of me. As I struggled to reclaim my breath, the shape in the center continued its metamorphosis. It was clearly in the shape of a human head, but the skin of bruised quicksilver remained mirrorlike. I could see my own features warped in its reflection. I was reminded of the horrid chandelier my mother had created from the heads of those who had stopped being of any other use to her. I'd lost my mother to this kind of magic, I would not lose Iris.

"What have you done?" Ellen asked Iris as Abby helped her back to her feet.

We all looked to Iris, and I breathed a sigh of relief to see her eyes had returned to normal. Then I felt a wave of anger. She knew better than to invite this kind of dark magic into herself, into our home.

I didn't focus on her for long, though, as it was impossible to ignore the floating cranium at the center of the library. Its eyes opened, but they too shone smooth and reflective; there was no difference between the composition of the eyes and the lids that had covered them. Its lips separated slowly, a thin film of bluish mercury covering the mouth, then popping inward like an imploding balloon.

"My girls, my beautiful daughters, are you to be my greatest torment?" The voice that came from the form had no intonation; it sounded flat, nearly mechanical. No, worse than that, it had been robbed of all hope. Still, it was clear the voice did not belong to a man; it resembled a woman's soft alto.

"Mama?" Ellen blanched. She broke the circle and approached the suspended figure, nearly touching it, but stopping shy of actual contact.

Iris walked a complete ring around the form. "Where is he? Was he too much of a weakling to face us himself?"

"Your father is not here. Only I. I am alone."

Ellen fell to her knees before the chrome apparition. "Mama, I have missed you so much." The look of wonder on her face told me she didn't give a damn about Iris's intended interrogation. "What happened, Mama? They said you ran the car off the road on purpose." This was news to me.

Ellen's question was met by silence then a heartrending moan. "No choice. I had no choice."

Abby had moved softly around the edge of the room to get a better view of the entity's face. The quicksilver face took a moment to register our presence, focusing first on Abby then turning toward me. Rather than looking at me dead on, she seemed confused by something on the periphery of her vision. "What kind of magic is this?"

Iris lowered her head in shame. "I'm sorry, Mama, I know it was wrong to use blood magic . . ."

"No," she said and turned her empty eyes on me. "This girl. She's wrong."

A touch on my shoulder nearly caused me to jump out of my skin. I looked back over my shoulder to find Maisie had come into the room unnoticed. I remembered that she had been resting. She wore a gray oversized T-shirt. Her hair was mussed. The room flashed with a pop then darkened. The smell of ozone wafted around us.

"I told you to stay in your room," Abby chastised her, but only mildly. She pulled Maisie away from me, trying to maneuver her through the door. "You get on back to bed, you hear?"

"Mama, we don't have much time. The power is fading," Iris said, her voice keening.

"We will find a way to free you, Mama," Ellen said. "We will. But you have to tell us why you are . . . where you are."

"Because she killed Grandpa," Maisie said, breaking free of Abby's grasp and taking a few steps closer to the orb. Her certainty sent a chill down my spine, as it echoed what I somehow also knew to be true. Maisie's words were answered by my grandmother's wail.

"Why?" Ellen's voice broke. She pushed away, scrambling a few feet back from the apparition.

"Because he had another family. A family before us." This time it was Iris who answered. She had seen it all with a single touch of Jessamine's hand. "Jilo's little sister." My mind flashed back to the night I first met Jilo. The night I had gone to her crossroads. She had hated us Taylors. Now I was beginning to understand why.

"His parents did not approve, but he rebelled." Iris wrapped her arms around herself. "When he took her to France and married her, they cut him off financially, revoked his access to the family trust. They knew their son was a man who loved his comforts. Eventually he grew tired of the poverty and tired of his wife as well. He never even divorced her. He left her and his children behind and came back to Savannah and married Mama."

"When we married, I knew nothing of his first wife and family. When I learned what he had done, how he had deserted them. How he had deceived me. I couldn't live with knowing he had made me his whore," the voice raged. "I wanted him to pay. For what he'd done to me. For deserting his children. For abandoning his real wife. I wanted him dead. I just kept driving faster and faster. Then I awoke in hell."

"Well," Abby said, a halo of golden light emanating from the crown of her head. "You've been there long enough. If you let me, I think I can lead you out of there." The light grew brighter around her until it shone like a gold and soothing aura. This halo. It struck me that this was what coming home looked like.

Abby took a step toward the metallic face, then another. Rather than drawing nearer the manifestation, Abby herself began to change, growing smaller to my eyes, looking as if she were walking down a long straight path into the horizon.

"Abby, no, you don't know what you're doing," Maisie called, a sense of urgency causing her voice to strain.

"Don't worry, sweetheart," Abby said and nodded. "I do. I'm going to help your grandma find her way out of there."

"No. You can't just reach in and pull her out." Maisie turned to me. "Gehenna isn't a place. It isn't a realm or dimension. It is a machine."

"Sweetie, we don't have time to entertain your fancies." Iris didn't even look at Maisie as she said the words. Maisie looked at me as if Iris had struck her.

"This has been too much for you." Ellen wrapped an arm around Maisie's shoulders. "You shouldn't be a part of this. Let me help you back to your room."

"I do not need help finding the room I have lived in my entire life," Maisie snapped. She threw my aunt's arm off. "You have to listen to me. I know things y'all don't," Maisie said, then turned to me.

The quicksilver face melted away, first returning to its spherical shape then morphing into a bulging disk. It floated out before us as Abby's form constricted.

"We have to stop her," Maisie said, shaking Iris's shoulders.

The convex face of the disk distorted into an absolute flatness, then began pressing backward on itself until it became concave.

"Abby doesn't understand. We have to bring her back." Panic had taken control of Maisie's voice.

I started circling the gateway, only to realize that while it remained perfectly clear when seen head on, the shape appeared distorted from the side. From the side, Abby's form was stretching out, falling to a dense point at the front, fainter and more dispersed at back. An arrowhead of light about to pierce a black hole's event horizon. Then her luminescence began to unwind, like spun gold, into the darkness. Gehenna began to show its teeth, revealing itself as an insatiable devourer, a perverter, of any goodness. The mouth of Gehenna opened wide, readying itself to feast.

My heart beat like mad. The vision I held of Abby hanging before the gate of Gehenna had remained unchanged for several seconds now. I realized, from our perspective, her image would remain there, frozen forever in this hellish event horizon. From her perspective, she might already be eternally lost. A string of light wrapped around me and tugged. I turned back to Iris just in time to see Maisie fling herself in after Abby.

The light that had lassoed me had also attached itself to my aunts. I realized Maisie had bound us all together, linking us to form a type of throw line. A tug pulsed down the length of the binding. As Maisie's image flattened and superimposed with Abby's, I tugged back with all the magic in me, but the gravity of Gehenna had no intention of surrendering prey that had come knocking at its door. The strand of light stretched as thin as one of Maisie's own golden hairs, and I felt certain it would snap, leaving the two lost at the portal of hell. The room filled with the sound of fearsome shrieks and howls. Maisie appeared, her tether wrapped around herself and Abigail, the mouth of Gehenna stretching, its darkness straining to reach into our world and swallow them whole. But then it fell back in on itself, collapsing under its own weight. Like a shattering hologram, the vision of Gehenna broke into pieces, each piece a smaller, yet exact duplicate of the whole, then faded from sight. Maisie stood before me, with her arms wrapped tightly around Abigail and a look of triumph in her eyes.

SEVEN

"All right," I said, "we are listening. What do you mean that Gehenna is a machine?"

Ellen crossed to the loveseat and sat down. She patted the seat next to her, and Maisie went to join her. Iris seemed unwilling to entertain Maisie's ideas. Instead she turned away and began to peruse the tomes that lined the wall. I surmised she expected to find more concrete answers therein than she would get from her niece's ranting.

"I know things you aren't going to find in those books, Aunt Iris."

Iris turned back and acknowledged Maisie with a nod. She signaled her acquiescence by holding her hands up toward us, palms forward, then sitting in one of the wingback chairs. Abby took the other, and I lowered myself onto the ottoman. "We're all listening," I assured Maisie.

She took a moment to compose herself. She drew a breath and spoke to us all, although she looked only at me. "You know Ginny taught me things only an anchor, like you, should know. Things about the line and its limitations. She stopped just short of telling me how it was created. You have the right to know everything, but the other anchors, they don't trust you. They've decided to keep you ignorant of these truths."

"Gehenna, baby," Ellen prompted. She was not going to sit through the unexpurgated version while her mother suffered through endless torment.

"Gehenna," Maisie echoed. "I'm getting to that, but you have to know the whole story."

"Okay." Ellen acknowledged the need for patience. She reached up and ran her fingers through Maisie's hair.

Maisie seemed oblivious to this sign of affection. A small line formed between her brows as she concentrated. She tugged at the collar of her T-shirt. "The line has limitations. Witches created it to protect this reality, our mortal world, from the old ones." She peered deeply into my eyes. "Like I said, I don't know how they did it, but I think deep down you do. I think the line has been trying to tell you. I know you've had the dream."

As she spoke the words, memory of the dream I'd been having on and off, sometimes remembering I'd had it, sometimes not, reached up to my conscious level. The sight of pyramids and obelisks being struck by lightning, silence giving way to the whirring sound of energy rushing around stone circles, a filament of energy racing along a magnificent stone wall. A faceless man, slithering away. Yes, I'd been having the dream, but I still had no idea what it had to do with the line. These places, these monuments, at least the ones I recognized, were built at different periods in history, epochs separated by millennia. It made no rational sense to me that Giza, Monks Mound, and Teotihuacan could have all played a role in the line's creation.

"The anchors would be furious I've told you about Gehenna," Maisie said. "I'm sure the only reason I am still breathing is because they believe y'all think I am crazier than a bedbug." She paused and examined each of our faces. "They will kill me if they learn I've shared what I know. They'll kill you if they realize you have listened. Except Mercy, of course. They won't kill her. They'll bind her. Y'all need to decide if you really want to hear this before I go on."

My heart sank as it acknowledged the truth behind her words. The other anchors should be my allies, not my enemies, but they seemed to have it in for me as much as my declared enemies. Maybe even more so.

Iris and Ellen looked at each other. Ellen placed her hand on Maisie's knee, and Iris relaxed back in her chair.

"Well, I sure as hell ain't going nowhere," Abby said. "Let's have it." She had been shaken by her experience, but she was determined not to show it. Still, her hands trembled, and the static electricity that had built up around her caused a slight pop as she tugged the last curler from her hair. Her eyes remained as wide as saucers.

Maisie licked her lips. "Gehenna lies beyond the line's reach, not even a hair's breadth beyond this physical dimension, but it isn't a place. Gehenna is a machine, a power plant. The old ones created Gehenna. Before Gehenna, when a person died, their essence could freely return to its source. The old ones realized if they could trap a person's essence, it could be converted to power. When it comes to magic, if the power of blood is like oil, then soul magic, the magic of Gehenna, is nuclear. Our world's is not the sole Gehenna. There are multiple ones, surrounding multiple worlds. Our souls, and the souls of sentient beings from a million different planets, a billion different realities, provide the power for much of the old ones' magic."

"If this is true, if Gehenna is a dynamo of some sort, why would Mama be trapped there?" Ellen's guileless eyes moved past my sister to me, carrying the wordless question of whether I believed any of this. I answered with a slight shrug. My brain was telling me it sounded pretty far-fetched, but my gut told me it felt all too true.

"When a person dies, the vibration of their essence speeds up, kind of like a jet engine coming to life before takeoff. If the essence doesn't reach the right frequency, it doesn't ascend. It was in this in-between frequency the old ones built the Gehenna machine. It is voracious. We all felt its gravity. People wonder why Savannah is so haunted? It's because in the same way the line's power is anchored by witches, Gehenna is anchored to this world at certain places. Savannah is one of those places. Gehenna may fail to capture a soul, but its pull may still keep a spirit from reaching the vibrational wave it needs to achieve to transcend our realm."

"What would stop a soul from ascending?" My lower back began to hurt from sitting on the ottoman. I leaned back against my hands to relieve some pressure.

"A sense of guilt. A soul ends up in Gehenna not because of what she did in life, but because of the shame she feels for her choices, her failures." She looked up at me. "Most of these people aren't evil. They aren't even bad. There's a story of a man whose soul spent years in Gehenna because he felt guilty over having his badly injured dog put to sleep rather than putting it through a painful surgery that offered only a slight chance of saving its life. The dog's spirit waited for him, just beyond Gehenna's gates, until it got tired of waiting and went in to pull his master out."

Abby held up her hands. "Wait. So where do the truly evil— the ones with no sense of remorse—go?"

Maisie shook her head and shrugged. "I don't know. I don't think anyone knows. But they don't end up in Gehenna." She lowered her eyes and bit her lip. I knew she was weighing her words. "The crimes of those in Gehenna may be real or imagined, but Gehenna is full of people like us. Like Grandma. Like you." She looked at Ellen. A sudden sob escaped Ellen. She pulled her arms tightly around herself, and she averted her gaze. We knew the guilt she carried with her for not saving her son. "Like Oliver, who, despite what he says even now, carries the shame of what happened with Grace." She turned to me. "Like Peter, who knows deep down he raped you."

I nearly jumped off the ottoman. "Peter did not *rape* me."

"He had a spell, a magical roofie, put on you, then took you to bed. You may have managed to rationalize what he did, but I can see the shame in him even if he can't."

I struggled up from the ottoman and went to the window. I stared out at the garden. I had never allowed myself to look at Peter's actions in this light. But today was not the day to do so. At the moment, I could not even begin to consider the feelings her words had stirred up. I'd file them away and look at them another day. After all, what was one more item on the list of things I'd queued up on my "to be processed" list? I kept my eye on the greenery on the other side of the glass.

"The dog." Iris's calm voice came from behind me, leading me to turn back to face her. "Is that just a sweet story, or is there actually a way to get Mama out of there?"

I could feel Maisie watching me. Her thoughts telegraphed her regret for having gone too far about Peter. Her unspoken apology caused the tension to leave my shoulders. The breath I'd been holding escaped.

"Some souls eventually let go of their pain and find their own way out," she said, slowly turning her attention from me to Aunt Iris. "Others stay trapped. The demonic faces you saw there—they aren't demons. They are humans who have been in Gehenna too long. Gehenna has twisted them. Squeezed every last drop of humanity out of them. They grow so dense, so dark, so heavy that sometimes one will drop out of Gehenna and back into our reality. Their perversion causes them to tempt others into doing things that may land them in Gehenna too." Maisie shuddered. "You've seen them," she said addressing Abby. "The shadow people who always seem to be flitting at the corner of your eye. They crave the light you carry." Abby shifted in her seat, pulling her robe more tightly closed.

"Your grandmother?" Iris tried to rein Maisie's thoughts back in.

"Grandma," Maisie said and nodded. "I'm afraid the only way to help her is to go in after her."

"How?" Ellen tensed and leaned in toward Maisie.

"Getting into Gehenna is easy. To get into Gehenna all you have to do is die." Maisie waited for us to absorb this.

"We can do this," Iris said. "We can stop my heart, and I will go to her." She focused on Ellen. "Once I have her out of there, you'll bring me back."

A crease formed between Ellen's eyes. "No. It's too risky. I won't risk losing you. Not even for Mama."

Iris stood and stepped quickly across the room. She knelt before Ellen. "We have to. I cannot live with myself knowing we never tried." She reached up and grasped Ellen's shoulders. "I'll never make it past Gehenna myself if we don't try."

"It's more complicated than you think." Maisie leaned toward Ellen and Iris. "Anyone can enter Gehenna, but only someone who has no sense of shame can leave." She focused on Iris. "You wear your guilt like an overcoat, and I am afraid most of it is about me."

"Who doesn't feel guilty about something?" Abby gave voice to the question nagging at my own mind. "Only babies and sociopaths, and chances are the sociopaths ain't gonna be lining up to help us."

"It's true," Iris said, sounding defeated. "Anyone who's lived long enough has some regrets, no matter how hard they have tried to do the right thing."

Anyone who's lived long enough . . . The words bounced around my mind. I knew someone who was constitutionally incapable of causing others pain. Someone who truly was an innocent. Someone who had only been in this world a matter of months. "Call Rivkah. Emmet has to come back to Savannah. He has to come home."

EIGHT

"Your grandparents were never legally married. Big deal. It doesn't change who you are." Peter held me tightly to his smooth chest. It was a big deal. Especially to Iris. She had always taken great pride in our family's history, pride in her pedigree. And it was a big deal to me that my grandfather had been such a moral failure that he could have deserted his first family.

Still, I didn't protest. Peter was only trying to make me feel better, and it felt so good to lie with him. I pressed my cheek against his skin and breathed in his scent. I was still struggling with Maisie's assertion Peter had used magic against me as a kind of date rape drug. I had long known he had gone to Jilo for a spell. Heck, I myself had gone to Jilo for a spell that would ignite my passion for Peter, only Peter had placed his order first. Still, Maisie's interpretation of events showed Peter's actions in a different light. It was just another one of those horrible gray areas I would have to navigate. One day, soon, Peter and I would have to discuss it, but today was not that day. I filed the thought away for safekeeping.

"Your grandfather's other family." Peter's words pulled me back. "Where are they now?"

"At least one of them is here. Jessamine. The rest I don't know. I mean, I don't even know how large my new family is." A pain twisted in my heart. "I don't even know if they'd consider me family."

"Oh, baby." He nuzzled my hair. "They would be fools not to want to count you as kin."

"I don't know about that. If the shoe were on the other foot . . ."

"If the shoe were on the other foot, you'd be making plans for a family reunion. Or would it only be a 'union' since y'all haven't met yet?" He laughed, but his humor didn't really help.

"How it must have hurt them, to be deserted like that."

"Yeah, I'm sure it hurt like hell, but it wasn't you who did the hurting. Don't you take any of that on."

"I think Iris has claimed all that guilt for herself."

"She's been thrown for a loop by all this." His large hand ran down my arm, slid to my stomach. "Learning about your grandpa's lies has made her feel like she isn't who she always believed herself to be. I think I understand how she feels."

I stiffened as my heart jumped to my throat. "What are you talking about?"

He sighed. "I've been trying to find a way to talk to you about something."

I could feel his heart beat against my cheek. He seemed to have lost his nerve. "You know you can tell me anything."

He planted a kiss on the top of my head. "Yeah, I know that. I shouldn't have even brought it up, though, at least not right now. You've got so much on your mind already." A pang of guilt hit me. I hadn't even broached the topic of my grandmother's fate, or the more difficult matter of Emmet coming home to Savannah.

I placed my hand against his rock-hard shoulder and pushed myself back so I could see his eyes. "Tell me."

He removed my hand from his shoulder and pulled me back in against him. "Before the baby is born, I think we need to talk to my parents about who I really am."

I was dumbstruck. What had we done to betray his origin? Had I said something? Had I not said something? Panic nearly caused me to blurt those questions out.

"I mean, look at them," he said, interrupting me. "Then look at me. Dad's barely five foot seven. He and Mom are both black Irish."

I felt myself relax. It was true, only the most miraculous combination of Claire and Colin's recessive genes could have created my redheaded giant.

"I know what you are about to say." Peter rocked me gently. "I've looked through all the family pictures. I don't look like any of my relatives from either side."

"So, you think you were adopted? Is that what you're saying?"

"I would have thought so, but no, there are plenty of photos of Mom when she was so pregnant she looked bigger than a—" He stopped himself. "Pregnancy didn't suit her like it does you."

Relief washed over me. He had no idea that Claire was not his natural mother. "Yeah, nice try there."

"I'm hers all right, but I don't think my dad is my father, if you follow me."

I didn't have the heart or the energy to lie to my husband actively. "How do you feel about that possibility?"

"Yeah, thanks, Doctor. It's more than a possibility. I feel it in my gut. I always have. I love my dad so much, it never mattered before, but now . . ." I pulled from his arms so that I could see him. His two-tone eyes, one blue, one green, looked down, as if he were imagining the confrontation he felt he should have with his mother. "I need to know who I am." He lifted his eyes to meet mine. "I owe it to our son. I mean, there are medical reasons." This rationalization didn't ring true, even though logically it sounded valid. He had obviously long suspected his parentage, and that he was becoming a father himself must have sharpened his desire to learn the truth. It hurt me to think I would be one of those forced to hide the truth from him.

"Tomorrow," I said. "We'll go to visit Claire. Together. We'll ask her together. All right?"

He nodded, and it broke my heart to see tears well up in his eyes. He brushed them away with the back of his hand, then reached over and turned off the light.

NINE

I awoke to find Peter gone. Again. I rubbed my eyes, amazed to see the clock showed it was past eleven. I should have been up hours ago, helping Iris finish up with preparations for Thanksgiving. I jumped out of bed and rushed through a shower. Makeup could wait. I dried my hair enough so it wouldn't tangle and threw on drawstring sweatpants and one of Peter's T-shirts.

I smelled no cloves, no cinnamon, no sage. I rushed downstairs and into a kitchen empty except for Uncle Oliver, who sat at the table examining the old tourist map we had marked with the locations where the body parts had shown up. His eyes were red. He'd been crying. The sight unnerved me. He always shrugged off emotion. Pain seemed to slide off him. To witness Oliver hurting was a new and unpleasant sight. I averted my eyes to the map. So much had happened since I last looked at the map, it seemed like a thousand years had passed.

"Peter's at the bar. Told me to tell you that you shouldn't worry, he would hold off on talking to his mom." That was a relief. I still had time to warn Claire. "Cryptic message delivered, my duties have been carried out." Oliver looked up and read my expression.

"Oh, and Thanksgiving's been canceled, Gingersnap." He gave me a sad smile. "At least in the Taylor house."

"Oh." I felt somehow cheated and guilty for feeling cheated at the same time. Halloween or Samhain wasn't a big day for us like it was for our Wiccan friends. For us it was a time to indulge in an overabundance of sugar and dress up the way popular culture told us witches should dress. Iris always went all hippie earth goddess, and Ellen did the pointed hat and green makeup. Fun, but not a big deal by any means. Thanksgiving was going to be my first big family holiday as Peter's wife. I'd been looking forward to combining our families. Maisie was back and on the mend. We needed to celebrate her return to health. A touch of guilt rose in me. This was to be my first Thanksgiving without having to suffer from Ginny's vocal, no, vociferous disapproval of my every action. And dang it, we'd faced so many horrible things over the last several months, I just wanted one nice day. A day to have everyone I loved together. To enjoy them before I lost anyone else. "Why?" Even though I essentially knew the answer, I had to ask.

"Something about learning our mother is trapped in hell killed Iris's spirit of gratitude. On top of that Sam called. He's decided to spend the day with his family in Augusta. Iris is upstairs in her room and won't come out for love or money."

"Grandma isn't in 'hell,' she's in Gehenna, and we will get her out of there."

"Well, if anyone can manage that, I'm sure it will be you." I noticed he had a large bandage taped on his hand.

"You hurt yourself?"

He examined his hand. "Yeah, a tiny cut. Nothing to worry about."

"Doesn't look tiny. You should let Ellen look at it."

"I will when she gets back. She rushed off this morning. One of her meetings, I guess."

One of her meetings, I hoped. I pulled out a chair and joined him at the table. He started laughing, but the laughter didn't really sound happy.

"What's so funny?"

He shrugged. "I dunno. I guess after all the times I've been called a 'bastard,' it's kind of amusing to learn that is indeed exactly what I am." Tears moistened his eyes, then rolled down his cheeks. He made no attempt to hide them or wipe them away. "I guess I no longer need to feel guilty about letting the family name die out with me."

I could take it no longer. I made my way around the table and bent over to hug him. He reached up and patted my arm. "Thanks, Gingersnap."

My eyes fell to the map. "There are more Xs." I released Oliver and traced the new marks with my finger.

"Yep. That's the other thing. Adam's going to be working today. We now have everything but the head." He tapped the map with his pen. "This morning a jogger in Forsyth stumbled over—literally—a leg across from Old Candler." He pointed a bit south of Madison Square. "Its partner was left on the sidewalk by the Scottish Rite Temple." He tapped his pen again. "An arm out by Saint John's." He reached out and angled the map a bit. "Last night, a security guard found the missing foot in a cardboard box on the steps of City Hall."

It all struck me as too much. I felt the blood drain from my face and almost swooned. *Swoon*, the word struck me as I felt my knees start to give way, and it was only the absurdity of the word that gave me the strength to keep it together and not crumple. Oliver sensed what was happening and jumped up to brace me. In one quick and graceful move, he slid his chair under me and guided my bottom to it. "See?" he said. "Dismembered body. There are worse things in the world than finding out your father was not quite the man you believed him to be."

I put my elbows on the table and held my head in my hands, fighting the sense of vertigo and its best friend, nausea. I took slow, steady breaths.

Oliver gently grasped my shoulders. "You gonna be okay, there?"

I nodded. I swallowed. "Yes. I'm fine now."

"Come on, Nancy Drew, pull it together. Take my mind off our family mess. Help me figure this out. Adam needs us. He isn't a man who asks for help often. This time he's asked."

I sighed in capitulation. "Aunt Iris thinks someone is attempting to work a spell." I pulled the map closer. "But I don't see any significance to where the parts have been left. There's no visible pattern. I cannot think of any historical connection to these particular sites and sacrifices."

"Okay, then." Oliver seemed strangely enthused by my less-than-insightful participation. "Let's start with the basics of what we do know."

"You start. I need some tea," I said and stood.

"You sit, let me get it," he offered, but I shook my head.

"No, I'm good now." I stood and made my way to the cupboard. I opened the door and reached for a mug that had somehow made it from Clary's Café to our own personal collection. It slipped through my fingers and broke into three heavy shards on the counter. I jumped back.

"You sure you're all right?" Oliver said looking up from the map.

"Yeah. Yeah. Just clumsy." I grabbed a towel from the counter and wrapped the sharp-edged pieces in it, carrying them to the garbage can Iris kept in the pantry. I stepped on the pedal to open the lid, and my heart broke. There, thrown out with other items to be forgotten, was the twisted silver of a photo frame. Shards of bloodied glass rested upon a photo, the photo of Uncle Oliver and Granddad on their fishing trip. I reached in carefully and extricated the picture from the detritus. I placed it on a shelf, determined to have it restored for Oliver. Once the pain had faded, once his pride had healed, he'd want it back. I shook the broken mug into the can and let the lid fall closed.

I returned to Oliver. "Unless the killer intends to go all jigsaw on the head too, I think it's safe to assume the body has been divided into ten pieces," he said and recorded this point on a legal pad I hadn't even noticed before. He drew a heavy asterisk next to it. "So far nine of them have turned up. What else do we have?"

"Well, if we are running with the obvious, magic was used to keep the parts fresh, right? I mean, I'm assuming the parts just found are in the same condition as the others."

"That's what Adam said."

"Okay, then, write," I ordered, and my uncle obeyed. "We know it's the body of a female."

He paused mid-scribble and looked up at me. "We know she had red hair."

"But they haven't found the head . . . Oh, I see." The realization of how they knew this was quickly buried under an even more unpleasant realization. Magical correspondences. Voodoo dolls. "Sympathetic magic." Maybe I was growing paranoid, but lately it did seem like the whole world was out to get me. I flashed back on the earlier discussion I had with my aunts about Alice Riley. Witch. Pregnant. Now we had a dead redhead. I crossed to the table and sat back down, feeling like the wind had been knocked out of me. "Has someone murdered this poor woman and substituted her as a proxy for me?"

Oliver said nothing, but his expression spoke volumes. For a few moments he sat drumming nervously with his pen on the pad. "I don't want to jump to conclusions. Shelve it for now." He flushed with anger. "Damn it, I wish Iris would get over herself and come down. She's the one who's good at this kind of deduction." He slammed the pen down, and it flew off the table. "I'm going to go get her. Drag her down here."

"There is no need for dragging." The swinging door into the kitchen pulled back to reveal Iris standing there. "And I am doing my best to 'get over myself.'"

Oliver regarded her with a guilty expression. His eyes darted from Iris to me then back to Iris. "You know what I mean. I feel every bit as bad as you do, but you don't see me hiding my head in the sand like an ostrich."

"No, little brother, it is much more your style to strut around like a peacock." A long moment of silence stretched out between them as they stared each other hard in the eye. I was about to crawl under the table in search of shelter, when they both burst out laughing. Iris approached her younger brother and placed a kiss on the top of his head. She reached out and grasped his wounded hand. "What happened here?"

"Just a cut."

"You show that to Ellen when she gets home." She stepped back and took my uncle and myself in. "What's so crucial that you two are plotting to storm the castle and drag me from my turret?"

"They found the rest of the body," Oliver said. "Well, other than the head. That is still missing."

"All right, we knew the parts were still out there, and they were bound to show up sooner or later."

"Mercy's worried, well, I'm kind of worried too." Oliver bit his lip. "The woman was a redhead."

"There's the connection to Alice Riley. Pregnant," I reminded my aunt. "Commonly believed to be a witch," I said, and fearing I hadn't made my case added, "and let's don't forget that half the magical world seems to have an ax to grind with me."

Iris sat next to her brother. "I'm listening. Go on."

"We're afraid," Oliver took over for me, "that whoever is behind this is, as you thought, attempting to work a spell of some kind using the body as a poppet. A poppet to represent Mercy."

Iris's lips pulled into a tight line. She looked drained this morning; the light that had been glowing in her since she slipped out from under Connor's yoke seemed to have all but faded away. "I see." She took a few seconds to study the map. "This doesn't feel like the work of a real witch. It just doesn't. An attack by proxy. That's for amateurs." She reached over and picked up the legal pad. "Ten pieces. Most magic workers get hung up on the numbers six, seven, and thirteen. What is the significance of that number of ten?" she asked, but then answered her own question. "Whoever is behind this knows more than about magic. Perhaps they know something about the ten united families. Something about the line and the families who remain loyal to it."

There were indeed ten united families who maintained the line. There were originally thirteen, but three families came to regret their participation. They had been perfectly happy to throw off their own masters, but hadn't taken into account they would lose control of the non-witches who had been subservient to them. My father, Erik, had been from one of these families. When Ellen, his wife, failed to give birth to the daughter the rebel families had hoped would come to destroy the line, Erik began an affair with my mother. Maisie and I were the products of this affair.

"If the person, or people, behind the dismembering of this unfortunate soul is indeed attempting to use the corpse as a magical substitute for Mercy, I suspect it may have absolutely nothing to do with her personally, and everything to do with her role as an anchor of the line."

Well, that's a comfort, I thought, drawing my arms around myself.

"You think an ordinary magic worker is out to destroy the line?" Oliver asked.

"This is no ordinary magic work. I'd say more an extraordinary magic worker. Someone on par with Jilo . . ." Her words died as we all shared the same realization.

"Jessamine?" I thought of the anger I sensed coming from her. I could understand her anger, her sense of betrayal, but would she, could she, use magic to attack me? To attempt to harm the line through harming me? Something about this theory didn't sit right with me. "Jessamine knows Jilo and I were close. I don't believe she would betray Jilo like that."

"I haven't laid eyes on her yet, but to me she sounds like the type who would bank on your thinking that way."

"I suspect your uncle is right. I think Jessamine might see your affection for Jilo as a weak spot in your defense. Think, Mercy, what better way to extract revenge against your grandfather than by taking down the one thing he had truly been loyal to? He may have been willing to make fools out of his family . . . out of both his families, but he would have gladly laid down his life to protect the line."

"How do we handle this?" Oliver asked, having already tried and convicted Jessamine.

"Let me think about it for a bit." Iris crossed to the counter and found her apron. She tied it around her waist. "In the meantime," she said smiling at me, "you go upstairs and fetch Abby. Tell her she's got some baking to do." She held her head high, putting her hands on her hips and striking an intentionally humorous pose. "Thanksgiving has officially returned to the Taylor household."

Fake it till you make it. One of the slogans Ellen had adopted from her meetings came to my mind. Iris appeared to be doing just that. Still, I felt glad she'd changed her mind. I pushed myself up from the table and exited through the flapping door and into the hall. I climbed the stairs to the upper floor and turned toward

Maisie's room. I'd only taken a step in that direction when from behind me I heard the screech of a hinge thirsty for oil. My heart stopped cold, then began beating wildly to make up for the lost contractions. I knew that sound better than that of my own voice. It was the noise made by the door to the old linen closet, the room that as children, Maisie and I had adopted as our place of secrets. The same room to which Jilo had linked her haint-blue chamber.

I stopped dead in my tracks. I knew beyond a shadow of a doubt if I turned toward that creaking sound, toward the door I knew had just pried itself ajar, I would see the haint-blue aura of Jilo's enchanted chamber spilling through the crack into the hall. I knew it would be so, even though I knew it to be impossible. At Jilo's behest, I myself had destroyed her enchanted chamber, a room capable of straddling both space and time, or perhaps more correctly space-time. The physics of the place was well beyond my ken, and even though I felt I had the power to re-create such a space, I lacked Jilo's insight into the intricacies of the necessary magic. She might not have been a born witch, but she proved herself a great magic worker many times over.

I turned to see the door open, and the hall was indeed scintillating like sun on a pool. Jilo had figured out how to straddle dimensions. Could she have found a way around death itself? No sooner had the question entered my mind than the impulse to dive into that haint-blue light became an absolute compulsion. I fled down the corridor toward the cerulean glow. I paused at the threshold of the now open door, my intuition suddenly registering a sense of fraud. This magic was counterfeit. I stepped back, away from the light, but it was too late. It reached out to envelop me; then everything around me dissolved in a bright pulse.

TEN

When the flash faded, I no longer stood in my home before the entrance of my childhood playroom. I found myself in Oglethorpe Square, but everything around me was in the wrong place. The familiar landmarks of the world I knew were all present, but they lay reversed. No, they were mirrored in aspect to their natural coordinates. North lay south, east lay west, and the noon sun hung high but shone down from the northern edge of the horizon.

The Owens-Thomas House sat at the park's southwest corner. I blinked, and upon opening my eyes, the mansion had shifted to northwest, with President and Abercorn Streets having spun around like spokes on a bike wheel. The sun stood high over a Savannah that was not my home. I stopped and turned a full circle, searching the silent world around me for any sign of intelligent life, but there was none. Silent nature stood frozen, without even a breeze to flutter the Spanish moss.

Not knowing what else to do, I began walking toward where my intuition told me my house should be, all the while sensing a growing heaviness, a condensing of the atmosphere. The edges of the sky faded from blue to gray, not to a gray that the sky would naturally wear, but a gray that had never known any color other than black and white. A memory prickled at the back of my mind. I'd seen this sky before. I picked up my pace, but with each step I took closer to where home should lie, I felt an increased sense of menace, as if I were being guided, being funneled into a trap. The streets of Savannah had become a type of kaleidoscopic maze, with my well-worn path home transformed into a dead-end trail.

I sought to escape this feeling by turning away from home, onto Lincoln, testing the reality of what my witch's senses were telling me. I could only continue a few steps in my new direction; then the air around me seemed to congeal, constrict, and drive me back to this caricature of my customary route.

I was not going to lose my head. If I couldn't escape on foot, I would turn to magic. The first trick I had learned once my powers had been returned to me was to teleport short distances, simply by concentrating on the place where I wanted to go. I learned quickly to close my eyes when I did so, otherwise the motion would leave me feeling seasick. I closed my eyes and concentrated on home. Instantly I began to feel the now familiar sensation of dropping down and sliding, but this time something struck me as different. I felt as if I were bumping up against a boundary, like I was pushing against an enormous rubber band. I heard a screech like metal scraping against metal, and my eyes flashed open. I still stood some yards away from the Owens-Thomas House and only a few inches from where I had started.

I felt unseen eyes on me. Somebody was toying with me. "I know you're watching me. Enjoying my fear. But we have arrived at the end of your good time." I scanned the empty street, the deserted square. "I am an anchor of the line, and you cannot use its power against me." I wished I felt more certain of that fact, but my gut told me it was true. At least mostly so. "That means you are tapping into a different source, and the magic you are using is dangerous. It will backfire on you. If you stop now, I'll help you.

I promise. Now show yourself." Even though my gut told me Iris was too quick to lay blame at Jessamine's door, I very nearly expected to see her appear before me.

I stood there waiting, but my words were met with silence, and well, that just pissed me off. "I said show yourself." The words came out in a quiet voice. They didn't boom through the ether or echo around me, but even I was surprised by the sense of authority they conveyed.

The world around me scintillated; then shadows danced with light. A darkness coalesced and took form before me. The sound of clapping met my ears before my eyes could resolve the figure there.

"Wow, you have gotten really bossy there, cousin." Teague Ryan stood mere steps away. Teague looked like the kind of guy who reported television sports. Good-looking, but not too much so, with closely cropped hair and broad shoulders. I'd think him handsome if his personality didn't come so much into play. Teague was a bully. Nothing more, nothing less. I hadn't seen him, I hadn't even thought of him, since the night back in early July when we drew lots to see who would replace Ginny as our family's anchor. Teague worked his square jaw from side to side until it popped, then took a few steps closer. His pulse throbbed in his temple. I stood my ground. "You wanted to see me," he said, "so here I am."

Teague had wanted, no, expected, the line to overlook us undisciplined Savannah Taylors, and settle its powers on his own broad shoulders. Of everyone who might have been chosen to replace my Great-Aunt Ginny as anchor of the line, Teague was the angriest I had been chosen. Well, other than Maisie, that is, and she tried to kill me to get her hands on the power. Did Teague hope to succeed where my sister had failed? "What are you playing at here?" I asked.

He folded his arms against his chest, trying to appear relaxed, and actually doing a pretty good job of it. "I'm not playing at anything. I'm not playing at all. I am here to do what no one else in the family has the spine to do. I'm here to protect the line. I am here to *deal* with you."

At that moment I made the connection between the spell he had been working, the dimming of light, the loss of color, the ever-constricting ring, and the attack that had occurred at Jilo's house. "It was you who attacked Jilo and me," I said.

He had followed me to Jilo's home and set the spell in motion that nearly collapsed reality in around us. We'd escaped with our lives, but Jilo's house had literally been wiped from the face of the earth, just as if it had never been there. The magic he was using was darker even than what I'd seen through Tillandsia. He'd tapped into a magic so toxic I couldn't even imagine its source.

He smiled. "So what if it was?"

"So what if it was?" I parroted him. I felt my skin flush as my fists clenched into tight balls. "You think it makes you a big man, attacking an old woman? If it weren't for you, for what you did, she might not have—"

"Not have what? Kicked the bucket? Bought the farm?" He leaned in over me, glared down at me. "That old bat was well past her sell-by date, and you had no business exposing the line to her anyway. She was too smart. Too crafty. What if she had found a way to hook into it? Do you think she would have put the line's interest over her own? Hell, why should she? You're an anchor, and you certainly don't."

I ignored his gibes and took a step back. He knew he was prodding a very sore spot, and I surmised he was taunting me for his own amusement, trying to push me to the point where I would lose control. A time not so long ago, he might have succeeded at tapping into my famous temper, but not now. Still, he sickened me. His jealousy and greed had made him a fiend. He must have been the one messing around Jilo's place of rest. "You are a ghoul.

Defiling graves. Making deals with demons. Dismembering an innocent woman. Do you even have an idea how lost you are?"

"I have no idea what you are talking about. I've come to protect the line. I got nothing to do with any other mess you've gotten yourself into."

I began to circle him counterclockwise, forcing him to turn with me. I'd learned much from Jilo. Even if my movements created no magical effect, they would affect him psychologically, put him on the defensive.

This was the first time I'd had the opportunity to examine Teague through a witch's eyes. Before I had my power, he managed to intimidate me, but no longer. For one thing, in spite of what his enormous ego led him to believe, I didn't sense he had much of his own power to play with. And when it came to smarts, he wasn't the sharpest point on the pentagram.

My instincts told me he thought himself a leader in the cause, but he was just a dupe, not a person who had the wherewithal to pull this off. "Okay, then. If you aren't relying on blood magic, how are you working these spells?" I stopped in my tracks and hit him where he was most vulnerable. "I know you don't have enough power on your own. Whose magic are you using? Whose skirts are you hiding behind, little boy?"

His head shook from left to right; then he lunged forward, erasing the slight space I'd maintained between us. His hands clenched into meaty fists, red sparks shooting out around them. I wasn't sure if he intended to use magic against me or punch me. Or both. I braced myself, but I'd be damned before I gave up any ground. "I've never killed anyone," he said in a hiss. "But I sure would like to start with you."

I should have felt frightened, terrified even, but a deep sense of peace descended on me as some important pieces shifted into place. "And you would if you could. If that were all it would take. But you can't, because if you did, the line would never, ever take you as anchor." I laughed. "If anything, it would cut you off completely from its magic. You'd be left small. *Impotent.*" I leaned in further toward him. "That is why you've been trying to trap me. You aren't trying to kill me. You're trying to contain me." I realized that even the spell that erased Jilo's home had been a snare, not a weapon.

His lips curled up into a smile. "Wanna try to bounce yourself home again? It was fun watching the barrier smack you right back down. Hell, keep trying. I could watch it all day."

He had begun to regain his footing, so I smiled and shook my head as if I doubted he'd thought the whole scenario through. "So what exactly is your plan?" I took another jab at his ego. "You do have a plan, don't you? 'Cause I got to tell you, only a loser would try to play something like this without a plan."

He straightened to his full height, and glared down at me through narrowed, contemptuous eyes. He licked his lips. "Of course I have a plan, and this place right where we're standing is it. I have caught you. You *have* been contained, and there isn't a damn thing you can do about it."

I looked around, doing my best to appear unimpressed. "What's so special about Kaleidoscope Land? Sure, it's a bit disorienting at first, but I'll figure a way out of it sooner or later . . ."

"That might just be true," he said and let loose with a howling laugh. "But later will be a hell of a lot later than you think." He winked at me. "Seems like a big-shot anchor like yourself would have learned a thing or two about how time passes differently in some dimensions than others."

"Oh, aren't you clever?" I asked. "Shift me to a place where time moves more quickly. Where I will live out my natural lifespan in months rather than years, so you don't have to wait long for your next shot. There's one big problem with that, genius. It looks like you are stuck here with me."

A lopsided smile came to his lips. "No, you're wrong there, Red. I've got a hall pass." He turned his forearm toward me, showing me still-inflamed skin that bore a fresh tattoo, a circle composed of symbols that resembled stylized lightning bolts or sharply jointed versions of the letter "s." He looked at me with such smugness, I should have hated him, but instead my heart broke for him. I recognized the symbol. I'd seen something similar in the file my grandfather had compiled on *Lebensborn*, the grotesque Nazi breeding project, the source of my very own existence. I had no choice about having *Lebensborn* written into my DNA, but Teague chose to place its mark on his body. It sickened me, but I couldn't afford the luxury of pitying him.

"How long have you been working with Emily?" I asked.

He reached up and wiped the smile from his lips with a swipe of his hand. "Who?" His eyes rounded in confusion.

He had to be faking it. "Don't play stupid. Emily. My mother." I shook my head at his gullibility. "She isn't your ally. She isn't working with you. She's been tricking you. She wants to end the line."

His head jerked back and shook involuntarily. "I thought your mother died?" His words had started as a statement, then twisted into a question. He wasn't pretending. He really didn't know.

But if he hasn't been drawing magic from my mother, where is he getting his juice? No sooner had the question formed in my mind than I was struck by a vision of Teague. Stranger still, rather than seeing him from the outside, I experienced that revelation as if I were he. Through his eyes, I watched his reflection in a mirror. He stood alone, in a room lit by a single candle.

Since he was a witch, I should not have been able to pierce his psyche so easily, even if I were much more powerful than Teague. Still, something, an unbidden power, had given me access to his memories. This vision, like a silent movie, continued to unfold in my mind.

Teague's was the only visible figure, but he wasn't truly alone. I sensed others, disincarnate intelligences surrounding him, guiding him. One was much stronger than all the others combined. Watching himself in the mirror, he stripped to the waist and drew a sign much like the one found near Jilo's grave on his own chest, over his heart. I saw an arc of energy appear from nowhere and strike him, driving him down to his knees. I intuited it wasn't just magic, it wasn't just power he had accepted into himself. He had welcomed a consciousness into himself. He had offered himself up for possession. No, that wasn't quite right—he had allowed himself to become an anchor for a power that had lost its rights to be in our world.

Rather than continue as a passive viewer, I decided to attempt to direct his consciousness to open even wider to me. It yielded with ease, and I pushed deeper into his psyche, following the line of dark magic that connected him to the font of his power. What I found there chilled me, for I recognized this entity.

What I uncovered was not a minor demon like Wren, nor even a greater one like Barron, the demon Emily had sacrificed in her attempt to deliver me over to the old ones. The source of Teague's magic wasn't a demon in the conventional sense at all. My mind flashed back to my first taste of magic, when I witnessed an image other than my own in the mirror. Then I realized, Teague had somehow joined forces with one of the most dangerous witches this world had ever know, Gudrun, onetime best friend of my own paternal great-grandmother, Maria Orsic.

"Gudrun." Her name escaped my lips.

Teague trembled when he realized how easily I had breached his defenses. His eyes fell, and beads of sweat formed on his forehead.

I laughed in his face. "Even if you could hold me here, and watch from some safe and distant perch as my life force failed me, you would still have one big problem with this scheme of yours."

He stared at me, shaking his head as if he were trying to force me out of it. "Haven't you felt it, Teague? The world has changed. The line has changed. You could wait a thousand lifetimes, and still it will never choose you. Never."

I took advantage of his confusion and closeness to reach out and snatch his tattooed forearm. "Let me teach you a little blood magic," I said, sinking my nails deep enough in him to break through his skin. He squealed as his blood covered the tattoo. I claimed the sigil's magic for my own purpose. "Come on, Pinocchio, let's go say hello to the puppet master."

I closed my eyes and slid. This time I felt no resistance; I moved easily beyond the borders of my cousin's latest trap, this time with Teague himself in tow. When I opened my eyes less than a second later, we stood in my own bedroom. Teague staggered away from me, falling to his hands and knees and vomiting all over my rug. He was going to clean that up himself, once I got through whacking him over the nose. I turned away from the sight of his stricken face, only to catch my own reflection in my makeup mirror.

I hated what I saw there, as the sheen of Gudrun's foul magic clung to me. I forced myself to shrug off the fear of what my return ticket might end up costing me. "Come on, Gudrun. I got your boy, and I know you can hear me." For a fleeting moment, I saw her face, ice-blue eyes and perfect nose framed by a black pageboy bob, but as with the first time I had used my mirror to see into her world, she waved her hand and faded instantly. This time, though, I heard a pop, and although the glass remained in its frame, a web-work of cracks shot out from the mirror's center toward its outer edges. I guess Gudrun had had enough of my popping in uninvited.

To think the families had wanted to send me to this woman for training. If I had acquiesced, if I had gone to her, would I have ever made it home again? The sound of laughter rang out behind me, and I turned to find Teague back on his feet. "You don't stand a chance, not against her. Not against us."

"There is no more 'us' as far as you and she are concerned," I said, trying to keep my voice firm but calm. "Get it through your thick head, Teague. Gudrun has been lying to you. Tricking you. She has no interest in protecting the line. If anything, she is the line's greatest threat."

"You're wrong. She's changed. She's no longer a threat to the line. You are."

I held my hand up to him. "Stop. Believe what you want, but I am going to send you home now. You've left me without a choice. The families, the other anchors, I will have to tell them what you've been up to. That you have been conspiring against me, against an anchor."

"You are either a liar or a fool," Teague said. His face was deep red with anger, but then his emotions seemed to turn on a dime. He broke out in raucous laughter, the mirthful outburst causing tears to fall from his eyes. He wiped at them with the back of his hand. "You know, you really are too much. You don't have as many friends as you think you do. Do you think I approached Gudrun on my own? That we somehow figured out a way to sneak behind the other anchors' backs so she could use me to host her magic? Some of the other anchors, Mercy, they already know, and they are rooting for me." Was it my instinct or only my fear that made me believe him? "And I am going to keep coming for you until I get the job done."

"Your scheming against me has nothing to do with protecting the line. This is all about your pitiable need to feel important." The hate in his eyes made me wince. "You are going to leave me alone," I said, but this time the words sounded much less convincing.

"Oh, no. I am going to do no such thing. The only way you are going to get me to leave you alone is if you kill me, and we both know you don't have it in you."

"You're right," a familiar voice replied. I had been so focused on Teague I hadn't even noticed Maisie standing in the doorway. "She doesn't, but I do."

Before I could even think to stop her, Maisie raised her hand toward my shattered mirror. The largest shard broke free from the frame and whisked around me. It reached Teague and sliced his neck open, clean to the bone. The life shot out from him in a rush of scarlet as he fell to the floor before me. I blinked at the splatter of his blood that touched my face.

When I opened my eyes, Maisie looked up from Teague's corpse to my face. "Oh," she said. "Let me grab you a towel for that."

ELEVEN

I'd seen so many horrors since the morning I'd found Ginny's body lying in her parlor. In so many ways, the sight of my cousin's corpse lying on the floor before me was just one more. I wasn't sure what I should be feeling, but all I did feel was shame. Somehow I knew that in fifty or maybe one hundred years, when my own granddaughter or even great-great-granddaughter charged the atmosphere of this room, searching for memories of me, this one, this sight of me covered in Teague's blood, would be what rose up before her. Would she feel the horror that remained frozen in my chest?

A scream caused me to raise my eyes. *Oh, good. That's covered.* The words went through my mind as my cousin Abigail stood before me hyperventilating. My legs collapsed out from under me, and I landed on my knees. My gaze returned to Teague's face, which lay turned toward me, his dead eyes glazed over but still full of surprise. I heard the heavy tread of boots running up the stairs, down the hall. Sam found my room before Iris could join him. I hadn't expected to see him here today. He must have had a change of heart about joining us. I bet he was rethinking that decision right now. He knelt beside me and lifted me, carrying me from the room.

Oliver met us in the hall. He dodged into my room, then came back just as quickly, the color having faded from his face.

Iris appeared in the hall, and Oliver grabbed her before she could go into my room. "Don't," Oliver said to her. "You don't need to see this."

The words that followed blurred together into an indecipherable barrage of meaningless sound. The light around me dimmed, and I closed my eyes. I drew a breath and forced myself to return to the moment. "I'm okay, now. Thank you," I said. "You can put me down." Sam shifted me carefully until my feet touched the floor. The room began to spin.

"I don't think so," Sam said and bent down to slide his right arm back beneath my knees.

"She killed him. Without a qualm. Her face . . ." *A gaze blank and pitiless as the sun.* Yeats's words surfaced in my mind. "No feeling. She just . . ." My voice failed me.

"I have a tarp and some duct tape in my truck," Sam said in an even voice. *Sweet, handsome, and willing to help hide the bodies without asking a single question. He really was a keeper.* I began laughing again even though none of this should have hit me as funny. So this was what hysteria felt like.

Iris stood before us, looking like she wasn't sure if she should hug Sam or slap him. "Hopefully we haven't come to that," she said to Sam.

Maisie reappeared with a dampened cloth. She had washed the blood from her hands, but there were still splatters on her shirt. The sight of her ended my laughter.

"I could see into him," Maisie said, and I raised my eyes to meet hers. "He hated you, and he was never going to give up until he had taken everything from you." Her eyes narrowed in disgust. "I saw that he dreamed, no, fantasized, about overpowering you, hurting you, killing you. It gave him *pleasure*." The word came out sounding sick and dirty. "While I was gone, while I was wherever the line took me, I found myself in a place of such certainty, such clarity. I knew then if ever I laid eyes on you again, I had to do everything in my power to protect you. I'm sorry if my sense of conviction makes you uncomfortable, but I will gladly kill a thousand Teagues if it means keeping you safe." I didn't know whether to feel gratitude or horror as her words hung in the air between us.

"Here." Maisie offered me the washcloth.

"I'll take it, darling," Iris responded. "Abby, can you take Maisie back to her room?"

Abigail had followed us into the hall, but she was still pretty much frozen in the same stance. "Yes, I'll do that, but then I'm packing my bags and going home. I thought I could help, but I'm afraid the girl's too far gone." She looked at me as tears brimmed her eyes. "I'm sorry, I didn't sign on for this." Maybe it was uncharitable of me after all she had tried to do for us, but I felt disappointed in her. The sight of blood caused her to give up on Maisie, even after Maisie had flung herself into Gehenna to save her.

"Of course, dear," Iris responded without taking her eyes off me. "We understand." I didn't, but I had enough to think about without picking a fight. Abby hesitated to take Maisie's hand, but then she grabbed hold of my sister and escorted her down the hall.

"Take Mercy to my room, please," Iris said to Sam.

Sam maneuvered me through the doorway to Iris's room and sat me on the foot of the bed. He knelt beside me. Oliver sat next to me, putting his arm around my shoulder to prop me up.

"Who is this guy Maisie killed anyway?" Sam asked Iris. He used the present tense. Iris didn't respond. Instead she used the washcloth to dab at the splatters on my face.

"Teague Ryan," Oliver answered for her. "He *was* our cousin."

I looked up at Iris. "He's been working with Gudrun to . . . trap me." Iris's head tilted up and her lips pursed. "He said the only way to stop him was to kill him, and Maisie, well, Maisie . . ." I didn't recognize my sister since the line had allowed me to bring her home. On the exterior she remained unchanged. On the inside, though, well, truth was I had probably never really known what was going on in her soul. I wanted to believe my sister was not the person who had offered me up as sacrifice. That she was not responsible for her acts, considering she had been driven mad as a consequence of Ginny's crimes. And I had hoped that somehow we could reach down into her and find the grain of the girl she had been born to be and nurture it. Abigail had much more experience plumbing the depths of souls. Maybe she was right, maybe Maisie was too far gone, but I wasn't ready to give up hope yet.

"He was conspiring against an anchor of the line." Iris's words broke into my thoughts.

"Yes," I said, "but he said the other anchors know all about it. He implied he had their consent, if not their assistance."

"That doesn't matter," Iris said. "Well, it matters, but not in regard to how we are going to handle this situation. Listen to me." She freed her hand and placed both her hands on my shoulders. "Maisie did not kill Teague. You did. Do you hear me?"

"I don't understand." I shook my head.

"You are an anchor. It is an anchor's right to *remove* anyone who threatens them."

"My right?" I asked. "That's horrible. I shouldn't have the right to kill anyone."

"It's their law, not ours. You were doing your duty. You were protecting the line. That is the story we need to stick to."

"I don't know what you two are talking about," Sam said, "but why do you need to give these people a cover story? It sounds like this was self-defense to me." Was it only my imagination, or had Sam started shifting away? He seemed to be trying to avoid Iris's touch. Even an accidental one. That didn't bode well for their relationship.

Had he seen too much? Just moments ago he was ready to act without judgment.

Iris reached out her hand, and he stepped back. A small twitch of her right eye told me that she, too, had noticed Sam's sudden coolness. "Of course it was self-defense, but all the same, if the families learn Maisie killed Teague . . ."

She didn't need to finish her sentence. I understood. They would use any excuse to take Maisie from us. This time once and for all.

Maisie's lack of any hesitation to kill or remorse for the murder she had just committed made me wonder if maybe this callous killer *was* the true Maisie. Our very conception was linked to black magic; we had been born as an unintended result of our parents' attempt to destroy the line through the sex and murder magic of Tillandsia. Had my sister and I been tainted, stained to our very souls by their acts? Had I made a mistake bringing Maisie home?

"Maybe we just can't save Maisie." Ellen stood in the doorway. She stumbled a bit as she stepped over the threshold, but managed to catch herself. "Maybe we can't save Mama either." Even from ten paces away, I could smell the alcohol on her. She took a few more weaving steps, then stopped right before us. "Sometimes people get too lost for the saving."

"Ah, damn it, Ellen, like things aren't difficult enough around here," Oliver said, removing his arm, and after reassuring himself I wouldn't flop over, he stood. "Come on, I'll put on some coffee."

He walked over to Ellen and grasped her arm. She shook it off. "I don't want coffee."

"Sorry, sis, but right now I don't give a donkey's damn what you want." He got a stronger grip on her and spun her around. He escorted her from the room, and Iris went to the door and stared after them. I heard Ellen protesting as Oliver ushered her down the stairs.

"I'd like to clean myself up now," I said, then realized I didn't want to use my regular bath in the hall, knowing very soon that hall would be swarming with witches. Iris's bathroom was en suite, and that meant I could have two closed doors between me and the rest of the world. The doors wouldn't provide much of a barrier against intrusion and offered none against magic, but in this moment the psychological separation they promised seemed precious.

"Aunt Iris?" I asked, and she turned to me.

"Yes?"

"May I use your shower?"

She nodded. "Of course, sweetheart."

TWELVE

I stood under the hot water for what seemed like forever, watching the pink of Teague's sticky blood rinse down the drain. Even after the water ran clear, and I knew my skin was clean, I washed myself again, wondering if I could ever forget the sensation of his life jetting out on me.

I stepped from the shower and dried my body, taking a moment to place my hand on my stomach and send loving, calming thoughts to my little one. I wrapped the bath sheet around myself, and borrowed Iris's blow dryer. I liked the way the whine of its fan helped to drown out the sound of the argument that had broken out downstairs. The second I turned it off, the voices rose.

I was grateful to see Iris had gone to my room and found clothes for me to wear. A teal-and-white sundress with a matching cyan sweater. My modest maternity underwear. I dressed to the accompaniment of shouts and tearful recriminations. The shouts came from Oliver, the tears from his sisters. I heard the door, and another angry voice joined in. This one belonged to Adam. That Sam's voice didn't rise to Iris's defense led me to surmise she'd sent Sam away while we handled the witch stuff.

Iris either hadn't remembered to provide me with socks or shoes or had begun to take the barefoot and pregnant idea a tad too much to heart. My comfortable trainers had been covered in Teague's blood. I'd never wear them again. I considered trying to stuff my feet into a pair of Iris's diminutive shoes, but I would probably only end up with blisters. I steeled my nerves and went down the hall barefoot to my own room.

Teague's body had been moved. I could only surmise the families had moved quickly to claim his remains, although they delegated the rest of the cleanup to us. We would have to burn the rug. My favorite quilt. The clothes Maisie and I had been wearing. Everything that had been splattered with Teague's blood. That was the only way to know for sure the magic that still resided in his blood couldn't be used to power spells that ought not be cast. Even though the room would be thoroughly and magically scoured, I couldn't bear the thought of sleeping here. Eventually, we might return to the room I'd grown up in, but for tonight at least, I'd ask to move my and Peter's essentials to Uncle Oliver's deserted room.

I heard a movement in the hall and turned to find Peter standing in the doorway. His normally ruddy complexion turned ashen, and he grasped the doorframe to steady himself. "I thought you'd be safe in this house," he said, shaking his head as he took the scene in. I didn't have to ask how he knew to come. I knew our child had called him, just as he had when Ryder had attacked at Magh Meall and when Emily had trapped me at the Tillandsia house. Peter released the frame and took a step into the room, his eyes fixed on the bloodstained rug. He drew nearer. "I'm glad she killed him," Peter announced. "I am."

I couldn't bear to hear his words. I began to turn away, but his calloused hand caught my arm. His mismatched blue and green eyes burned with an anger that was seasoned by fear. "It saved me the trouble."

I couldn't look at Peter. It broke my heart to hear his words. "Don't talk that way." I grasped his hand in mine, pulling it down to my protruding stomach. "You know he hears you. He understands more than you think. I don't want him thinking his father is a killer. That isn't you."

He leaned forward and placed a kiss near where our hands rested. "I know he hears me." Peter looked up at me, his sweet smile returning to his lips. "He talks to me too, you know. Not in words. In feelings. In pictures." I knew Colin could call his father in moments of crisis, but I would have never guessed the two were so linked.

Peter's smiled faded. "He's felt fear. Real fear, and I will not have that. I want him to know I would do anything to protect him. To protect both of you. If killing is what it takes to keep you safe—"

"Please don't say it. Please don't."

He stopped talking, but his expression, the set of his honest eyes, the way his right eyebrow arched a bit higher than its mate, the tilt of his head, these things finished his thought wordlessly. "He tried to hurt you and the baby." His words forced me to be honest with myself. It wasn't that Teague didn't need killing. I just didn't want blood on my husband's hands, or my sister's for that matter.

"Let's not talk about it anymore," I said. "Let's go join the others and see where things stand." I pulled away and went to the closet. An old pair of canvas sneakers sat on the top shelf. I went up on my toes, but Peter reached over me and pulled them down for me. I skirted the bloodstains on the floor and rug and fished a pair of socks from a drawer. I slid the chair away from my smashed makeup mirror, far away, and finished dressing. Peter remained within an arm's length of me the entire time, then shepherded me downstairs with his arm around my waist. He held on to me like he was afraid someone might snatch me away, and I let him.

"I thought she'd be safe here." The sound of Adam's frustration met us in the hall. "I thought y'all had magic-proofed this place after you found out Jilo had enjoyed her run of the house." It surprised me to hear their voices were coming from the library rather than the kitchen, our regular meeting place during times of crisis.

"We've tried," I heard Iris say, "many times over the years. General, all-encompassing protection spells are weaker than ones a witch might create to deal with a particular threat. A strong will combined with the right amount of magic can blow right past them. The ones aimed at fending off particular types of attacks are stronger, sometimes much stronger, but only good for dealing with that particular threat. Besides, even perfectly adequate charms age and weaken, and magic is always evolving. What worked last year might prove worthless today."

"Ginny always kept our protections in place," Ellen said, her words still a little slurred. "I'm not making excuses"—a fire rose in her tone, probably in response to Adam's unspoken challenge— "but the truth is, none of us have her skill."

"None of us have Ginny's ability to focus," Oliver said. "The old biddy had security well under control."

"What my family is not saying," I whispered to Peter, "is the responsibility for ensuring our security really lies with me, but I haven't a clue how to handle it. Those who could teach me how, the other anchors, treat me like a pariah. They don't want me to know the best ways to protect myself and my family . . ."

Peter put his finger to my lips. "To hell with them all." He lowered his hand and kissed me. "Tell me, where would you feel safe?"

At this point I wasn't sure I could feel safe anywhere, but I knew what he wanted me to say. "Take me to Magh Meall," I said. "I want to see your parents."

"That's my girl." Peter beamed down at me. I wouldn't feel a lick safer in the tavern where I'd been attacked by Ryder than in the house where Teague had attacked me, but Peter wanted to believe he could help by taking me where he himself felt more secure. One more lie, a little white one, perhaps, but still another lie between us. All of a sudden, Oliver and Adam began verbally tearing into each other. Their words came too quickly and over-lapped each other. I couldn't make out what had been said, but the anger came through loud and clear. "We'll go out the back way," Peter said and took my hand to lead me through the kitchen.

He eased the swinging door open and closed, and ushered me past the table toward the back door.

As I passed, something caught my eye. "Wait," I said, my hand slipping from his grip.

"What is it?"

"I'm not sure." I crossed to the table where the map of Savannah still lay open. A mug of coffee sat on it. The ring of a coffee stain showed a few inches to the left of the mug's current placement. A perfect dark circle had been made over one of the marks Adam had made on it, so that his X stood at the circle's exact center. I lifted the still warm mug to find a second, lighter stain had formed there also. The perfect circles. The crisscrossed lines. "Go get Oliver."

"Are you sure? I think you should take a break from all this."

I shook my head. My heart began to thud. It was all so clear now. "No. Please go get my uncle." When Peter didn't move, I looked up at him. "Please. Now. Tell him I've found the Tree of Life."

THIRTEEN

My aunts filed into the kitchen, with Oliver and Adam on their heels. "I sent Sam home," Iris answered before I could ask. I nodded as Peter slid out a chair for me. "I worry about how he is doing with all this," she said. "It's true he doesn't share the antipathy most civilians feel for us witches, but if things get too complicated, too strange . . . Well, he is only a man after all." Iris pulled out a chair and sat across from me.

"If he loves you, he'll handle it just fine," Peter said and beamed at my aunt. "Look at me. There isn't any amount of weird that could come between Mercy and me."

"Yes," Iris said and offered a drawn smile. "But you two are blessed to have found each other. I don't seem to share your luck in love."

I reached out and took her hands in mine. I clasped them tightly, and did my best to send every ounce of love I could to her through that physical connection. I couldn't lie to her, and I didn't want to diminish her concerns by whitewashing the truth. Sam had taken the sight of my standing over my cousin's corpse with aplomb; then in the next moment, he seemed overwhelmed by the high strangeness that was our life. He behaved as if the very thought of Iris's touch reviled him. Adam had almost walked away from Oliver. God knows he had reason enough to. Until Adam showed up at my wedding, I'd thought for sure he'd had enough of the Taylors and our magic, which had over time cost him his son and very nearly his own life.

A new wave of gratitude for Peter washed over me. I was lucky to have him, especially after the way I let myself get confused first over Jackson—again I shuddered at the thought that I had let that demon touch me. Then again, there were the mixed messages I'd sent to Peter over Emmet. I suddenly realized I still hadn't told him about Emmet's impending return to Savannah.

"I wish I could somehow compartmentalize my life," Iris said, pulling her hands from mine. "Put Sam in a comfortable, safe place, where he wouldn't be at risk. As we all know, though, no amount of magic will allow that."

Adam grunted. "It takes a tough man to love a Taylor." He patted Iris on the back. "If he isn't strong enough to hang in there, then he doesn't deserve you."

"That's right," Peter said and smiled.

"If you two are through congratulating yourselves on your grit," Oliver said, trying to look cool, but not doing a very good job of covering the fact Adam had once again swept him off his metaphorical feet, "Mercy can tell us what she means about finding the Tree of Life."

I pointed at the coffee rings on the map. "Make you think of anything?"

"Hmmm . . . maybe." He fished a compass I hadn't seen since high school from the same drawer that had housed the map and drew nine neat circles with the Xs at their centers. He sat down and stared at the map for a few moments, considering the marks he'd just placed on it. "You may very well be right, Gingersnap," Oliver said and laid down the compass, "but I don't see any correspondences between the placement of the body parts and the sephirot."

"The what?" Adam loomed over me, staring over my shoulder.

"The sephirot." I touched each of the nine circles, and looked back at him. "In Kabbalah—" I began, but the way he raised his eyebrows and looked down his nose at me told me he had no idea what that was either. "It's a kind of Jewish mysticism. The sephirot circles represent the ten attributes of the infinite mind. Together with some connecting lines"—my finger traced the marks Adam himself had made on the map—"they combine to form the Tree of Life."

Oliver looked at Adam. "Not much of a tree really, more like a mystical Twister mat. When the head turns up, we'll have the tenth sephira."

"'Ten Sephirot of Nothingness, ten and not nine,'" Iris quoted although I had no idea of her source, "'ten and not eleven.' The *Sepher Yetzirah*, the Book of Creation." She scooted her chair closer to her brother's. As she did so, it struck me that this was our Thanksgiving. Other families would be sitting down to candied yams and pumpkin pie. Not us; we were gathering around a murder map.

Adam stared at me blankly. "I'm sorry, I evidently don't speak witch."

"God is eternal. God is indivisible," Ellen said, brushing back the hair from her reddened but sobering eyes. "God is perfect." She focused over my head at Adam. "Where God is, there is no need or even room for change or growth. For God to create, he, she, it . . . whatever you want to call God, had to get out of the way. God created ten blank spaces, ten points both within himself and yet where he was not. Together these points form the great void, where all realities come into existence."

"So what you're telling me is Genesis was actually a sequel."

"Yes," Oliver said with a glint in his eye. "That is exactly what we're saying." I was glad to see their anger had faded. I didn't want them fighting, especially over me.

Adam passed around behind me to look at the map from a different angle. "Tell me, how does any of this philosophy apply to the concrete and actual problem at hand?"

"We," Iris answered for us, "have been working under the hypothesis that the woman's murder and dismemberment is an attempt at working a spell. An attempt at invoking sympathetic magic as a means to power the spell."

"We think," Oliver continued, "the spell might be aimed against Mercy, perhaps an attempt to weaken the line through harming her."

"Is it over then, this business with the body? Was it this Teague jackass behind it?"

"No." I shook my head. "The desecration of Jilo's grave, the berserker spell. I don't think that had anything to do with Teague. At least not directly. His goal was to protect the line. He would never knowingly participate in an attack against it. This business with the sephirot, it may be connected or perhaps it's only intended as a distraction."

"Someone would kill and dismember an innocent woman as a mere sleight of hand?"

"I don't know, but I want to visit the places where the parts have been found. I am certain the locations are not random. I want to look at them through the lens of the sephirot. If we can figure out what the spell is attempting, we will know who is actually behind its working."

"Who do you think is behind it?" Adam asked. A good and logical question everyone else had been afraid to pose.

"That depends on the aim of the spell. We know Emily is out there, but my gut tells me she wouldn't bother using a dead body as a poppet to come after me, and I doubt she'd have to rely on whatever magic clung to Jilo's bones. If the spell's goal is to hurt me, but not damage the line, it could be any number of disgruntled witches trying to work magic without setting off any alarms along the line."

"This simply doesn't feel like a witch's work to me." Iris leaned toward me. "I sense you don't want to accept it as a possibility, but Jessamine is so full of rage." Iris raised her hand to emphasize her words. "She's Daddy's granddaughter, the same as you. Who knows how much magic of her own she might have? You know I loved Jilo too, but you and Oliver exposed her to the Tree of Life. Who knows how much of her experience she shared with Jessamine? It may have been Jessamine herself who defiled Jilo's grave."

"Do not go there—"

She twisted her palm up as a signal for me to stop. "I am not saying Jilo would have ever intentionally done anything to put you or any of us in danger, but who knows what Jessamine might have gleaned from a careless statement made here or there?"

I sat and let her words settle. I bit my lip as I weighed whether I should dare speak the truth. I didn't want to hurt my aunt, but for my own sake, I couldn't afford letting her carry on with blurred vision. "I'm sorry, but I think you want Jessamine to be guilty."

Iris made a sharp intake of air and stiffened as if I had physically struck her. "I have no desire to pin guilt on the innocent, but—"

"But," Oliver said, placing a hand on her shoulder, "a part of you wants to get even with her for taking away your sense of self, your regard for our father, for alerting us to the fact Mama has been wasting away in Gehenna for over two decades. Jessamine, innocent or guilty, has turned your world upside down. You want to punish her for that."

"How could you even say that, Oli?" Iris shook her head.

"Because I feel the same exact way," he said.

"As do I," Ellen added weakly. She raised her fingers to her temples. The hangover had set in. Her own healing powers would ensure it wouldn't pain her long, but I could see it was fierce all the same.

The swinging door eased open, and Maisie stepped quietly into the kitchen. All eyes turned toward her. She moved cautiously to the table and sat, never daring to raise her eyes to meet ours. She reminded me of a photo I'd seen of a wounded soldier returning from Vietnam to an ungrateful hometown. She had wanted to defend me, but I had rejected her as a murderer. Had the line actually preserved her, groomed her, and returned her to me as my protector? No one else here, including myself, would have acted so decisively against Teague.

"I'm not saying Jessamine is innocent." I focused my thoughts. "I'm saying we need to investigate without prejudice."

"I am fine with doing that," Oliver said, releasing Iris and turning his attention back to me. "As long as you are willing to keep an open mind about this sephirot theory of yours." He folded his hands on the table, reminding me of the many times I'd been called to the principal's office to receive the message that a bright girl such as myself could do so well if only I would focus. "Yes, there are ten sephirot, but if we are looking for magical correspondences—" He interrupted himself and explained to Adam. "Using like to draw like, as above so below and all that—I don't see any link between them and the locations on this map. They aren't laid out in anything resembling the traditional arrangement of the sephirot on the tree. And here"—he tapped on the caricature of City Hall—"they found a foot. Just a foot. Here"—he pointed to Hutchinson Island—"they found a hand by itself." He looked to Adam for corroboration. Adam nodded. "This doesn't match the classical correspondences of the parts of the body to the sephirot. You never see the separation of hand from arm or foot from leg." He ran his fingers through his lengthening gold curls. "I'm sorry, but when it comes to the different sites, I can't even hazard a guess what the magical correlation to the sephirot might be." His eyes scanned over the circles once more. "I see none."

"I think," Maisie began, her voice cracking. She looked up at me, and I nodded in encouragement. She licked her lips. "I think that's because you are only considering the positive aspects. Whoever is behind this spell is working dark magic. They would take the left-handed path. You should look for any negative correspondences."

"And that is exactly what we are going to do," I said. I reached out and took her hand. "Close your eyes," I said, and together we slid from the room.

FOURTEEN

I had no reason to begin at City Hall, other than the location was at the top of my mind due to Oliver's attempt to convince me of the unsoundness of my theory. When I opened my eyes, Maisie and I stood hand in hand at the corner of Bull and West Bay, facing the four-story neoclassical confection. Sun glinted off its gold-plated dome, but it was the gold of the marigolds showing from the flower boxes on the second floor that caught my attention. My eyes followed the lines of the twin Ionic columns up to the sisters who adorned the space immediately beneath the dome.

"Art and Industry," Maisie said, showing me how connected we still were, even after all that had happened between us. "What was it you used to tell the tourists they were called?"

I smiled in spite of myself. "Fannie and Rita Mae." I named the statues after my two favorite authors when I was twelve, weeks after I'd started the Liar's Tour and days after I learned what the word "lesbian" meant. "Well, Uncle Oliver thought it was funny." Maisie smiled back at me, and I squeezed her hand tighter. I turned back to face City Hall. "What do you think, do you see anything?"

"I think Oliver was willfully ignoring the most obvious correlation." She reached up with her free hand and pointed at the golden dome. "Looks enough like a crown to me."

"That's Kether, right? The crown?"

"Yes, when you are considering the positive aspects, but I suspect it's Rita Mae and Fannie we should consider. Look at them." She lowered her hand to the stone ladies. "They are the same but different."

"Kind of like us, huh?"

Maisie dropped her hand, and I turned to face her. "Possibly. I know you are worried the woman's body is being used as a magical substitute for you, but I was thinking more about how the demonic orders correlate to the sephirot." She blinked and turned her head at an angle. "See, when you were out destroying Savannah's reputation, Ginny kept me inside to learn about demonic orders." Her hand slid from mine as her shoulders sagged. "Maybe I am crazy after all."

"No." I grasped hold of her hand again. It seemed impossible that this same soft hand had executed Teague, but I couldn't let myself dwell on that. "I don't think you are crazy at all. Tell me. Tell me what you see."

Maisie's eyes pointed back up toward the statues. "Like I said, they are the same but different. In its positive aspect Kether represents the crown. In its negative aspect it represents duality."

"How is duality negative?"

"It stands for duality in what should be indivisible. Duality in God. God . . ." She seemed to ponder something that really had nothing to do with the holy. "They found something out near the Cathedral too, right?"

"Yeah, they found an arm."

She stood still, but I could almost hear the wheels turning in her head. Then she nodded. "What is unique about Saint John's?"

I considered her question. "Well, it's big. It's beautiful." Our mother had once possessed the body of a tourist on its steps, but I doubted that was what she was looking for. "Savannah didn't start out friendly toward Catholics." Savannah had been established as a buffer between the British port of Charleston and the Spanish territory of Florida. Oglethorpe had feared Papists would be more inclined to support Catholic Spain than support Protestant England.

"You're getting warmer. The squares."

I realized instantly where she was going. Oglethorpe had laid out Savannah's squares, and surrounded them with what he termed "trust" and "tithing" lots. Tithing lots were intended for private houses, trust lots for public buildings such as churches. "The Cathedral is on the wrong side of Lafayette Square. It's on a tithing lot."

"I suspect the Cathedral might represent 'Chaigidel' to our secret sorcerer."

"Chaigidel?"

"The confusion of the power of God, represented by a church where a church was not originally intended to exist."

It seemed like a bit of a stretch to me. I had begun to lose confidence in our theory when Maisie turned west. "Wasn't the other arm found right around here?"

"Yeah." I pointed left down Bay. "They found the arm somewhere over behind Moon River." Then I pointed right. "The torso was out by Old Rex."

"The torso? Not a hand?"

"That's what Adam and about thirty traumatized tourists said. Why?"

"The lion at the Cotton Exchange fountain," she said, but I didn't follow. "Rex? King Cotton?"

"Okay." I pretended I had caught on.

"The eighth sephira. In its positive aspect it stands for 'Majesty.' In the demonic order it represents Adrammelech, the great king."

"So why the confusion?"

"It's also known as the 'left hand of God.' I would have expected to find a hand, but maybe that only means the correspondence of the part to the site is secondary."

"Or maybe it means I've brought you on a wild-goose chase."

"I don't mind if you have. This feels almost like old times, back when you loved me."

I started to protest.

"Back when you really loved me. Back before I gave you reason not to."

"I love you. I never stopped loving you. If I had, I would never have risked everything to bring you home. I just worry the sister I've loved my entire life never really existed," I said and instantly regretted my honesty. Still, the truth had come out, and I felt it would be wrong to backpedal. "I'm just trying to figure out who you are."

"That makes two of us." She forced a smile and moved on. "What do we know about where they found the arm?"

I wrapped my arm through hers and led her back south on Bull Street, then right onto Bay Lane. "Moon River is haunted. That much I know."

"Okay, but the arm wasn't found in the bar. It was found near the bar. What about this area here?" she asked, making a small circle that took in a portion of the street and the sidewalk. "The basement areas and portion below the street here." She looked up at me. "Don't you hear it? The sound of abject misery."

"Before the Civil War, slaves were kept in holding pens down there."

She knelt on the sidewalk and placed her hands on the concrete. "Yes. Nehemoth. The groaning." She stood and stared to the east. "They found something by Columbia Square. By the Kehoe Mansion?"

"Yes."

Her face lit up. "The king of cast iron. Tubal Cain. The lord of sharp weapons." She tugged on my arm. "Old Candler. It was an asylum for years, right?"

"Yeah, I guess so." I knew it had been, but I didn't want to dwell on issues of mental health with her.

"God only knows how many have died there," she said.

Josef and Ryder had committed murder to free the demon my grandfather had trapped there. Ryder had sacrificed his own girl-friend, Birdy, and their unborn child without a single qualm to draw the demon and its power into himself. My mind flashed on the image of Birdy's ravaged corpse. I pushed it quickly away.

"Belphegor," she chirped. "Lord of the Dead who reigns over those who bellow grief and tears." I would have never imagined I'd hear these words spoken so cheerfully. "You had a circle on the map over by Christ Church."

I nodded.

"Take us there."

In the blink of an eye, we stood on the red brick sidewalk before the Episcopal meetinghouse.

Maisie looked the building over as if it were the first time she had seen it in her life. She turned 180 degrees to face Johnson Square then turned back to face me. "This isn't quite right. It wasn't here." She took quick steps to the corner, then turned on Congress and headed east. I struggled to catch up with her, wad-dling as fast as I could. Suddenly she stopped and pointed up at the parking structure. "It was here, wasn't it?" She burst out laugh-ing. "I'm sorry, I know it isn't funny, not really, but this convinces me you are right. There is no doubt this is a spell connected to the sephirot, and whoever is behind it has a sense of humor. The demon Astaroth. His title is 'One of the Flock.'" I waited silently for further explanation, but she looked at me like I was hopeless.

Finally she sighed in exasperation. "You have told me a thousand stories about what used to stand here."

I felt so embarrassed by my thickness I blushed. "Bo Peep's Pool Hall." I no sooner said the words than a car horn caused me to turn.

I registered the trident symbol on the front of Oliver's new Quattroporte; then he pulled up next to us and rolled down the window. "You two need to get home now. Your aunts are worried, and I'm on my way to the airport."

"The airport?" I echoed.

"Yep. Going to pick up Rivkah and Emmet. Get on home now," he said and pulled away before the window had even finished closing.

FIFTEEN

I still believed only Emmet could free my grandmother, but a very large part of me regretted telling Iris to contact Rivkah. I didn't want to see Emmet; I didn't want to be near him. I didn't want to feel my pulse rising when I laid eyes on Emmet, but I told myself we had no other option. I hated the butterflies that danced in my stomach as I heard his voice in the hall. I didn't greet him as he and Rivkah came through the door. I couldn't risk his seeing just how happy I was to see him. Instead I remained seated at the table, nursing an already lukewarm cup of chamomile.

I was grateful to Uncle Oliver for "inviting" Peter to spend the evening with his parents. I couldn't have dealt with having him and Emmet under the same roof. I had alerted Claire to Peter's suspicions about his parentage, but worked both sides of the equation by making Peter promise not to broach the subject until I could be there with him. I hoped that issue was diffused for now.

The swinging door flung wide. "Darling, it's so good to see you up and about," Rivkah said as she pulled Maisie into a tight embrace. Maisie looked over her shoulder at me, her eyes widening as she pulled a face. I'd grown used to Rivkah's enthusiastic hellos and had already braced myself for my turn. I was warming up my smile when Rivkah released Maisie and turned to look down at me. "What is this nonsense about you wanting to kill my boy?"

"Rivkah," Emmet said, "you promised you wouldn't do this." His face flushed, like a teenager who'd been embarrassed by his mother. Well, perhaps that really didn't fall too short of the mark. The two had developed a familial bond.

He looked good, having struck a balance between his original overly manicured look and the feral appearance he'd perfected before he left Savannah. Before I sent him away from Savannah. The memory of Tillandsia, how it felt to be in his embrace before everything went so horribly wrong, washed over me.

"Do what? Find out why this girl thinks she has the right to order us to drop everything and attend to her desires? It would be bad enough if she only needed help moving, but she wants to *kill* you."

"Not permanently," I offered, realizing instantly how inept my attempt to diffuse her anger was.

"*Not permanently. Not permanently.*" She slammed her purse on the table so hard I jumped.

"Rivkah, enough," Emmet said, putting his hand on her shoulder.

"No." She turned to face him. "What she's asking of you is too much."

"Yes," Iris concurred. "It is too much to ask, but it isn't only Mercy who's asking. It's our entire family." She stepped up behind me and gripped my shoulders.

"But he wouldn't even consider this if it weren't Mercy asking."

"However, she has asked," Emmet said in a calm voice, "and I have said yes."

"I know you see this as some grand romantic gesture, my boy." Rivkah spun toward me and flung out her hand. "Look at her. I mean it, look at her. She has another man's ring on her hand and another man's child in her womb. She isn't yours. She never will be yours."

"I know that." Emmet lowered his eyes, focusing on the floor a few inches before his toes. "But I will always be hers." My heart broke at his words. I knew I had taken advantage of his feelings for me to enlist his help. I was using him, asking him to die for me, and when I was finished, I'd send him away. I would have to. I could never give myself to him the way he wanted. I hated myself for bringing him into this.

Rivkah reached up and took his chin in her hand. She started to speak, but stopped herself. Her shoulders rose and then she sighed.

My pulsed pounded in my head and the room darkened. The room felt hot and close. "No." The word came out before my conscious mind was sure what I was objecting to. "Don't do this. We won't do this. I won't do this. I'm sorry." I looked up over my shoulder at Iris. "We cannot ask this of Emmet. I'm sorry about Grandma. I am."

The tension in Rivkah's face melted. The tightness in her lips released. Her brow descended, and her eyes warmed. "There's the girl I know and love."

"However, this is not your choice to make," Emmet said. "It is mine." He knelt before me. He had no words for me, but the way he stared at me, the lids of his eyes covering the onyx irises nearly to his already concealed pupils, told me everything he wanted to say. I closed my own eyes as I couldn't bear his message. I loved my husband. I had no doubt of that in my mind. For the shortest of moments, though, I wished I could split myself in two, setting free the part of my heart this golem-turned-man had claimed. I buried that wish and opened my eyes.

He looked over my shoulder at Iris. "Shall we proceed?"

"I'll get Ellen and Oli." Iris started for the swinging door, but stopped and turned back. "Thank you," she said addressing Emmet.

"I warn you, Iris." Rivkah pointed at Iris's face. "I have always loved and supported your family, but if any lasting harm comes to Emmet . . ."

"I appreciate your support and return your affection whole-heartedly. We won't fail Emmet."

"But if you do . . ." Rivkah insisted.

"I will give my own life to return him to you." The two women regarded each other for a moment as the pact between them was sealed. The moment having passed, Iris turned and left the room. I wondered if it were truly possible, to trade one life for another.

"I'll go run the bath," Maisie said. "Excuse me." She followed Iris out of the room, her movements cautious, nearly silent, as if she were afraid to upset the delicate balance we had found.

"Please, my boy. Don't go through with this." Rivkah looked at me, commanding me silently to back her up.

"I'm sorry I asked you to do this," I said. "It was wrong of me. I don't want you to."

Emmet stood to his full impressive height, causing me to crane my neck to take him in. "You are lying to yourself," he said, crossing his arms and looking down at me with his irritating, smug smile. "You want me to help your grandmother, but you don't want to be the one responsible for my taking the risk of doing so." He reached down and placed his warm palm against my reddening cheek. "I hereby absolve you. This is my choice," he said, then regarded Rivkah, "and I would do the same thing even if there were no Mercy."

"Now, who's lying to himself?" Rivkah made a huffing sound. "I see you are determined." She lowered her head.

"Sooner started, sooner done." Emmet smirked at the cliché. He held out his hand to help me stand.

"No." I refused both his courtesy and his sacrifice.

"Yes," he said. "You must be there to serve as my beacon." He reached down and took my hand. I couldn't bring myself to look him directly in the eye. "Mercy." His voice came out sharp and shocked me so that I had to face him. Despite the harshness of his voice, his face was smiling. "Don't worry. Nothing will keep me from returning. As long as I know you are waiting for me." Guilt, love, annoyance, gratitude, confusion. In my father's native German, there was probably a single word to describe the feelings that washed over me. My own vocabulary had no such term. "Come now." His smile turned back to a smirk. "Many hands make for light work."

"You two go ahead," I said. "I'll come up in a moment."

They left me alone in the kitchen, Rivkah cackling like a hen at her newly adopted chick. I leaned back in my chair, placing my hands against my lower back and stretching. I ran my hand over my stomach. I halfway expected to feel a reproval coming from Colin, but I only sensed he was at rest.

I took my cup to the sink and emptied it. I washed it by hand and sat it on the drain board. I contemplated the chip in the sink's porcelain. I pondered the spots on the splash. "They're ready." Maisie's voice startled me. "Sorry."

"It's okay. I'm a bit jumpy. It isn't every day you kill somebody, you know?"

"I'm trying to keep it down to two a week." We caught each other's eyes, and even though I knew it was wicked of us, we both burst out laughing. "Go on, they're waiting for you."

"You're not coming?"

"No. Rivkah is very happy to see me up and well, not so happy with the thought of my helping to drown her son." She sensed I was trying to find words to comfort her and held up her hand to stop me. "No, seriously, I'm trying to keep my homicides down to two a week, and I have the feeling I might need to save my second for a day or two."

"You are terrible," I said.

"And you can be a pest. Get out of here and leave me alone."

I reached out and gave her hand a squeeze, then made my way upstairs. I could hear voices—Emmet's voice, my aunts' voices—coming from the far side of the door of a rarely used bath at the far end of the hall. I stepped into the doorway, focusing on the floor where the deep claw-foot tub dug into the checkerboard tile. The room would normally have been far too cramped for a crowd of six, but the boundaries had been stretched.

I wondered which of us had become so skilled at borrowing space from other dimensions, until Emmet stretched out his arm to display the expansion. "Not bad, huh?" His pride glowed in his eyes; a wry smile reigned on his lips.

"Not bad at all," I said and stepped over the threshold.

"Three minutes." Rivkah's voice caused me to look up. Emmet began disrobing, laying his clothes out carefully over a defunct towel warmer. I seemed to be the only one of us bothered by the waxing state of his nakedness. He noticed my consternation, and the devil's own smile curved on his lips.

"Three minutes." Ellen nodded. "Then I'll pull him back." I was glad to see she had recovered from the effects of her latest bender.

"Not a second longer."

"You have my word, Rivkah," Ellen said, placing a stopwatch in Rivkah's hand. "From the second his heart stops until it beats again."

Emmet caught my eye, then fanned out his large hands to cover his genitals. I begged my eyes not to follow, but they did as they wanted, caressing the patch of hair that began between his hard pectorals and traced a line over the center of his abdominals, fanning out again on his taut lower stomach.

"You are shameless," Iris said taking note of his flirting.

"Yes, I am. Isn't that the point of this exercise?" Maybe it was gallows humor, but for the second time in a matter of minutes, I found myself in the middle of an inappropriate laugh. My eyes bounced up and were caught in the dark glimmer of his. Then I looked away.

"We should get started," Iris said. "Climb in, please." Emmet turned his back to me, casting one last naughty glance over his shoulder. His suave expression turned to shock as his foot hit the water. "I'm sorry it's so cold, but it's going to have to get even a bit colder yet."

Emmet reached down, grasping both sides of the tub, and put his foot in. A second, and he lifted the other over the rim, touching the water with his toe then pulling it back.

"Mercy," Iris called, and my head jerked in her direction. "Who is this timid little girl getting in the bathtub?"

Emmet's face flashed a blend of shame and anger, but then his eyes narrowed. "You almost had me there," he said, but still he seemed determined to demonstrate his toughness. He bent his knees and slid waist deep into the water. Even though his face remained stoic, he nearly panted from the cold. Finally he settled, his knees poking up high above the water. "It isn't so bad."

"Good, then we are ready for the rest of the ice." Iris turned and opened up the old camping cooler I hadn't laid eyes on since grade school. Oliver heaved a sack out of the cooler and tore open the bag. The cubes fell first in plops then with one final glacial splash.

Ellen and Iris glanced at each other. "Not quite deep enough," Iris said. "He'll have to kick his legs up over the sides so we can hold him under."

"Why do we have to make the water so cold?" I asked, feeling a sympathetic chill run up my own spine.

"Just a precaution," Oliver said as he grabbed another plastic bag. "Lowering his temperature may help prevent . . ." He stopped himself and threw a guilty look at Rivkah. "It makes any permanent damage from a lack of oxygen to the brain somewhat less likely." He dropped the bag back into the cooler without daring to meet any of our eyes.

Iris unhooked the necklace she had been wearing, a gold chain and pendant. She approached the tub and leaned over Emmet. "Here." She held the necklace out. "This was Mama's, it still carries her charge. Focus on her energy, and it will help you locate her in the darkness."

Emmet held up his bluing hand, palm up, and she dropped it into his hand. He clasped his long fingers tightly around the piece. Iris nodded at Oliver, who circled around her to take a place behind Emmet. They each put both hands on one of his broad shoulders. Ellen approached and took his left wrist in her hand. "Before we do this," Emmet said suddenly, fighting to keep his teeth from chattering. "It's only that I've heard ghosts are often seen wearing what they wore last. If that's true . . . If I don't make it back . . ."

"Yes?" Ellen asked.

"Please remember that this water was very, very cold." He barked out a laugh and plunged his upper body under the water, a wave breaking over the rim as he flung his long legs over the sides. Oliver and Iris combined their weight to help hold him under, lest his body rebel and struggle to break the surface. It was unnecessary. He didn't struggle. He gave himself up a willing sacrifice.

SIXTEEN

I approached the tub, moving slowly over the slick, wet tiles, just in time to see the bubbles from Emmet's last breath break the surface. His body shuddered once, twice, and went limp. "He's gone. Start the watch," Ellen said, but I could already hear the watch's ticking. Rivkah had no intention of this adventure lasting one millisecond longer than the time agreed upon. The floating shards of ice had gathered above his face, obscuring his features. I sensed, more than saw, that his eyes had remained open, staring out at us from the other side of the void he had crossed. I leaned closer to the water and scattered the ice. I stepped back and flung the frigid droplets from my fingers.

Iris and Oliver reached in and tugged at his slippery frame. I wondered why they insisted on doing things manually. I wiggled my finger, and his head broke the surface. His torso, cold, purplish tinged, followed, and his legs slid easily back into the tub. The body, Emmet, was now in a sitting position.

"You got a little over two minutes, then we pull him back." Rivkah held the watch so tightly, her knuckles had turned white. Ellen nodded.

A rap on the doorframe caused us all to turn. Sam stood there, leaning against the wall. He folded his arms across his chest. "Sam, honey," Iris said, pulling the sleeves of her top down over damp arms and moving toward the door. "I'm so glad to see you, but you shouldn't be in here right now. I need you to go downstairs and wait." She reached for him in an attempt to usher him out, but he stepped aside.

"What fun would that be?" It was Sam's body, Sam's voice, but it was not Sam. I seemed to be the only one to notice the dark aura surrounding him.

"Get away from him." I was too late; he grabbed Iris by the arm and twisted it violently enough to pop it out of the socket.

She screamed from pain and shock. "Sam, what in the hell?" Ellen said.

"Ninety seconds," Rivkah said.

Oliver barreled around me and lunged at Sam.

"It isn't Sam," I said, tugging on the back of Oliver's shirt, trying to pull him back. He broke free from my grasp and dove at Sam, but Sam flung Iris to the floor and swung his fist. Oliver was knocked backward, his head hitting the edge of the tub. Red began dripping from the point of contact.

"I have been aching to do that for years." The voice came from Sam. Iris had managed to sit up. She held her good arm up toward him, a ball of blue light forming at her fingertips. It shot out and encased Sam's body. For an instant, he stood there frozen, but then the casing curled open like a blooming lily. "It is so good to be home." A childish voice piped from Sam's mouth. He kicked Iris in the stomach, and she crumpled over.

"Wren," she said between coughs.

He licked his lips and shrugged his shoulders. "This body is so comfortable. It is so spacious and solid. Fits like a glove, you might say." He winked at Iris. "I hope you don't mind I took it out to Jefferson Street for a bit of professional companionship. I was aching to take this body for a test drive, see how well it handles the curves." Sam's tongue shot out and moistened his lips, then he laughed and advanced on us. "Crack whores carry such an exotic aroma, you know? Something like sweet burnt plastic. Or maybe candied ballpoint pens."

"How could you have taken control of Sam's body?" Iris asked.

"How could you have taken control of Sam's body?" he mimicked her.

Rivkah beamed him between the eyes with the stopwatch. "You two bring Emmet back now. I will deal with this weakling son of a bitch."

Ellen ignored Rivkah and scrambled around me to examine Oliver. She raised a hand and caught a towel as it jumped into her grasp. "Oli," she said. "Open your eyes. We need you." Oliver gave no sign of hearing her.

"Weakling?" A venomous laugh the real Sam could never have produced burst from his mouth. "No. Not anymore, and given your help in this little experiment, that is partially thanks to you." He slapped his hands together, and a ball of dark energy, a force so black it seemed to devour light, shot from them. "In return, a gift from Gehenna." Rivkah screamed like an enraged banshee and braced herself, but the burst of concentrated darkness hit her, lifting her and slamming her against the wall. Sam's lips twisted up. "Oh man, I could do this all day."

Ellen rose to confront him. "Sleep," Sam's sharpened voice commanded, and Ellen fell limp over Oliver's prone frame. "I always liked that lush. I'll take it easy on her." Sam walked toward me, and as he did, the room's periphery rolled back further and further. It was like his stride pushed the rest of the world away, and Rivkah and my family with it. "You, though, I do not like at all."

I focused on Emmet, placing a hand on each side of his head.

I willed the tub's drain to open, and the frigid water began to work its way out. *Time to come back to us.* I willed his heart to begin beating. I felt a bit of an electric shock myself when I realized I had succeeded. Still, he didn't stir.

Iris's sobs faded as her image slid yards, then miles away. Rivkah faded almost as quickly on my other side. I tried to sense Emmet's essence. I could feel it, dimensions away. *Come back.* Another force, strong, stronger than my own, was pulling him back in the opposite direction.

"You don't need to worry about the golem's body," Wren said and chuckled. "It may be vacant, but now that you got it ticking again, it may live forever, or at least until Gehenna goes out of business. And we both know that is as good as forever." Wren poked a finger into Emmet's chest.

Emmet. You have to fight. I need you. I kept trying to get a strong enough hold on him. Ellen and Oliver had now disappeared beyond the horizon.

"It's just you and me now, princess, and thanks to the circuit you have completed, I've got all the power of Gehenna behind me." He flung his arms out wide, and sizzling bits of darkness danced along his fingers. Bile caught in my throat as the air around us took on the scent of rotten eggs—no, sulfur. "That's the smell of power. Not blood magic. Not witch magic. This here is the real stuff. Soul magic." He lifted his nose, and breathed in. His face took on a maniacal expression, his eyes nearly bulging out of his head, his brows lifting comically. "Breathe that perfume in. You can learn to love it, you know? I sure as hell have." He laughed. "Get it? Sure as hell?"

"How can you be here?" I said. "How can you be inside Sam?"

"You can thank your little brother, Josef, for both of those things." He folded Sam's arms across his chest. "Josef caught Iris's new toy here and carried us out to Sapelo. That corpse of your Jilo, it's rotting away underground, but it still had enough of

Tillandsia's magic to power one more tiny spell. Left me with this nice package, and made sure that high yellow cousin of yours would come knocking. We knew if Jessamine came, one thing would lead to another, and you all would end up finding out that poor sweet Adeline was trapped in Gehenna. Once you knew that, you would be stupid enough to try to get her out."

I slid my hands down Emmet's sturdy neck to his shoulders. They were growing warmer to the touch. I risked taking my eyes from Sam only long enough to confirm Emmet's chest still rose and fell. "So this was all another one of Emily's tricks?"

"I wouldn't say it was so much of a 'trick,'" Sam said and shook his head, "as a well-timed disclosure of truths. Your mother, she played her cards close to her still-perky little tits. She's held on to these tasty tidbits for decades now. Nice, huh? I knew your grand-dad had trouble keeping it in his trousers, but damn! Not only sowing his seed in that dark soil, but buying the field he plowed. I cannot tell you how much I love it that your prissy stuck-up bitch of a grandmother was never even legally married to your grandfather. Imagine. You all were born on the wrong side of the sheet. Illegitimate." He sounded each syllable out as if it were a separate word.

My emotions blurred. I had begun to grow fond of Sam, but I detested the creature who had taken him over. "What happened to Sam? Is he in there with you?"

"Sam? Sam, you in here?" Wren called and rocked from side to side, rapping his knuckles against his temple. He stopped and shook his head. "Nope. He isn't home."

"Then where is he?"

"The little bitch has been buzzing around me all day, trying to get back in, but I got things locked down in here. He won't manage to hold out longer."

"That's all I've been waiting to hear." Maisie's voice came from nowhere. She stepped sideways from nothingness into my field of vision. My eyes caught the flash of a knife's blade slicing up through the air, and twisting into Sam. Sam's hand moved to cover the wound, but Maisie slapped it away. Her lips began moving silently at first; then her voice built to a whisper. I knew her words to be an incantation, but they were in a language I didn't understand.

She dropped the bloodied knife to the floor, where it bounced and slid beneath the tub. Sam's body stood rigid, frozen in place by Maisie's spell. She stiffened her fingers, and placed their tips against the hole in Sam's abdomen, wiggling them back and forth until her hand disappeared all the way to her wrist beneath Sam's skin. Sam's mouth fell open, and a horrible sound, something lost between a scream and an angry teakettle's cry, escaped his lips.

Maisie pulled her hand back, a small tarlike orb struggling within her caged fingers. She tightened her grasp, and her chant grew in intensity. The struggling substance in her hand caught fire. "That's enough of him," she said and wiped what was left of Wren from her palm on her jeans. Sam's body went limp, and Maisie used her magic to guide it gently to the floor. The room's walls rushed back into their customary positions, but my family had not returned with them. Maisie knelt next to Sam's limp form, pressing her hands over the wound she'd put in him.

She looked up at me. "Now would be the time to find Ellen."

SEVENTEEN

We hadn't even had a full day to recover from our disastrous holiday when we received a summons from the other anchors. Teague's remains were to be disposed of in a way that was intended to serve as warning to any who might consider challenging an anchor.

Now my family and I stood in a place that was nowhere, and yet everywhere at the same time. It was a blank space, existing only in the imagination. This void was "where" the anchors convened, and it was normally open only to the line's anchors. Here they could project their avatars, mental images of themselves, without ever truly leaving their own backyard. I had never visited before. Even as an anchor, I had never before been invited, and I suspected my invitation to visit would not extend past the current gathering. Tonight, though, my fellow anchors had made the space accessible to any witch from the ten families who remained loyal to the line. The doors wouldn't open to general admission, though, until after the little meeting that had been called between myself, my family, and the line's other loyal anchors.

I wondered if Emmet would take advantage of this gathering to find me. He had succeeded in freeing my grandmother from Gehenna, leaving her soul to ascend to wherever it is unburdened souls go, but Rivkah had been left apoplectic by Ellen's failure to favor Emmet over Oliver. She insisted he return to New York with her, and honestly, I think she was right in doing so. Emmet wanted to remain in Savannah, and I felt sure Emmet would have stood his ground had I offered him the slightest encouragement. Instead I did what I knew I must. I clung to Peter as if he were the only man I could ever love, for I did love Peter with all my heart. I had made my choice, so that was the way it had to be.

The anchor's meeting space itself was totally malleable, capable of reflecting any mental image projected onto it. The others who would join us might envision their surroundings as resembling Paris's Père Lachaise cemetery, a tiny country graveyard, or even a dumpster in some dark alleyway for all I knew. My family had agreed to use the beach on Hunting Island as the template for our shared experience. It was there that we had taken on the line's other anchors, and we had won. We agreed the memory of this victory would put us on a better psychological footing. Of course, if it hadn't been for Jilo, the outcome of that confrontation might have been very different. Again I felt the already familiar stab of pain in my chest that meant I was missing her.

"Welcome to the 'grand imaginarium,'" Oliver said with no great enthusiasm. "Hope the gift shop's open." I was sure many of the witches who would visit this space tonight would find all this terribly impressive, but Oliver and I had seen better. Much better. This setup seemed amateurish in comparison to Jilo's haint-blue room, which had truly straddled dimensions of both space and time. "Just think what the old buzzard could have done with this much magic," Oliver said to me, confirming that we were sharing many of the same thoughts, if not the same feelings.

"We should not be wearing black," Iris warned for the umpteenth time, speaking of the avatars of ourselves that we projected into the invented space.

"It's a funeral—" I began.

"It's a celebration," Iris interrupted me. "It's dangerous for us to ignore tradition, at least when tradition is working in our favor."

After Ellen patched Sam up and got him on his feet, he took off without a single word. He had been spooked all right, and understandably so. I knew my aunt was hurting, so I overlooked the sharpness of her tone. I knew it had nothing to do with me.

"No, I refuse to celebrate Teague's death," I said in a calm voice.

"Well, Gingersnap, you can be damned and well certain that little son of a bitch would have celebrated yours, had he been given the chance." Oliver had acquiesced to my request for the appearance of somber dress, but he hadn't done so quietly.

"Uncle Oliver is right," Maisie said. "Teague would have killed without a second thought, if it would have got him the power he craved."

Ellen touched my shoulder, whether in reality or only in this realm, I wasn't sure. The gesture felt real, so maybe it didn't even matter. Things that took place in these magical spaces had a way of affecting the dimensions they touched. I suspected whatever happened in this realm would ripple out to our reality, maybe even all realities. "It's only the others might find us showing up in mourning attire confusing. Tradition holds that we celebrate the demise of those who would harm the line or its anchors. This is meant to be a party."

"You should listen to your elders." A voice came from nothingness. I recognized that voice. Even though I had learned his real name was Fred Firth, I would always think of him as "Mr. Beige." The air shimmered, and the man who had expressed the sentiment, or at least his projected image, stood before us, medium build, thinning light-brown hair, middle-aged, wearing tan khakis and a blue button-down shirt. To this muted fellow, the color combination he wore must have seemed nearly garish.

He was one of my fellow anchors, and we should have been allies, but our only true face-to-face encounter had ended with my nearly ripping out his solar plexus along with his connection to the line's power. He threatened my child; he would never be that foolish again. None of them would, but neither would any of my fellow anchors let me within a stone's throw of them again either. No sooner had I thought of the other anchors than I witnessed sparks and shimmers coalesce behind Beige. One resolved into the diminutive Asian woman I now knew to be Ayako Izanagi. In a different world, I think we would have been friends, but given the way my fellow anchors viewed me, probably never in this one. The remaining anchors materialized in nearly the same instant. Beige took their arrival in. "We will soon let down the barrier and let the other witches enter, but before we do, I feel we should make sure we are all on the same page as to what we need to accomplish today."

I had no interest in Beige's agenda. I let his words roll over me as my eyes coasted from one anchor to the next. A part of me found it amusing that the avatars with which many of them presented themselves hid the actuality of their true form's physical defects, or showed them as taller, slimmer, and often younger than they truly were. It was almost as if half of them were basing their avatars on old or airbrushed photos.

Only one showed himself completely as I remembered him. The young, nearly sexless man with flaxen hair and horrible blank eyes. I knew more than the odd one's name; I had made a study of him, as he was the one who had made the connection between my baby and the change that had been effectuated in the line. As my fellow anchors worked to bind me, the line had reached out through my little Colin and tapped into Fae magic. By doing so, it strengthened itself and loosened the witch anchors' control over it.

The pale one was Fridtjof Lund, from a city of the same name in southern Sweden. Lund, the municipality, stood as the oldest town in Sweden, but it remained unclear whether the town took its name from Fridtjof's family, or vice versa. The truly odd thing about this sexually ambiguous witch was that he had not been born from a union of male and female. He had only one parent, a self-fertilizing being identical to himself. In effect, each new generation was a clone of the preceding. How far back this chain went was anyone's guess, but descriptions of a witch resembling Fridtjof could be traced back to the point where history blurred with folklore. How far this chain would extend into the future depended on whether he respected my warning to leave me and my baby alone.

Behind the other anchors, in the distance, I noticed a group of tall and extremely slender pallbearers, winding their way toward us, their unnaturally long arms carrying Teague's exposed and naked body on a bier. They didn't jostle the body as they drew near, as those who bore it approached us without any apparent form of locomotion. Their feet hovered a good six inches above the ground. The pallbearers themselves wore a somewhat anachronistic getup, including stovepipe hats befitting Victorian-era undertakers. I very nearly pointed out these men wore black, but then they came close enough for me to see their faces, or at least where their faces should have been. These voids held no features, only a blankness that looked like pale silk had been stretched over a skull. Shadows filled their eye sockets; two narrow snakelike slits sat where a nose should have been. Their mouths were gaping holes filled with tiny steel blades whose alignment made me think of barbed wire. "What are they?" I asked.

"As I said, they are scavengers." Beige cocked his head to the side and regarded me like I was an ignorant child. I guess my question showed I hadn't been paying attention. "They are here to consume your cousin's body, and along with his body any magic that is still bound up within it."

"Oh, no," I said. I felt repulsed by the idea. "Nothing like that is going to happen." The six pallbearers turned their heads toward me, groaning and gnashing their horrifying dental work together. "They're very hungry." Beige spoke on their behalf. "They haven't eaten in nearly six hundred years." His avatar took a step closer. "This is not simply tradition. It is law. Young Teague here tried to harm one of the line's anchors." I felt him will my eyes to meet his own, but I denied him the pleasure of thinking himself capable of controlling me. His tone turned even more bitter. "And this is the prescribed fate of those who would harm an anchor of the line. At least those who aren't lucky enough to have somehow charmed the line itself."

He meant his comment to send a shudder down my spine, but instead it reinforced the steel I felt growing there. I had nearly forgotten, but his words reminded me: I was in charge here. The line had loosened the other anchors' grasps on it. I didn't know why, but it had chosen to align itself with me.

"This is all just for show, right?" Oliver asked. "That isn't really Teague's body. That's only a projection here, like the rest of us."

"No, Mr. Taylor. Those are young Mr. Ryan's remains. This realm isn't capable of supporting human life, at least for more than a few moments, but that is no longer an issue for him."

"And those creatures?" I asked.

"Oh, they are really here too."

"This is atrocious," Ellen said, pulling me back into her embrace. "Why can't we burn him and be done with it?"

"Because, Mrs. Weber"—he addressed my Aunt Ellen using her married name, my father's name—"he died at the hands of an anchor. A connection, a type of open wound, has been created. These creatures will draw those toxins into themselves, keep the wound from turning gangrenous. Keep the poison from infecting the line. Now, if he had died at the hands of someone other than an anchor, well, then yes, we could . . ." He let his sentence die, held his hands out, palms up, and shrugged.

He's lying. The knowledge came to me. I turned my head involuntarily to find the source of the words, but couldn't pinpoint it. "Yes, I did kill him." I pulled away from Ellen. "But I know you're lying. This horrid show you want to put on. It's unnecessary."

"Well, perhaps I am not speaking the literal truth, but metaphorically I am being completely honest. A situation I'm sure you can appreciate," he said, his bland face pinching in on itself as a twisted smile rose on his lips. He knew I hadn't laid a finger on Teague. "This 'horrid show' you speak of is indeed very necessary. Thanks to your mother—" He shook his head. "No, thanks to you"—he pointed at me—"we anchors must provide pageantry such as this to let the witches under us . . . under the line," he corrected himself, "know that we are still in charge. That we are still in control of the line. That we are still acting in unison."

"I sense very little unity here," Iris said, "and we all know your control over the line is at best tenuous. This precious passion play of yours is for your own benefit. You need it to maintain the illusion of being in control, to convince everyone else to have faith in you."

"I'm not saying otherwise, Mrs. Flynn." He held up his hands and forced an innocent smile on his face. "I'm sorry, Ms. Taylor. I understand that unlike your sister you have cast off your husband's name." He said this as if Ellen's failure to do so betrayed a disloyalty to the line, if not an absolute endorsement of Erik's attempt to end the line. I nearly told him what I thought of his tone, but he carried quickly on. "All I ask is that you consider this: If we lose the confidence of the families, we might lose control of the line altogether. If we lose control of the line, it may very well come crashing down around us. Should that happen, I doubt any of us would survive the return of our old masters. It could quite literally be the end of the world for both witches and humankind."

He sighed deeply. "Listen, I know this all feels very personal. Like everyone is out to get you, but that isn't the truth. We as anchors have one simple goal: to protect the line. Many are frightened by what they perceive as your reckless behavior. Even your own cousin turned against you because he believed he was acting in the line's best interest."

"Teague turned against me because he was jealous and greedy. Not for any other reason."

Beige nodded. "That may very well be, but there are others, and it may surprise you to learn I am not among them, who feel he was justified in his efforts to *contain* you. It is in your own best interest Mr. Ryan should be made an example of. We must demonstrate that his attack against you was an attack against all of us, regardless of his motivation or the perceived righteousness of his cause."

"So it's true then," I said addressing the other anchors. "You were supporting Teague. You did clear the way for him to make use of Gudrun's magic."

Beige shook his head. "Oh, no. Not all of us, and certainly not I personally, but one of our little family did." He turned back toward the others. "Isn't that right, Ayako?"

She flushed red and took a step back stammering. "It seemed a peaceable solution. You would not have been harmed."

Nope. We would never be friends. "No, my child and I would have just been stolen from my husband and family and sent to a dimension where I could die from old age before they sat down to dinner."

"The time differential is not that great. And you were not to be alone, you were all . . ." Her words trailed off as she realized she had given away much more than she had intended.

Oliver stomped forward. "Well, I will be damned." He turned to face us. "Do you hear that? She was going to ship us all out. Get rid of us pesky Taylors once and for all."

"No, it wasn't like that. I wanted you all to be together." I could hear the buzzing of the other anchors as they communicated telepathically with one another. They were blocking their words, but I felt a world of condemnation falling on Ayako. "I am sorry," she squeaked.

"No," Beige responded. "We are sorry." He shook his head and sighed. "Ayako Izanagi, I bind you. May the power reject you. May it not claim you as its own."

Fridtjof stepped forward. "Ayako Izanagi, I bind you. May the power reject you. May it not claim you as its own." Ayako's avatar blinked in and out like a flashing Christmas tree bulb. When the avatar had finally resolved itself, the stocky Russian woman whose name failed me began to add her own addition to the binding.

"Stop," I called out. "Stop it. You are hurting her."

Both Beige and Fridtjof looked up at me with shock written on their faces. "But she tried to harm you," Fridtjof said.

I knew he hadn't spoken in English, that his words had been Swedish, but still I understood their meaning. I hoped the reverse would hold true. "If you bind her, it will wipe her mind clean. She will live the rest of her life like a vegetable."

"Of course. That is the point," Fridtjof replied.

"Binding her is worse than killing her outright."

"Killing her could endanger the line," Beige said. "I don't think you fully understand how we anchors had to scramble when your Ginny was murdered."

I turned to my family. "Do something. We can't just stand here and watch this happen."

Ellen looked at me. "I love you so much. I love your dear, kind heart. But this woman"—she motioned toward Ayako with a careless gesture—"she conspired against you. I'm afraid I don't have your depth of compassion."

I turned from her to Oliver. He lowered his head and looked away from me. I reached out and took his hand. "I'm sorry," he said without looking at me, "but I agree with Ellen."

My eyes locked with Iris's. That she didn't want to cause any further trouble with the anchors was written all over her face. She began to turn away, but then stopped herself. She drew a deep breath, and her face relaxed. "We no longer live in the Dark Ages. I'm sure we can find some rational alternative," she said, looking away from me toward Beige. Her face lit up with inspiration. "Since Ayako's such good friends with Gudrun, send her to live with her."

"I am touched." Beige looked at me and put his hand over his heart. "Really touched that you are pleading on your attacker's behalf, but the punishment for her actions was long ago prescribed."

"Really? Gudrun was responsible for the death of how many millions of innocents, and still she got off pretty much scot-free."

"Gudrun cannot be bound," Fridtjof spoke up. "Nor can she be killed. If either of those options were possible, it would have been chosen. The best we could achieve in her case was containment."

"Have you not wondered how Gudrun could have existed unchanged for decades of our time in a place where time moves so much more quickly?" Beige asked. "She doesn't age. As far as we can tell, she is immortal. Worse than that, she appears to be indestructible."

"Then how could you have possibly sent my sister to study under her?"

"Gudrun expressed remorse for her past." Beige's gaze fell down and to the left, before returning back to me. "You are not the only one susceptible to the allure of clemency, and we had hoped Maisie might learn from Gudrun's mistakes. Just as we are still hoping that you will learn. That you will stop working at cross purposes to your fellows."

"I won't help you," I said. I shook my head. "I won't consent. I won't participate in this binding." I watched Ayako's face as I said this. Rather than gratitude, I saw anger building.

"You have no respect for authority. No respect for tradition. You *are* a danger to the line," she hissed, her brow lowering as she looked at me through the lashes of her narrowed eyes. She turned from me and advanced on Beige. "Do it." My jaw dropped in surprise at her words.

The stocky Russian stepped forward and warbled. "Ayako Izanagi, I bind you. May the power reject you. May it not claim you as its own." She stepped back and a man with cinnamon-colored skin and glossy straight black hair came forward.

"We don't need your consent," Beige explained sotto voce. "The binding of an anchor doesn't require unanimity, only a majority."

I started to protest, to do something, anything, to get them to slow down, to reconsider, but a clamor arose from the pallbearers, shrieks and metallic clacks combined as the bier rocked and fell from their grasp. The bier crashed to the ground, or at least what passed for the ground in this place. The noise made by the collapse seemed real enough, and the pallbearers slid back in a dismayed unison, appearing to grow both angrier and more frightened in each passing moment. The corpse rolled a few feet, ending face-up. At first it lay still; then a slight quiver moved through the body. Had we been mistaken? Had Teague somehow survived? No, Ellen hadn't uncovered a single sign of life when she examined him. Still the body moved, convulsed. I took a few steps forward, my curiosity leading me to break through the extended circle the pallbearers had made around their intended meal. It bucked up once, twice, then stood, like a marionette being jerked upright. His nearly severed head bobbed then dangled sickeningly to the side.

Something was moving beneath Teague's skin; his abdomen extended as if an elbow were pressing against it. The projection slid to the side, giving the impression that whatever was inside was turning around. Teague's hands rose, then his fingers tore at the skin of his chest, piercing it and prying it open. Like opening a zipper, Teague's hands tore at the wound, enlarging it until an abdominal cave split open in a shower of blood and offal. Another being emerged from its center, shaking off Teague's form like an ill-fitting suit. The casing lay still now, but my eyes had already abandoned it and were transfixed by the shape that had burst from the corpse as if it were a chrysalis. It stood before us, slippery and red, naked except for the sheen of Teague's fluids. I took the image in first as being human, second as female. Her laughter punctuated the screams of the pallbearers whom she turned to ash with a wave of her hand.

"Gudrun," a voice behind me said, dread falling on me as I realized it was indeed the witch who had worked with my own great-grandmother in her efforts to bring down the line. I turned away from the sight of her just as a pain in my midsection shot through me. A sharp quiver bent me, forced my eyes closed. I drew in a deep breath after it subsided. I opened my eyes and found myself, my real self, not an avatar, back home, sitting across from the vacant forms of Maisie, my aunts, and my uncle. Another pain, like I had been punched in the stomach, caused me to gasp in a sharp intake of air.

I saw a flash, and my consciousness returned to my avatar. Beige was speaking, but I couldn't make out his words. Everyone, even my aunts and Oliver, remained fixated on Gudrun; they hadn't realized I was in distress. Another pain, like a burning knife, shot through me, and the world went black. I gasped in air and began to cough. I could barely see. The only illumination was the flames that consumed the space around me. My heart fell as I realized the space around me was Magh Meall.

EIGHTEEN

Smoke, thick, whitish blue changing to black, filled the air. I called to my family with all my soul, hoping they would suddenly appear at my side, but there was no response to my call. My eyes burned. I got on my hands and knees to try to crawl beneath the noxious fumes. The heat was unbearable. The lack of air was worse. I used the position of the jukebox to orient myself. I went up on my knees and attempted to look around.

"Claire," I called and was instantly overcome by a cough. I lowered myself to the floor as an explosion coming from the kitchen area tore through the room. A beam fell from the ceiling, missing me by only inches. I focused on the flames. I willed them to fall back, to die away. Darting in and out and dancing among the natural flames, I recognized fire elementals, salamander-like beings, conscious flames. The same creatures who had saved me when I had been left to burn in Ginny's house.

They advanced on me, moving in unison as if they were a multiple expressions of a single mind. Their heads bobbed up and down as they vocalized in their ancient tongue, a chant alternately dissonant then harmonious with the fire's roar. The elementals turned and chased after the natural flames, swallowing them, but the fire was burning too strong. After a few moments, one of the entities returned to me, nodding up and down, half turning, then fully turning. Walking away and stopping. Looking back at me. I realized it wanted me to follow, follow it even deeper into the inferno. I hesitated and considered once again sliding away, getting my baby and myself to safety, but the thought brought another pain, not as sharp, but strong enough to get my attention.

This pain, I realized, was little Colin's first kick, and he was serious about getting my attention. Somehow my child knew something I didn't. "Okay, baby. Mama's listening." I crawled forward, keeping my head low. The elemental was leading me back toward the kitchen, but stopped near the bar. There, sticking out from beneath a pile of smoking rubble, I saw a hand. I recognized it as Peter's. My crawl turned into a desperate scramble as I fought to draw near his side. I leaned up and waved my arm, allowing my magic to remove the destruction that lay on top of him. I realized he was not alone beneath the pile. He was lying on top of Claire. It looked like he had tried to shelter her. I knelt next to the two, leaning in to hook my left arm under Claire's neck and grabbing hold of Peter's arm with my right hand. I feared that big Colin was still trapped in here somewhere. I needed to find him, but first I'd get Peter and Claire to safety.

Another sound, the wailing of sirens, came from beyond the wall of fire and smoke. I could hear voices barking succinct orders. The front of the bar had only one small window. The side wall was made up of old-fashioned bubble glass panes. With a single blast of a condensed stream of water, these panes shattered into crystals. Tiny shards were spraying everywhere. I closed my eyes and focused on the street outside. When I opened them, Peter was lying next to me, my fingers dug deeply enough into his arm to leave bruises. However, Claire was nowhere to be found. I looked up, sick with fear. Peter began stirring, but I had to go back. I had to get Claire and find Colin and get him out as well.

I squeezed Peter's hand in mine, then released it as I prepared to slide back into the burning tavern. In the moment before I closed my eyes, someone stepped between me and the flashing lights of the emergency. "Don't waste your effort." The whirling red, white, and blue lights of the emergency vehicles lit Josef, my half brother, my mother's lover, up from behind. "Your little teleportation trick only works on the living." He tilted his head, and the light found his face so that I could observe his tight smile, the curve of his lips only serving as the underpinning for the cruel gleam in his icy blue eyes. "Your mother wanted you to know you were always in her thoughts." Josef laughed and faded into the darkness. An EMT turned at the sound of Josef's maniacal laughter and ran over to examine us.

"My in-laws are still inside," I tried to yell, finding my voice coming out only as a froggy whisper. She understood and called out to her fellows. One of them, a fireman, took off his helmet and wiped away the sweat on his brow with the back of his sleeve. He shook his head slowly before donning the hat again and returning to the fire. I understood the meaning of his gesture, but he had to be wrong. I sent out a psychic ping into the ruined bar, trying to locate Claire and big Colin. It came back to me empty. There wasn't a living soul inside.

The next few minutes were a blur. Peter was hoisted onto a gurney and loaded into the back of an ambulance. "I'm fine," I protested to the forms in uniforms that encircled me. "Look after my husband." More sirens. More lights dazzling the night sky. Police cars. I heard the word "accelerant." I called out again to my family, but still could find no connection. Had Gudrun harmed them? Was her arrival somehow connected to this destruction?

"Mercy." My name pulled me from my thoughts. My heart leapt at the sound of Peter's voice. He pulled the oxygen mask from his face. He was so pale. His hand trembled so violently it broke my heart.

"What happened here, buddy?" The voice behind the question combined authority and concern. I turned to see Adam looming over me.

Peter tried to force himself up, but winced and remained supine. "The place was empty. We were closing up. Then it showed up out of nowhere," he said to Adam. Or I guess Detective Cook, as he appeared to be here in his official capacity. Peter coughed, and another EMT tried to put the mask back in place, but Peter pushed it away. His staring eyes held no luster. His breath was coming fast and shallow. "It mauled my dad. Oh, God. Oh, God." His eyes focused on the memory of what happened next. He looked up at me, white as a sheet and tears brimming in his eyes.

"What showed up out of nowhere?"

"This guy's in shock." The EMT stretched the elastic band and forced the mask back over Peter's face. "Keep that on, buddy." He flashed a light into his eyes. "Looks like he may be concussed, and that arm's broken." He nodded at Peter's right arm, which the EMT had managed to work into a sling without my even noticing. He turned to Adam. "You should save the questions until after he's checked out in the ER."

"Detective," a uniformed officer called to Adam. "You need to see this."

"Okay, I'll be right there." Adam reached toward me and pulled me into a tight embrace, placing a kiss on my temple. He released me, staring intently into my eyes, nostrils flaring. He was starting to say something when the officer called his name again, this time with a greater insistence. "You have her examined too," he said, pointing at me and giving the EMT a stern look to let him know it wasn't merely a request. I started to protest that I was fine, but Adam wagged his finger once in my face, then went to see what the patrolman who had called him had to say. The EMTs packed Peter into the back of the ambulance, and I sat by his side. Peter kept trying to sit up, but the tech had the foresight to strap him down to the gurney. Peter turned his head toward me. "You've got to tell Adam," he said.

"Tell him what, sweetie?" I asked, assuming he was delirious.

"The fire. It was a wolf that started it." The ambulance whisked us away to the tune of its shrieking siren. I held tight to Peter's free hand, but my eyes remained fixed on the ruins of Magh Meall until we turned the corner, and there was nothing left to see except the smoke that rose up to blot out the stars.

NINETEEN

I'm sure the anchors would have counted themselves as lucky. Even though Gudrun had broken out of her dimensional prison and was once again free to wreak havoc on our world, from their vantage, Gudrun's escape had so far been bloodless. Of course, they wouldn't count the scavengers Gudrun had turned to ash. Nor would they overly concern themselves with the losses to my family.

I sat alone at the kitchen table, watching an easy rain fall on Savannah and painting my nails a demure pink. Seemed as good a shade as any for a funeral. Rather than the jagged grief I would have expected to descend on me, I just felt numb. I couldn't really comprehend that Peter's parents were both gone. Murdered by my own half brother.

I should have realized how vulnerable the Tierneys had been. Done something more than weave a few protection spells against a magical attack. I should have realized that if those who wished us harm were prevented from attacking using magic, they would rely on everyday violence.

Colin had died directly at Josef's hands, or should that be claws. Josef was a skin-walker. He had chosen to make his attack in lupine rather than human form. A wolf capable of human treachery. The thought made me shudder.

Josef hadn't touched Claire. She had succumbed to a beam that fell in during the explosion. Peter had carried her lifeless body as far as he could before giving in to smoke inhalation. He broke his arm in the fall and was concussed by debris dropping from the Tierneys' apartment on the floor above the bar.

Part of my mind kept telling me that there was no way any of this could be real. That soon, I'd wake up and realize it had only been a nightmare. But the world around me kept moving.

I blew on my nails to help dry the lacquer, then reached for my chamomile tea. The heat of the cup warmed my right hand, while the fingers of my left hand examined the cool smoothness of my best pearls. White pearls, black maternity shift dress. My feet were too swollen even for my flats: early onset swelling, another perk of my unconventional pregnancy. At least I finally had a practical use for my worthless magic: I'd spell them into fitting.

I'd have to go up soon and rouse Peter. He had barely left our room for three days now. He hadn't shaved or showered. Iris had done her best to see Peter was fed, cooking all his favorites and stopping just short of spoon-feeding him herself. Oliver had tried both drinking with him and leaving him to drink alone. Peter wouldn't even let Ellen come near him. She wanted to heal his arm; he said he needed to feel the pain. Me, he was barely even talking to.

He didn't want to blame me, of that I was sure, but how could he not? He'd look around me rather than at me. I spent what seemed like days on my knees, begging my husband to turn toward me in his pain and not away. He didn't want to talk. He blamed me for his parents' death, and honestly, I blamed myself too. I set my mug on the table and applied polish to the fingers of the other hand.

I studied the back of my hand as the fresh lacquer dried, making a connection between the number of fingers and the five deaths my family had endured in six months. I counted Ginny in that number, because part of me said I had to. I included Jilo, and even Tucker, because my heart told me it was true. I certainly did not count Connor or Teague.

Nor did I include my mother.

The uniformed officer at the site of the fire, the one who had been so anxious to catch Adam's attention, had found Emily's head in a satin-lined chest outside the ruins of Magh Meall. Why Josef had turned against her we might never know. She had chosen to align herself with a sociopath, undoubtedly believing she could control him, certainly never suspecting that his violence might one day be turned against her. Josef had aligned himself with Gudrun, and this alliance had proven deadly to my mother.

"The burning bodies, the last sephira," Maisie whispered when Adam revealed the find to us. Emily's dismembered parts, a nightmarish jigsaw, were being held at the medical examiner's office under the name "Jane Doe 42." We had not stepped forward, nor did we plan on stepping forward, to claim her. As far as the world was concerned, Emily Taylor had been dead for more than two decades. I for one was more than happy to have them go on thinking that.

At first I was certain this was just another of her tricks. She had the power to create doppelgängers of herself and send them out into the world to carry out her subterfuge. I myself had witnessed one of them being impaled with a shard of glass from a crumbling dome. But Iris and Oliver visited the morgue and worked a spell capable of disintegrating anything created using magic. The spell had no effect; the parts that had been strewn over Savannah proved to be of organic, not magical, origin. It was indeed my mother's body.

It was so confusing. All along I had feared Emily had been the one behind the spell; I still couldn't wrap my head around the fact she had been the sacrifice that would allow Gudrun to free herself and wage a new war against the line. None of this made any sense. Had her murder been a punishment for failing to entrap me with Tillandsia, or had she given herself willingly to the cause of destroying the line? Maybe the truth lay somewhere between these possibilities. Perhaps she had no choice about dying, but she'd been allowed to go about it in a way that took the most from me?

Yes, even with her head in a box, my gut told me Emily had machinated the attack against Colin and Claire as a way to punish me for siding against her and her insane scheme to bring down the line. Unlike Gudrun, Emily had never been one to risk a full-on frontal assault. Her preferred method of war was to wear away at the edges and sow seeds of uncertainty and doubt. She removed the people who were important to you, eating away at any sense of security and doing whatever she could to unsettle you. It was so like her to attack on the periphery, even as a parting shot.

The purpose of the spell for which Emily was sacrificed was now evident, even if the workings behind it remained unclear to me. Gudrun had freed herself from the dimension that had held her since the end of World War II. I knew it was too much to hope that Gudrun intended to escape to my great-grandmother Maria's Aldebaran Aryan paradise. Now that she had freed herself, and returned to our world, I knew Gudrun's ultimate goal would be finally to bring about an end to the line. Common supposition held that if she succeeded in falling the line, the old ones would reward her, and reward her well. She would probably end up the queen of us all.

The other anchors were holding emergency summits. The united families were preparing for war. My family and I had been excused from participation as we were considered part of the problem, not the solution. The fact that my paternal great-grandmother had helped Gudrun orchestrate a world war didn't help me when it came to being considered guilty through association.

Witches around the world now shared a common opinion about me. I was indeed the Scarlet Woman of prophecy, the witch who would cause the line to fall. The only surprise for them was that I had never intentionally tried to harm the line. They saw my attempts to save my family and my hometown as immature, impulsive, hardheaded, and selfish. They agreed it would prove to be my numerous character flaws rather than any intentional evil that would bring about the end of the world. That opinion had developed as the general consensus even with Oliver handling my PR. I halfway expected an inquisition to arrive on our doorstep at any given minute. Probably the only thing standing between me and that fate was that every witch in the world whose last name wasn't Taylor was terrified of me, due in part to my uncle's efforts. When he realized he couldn't inspire loyal support for me, he decided abject terror of me might prove our next best hope. "Just until things blow over," he had said to me with a confident, if unconvincing, smile.

Truth was I couldn't give a damn what the other witches thought of me. I'd been on the outside of magic my entire life, one way or another. I didn't care about them. I could count the people I loved, truly loved, on my fingers, and now I'd lost two more of them. Maybe three. I didn't know if Peter would ever recover emotionally, if he could ever forgive me for what my mother and brother had done. Intellectually he knew the fault didn't lie with me; emotionally he knew his parents would still be alive if he had never laid eyes on me.

Emily had kept at least one promise to me. She had taken the truth regarding Peter's Fae origin to the grave. Still, even though she had kept her word regarding not alerting Peter to his true nature, Emily had certainly driven a huge and splintered wedge between us. Peter had shut me out, and the only other woman on earth who might have been able to tell me how to reach him, well, we were burying her charred remains alongside all that could be found of her husband in Laurel Grove in about three hours.

Perhaps if Abigail were still around, she might have found a way to help ease his emotional pain, take the edge off a bit, like she had done for Maisie early on in her healing process. No, I realized, I would have turned any such offer down. I wouldn't feel right about going behind his back. Besides, what with the whiskey he'd been downing, that edge should be pretty blunted already.

"Arson Turns Deadly" was the headline of the newspaper the day after the fire. The article noted that even though the cause of the fire was still under investigation, a police spokesman confirmed that evidence of an accelerant had been found. The paper made no mention of the discovery of the silk-lined box. The department had decided to keep that quiet until identification had been made.

Still, people talk, and when allegations that the Tierneys might have set the fire themselves began to surface, Adam attempted to have himself recused from the case. To me he had confessed, "It pisses me off more than you can begin to imagine that I know who was behind this, but I can't do anything about it. I can't just walk in and tell the chief that the fire was an exercise in magical correspondences." Since Adam couldn't admit the link between my family and the dismembered corpse, his request to be removed from the case had been denied. The official reason given was it would eat up too much valuable time getting another detective up to full speed. The real reason was that Adam's superiors had hoped it would put a fire in his belly; now it had all turned personal for him due, of all things, to his relationship with my uncle.

Adam insisted that all rumors be squelched by informing the press that the Tierneys had been victims of an as yet unidentified assailant, and that neither Peter nor his parents had anything to do with setting the deadly fire. Seeing his parents' names cleared seemed to help Peter. A little at least. But not for long. He fell quickly back into a dark and unreachable chasm. I took another sip of tea and steeled myself before going upstairs to wake him.

I felt a tingle, a vibration I had come to associate with Maisie. I turned to face her before she could even physically enter the room. She looked like a lovely librarian, all done up in understated mourning garb.

"I hope it's all right," she said softly, creeping up to me as if she were afraid the slightest noise would cause me to take flight. "I loved Claire and Colin. I want to say good-bye to them. Please say I can come."

I held my hand out toward her, and she came and clutched it between hers. "If you feel you are ready to face the world, I wouldn't dream of saying no." Then a discomforting thought hit me. "Stay out of Peter's line of sight, though, okay? He's not himself lately."

TWENTY

The rain had stopped, and though the air still felt chilly, a few rays of light reached out from behind the dissipating clouds. Claire and Colin had been beloved fixtures in Savannah, and even though not everyone from the church had followed us to the cemetery, still mourners stood in concentric circles eight deep around the open graves where Peter's parents were to find their final rest. Maisie did her best to remain unobtrusive at the outer edge of the gathering.

I watched Iris's eyes scan the crowd, reaching further and further back all the way across the cemetery to its entrance. I knew she was on the lookout for Sam, hoping he might decide to join us. She had phoned him, and left him a message with the time and place. Still, if he hadn't made it to the church, I doubted he'd show up here, but I didn't have the heart to strip Iris of hope. Sam might not have shared the common aversion to witches, but having your body taken over by a boo hag could push anyone over the edge. Iris felt the weight of my stare, and her eyes met mine. "You got to be tough to love a Taylor," she said reaching out and patting my hand. "Guess our Sam just wasn't tough enough."

I wondered if Peter would, in the end, prove tough enough. His buddies had pulled him aside. They encircled him, and I felt sure they were carrying on an abbreviated graveside wake. Oliver had followed to watch over Peter, hopefully limiting Peter's alcohol intake rather than facilitating it. I would have felt better if Adam too had been on hand; he had no magic, but he was a rock. I knew beyond a shadow of a doubt where his allegiance lay, a certainty that felt like a near luxury in recent days. Sadly it was starting to look like his job would make him miss the entire gathering. I could only catch glimpses of Peter through the wall of friends surrounding him. I strained my eyes and willed the crowd to part.

"I hope it isn't inappropriate for me to have come." A voice broke through my intention and pulled me back to the present. I looked up to see Jessamine standing a bit off to my side. She had come close enough for us to hear her, but held cautiously back. "Listen, I know this is neither the time nor the place for a discussion, but"—she reached up, self-consciously patting her auburn hair—"I'm going home today. I fly out this afternoon." She looked away from me to Iris. "I know you know . . . about me. Who I am. When we touched, I saw it in your eyes." Her eyes fell back to mine. "I heard about all . . . this. I just wanted to offer my condolences. I'm sorry. I shouldn't have come."

I reached up quickly and caught her arm. "Why did you come? Not today. I mean before."

Jessamine began to speak, then thought better of it. She pursed her lips. Finally she seemed to find her words. "I felt that Jilo had betrayed us. When I learned she had befriended you, I couldn't believe it. I had to meet you all." A cloud passed over the sun, and I saw tiny goose bumps prickle her flesh. "I was sure I would hate you." She rubbed her hand over the exposed skin. "I wanted to hate you. I had grown up believing you were monsters, but seeing you in the flesh, I . . ." She wrapped her arms around herself. "I realized you were no more responsible for my grandfather's desertion than I was. I saw you were just . . . well, not ordinary people, but certainly not fiends. It made me wonder if my family had not been the lucky ones." Her eyes swept over the open graves. "All this magic doesn't seem to bring you happiness." Her voice trailed off, then she grew flustered. "I'm sorry. I have no right being here, talking like this to you. Especially now. I'll go."

"Please stay." The words came to me by reflex. Jessamine seemed hesitant. Her mouth puckered slightly, and she leaned back away from me.

"Please," Iris added, and Ellen shifted over a seat so Jessamine could sit between them. Jessamine flashed me one last uncertain look, but then took the seat between her aunts. I knew Iris regretted having jumped to conclusions about Jessamine being involved in all of this. Her desire to blame Jessamine had come from a place of pain, a deep disappointment at having the false image of her father toppled. I sensed she had come to realize this with both mind and spirit, and was glad to have a chance to set things right with her unexpected niece.

Ellen, who had been hiding her red eyes behind the nearly impenetrable black lenses of her sunglasses, pulled the glasses off and put them on her head. "We have siblings we've never met," she said as if the idea had finally hit home. Perhaps emotionally it just had.

"Yes, a sister and a brother, my dad." Jessamine glanced over at me. "And you have other cousins too."

Iris reached out gingerly, and placed her hand over Jessamine's. "The circumstances that led to our meeting were"—she looked for a precise term, but seemed to settle—"*unfortunate*. I hope we can try this again. When all this is behind us, that is."

Jessamine stared dead ahead, saying nothing. Then she nodded and turned toward Iris. "I cannot speak for my family, but yes, I think I would like that."

The priest cleared his throat, causing a silence to ripple out from a circle where he stood as the center. Peter's friends scattered slowly, and I saw Oliver maneuvering Peter in our direction. Peter was speaking, and Oliver responded by nodding silently. If Oliver was surprised by Jessamine's presence, he gave no sign. I wasn't sure the new arrival had even registered with my husband.

Those gathered tightened the circle around us. The scattering of white wooden folding chairs could not begin to meet the demands of all the mourners gathered at the grave, so many were left to stand shifting from foot to foot, some leaning one against the other for support. I was glad I wouldn't need to stand, but the sight of the white chairs reminded me of my wedding not so many weeks ago.

It had been such a short time since Peter and I had made our vows to each other. Still, it felt like many lifetimes had passed since then. I could barely recognize the man who stood at my side.

He looked uncomfortable in his new dark suit. The only other suit he owned, he'd been wearing since high school, and the pants no longer held quite the same color as the coat. There had been no thought of getting Peter to a haberdashery. He'd barely even gotten out of bed since the fire. Oliver took the size from the old suit and eyeballed the necessary alterations. The slim cut of the jacket would be perfect once Peter's cast was removed. For now it hung over his shoulders, and he looked for all the world as if he might shrug it off. The way he continued to look past me made me wonder if he wouldn't rather shrug me off too.

I reached up and grabbed his hand. Peter looked down at me, and for a moment, just a moment, I saw a tenderness in his eyes. The moment passed as the priest began to speak. I wished I could have held his gaze even a second longer. A shudder went through me, and along with it a presentiment he would never look at me that way again. Peter held on to my hand, but looked away. I could tell he wasn't focusing on the priest's words. His eyes continued to scan the horizon, as if he were expecting an arrival.

"In sure and certain hope of resurrection." The words pierced my consciousness, drawing my gaze back to the twin AstroTurf-bordered openings at my feet. Something about the phrase struck me. The resurrection wasn't guaranteed; the only thing that was sure and certain was the hope. As the thought crossed my mind, Iris, who was sitting on my right, reached over and pulled my head against her shoulder. I let it rest there, happy to close my eyes and let the peekaboo sun warm me.

Peter's grasp on my hand tightened, and a charge of tension pulsated through the connection. I sat up and turned toward my husband. His face wore an anxious expression, his forehead bunched up to form creases. A bead of sweat trickled from his temple. He seemed to sense something at the edge of the cemetery. His eyes scanned the bushes at its boundary. I let my gaze follow his. I couldn't see anyone, but I, too, could sense an uninvited guest. I touched Iris's shoulder, pointing toward the spot where my instincts told me the interloper waited. Iris craned her head forward and narrowed her eyes to focus on the spot, only to look back at me and shake her head. She raised her eyebrows and gave her shoulders a slight shrug. She could sense nothing.

Peter turned to face me, and as he did, the beautiful mismatched color of his eyes changed to pools of mercury, the silver betraying his Fae blood. I wasn't sure if this change would be evident to anyone else, or if it was my witch blood that allowed me to see it.

"Do you hear that?" He voiced his question loudly, drowning out the priest's final petition. "They're laughing." He dropped my hand, his own anomalous glee leading him to echo the sound of the laughter he heard.

The priest stopped in midstream. "Of course, they are home with the Lord," he said, either misinterpreting Peter's words or willfully covering what he had interpreted as a psychotic break.

The priest granted us a beatific smile, then rushed to the prayer's conclusion. He had moved too slowly, though. Peter had already dropped my hand and bolted, breaking through the assembly like he'd been called in a game of red rover.

"I got this," Oliver announced. "Peter, come back," he called after Peter in a tone that made it clear to those of us who were familiar with Oliver's magic this was not a simple request; it resounded with his tried-and-true power to compel others to do as he wished. Oliver turned toward us, flummoxed when Peter carried on, ignoring his command.

"Well, don't just stand there," Iris said, "follow him."

"I am not wearing the right shoes for this," Oliver said, shaking his head. Then he went off, bobbing and weaving his way through the mourners who had, at least for the moment, all but forgotten Claire and Colin as they turned as one to follow my disappearing husband with their eyes.

"Peter," I called out after him, but he didn't stop. He didn't even slow. He carried on in a straight and singular line, leaping over the gravestones that had lined up between him and his goal, a goal I couldn't even see.

TWENTY-ONE

After Peter's quick exit, the other mourners made their way quietly and awkwardly back to their cars. The funeral procession that had arrived in such a neat and orderly fashion resembled the final lap of a dirt track stock car race as it made its exit. Only a few people even bothered to approach me, take my hand, or give me a quick peck on the cheek. I suspected more than a few felt it in their bones that somehow the Taylors were to blame for Colin and Claire's meeting an early death, and Peter's behavior was merely further proof that he had to be crazy to marry one of the Taylor girls. What could I say? They were right on the first count, and more than likely right on the second too.

Still, I made nice with those who did come up to me, although I kept one eye toward the gate and one ear open, hoping against hope we'd shortly get word from Oliver. As soon as the graveside crowd had cleared, I stepped behind a tree, where no one could witness my slide, and closed my eyes, concentrating on my husband and expecting to find myself standing beside him when my lids reopened. I could feel a cloud blot out the sun. I felt a drop of rain, then another in quick succession. I could not feel Peter.

"I can't find him. I can't even sense him." I felt panic begin to tingle in my lower back and work its way up me, cascading over my shoulders as my scalp began to prickle.

"It is going to be all right, sweetheart." Iris's voice came from around the other side of the trunk. She came to me and put her arm around my shoulder, leading me back to our group.

Jessamine placed her hand on my forearm. "I hate leaving you like this, but my flight . . ."

"Of course," Iris responded for me. "We understand. It was lovely of you to come."

I reached out and took her hand. "Thank you."

A tremulous smile came to her lips. "Don't worry, I'm sure your husband will be all right. He's hurting right now, but his heart will mend." She held my hand in hers. "I'll be in touch. Soon." She released me and made her way down the drive to her rental car.

"I'm sure she's right. Peter is fine," Maisie said, although her uncertainty came out in her tone.

Ellen nodded her agreement. "Let's just get home. He'll probably be there waiting for you when we step through the door." We all knew he wouldn't be, but the rain had begun to fall in earnest and the limo was waiting.

The chrome sky was darkening, enhancing through contrast the forced jolliness of the fandango holiday lights strung along the porches of the houses bordering the cemetery. A glowing, inflated snowman danced in the wind, stung no doubt by the grapeshot rain. More lights, brighter red-and-white ones filled the automobile's interior, casting whirling funhouse shadows around us. A siren wailed behind us, and the driver smoothly maneuvered the limo to the side of the road.

"Sorry, ladies," the driver said. "I don't know why—"

A rap on my window caused me to jump. The window was misty and the image on its other side distorted by the droplets. Still,

I recognized Adam's face looking at me. I pressed a button and the glass barrier descended. "Mercy, I need you to come with me."

"What is it?" Iris asked, leaning over me.

"We've got a bit of trouble with Peter. No time to explain." He opened the door and reached in, unfastening my belt like I was a toddler. The water from his waterproof jacket cascaded onto me, but he extricated me from the backseat of the limo without another word. Soon, I was standing in the full downpour, being shuffled along and stuffed into the backseat of the patrol car. Adam's hand pressed against my head to keep me from bumping it as I climbed in. He pulled the safety belt about six inches longer than he needed to, then buckled me in. I shifted the restraint into a more comfortable position as he shut the door behind me. I felt a bit of relief that this car didn't have one of those cages separating the seats.

Adam took his place in the passenger seat and addressed the uniformed officer behind the wheel. "Hit it." The siren raged anew as we began flying down the street, disregarding all stop signs and red lights after nothing more than a slight hesitation at each. Through the rear window, I could see a pair of headlights keeping pace with us. My aunts and Maisie had obviously convinced their driver to follow.

"What has happened? Is Peter all right?" I asked, causing Adam to look back over his shoulder at me.

"Peter is on the Talmadge Bridge, looking for all the world like he's thinking about jumping."

"That can't be," I said reflexively.

Adam sighed. "Well, I hope you are right about that, but even if he isn't thinking about jumping, he is on the bridge, and he's dangling off the side. Our officers have been trying to talk to him, but he doesn't respond. I thought he might. To you."

"Is Oliver with him?" I asked. "He went after Peter."

"He must have given him the slip." Adam's forehead wrinkled, and he looked away from me. Was he concerned that Peter might have harmed my uncle? No, even as peculiar as Peter's recent behavior had been, he wouldn't harm a fly. I felt that in my soul. I began shivering, as much from fear and adrenaline as the cold. Adam undid his belt and worked off his jacket. "Put this on." I did as I was told, taking more comfort from his concern than from the jacket itself. He forced a smile to his face. "Almost there," he said to me and reached over to kill the siren.

The bridge itself had been shut down in both directions, police cars and fire trucks parked at odd angles and blocking the span. My heart sunk at the sight of an ambulance. "Just precautions," Adam said, seeming to read my mind.

"What are you, some kind of a witch?" I joked halfheartedly as the police car pulled to a stop.

He acknowledged the joke with a smirk. "No, if I had magic powers, I'd be living in the sunshine on my own private island. Seems like what any witch with half a brain would do. Now, let's go get that man of yours, shall we?"

I nodded, and Adam opened his door and hopped out. I reached for the handle, only to find there wasn't one, but as soon as that registered, Adam opened the door for me. The rain had eased and for the moment was nothing more than a light drizzle. He motioned with a slight jerk of his head. "Over there."

I followed the arc of his gesture, only to see an unbroken semicircle formed by the broad backs of Savannah's first responders. Adam put his hand on my shoulder and guided me toward the curtain of reflective raingear. "She's here," Adam said, and the curtain opened before me, just enough for me to see the back of my husband's head, and realize how precariously he was perched on the bridge's edge. He sat on the edge of the bridge, legs hanging over into oblivion. Adam gave my shoulder a comforting squeeze, and threaded me through the break in his colleagues' living barricade.

"Peter," I said softly, my voice catching. He didn't respond. He seemed fascinated by something on the horizon. "You sure are causing a lot of good folk a lot of trouble," I said, nearing him, but afraid to touch him.

He turned to face me, and my heart nearly stopped. He reached over and pulled me to him, nearly causing me to topple over the barrier.

"You're scaring me." I tried to pull my hand free as he tugged on me with his right hand, pointing to the sky with his left. I realized his broken arm had healed, and the cast had disappeared. All this in the short time since he had run away from the graveside. He might not be working magic, but magic was certainly working on him. In the same instant, I felt Adam grasp my right arm in his viselike grip. I stumbled backward into him as Peter, oblivious to my fear shifting into anger, let my arm drop.

"It's right there, Mercy," Peter said as his left arm slid back to his side. I fought against my desire to grab him by the hair and pull him back to safety.

I took a breath. "What's there, sweetie?"

My heart melted as he turned his face up toward me, and smiled at me then down at my stomach. "Hey there, boy," he said addressing our son. His eyes rose back to my face. "It's going to be all right now." He nodded, but his eyes shone silver.

"Yes. Yes it will," I said, working with my fingers to loosen Adam's grip on me. I took a step closer. "Everything is going to be fine, but it's time to go home now."

"Which home?" He looked away and scanned Savannah's low skyline, then peered straight ahead in the direction of the river's flow. "There's my home. It's right there. It's just a bit out of reach. My real home. I know that now. Our little Colin told me so."

"Mistletoe." The incongruous thought rose up from my subconscious, even though my rational mind had no time to process its meaning. My hands jumped reflexively to my stomach; then for a brief moment I caught sight of the thing on the horizon that had been the source of my husband's fascination. A window, a portal that shone into a glimmering green world where a sun still shone and it was always midsummer. None of the non-magical crowd even noticed it; I scanned Adam's face and surmised he didn't have a clue it hovered there, just out of reach. I had caught a glimpse of this world once before, when the line reached out and mingled its magic with the bit of Fae magic growing inside me. Peter slid an inch or so forward, and I nearly screamed as he teetered forward. He righted himself at the last possible moment.

"Do you want to go there?" I called to Peter. He turned to face me. In this moment, I had his complete attention.

"I want to go home. More than anything." His words scraped a layer off my heart. More than being present for the birth of our son. More than sharing a life with me.

"I can do that for you," I said. "I can help you go home. You know if anyone can, it's me."

Enraptured. That was it. That was the only word to describe his expression.

"I'll help you, but you have to come to me." *Yes. I can help you leave me. I can help you leave your son.* I felt a sharp and icy blade cut through my heart, but I held out my hand. "You have to come." He stood, nearly losing his balance for a breathless moment, but then found sure footing. He jumped down off the barrier wall and grabbed me, swinging me up in the air. The first responders were ready to fall on him and pull him off me. "No," I said to stop them. "We're okay." Peter held me tightly in his arms, kissing the top of my head, my forehead. He pressed his face into my hair and breathed in deeply, then kissed my lips, my brow, my cheeks, never noticing the tears that were running down them. I allowed myself to step away from my emotions, to turn off my feelings and to switch to automatic pilot. People say no one has ever really died from heartbreak, but even if that were true, in that moment I was sure I would be the first. I would handle what needed to be dealt with now. I would process the feelings later. Peter lowered me to my feet and kissed me on the forehead, then once more on the lips. It wasn't a kiss that spoke of passion or love. No, this kiss said good-bye.

He stepped back and docilely allowed himself to be led to the back of a waiting ambulance. His second in a matter of days. I allowed myself to take a breath, watching as the EMT shone a light into his eyes. "What are you on, buddy?" Was it her voice I heard, or had I only read what she'd been thinking?

I stood back and watched it all happen. An officer approached the ambulance and, after a quick consultation with the tech, cuffed Peter to the gurney. "Seventy-two-hour psych eval." Variations of the clipped jargon rose up from the minds of several of the officers and firemen, the words weaving themselves into a near chant. On the periphery, I became aware of Maisie and my aunts, working their way past the protesting police officers. "We're family." I picked out Iris's voice saying, as if her statement reflected a much older and more essential law than any they represented. Maybe it did.

Adam stood near me, a little bit behind, a little to the right. He was on his phone. The "love you, too" told me he was speaking to my uncle rather than to the station.

The sound of the siren surprised me. The ambulance began pulling away, and I turned to chase after it. Adam reached out to catch me. "I want to go with him." I tugged against his strong grasp.

"I'll take you. Don't worry, he'll be okay now. This will all work out fine."

"No," I said, watching Ellen, Maisie, and Iris thread their way through a field of first responders. The ambulance took off at full speed, lights and sirens blaring full blast. "It won't."

TWENTY-TWO

What is magic? Once I believed it was the key to belonging, a shortcut to all success, safety from danger, and security from loss. I was wrong. Like with all other things in life, magic is just a solution that offers its own set of complications.

It isn't true that magic is everywhere you look, but the potential for magic is. Everything is made up of energy, and where there is energy, there is potential. Magic is nothing more than unlocking potential and molding it to your own use. Real witches carry the ability to tap into the well of potential right in their DNA.

Magic workers, people who are born without power of their own but who find ways to tap into the stream of magic, people such as my dear friend Jilo had been, have to work at it harder, relying on correspondences and attunements to achieve their goals. But even real witches, at least the smart ones, had learned a thing or two from those who had to earn their magic rather than inherit it. When working big magic, a spell you dared not risk going wrong, even real witches would use tools or props to help focus their intentions. They would choose the most auspicious time and place for the working.

We stood at Jilo's crossroads, my family and I. This spell we were now to attempt called for a location that was both natural and enchanted. The crossroads stood hidden in a grove and had served as the locus of Jilo's spell work for decades. Besides, being here, in a place that had been hers, made me feel stronger. Tonight, I would need all the strength I could beg, borrow, or steal. I pointed toward the earth with my index finger and drew a circle-bound pentagram. The white light from which it had been composed shone up on Oliver's face in a way that accentuated his skull. Death and loss. Growing up I had been so hungry for magic, openly accepting but secretly envious of my family's abilities. I'd been such a fool. Magic had brought me no happiness. All I had gained from magic was loss. Now I was being called on to use that magic to cast the spell that would take Peter from me.

After the incident on the bridge, the county had held Peter for three days. Certainly Oliver could have finagled an earlier release, but he and my aunts had spent days and sleepless nights poring over every available source, desperately trying to find a way to undo the harm my baby had inadvertently caused while trying to comfort his father. I let them only because I knew for them to find their own peace, they would need to know they had done everything they could have.

I'd been allowed to visit Peter, although I suspected the liberal visitation policy had been the result of Oliver's influence. I sat with him, hour after hour, watching him pull back from our world. He had grown more silent as the days wore on, until there were no words between us, no communication other than his pleading eyes.

For their part, the doctors tried to be reassuring. They ran tests and consulted. They provided medications. They questioned and rationalized away any outlying answers. What was wrong with my husband didn't fall within their frame of reference. They were good people, these doctors. They did what they could. Still, I knew all along they were only delaying the inevitable. Peter had been more than a mere part of my life, he had *been* my life for more than half of it. We had been inseparable since childhood; we had played, explored, broken rules, and at times broken each other's hearts. I loved him to the core of my soul. I couldn't really imagine my life going on without him. I felt somehow betrayed it could. Still, I couldn't allow myself the luxury of denying we'd come to the end of our adventures together. I had tried to prepare myself. I had tried to brace myself for impact.

Now in the moment of that crash, I felt the world should stop. That my heart should stop beating and my soul should be sucked into an insensate void, but that was not to happen.

Without a word, we assumed our natural points in the star. From my perspective, our lovely Ellen stood at the star's lower right leg. She had the greatest ability to unlock the potential of the earth, the material world. Diagonally across from her at the star's left hand stood Oliver, our family's golden boy, blessed by what seemed to be a nearly eternal youth and the ability to get his way no matter what. His was the essence of water, the patience and energy by which it grinds rock to sand. He met my gaze. He smiled at me to reassure me, but I saw the fear in his eyes. He was afraid I wouldn't survive this, or if I did I wouldn't be recognizable. He was right to worry. His heart was breaking for me, but I couldn't let myself feel the pain. Not yet. I had to do this. I turned to face Iris, who stood next to me at my right, the point of the pentagram associated with the potential of air. She could fly; the thought that she could take to the sky at will never ceased to amaze me, even in moments such as this.

Maisie stood at the point of fire, the element we shared, an inheritance from both of our parents. Her desire that I trust her, that I take strength from her, was palpable.

As we took our respective points along the pentagram, I couldn't help but reflect on how our magic had failed or backfired against each of us. Ellen could so readily heal others, but had come to rely on daily AA meetings as the cornerstone of her own well-being. Iris, capable of catching the wind and escaping to the heavens, had spent a good part of her life chained to a man who abused her emotionally and, we had come to learn, physically as well. Oliver, whose ability to compel others had led to the death of a young woman as well as her unborn child, tried to pretend he'd moved past the guilt, but I could see it wrapped around and rooted in his heart. I knew every time he looked at Adam, he wondered what Adam's son would have looked like, the type of person he would have grown into. I suspected Adam often wondered the same. Had they found a way to deal with this, or did they tap-dance around it?

My sister. Magic had nearly eaten Maisie alive. It corrupted her every word and deed. Did I ever really know my sister? The betrayal between us had been seeded into the very womb we had shared. I was choosing to trust her. Choosing to believe the evil that had taken her over was not her own. Would I pay the price for this choice? I felt sure in one way or the other I would.

Then there was me. The one who'd grown up on the outside of magic, only to have it hit me like a freight train. I stood at the head of the pentagram, the point of spirit, the place of power, as this was my spell to work. "Peter," I called into the darkness. "I need you to stand in the center." He approached in measured, cautious steps.

I wanted to scream at him that I loved him, but I knew it would be like dropping a pebble into a bottomless well. My heart and my mind held counsel with each other, and somehow they both agreed: the man I'd known, the man I'd married, was gone. If his parents' deaths hadn't broken Peter, our son wouldn't have tried to comfort him by revealing Peter's birth mother was still out there, still there in the world of the Fae, loving him, but what was done was done. "Face me," I commanded with a break in my voice. His eyes shone a cold silver in the night. Any love he'd known for me was gone.

I'd watched him struggle, fighting a losing battle against his true nature. I watched the Peter I loved die a bit more each day, until he was gone, leaving only a wounded creature desperate to escape this world where he didn't belong. Desperate to return to the people who had been denied to him for so long. The child who had once danced in my womb at the sound of his father's voice had fallen still. I would find a way to give my son the life he deserved. I'd probably never fill the void left by his father, but I'd do my best. I closed my eyes for a moment and drew a deep breath. *I promise you, my little one. Somehow I will make this right for you.*

If magic were wish fulfillment, when I opened my eyes, Peter and I would have found ourselves home, together, stringing tacky blinking holiday lights across the front of my family's already over-whelmingly large and ornate Victorian. The thought of the holiday caused my mind to flash again on the story of mistletoe. Such an innocent bit of vegetation, but so deadly when overlooked. Just as the Norse goddess never considered the harm it might bring her son, I never thought that it could be my own son who would reveal to Peter his link to the Fae.

But no celebrations for us. The only light I could see shone not from holiday lights but from the encircled star and from my husband's eyes. His eyes were turned upward, toward the portal opening above us, a doorway that would carry him home. A rustle at the edge of the trees caught my attention.

The blackest of hair, the palest of skin. Her lithe neck was stretched tall, her bearing regal. Even cloaked by shadow, I knew her to be the most ravishing creature I had ever witnessed. A crimson gown and rosebud lips. The fairest princess of them all. She embodied all fairy-tale superlatives and epithets, and I despised her to the depths of my very soul. A soft moan escaped my lips as a sense of finality washed over me, a finality that offered not even the flimsiest hope, for before me stood Peter's birth mother. She had come to collect her boy.

Peter turned to her and recognized her instantly. He attempted to rush to her, only to rebound against the boundary of the circle. He groaned and rushed at the circle like an animal trying to burst free from a cage.

"This witch magic is unnecessary," she said, her voice ringing through the night like crystal bells. She held up her hand and the light of the circle was extinguished. Peter broke free and rushed into her arms. "*Mo mhac.* My son." The portal that had always been just a bit out of Peter's reach slid down beside him. His face lit up with rapture and without a word, without a glance in my direction, without a moment of hesitation, he rushed through it, past the horizon, and he was gone.

TWENTY-THREE

I gasped as the cold blade of grief that had lodged itself in my heart twisted once more. I had come to the point where I had found strength enough to let him go, but there remained so many things I wanted to say to him. Words I wanted him to hear. Words of regret I'd hoped to hear from him. Promises that someday he would return to me, to our son. This utter lack of hesitation, his joy in abandoning us, was more than I could bear.

Like a boy fleeing school at the beginning of summer, Peter raced through the portal connecting this world to that of the Fae. He didn't hesitate. He didn't look back. Not a single farewell, not even a wave. As my eyes followed him into his new horizon, a hole formed in the material of my existence. He was as good as dead to me now. No, worse. There were plenty of pretty stories promising reunions in the world beyond death. I'd never heard any such tale about those separated as I had just been from Peter.

I gasped, struggling for air, unable to catch my breath as the realization that he was truly gone, that I would never see him again, sank in. So many times over the years, I'd had the chance to reach out to him. To take his hand. To tell him I loved him. So many times I'd had the opportunity, and I hadn't taken advantage of it. I despised myself now for those overlooked, unappreciated chances. The woman, the Fae, his mother, somehow she knew the spell had been broken and that the moment had come to reclaim her son. She stood off to the side watching as my heart was wrenched from my chest. She was so calm, so poised, I very nearly thought her heartless, until I looked deep into her silver eyes. Even though those eyes were not human, I could tell what I saw there was perhaps as close as the Fae came to sympathy. She might be the source of my anguish, but I felt she took no pleasure in it.

I felt a stabbing sensation in my chest, and my shoulders hunched up as my back bent. Hot sobs came from such a primordial place in my soul they could have been confused with laughter. I didn't feel sure I could survive this pain. I didn't know if I really wanted to. A part of me wanted to let the pain take me, to carry me away from the land of the living. Another part of me wanted nothing more than to rush through the entry that still hovered only a few feet away, mere inches off the ground, and drag Peter back through it, force him to come back to me. I knew deep down that even if it were possible, I could never be that selfish. I could never be that cruel.

I felt a black rage bubbling up within me. My anger craved a target. "How could you?" I turned to his mother. "How could you monsters send your children to us, let us love them, then take them away?"

"Monsters?" She looked at me with her luminous silver eyes. "If we Fae are monsters, then you witches have made us such." Even though her words had been said as a reproach, there was no anger behind them. Her voice caressed me. "No, I would never have caused you this pain, a pain very much like the one I myself felt when I gave my son up to this world."

"Then why do you do it?" Ellen asked. "I lost my boy. If I had had the choice, I would have given my very soul to save his life, to keep him here with me. I cannot imagine simply handing him over to strangers."

The Fae's eyes opened wider. "Is it possible you witches have forgotten your own history?" Our silence served as our answer. Her lovely face fell on me. "Then you must think me a monster."

"Tell us," Iris said, abandoning her point on the star and coming to put her arms around me. "What causes your kind to behave as you do? Why do you trade your own babies for human children? What purpose does having your changelings in our world serve?" I noticed Oliver had gone to Maisie, that he was sheltering her. God. She had loved Peter too. Was her heart breaking like mine?

The Fae broached our circle. I was quickly coming to the conclusion that witch magic was nothing more than minor prestidigitation compared to the magic of the Fae. "Your husband," she said, reaching out to me with her long slim fingers, "my son. He's not just any Fae. He is royalty. He is a prince." She held her head high, her delicate neck lovely in the moonlight. Around that neck she wore a pendant that might have been mistaken for an enormous ruby if rubies could glow in the dark. A scent reminiscent of sweet olive flower surrounded her. "I do not tell you this out of conceit, I tell you this so you will understand the desperate position in which you witches and your 'line'"—the word sounded sharp coming from her mouth—"have placed the Fae."

"The line?" Somehow, before she even explained herself, a wave of guilt washed over me, an emotion oddly out of place in the current circumstances, but the knowledge that we as witches were somehow responsible for where I now stood struck me as both an unpleasant and undeniable truth.

"Yes, that is how the web of magic you witches wove is known among your kind, is it not? The device by which you claimed this world, this dimension as your own, it was known as 'the line' at the time of its creation."

Iris squeezed me a tad more tightly. "We do still call it that, but how could it be of any consequence to the Fae?"

"When you draw a line, when you make a demarcation between one zone and another, you are creating a barrier, cutting the one thing off from the other. To protect yourselves from the dimension through which the great demons entered your reality, you witches gave yourselves a much wider berth than you needed. Once our dimension shared much of the same physical space as your own. Your line cut our world off, separating us from our shared source. Its creation was more than devastating. Greater than decimating. In the blink of an eye, a world of actualities was wiped out. Only a small remnant of the Fae survived. We tried to rebuild. We tried to start anew, but many of our children had been poisoned by your act of treachery. They were born deformed, their cognitive abilities damaged beyond any hope of healing." Her face lost some of its luster. "The worst is the reverberations of your magic set our reality adrift. Our wise ones determined we could slow this drift by placing our own equivalent of your line's anchors in your reality. It will live on as an eternal point of shame for us, but we were so angry, so desperate, for generations we stole human children from their cradles and put our own damaged children in their place."

"But my Peter, he's beautiful."

She smiled at me with obvious pride. "Our efforts worked. The exchange of children has almost stopped our drift, not completely, but still, we now have time to strive to find a permanent solution." She approached me in a nearly liquid movement. She touched my cheek, and I felt my body relax. "After many generations, we began to heal. The developmental problems that faced many of the first generation after your magic nearly destroyed us have for the most part disappeared. Our children are again physically beautiful and intellectually blessed. Their magic," she said as her eyes widened and shone with what I felt had to be joy, "it is wondrous, even by the standards of the Fae."

She removed her hand, and I felt instantly sadder, somehow diminished by the loss of her touch. "Why did you send Peter, if he was a prince?"

"Because, lovely one, a leader should never ask her people to pay a price she isn't willing to pay herself." A tear, luminous and as silver as the eye from which it fell, traced down her cheek. "We Fae are not monsters. We are living, breathing souls fighting for our lives. I am not heartless. I am a mother. Even though I rejoice at the return of my son, my heart breaks at your loss of him. I sense you loved him, perhaps even more deeply than you realize yourself."

"How could he leave me so easily?" With those words I swung again from heartbreak to anger. "How could he leave our baby?"

She looked down on me sadly, then turned to step nearer the portal that I'd only just realized had been shrinking, dissolving. "Don't hate him for leaving you." She paused. "I cannot find the words to explain to you in the time we have left, but when we place our children in this world, it is more than a change of physical locations for them. It is an absolute rewriting of their potential at a level deeper than what you have come to call 'quantum.' This *twisting*, it is done at the point of nothingness."

"The great void," I said, more to myself than anyone else who might have heard me.

Her look of approval told me she had appreciated my description. "Yes, the great void where nothing exists but from which all potential springs." In the passing moment, I sensed she was weighing her words, wondering how much more I might take without breaking. "He didn't forget you, my beauty. If it were a simple matter of forgetting, you would have never left his heart. He has been returned to his natural course. A course where you are a stranger, a stranger he never has and never will meet." She cast an uneasy glance at the fading portal.

"But our baby . . ."

At my words, she seemed to forget her anxiety about the closing window on her world. She was suddenly before me, her lovely face a mask of pain. She reached out with both hands and placed them over my stomach. For the first time in days, I felt little Colin jolt to life. I could feel his joy at meeting his natural grandmother flood through me, but her face told me this was in no way going to be good news. "You must be strong," she said, her voice taking on a musical quality, as if she were trying to sedate me through sound. "If I could give my own life to change this for you, I gladly would."

I pulled back, dragging Iris with me. "You're scaring me."

"I am so sorry, but there will be no child."

"What are you saying?" I lunged at her in desperation. I grabbed hold of her arm. A gentle pulse of electricity caused my fingers to tingle. My hand relaxed, and she slipped from my grasp. "You held on to my son with your hope. I suspect your hope will enhance your magic so that you continue to sense the child, for a period at least, but the child will cease to exist. It will cease to have been." She placed her hand over her heart, and moved gracefully backward toward the portal that had dimmed so as to be nearly imperceptible. "I am sorry, dear one. I am. Please know this." She paused beside the portal and looked once more into my eyes. "May you find a love who will never leave you, who will never forget you. This is my wish for you." With that she stepped into the fading window. She and the light were gone.

In the next moment I had fallen to the ground, digging my fingers into the dirt of Jilo's crossroads. I could hear my own screams as I reached out to any magic that might still lie buried there.

TWENTY-FOUR

I could not remember how I came to be home. I had been bathed and put to bed, Iris's bed, but how that happened remained a blank. Reality began taking sharp bites from the comfort I felt upon waking. Everything, my husband's abandonment, his parents' murder, my mother's death, Gudrun's escape, and the Fae's warning that my baby would soon be no more, competed to bring the emotions attached to them to the forefront. Bereavement and rage, horror and despondency bent around each other like a kaleidoscope of every shade of anguish.

For a moment I let myself slip into the fantasy that it had all been a bad dream. Any second Peter would come through the door and fall on the bed next to me, leaning on his elbows and crawling up along the mattress to place a Killian's-flavored kiss on my lips. I closed my eyes and pushed the fantasy away. I knew only madness lay in that direction. With my magic, with my pain, I might just manage to create a fantasy world for myself, where I could deceive myself with a false happiness, but lose any chance of saving my child.

An unpleasant scent pierced my awareness. Ammonia? Panic jolted through me. I felt for my distended stomach, so grateful to feel it was still round and hard to the touch that I began to cry. It was more than that Colin was all I had left of Peter, more than that he was a link to the person I had been. I hadn't even laid eyes on Colin yet, but he was my son. I felt him. I knew him. I loved him. He was real to me. He was real. I would be damned if I'd simply let him dissolve into the ether. I pushed the sheet down, surprised to realize I was completely naked beneath it. I startled at the sight of runes, the ancient magic symbols of the northern peoples, that had been drawn on me from just beneath my breasts all the way down my thighs. I realized the ammonia smell came from the India ink used to make the marks.

The character *Uruz*, the symbol of health, strength, tenacity, was repeated in a large circle on my stomach. My finger traced over one of the markings. I felt Ellen's magic in this rune and knew she had drawn it with her own hand, filling it with both her love and her power. *Laguz*, representing life energy, formed a second circle that lay within the borders of that formed by *Uruz*. This character and others I did not recognize—Chinese? Hebrew?—had been drawn by Iris. I knew Iris had connected her powerful intellect with a level of magic I doubted she had ever before attempted. It struck me as odd that I didn't feel Uncle Oliver connected to any of the magic, but maybe since giving birth was a female act, the spelling was left to the women?

I was so entranced by the discovery of the symbols, I didn't realize I wasn't alone until I heard a book hit the floor. I turned to see Iris curled up in a wingback chair from our library. She was sound asleep, soughing, her legs pulled up under her. The noise from the falling book didn't wake her. I recognized the book as one of my grandfather's journals. He had been a specialist in creating spells using runes and other magical symbols, and if his knowledge could help save Colin, I was sure it would go a long way for all of us toward finding forgiveness for him.

The shutters had been pulled tight; the only light in the room came from the floor lamp Iris had slid over to the side of her borrowed chair. I was unsure what time it was or how long I'd been sleeping. A feeling of déjà vu came to me. I soon realized I'd felt this same disorientation when I awoke in the hospital after Ginny's murder. It felt impossible that the previous awakening could have occurred only six months before. The memory of discovering Ginny's body was still sharp and clear. I could still hear the ticking of Ginny's dime-store clock competing with the buzzing of flies. Had it been that moment when everything in my life had changed from dull to full-speed? Or had it been the night before, when I got it in my head to turn my romantic problems over to a certain surly conjure-woman?

I thanked God I'd taken my tour into Colonial Park Cemetery in time to see the old woman of the crossroads working her way through the monuments like a needle through cloth toward the exit, holding on to her bright-red cooler and using her lime-green lawn chair as a makeshift walker. Her progress was slowed by an unfortunate woman who'd sought the death penalty against her husband, then wanted the magic undone once she realized she'd convicted him under false evidence. Did Jilo undo the curse in time, or had the poor innocent man been punished over a stupid misunderstanding? I wished I'd asked Jilo. I should have cared enough about what is right and what is wrong to at least find out. Or had I simply been too afraid to learn the truth? I wanted to believe Jilo had undone any harm before it became permanent.

Jilo didn't always take the concept of right versus wrong into account when practicing her magic, but still I came to love her and she me. My family could access exponentially more magic than Jilo ever dreamed of having, but I knew if she were here, she'd find a way to protect Colin. I wondered if I'd worry about her methods if she were still with me, or if I'd back her in whatever steps she thought might prove effective.

Still, as much as my friendship with Jilo had changed me, I knew the adulteration I'd experienced had been triggered before that encounter in Colonial. I tried to cast myself back into the girl I had been the day Maisie first brought Jackson home and introduced him to the family. I had grown so used to living on the outside of magic, on the fringe of my family, that I had become a solitary soul. Not exactly lonely, but not a part of anything either. Perhaps I'd enjoyed leading tourists around, telling them tiny white lies, because for a brief moment I was more than the center of attention; I was connected to them. Then, before things had the chance to turn messy, I was able to wave good-bye and send them off to City Market or the Pirates' House.

Still, I'd been happy. Happy, adventuresome, curious, committed to Peter through a promise that had never needed to be spoken, but one I'd very nearly broken. When I laid eyes on the beautiful lie that was Jackson, I saw my own magic in him. A magic that had been stolen from me. I loved the magic, and because I loved it, I, for a brief and foolish moment, had believed I loved Jackson. My callousness toward Peter drove him to take desperate measures to win me over, the result of which was the beautiful being I now nurtured in my womb.

I placed my hands on my stomach and sent all the love in the world to the little boy growing inside me. "You're gonna be all right, baby. We both will. Mama promises." I whispered the words knowing full well I couldn't really make that guarantee, but my love was so strong I felt sure it had to count for something. I felt an incomparable joy when I felt my feelings being returned. Colin believed me. More than that, he believed *in* me. He knew I was not simply going to give up on him and let him fade away, regardless of what his fairy grandmother had told me. I opened myself with all my heart and soul to my child. I made a promise then and there, that no matter what, I'd do what it took to protect him, to make sure he had the chance of having a life in this world, even if his life turned out to be every bit as messy and confusing as his mama's.

As my soul resolved to protect him at any cost, I felt a tug. An unfamiliar and powerful magic called to me. I recognized the magic's source by the fact it felt so entirely different from my own. This power was wholly alien in every sense of the word. Gudrun was nearby, and she called to me.

Still, it felt like an invitation, not a summons. A promise of assistance, of security, of enough power to take care of myself and those I loved. Enough power to save my son.

"No, this is all your fault. Josef may have set the fire, but you wove the spell that killed Claire and Colin," I said aloud as if Gudrun were there with me. Iris shifted, but did not wake. "My son lost his father trying to ease his father's pain, a pain you caused. And now . . ." My words failed me as I couldn't, wouldn't, allow myself to give voice to the idea that I might now lose my son.

Gudrun's answer came to me through impressions rather than words. A declaration of innocence. A promise of retribution against the guilty. A tickling reminder of how those who should be my allies had betrayed—and continued to betray—me was woven into the fabric of the calling. An offer of camaraderie. Hadn't we both suffered at the hands of the line's other anchors? Wasn't it true that we two were somehow special? Those who should have rightly formed a sure foundation beneath our feet had bound themselves together in their attempt to weigh us down. Yes, we had much in common.

I knew it would be foolish to answer the summons. Gudrun's magic came from a place of darkness, a place I'd never want to visit. My good sense screamed out at me to wake my aunt, tell her what I was experiencing, but my good sense had no idea of how to protect Colin. If Gudrun had even the flimsiest of ideas how I could save my son, I had to take the risk. I had to hear her out.

I waved my hands down the length of my body, and my nakedness was traded for street clothes.

I closed my eyes and focused on the tug. I had no idea to which unholy realm it might lead me, but I would walk barefoot over the coals of hell, the real one, if there were indeed such a place, to give my boy a chance of being born. I heard the familiar sound of a tourist trolley loudspeaker and opened my eyes to find myself in Oglethorpe Park, standing beneath the tree Peter and I had long known as the "climbing tree," the very spot where we had wed only months before.

On that day Peter had asked me, "I'll meet you beneath the climbing tree?"

"Always and for the rest of my life." That had been my response. I touched the bark of the climbing tree's trunk and asked it to remember that day for me, even if everyone else let it slip away.

Like a magnet collecting iron shavings, I felt my attention being pulled away from the tree, away from the memory. There, on a nearby bench, Gudrun sat with her back toward me. She held up a hand and signaled me to join her with a wave.

I took a breath and circled around to the front of the bench. "Thank you for joining me." She spoke with a clipped German accent that reminded me of Erik Weber, the man who had been both my uncle and my father.

There before me were the exquisite yet unforgiving features that twice had looked back at me through my mirror. Gudrun had now stepped through the looking glass into the heart of my world. She occupied the bench as if it were the throne from which she ruled. She sat there surveying me, waiting for me to respond, but I stood speechless before her. Her magic was visible to my naked eye, shimmering around her like an August heat rising off blacktop. She tilted back her head, her eternal black pageboy cut falling at an angle along her delicate jawline.

"I have no interest in harming you," she said. "However, I would have done anything to escape my prison. I would have sacrificed you, your child, your family, *anything* to free myself, but I am not your enemy." I examined the gray eyes that shone out from porcelain skin. They radiated a calm certainty that only a person who suffered from no self-doubt could obtain. "I merely took advantage of your true adversaries' hatred. I used it like a lever to pry loose the hold your fellow anchors had on me."

I finally found my voice, even though I was still overwhelmed by the strangeness of the aura around her. "Call yourself what you want. You've destroyed my life. You murdered my in-laws. You've taken away my husband. And by taking away my husband, you've endangered my son's life."

She held up her hand. "Enough of your litany. I am not responsible for your tribulations."

"It was your spell—"

"Yes, it was my spell, but my *assistant*"—the way she said the word suggested she found it a poor translation of the word she would have used if I could speak her mother tongue—"your brother, took liberty with my instructions. Josef wanted to strike out against you personally. I had no such desire." She offered a slight shrug as if to underline the fact she was confirming the obvious. "I had intended it as a form of penance on his part, forcing him to distribute his lover's remnants at the points of the sephirot. The sealing of the spell required the presence of burning bodies. I had intended that he offer the tribute to Asmodeus at a crematorium. Instead he took his revenge against you by setting your in-laws' establishment afire." She folded her hands on her lap. "Again, I will not lie to you. If my freedom required burning this entire city down around your ears, I would have done it without flinching, but Josef's actions were unnecessary. They were motivated by his own anger, and I regret not holding the reins tighter."

My bitterness blunted any sense of caution. "Well, I guess that makes it all right then," I said, each word laced with sarcasm. "Why are you here? I don't think you've come to ask for my forgiveness."

She burst out laughing, a pointed sound that brought images of beer halls and heavy weaponry. "Forgiveness? I have long ago lost the need for that saccharine validation." Her face smoothed back into a cool mask, with only a small twist on her lips still betraying amusement. "No, I do not seek your forgiveness, nor have I come to sue for peace." She leaned in toward me conspiratorially. "I could squash you and your frail magic with only a thought." She paused. "You don't believe me?"

So far our little talk wasn't living up to its promise. I felt my face redden. My hands balled into white-knuckled fists. I had grown sick and damned tired of threats, whether they could be backed up or not. "I believe you could try."

Again she laughed. Her eyes lit up with an odd shade of fondness. "Oh, so you do have some of Maria in you after all?"

She meant it as a compliment but I felt the words curdle in my soul. "If you consider me so inconsequential, why bother with me at all?"

"Sit," she commanded me as if she were talking to a young child. I didn't move a muscle. Then came what I perceived as an uncharacteristic gesture. She rolled her eyes and patted the empty spot on the bench. "I never said you were 'inconsequential.' Please." She moved her hand away so I could join her on the seat.

I nodded and sat next to her, turning sideways so she was in the center of my vision. She had been my paternal great-grandmother Maria's best friend, and from what I'd learned about Maria, that was not a good thing. She turned toward me as well, draping her left arm over the bench's back. My eyes were drawn to the large opal she wore on her finger. She followed my gaze toward the ring. She held her hand toward me so I could examine the fiery stone.

"Lovely, isn't it?" She tilted it back and forth so the oval stone burst to life beneath the sun's rays. "They die, you know? Opals. The fire drains out of them, leaving behind nothing but a cold and worthless stone." She pulled her hand back and returned her arm to rest on the bench. "Undoubtedly this one too would have faded long ago were it not always on my finger. I never take it off." Her eyes reached out to grasp mine. "It was a gift to me from Heinrich." She waited a moment, seemingly disappointed by my lack of reaction. "Dear me, are you so ignorant of your own history?" I bristled at her question, Peter's natural mother having asked me almost the same thing hours before. "Does the name Himmler mean nothing to you?"

I slid back involuntarily, moving myself away from the ring. Of course I knew the name. Himmler was the epitome of human evil, a Nazi leader as responsible for the death of more than eleven million people as Hitler himself. My eyes narrowed in on the stone. "I would crush the stone to dust and melt the gold that holds it."

Gudrun pulled her hand back to examine the ring more minutely. Her lips curved up ever so slightly. "It is only a bauble, and a pretty bauble at that."

"It was given to you by a monster."

"In your eyes it is somehow guilty by association?"

"Guilty no, tainted yes."

She raised her head proudly. She pulled the ring from her finger and held it up. It dissolved to dust before my eyes, a gentle breeze rising to carry the fines away. I coughed as I breathed in some of the powder.

"Thank you," I heard myself saying, even though it seemed an odd act to thank her for. All the same, I did feel more relaxed with the gem gone.

"It was politically advantageous at the time to accept the jewel from Himmler; it is politically advantageous now for me to destroy the gem." She pursed her lips and appeared to weigh her words. "You have much power at your disposal, but you are far too concerned about what is right, what is wrong." Her eyebrows rose a little. "You still believe in God, don't you?"

"Of course I do," I said, a bit taken aback by the turn this conversation had taken.

"Of course," she echoed me. "How do you imagine this God? Is he the great judge? The ultimate arbiter? The father?"

"Well, honestly, I'm not sure that he is a he at all."

"That is fair enough," she pushed on before I could express my full thought. "Still, you view this being as the definitive rule-maker. The final source as to what is right and wrong." She slid her hand down my arm. "What if there were no God? Who would be left to make the decisions then?" She shifted in her seat, looking away from me and following a pack of giggling children running down the path before us.

"Really?" I asked when she fell silent. "You've come all this way to discuss moral relativism?"

She turned back to me with a satisfied smile on her lips. "I've lived a long time, centuries on the timeline of the dimension where I was imprisoned, and even a century in your own sense of time." Her eyes narrowed. "Never, never have I seen a single shred of evidence that God exists. I've witnessed, even interacted, with beings, ones with powers beyond the human comprehension, who have called themselves 'gods,' but no, never has the great ineffable shown even its shadow. But I tell you this only as a kindness." Her eyes fell to my waist. "You should feel proud. Your tiny one, he is putting up a valiant fight. Still, it is a fight he cannot win. There is a world of reality forming around him that says he does not, cannot, exist."

My arms fell protectively around him. Gudrun clicked her tongue, and shook her head sadly. "A lesser witch, a weaker fetus, it would have been settled days ago. And you, yes you, would already be well on your way to forgetting him as well as his father."

"I could never forget either of them." Horror fed into anger.

"I assure you, you could." She let the words hang there between us, as if she were waiting for them to sink in. "And you will. When did you feel him move last?" She narrowed in on my protruding stomach. "Now, honestly, don't you feel that your womb is contracting, growing smaller?" She reached out, almost ready to touch me, then seemed to think better of it and pulled back. "I'm sure the fetus's growth has halted, even if devolution has not as yet set in." Her eyes drifted back up to my face. "Oh, you poor girl, you've gone absolutely gray." She reached out and took my hand in hers. She held it as if we had been lifelong and the most intimate of friends. I didn't feel the repulsion I would have expected at the contact. "The reality of your situation is finally dawning on you, is it not? You're losing everything. Your life is spinning out of control, but you could change all that."

She released my hand. She wrapped her arm around my shoulders, then pulled me into her bosom. She stroked my hair. "Aren't you tired, Mercy? Aren't you tired of all the lies and betrayals? Those who should have dedicated their lives to protecting you, nurturing you, they have deceived and endangered you. Your fellow anchors plot against you even as we speak. I cannot do anything about them, yet, but I have seen to it the worst of your enemies has been punished. Emily has been removed."

"You killed and dismembered Emily to complete your spell." I tried to struggle from her grasp, but found I couldn't, not because her strength held me, but because suddenly I could not bear to break away from the comfort I was feeling in her arms. I knew it was like welcoming the embrace of a boa constrictor, but I couldn't even work up a good enough damn to give to fight her off. "Only I don't understand what the spell had to do with your breaking free."

"Shhh . . . Shhh . . ." she said as I weakened in her arms. She was charming me. I sensed it, but the charm sedated my ability to care. "I could have taken anyone to seal the spell, but I wanted to make a statement. I killed her and sundered Emily's body limb from limb as a punishment to her and as a warning to those who would betray you, Mercy. The world has waited for you"—her voice betrayed a simmering anger—"I have waited for you for so long. The woman who bore you, she risked your destruction so she could claim the glory that is only yours to claim."

It ought to have horrified me, but somehow it seemed fitting Emily should be made an example of. "You are special, Mercy, even among witches. There is a well of power right at your fingertips, if only you would reach out for it. The magic is waiting for you, aching for you to use it. Think about it. All you need to do is claim your birthright, and the world will fall at your feet before you. Your little one, what have you named him?"

"Colin," I responded, with only the slightest warning from my subconscious. I had given his name to her, might I have given her control over him as well in doing so?

"Colin," she said as the fear washed away. "You could preserve his life, watch as he grows into manhood. If you claim your rightful power, acknowledge that power gives you the right to determine what is right and wrong. You, not some imaginary God. Stop and feel it within yourself. Isn't that what you want to believe? That somehow there is a great father in the sky looking out for you? Believe me, even if it were true, your God lets down millions of people each day. They age. They grow sick. They watch their loved ones die. I am not offering you platitudes and dreams. I am not some dry and effete priest asking you to have faith in an absentee God. No"—she was getting caught up in her own words—"I am trying to show you that you can be a god yourself. We are the only gods here, you and I." Her enthusiasm tugged at my will and weakened my conscience. She released me and nodded toward a toddler riding by on a pink tricycle, followed closely behind by her father.

He watched over his daughter as if she were his entire world. I should have felt joy at the sight; instead I felt the darkest shade of envy gnawing at my gut. Gudrun's voice sang in my ear. "Is it 'right' this ordinary child should live and your own special, magical infant should not? If there were a God, a divine will, what type of monster must he be to allow such a miscarriage"—her inflection made her sound as if she'd just realized an unintentional pun—"of justice? No, I think it much more likely there is no supreme will, no grand scheme, only the survival of those who will do what it takes to survive." She watched as the small girl turned back on her trike to circle her father. "What if you could trade that child's life to save Colin's?"

The suggestion sickened me. "That is a monstrous—"

"Well, of course, she is an adorable little one, isn't she? We wouldn't want to harm her." Her eyes scanned the area before us, and she pointed at another child. This one was older and had moved into the awkward phase where external beauty was both a memory and a hope for the future. He was picking on a smaller child, shoving him and making him cry. "How about that one?"

"It would be wrong. I don't have the right."

"Of course you have the right. If you have the strength, you have the right. With the kind of power you have at your access, there is no such thing as being wrong. There is only the choice to survive or leave the world to those who will." She raised an eyebrow. "Or perhaps you love your antiquated moralistic ideals more than you love little Colin?"

"No, you are twisting things, trying to confuse me." I knew the spell she had placed on me made me more compliant. More susceptible. It had something to do with the opal, perhaps even carried to me in the dust I had breathed in. The damnedest thing about her enchantment was it left me incapable of caring that she had enchanted me. I felt like I was bobbing up and down in the sea. On the brink of drowning, but still indifferent to that fact.

"Child, I am trying to open your eyes. I am trying to give you the strength you need to throw off the shackles that bind you. I am trying to save your son. I had hoped you would appreciate that." She looked away from me and down the path leading to the swan-and-merman-encircled fountain. "What if saving Colin didn't require the sacrifice of a child? That man there—" She pointed at a homeless man, weaving as he made his way to a bench. He had a bottle wrapped in brown paper, and alternated between singing out of key and swearing at anyone who looked his way. I sensed he was very lucky not to have noticed Gudrun noticing him. "That one, why should he have such a strong hold on this reality when our Colin is being *erased*? Look at him, what about him? If we could trade his miserable existence to buy even another single day for our Colin, why wouldn't we?"

I looked at the sad fellow. He held his bottle tightly as if he feared one of the passersby would covet it as much as he prized its contents. He swung around to argue with someone who wasn't there. Looking through my witch eyes, I discerned there was no spirit, no invisible assailant threatening him. He fought a projection of his own alcohol-soaked brain. Would he be missed? Would his death leave a void in the fabric of this world? Wouldn't it be so easy to reach out and draw the life force from him and offer it . . . ?

The heinousness of the crime I'd begun to contemplate woke me from Gudrun's spell. The story of Eve and the serpent flashed through my mind. With how many greater sins had she been tempted before giving in to that seemingly innocent bite? "Oh my God," I said in a gasp. "No. It's his life. I am not a killer."

Gudrun breathed deeply, as if she were trying to keep her cool as I tested her patience. She didn't try to interrupt me.

"No. God or no God, the way you think is wrong. It's true, I'm desperate to save my child, but I will find another way." I flung myself from the bench, nearly toppling over as I did. I backed away from her. "The world you describe. I wouldn't want to bring Colin into that world."

"You are dooming your child to nonexistence. It may be that the only honorable outcome of that bum's life would be to stand as sacrifice to protect something greater." She waved her hand in the man's direction, and he arose and made his stumbling way out of the park. "I believe I comprehend your difficulty." Gudrun looked at me, her head tilted to the side, her eyes lowered. She was the picture of sympathetic understanding. "When one person is killed, it is murder. When a group of people are killed, it is slaughter. You find these things unimaginable, but believe me, Mercy, when a hundred thousand die, it becomes a matter of statistics. Once the count grows high enough, one's mind loses its ability to consider the individuals behind that count. The emotions dull, and the conscience stops wheedling." She paused. "When you've reached that point, you yourself become a god."

"I don't want to be a 'god.'"

"Not even if for every death, you could buy another day of life for your little boy?"

I responded before any further temptation could penetrate my weakened defenses. "No, not even then," I said, knowing what I said was right even if it felt oddly like I was betraying Colin. "I'm leaving. Don't try to stop—"

"What about those the line destroyed? You have heard firsthand the effect it had on the world of the Fae, and you only know of their fate because enough of them survived to tell the tale. What about the others whose worlds were ended by the creation of the line?"

"There were others?" Again I felt responsible. Guilt washed over me.

Gudrun looked back at the Confederate Monument and shrugged. "I don't know about that, but I do know the witches who created the line demonstrated absolute indifference about anyone other than themselves." A shirtless guy, about a thousand years too young for Gudrun, jogged past us for what I realized was the fifth time. His gaze met with hers many times at each pass. "Foolish child," she said, but I wasn't sure if she meant the runner or me. "Today's anchors are no different. Ayako told me the other anchors have kept many things secret from you. Even now they have left you to believe that Ayako has been bound, but I assure you she has not been. Your fellow anchors have decided in your case, her actions were understandable, even if they did lead to a result Ayako herself had not intended." She smiled and placed her palm over her heart. "They have agreed they need Ayako for the final battle they plan to wage against the two of us." She nodded at the fact the other anchors had judged me as being as dangerous as the great Gudrun herself.

She folded her hands together like she intended to say grace. "I realize I am asking you to think in ways that go against your current convictions, perhaps even against your very nature, but I sought you out because you are special. I am convinced you are the witch we have waited for. The witch who can bring an end to the abomination you call the line. I promise you, though, if I cannot bring you around to my way of thinking, I will go. I will leave you and yours in peace. I have no desire to be at odds with you, Mercy. After all, we are of the same blood."

Well, there you have it. Her words struck me as a despicable and incontrovertible truth. I hated it, but for the first time since Gudrun had begun flapping her gums at me, I believed her. Really believed her. "You are a Weber?" I was related to Jilo—sort of. Now I was related to Gudrun too. I evidently shared DNA with half of the flipping world.

"No, not a Weber, but your father, Erik, was a cousin to me."

I couldn't even begin to process this at the moment. It was like learning I was second cousin to the boogeyman. It seemed just as impossible and twice as frightening. Right now, though, our shared blood might be the only thing keeping me alive. Hoping she would be bound by a thief's honor, I decided to pin her down to a promise. "So, we agree to disagree, you let me leave? You leave me and mine alone?"

"Your fellow anchors would consider your proposal the final proof of your treachery." She seemed pleased by the thought. She nodded. "You have my word. I only have one more issue to discuss with you, before we part."

I felt a rising suspicion at the same moment I felt my stomach dropping. "What's that?"

"All right. I acknowledge that you're not a killer. At least not in this circumstance. What, though, if it constitutes a matter of administering justice?"

"I am not a judge, and I am certainly not an executioner."

"No? Well, I think I should grant you the opportunity to be both." She raised her hand and began drawing a small circle in the air next to me. "You blamed me for your losses, but I am, in truth, not to blame." The empty space next to me began to solidify, darken. "He is," she said as Josef appeared by my side. The moment he assumed full corporality, he spat in Gudrun's direction. He strained against bonds of dark matter that fettered his feet and held his arms in place behind his back. "I hand him over to you for judgment."

"Bitch." The word no sooner escaped his lips than a band of the binding darkness formed around his mouth.

"Perhaps," Gudrun replied, "but it is you who has need of a muzzle. He is yours," she said, turning her focus back to me. "At least for the next twenty-four hours. I have put a kink in his magic, and until this time tomorrow, he will be without power. After that, he will again be free, to go on harming all those you love, and who knows how many more." Her eyes scanned him. "He's killed over fifty humans and"—she tilted her head inquisitively—"three witches." Her face took on a bemused look. "Really, Josef, if your sister is weak enough to let you live to see another day, I would love to hear about those three witches." She focused on me. "Of course, if she is weak enough to let you escape, I suspect that number will have risen to four by the time we meet again." She waited for the meaning of her words to enjoy their full effect. "I trust you can find your own way home." With that, Gudrun was gone.

TWENTY-FIVE

We stowed the still-gagged, bound, and powerless Josef in my old room. Stained as it already was by the memory of Teague's death, I didn't mind. My emotions had begun to let go of the space, and I had decided to take over the room on the other side of the nursery. It was smaller and didn't have the same view my old room did, but it also didn't have the old room's memories.

For Maisie's own good, Iris insisted she be locked in her room until we figured out how best to deal with Josef, a fate to which Maisie acquiesced with stoicism. "You understand?" I asked her before the family used our combined magic to seal the door.

"Yes," she replied with a mischievous grin. "Oriental rugs are expensive and hard to clean." Darn, I loved that girl.

On the other end of the spectrum stood Josef, my younger brother, well, half brother. I wondered how things might have been, if it weren't for my mother and her friends having twisted him. Would we have eventually met each other and bonded? Or was he damaged from inception? My own word choice struck me. Inception, rather than conception. Somehow it seemed to be the right term when thinking of Erik Weber's four children. We, his offspring, seemed to have been plotted rather than the products of ordinary physical intercourse. Rather than fathering children to preserve his memory or to pass on his traits, it seemed like he had been breeding pawns to be moved around in a game. I wondered if his children really numbered four, or if he'd managed to breed an army of damaged progeny.

"I don't like having him here." Oliver slapped his hand down on the table and pulled me back to the present. "He seems so damned cocksure someone is going to come riding to his rescue. I'm telling you the little prick is a Trojan horse. Gudrun wanted him here for a reason."

"Well, I couldn't leave him standing outside Sentient Bean, could I?"

"Gingersnap." He shook his head. "I'm not saying you did anything wrong, I'm just saying it's too neat of a package simply to have Josef handed over to us by a card-carrying member of the 'Spear of Destiny' club."

Adam turned to Oliver. "Do you find this boy attractive?"

Oliver startled and his eyebrows rose high. He seemed genuinely shocked. "How could you even ask that? He's a total psychopath."

Adam looked at me rather than at my uncle. "All right, my bad." He smiled at me. He was trying to lighten the mood, and I loved him for trying, but my heart was having none of it. The glint faded from Adam's eye. He ran his finger around the rim of his glass. "I agree, we would be foolhardy to take this Gudrun at her word for anything." His eyes grew unfocused, and his face hardened. "I must admit, after what the little bastard did to me, it is taking every ounce of self-control I can muster not to beat that smug face of his until there's nothing left of it 'cept broken bone and table scraps."

"You aren't going to do that, Adam," Iris said and shook her head. "You are not going to sink to his level. You are a better man than that."

"I think you see me as better than I truly am, ma'am." Adam's voice sounded calm, measured, but the look in his eyes told me Josef was pretty lucky Iris was there to serve as Adam's conscience.

"Your desire for revenge is understandable, but no, I see you plainly as you are. Otherwise, you would not be allowed to date my baby brother."

Adam's entire body rocked, then he laughed. He turned to Oliver. "Did she just say 'allowed'?"

Oliver nodded once and chuckled. "She sure did."

"She means it too," Iris added with mock severity.

Another attempt at levity landed like lead. Ellen began shivering. Even from the far side of the table, I could see goose bumps forming on her arms. "Bound or no," she said, pulling her arms around herself, "I feel really uncomfortable having him around." Her eyes made a circle of us there at the table. "After Tillandsia . . ." Her voice failed her.

"Oh, honey." Iris leaned over and wrapped her arm around Ellen's shoulders. She pulled Ellen's head to her bosom and rocked her gently. Iris took her big-sister duties to heart.

"It's either laugh or murder him," Oliver said. He reached over and took Ellen's hand. "We know what he did to you, sis."

Ellen's eyes widened for a moment; then her lips quivered. "I vote we kill him."

Oliver released her hand, then pushed back from the table. He stomped across the room and grabbed hold of the sink. His shoulders rose and fell a few times before he turned back to us with a stern look on his face. "I think I second that."

Iris bounded from the table, her movement lost between a leap and actual flight. She landed before her younger brother and delivered him a slap that reverberated in the air. Oliver stumbled back from the force. "I will have no more talk of murder. Do you all hear me? No more talk of beating."

"No." Oliver recovered himself and stood seething before his sister. "Just actual beating and on me rather than on the bastard who's earned it."

Iris's temper cooled. "I'm sorry." She reached out for him, but he pulled away. "But you were raised better than that." She stopped and looked at her own hand. "So was I. I am truly sorry I struck you, Oli."

"Well, damn, did you have to hit so hard?" Oliver bobbed out of her reach as he made his way back to the table. My eyes traced a path past the red mark on his cheek to his temple. I blinked, convinced it was just a trick of the light, but no, there were gray hairs growing in there. Even though they were aging gracefully, my aunts looked like they should be my aunts. Uncle Oliver, on the other hand, could easily pass for my brother. My entire life Oliver seemed to have been suspended around the age of twenty-five. Had his long stretch of seemingly eternal youth drawn to a close?

"I am so sorry," Iris said, pulling my focus back to her. Iris closed her eyes and drew a deep breath. She sighed it out then looked at us. "We are not vigilantes, and we are certainly not murderers. I am well aware of the harm this young man has done to this family. We live in a society of laws. We will obey those laws. Right, Adam?"

He ran his hand over his face, then reached out to take Oliver's hand. "Yes, Iris," he agreed with much less conviction than I would have expected from one of Chatham County's finest. "You are right about how we should handle this situation."

"*Should* handle?" Iris too picked up on his reticence.

Adam held his free hand out. "We, and by we, I mean the police, cannot handle him. Sure, if he were a regular man, but as soon as Gudrun's temporary binding gives way, Josef would kill every last officer in the county. You know it's true."

"He will kill again," I said, not having meant to speak out loud. I felt all eyes on me. "I'm just thinking that Georgia is a death penalty state. If it were possible to turn him over to the police, the result would probably be the same."

Ellen pounced on my words. "Yes." She turned to Iris. "You see, even Mercy realizes we have to do something to end this sociopath."

Iris looked at me. Disappointment was written all over her face. "Are you proposing we skip any kind of judicial review and simply execute the boy?"

"Well," I began to stammer, "I didn't say that, not really. I mean, we have to deprive him of his ability to harm people, but . . ." Honestly, I didn't know how I felt about any of this. Until this moment, I'd never given capital punishment a second thought. He'd tortured both Ellen and Adam, and he killed Colin and Claire. By doing that he had set my own life to unraveling. He'd as good as killed Peter, for my husband was as gone from this world as if he had died. Did I want Josef punished? Absolutely. Did I want him dead? Probably. But did I have it in me to *endorse* his killing? Did I have it in me to kill him myself?

"We all know the best way to do that." Ellen's voice grew raspy. "Iris, even you know some people just need killing."

"Ellen, this is not you speaking, not really." Iris pleaded with her eyes. "You are speaking from a place of dark pain."

"Why?" Ellen shrieked as every cupboard began to open and slam shut again and again. "Erik had two sons. Why would Josef be the one to live instead of Paul?"

And there we had it. Worse than Josef's being another living monument to Erik's colossal infidelities, a truth to which Ellen had long ago become accustomed, worse than the torture Josef had practiced on her during our night of horrors at Tillandsia, was the hard, cold stone of pain Ellen had been polishing since her son had died.

I felt my own fear for Colin, and for the first time ever, I thought I could begin to understand Ellen's agony. God, all the times I resented her for giving in to another messy drunken bender. *She needs to pull herself together. Move past it.* What an insensitive little bitch I had been. I thanked God I'd always kept these ignorant thoughts to myself, rather than proving myself a fool by sharing them with her. Now, I could feel the gravity of her pain, how nearly impossible it had been for her to get out of bed some mornings. Still, she had, she'd gone on, and dang it, if she found herself too weak from time to time to go on without a crutch, I had no right to judge her. Help her, encourage her, remind her she could do better, but judge her, no.

"Please, Aunt Ellen," I said, hoping to quiet the noise, "you're scaring me."

Ellen trembled, but the shaking around us stopped. Iris watched her sister, hesitating to speak, but finally said what the rest of us all were thinking. "You're right, Ellie, it doesn't make one damned bit of sense." Iris fell silent, and the distant look in her eyes told me she was doing a bit of soul-searching. "Honestly, if putting Josef down would bring you back your boy, I think I might just do it myself. Single-handedly." Ellen and Iris locked eyes. "But killing Josef is not going to bring Paul back to us. You know that."

Ellen closed her eyes and nodded. "Yes, I do. I know you are right. My head tells me you are right. We have to handle him humanely. Oh, but Iris, my heart. The dark things it calls me to do."

Iris joined the rest of us at the table. She sat between me and Adam, and took each of our hands. I, in turn, reached out for Ellen, she for Oliver, then my uncle completed the circle by tightening his grasp on Adam's hand. We remained there for a minute or so, still, silent, connected. I felt my little one kick and gasped.

The combined will of my magical family had woven a protective net around my son. It was working. My boy was a fighter. He wouldn't simply fade away. I believed it in my soul. The faces around the table lit up as they realized what had happened. I tightened my grip on my family, and wished Maisie were there with us to enjoy this rare and glowing instant.

Then that moment ended. Iris released her grasp on those next to her. "Maisie," she said, and I turned to find my sister standing behind me. "How did you get out of your room?"

"A bit of advice, Mercy." Maisie wrapped an arm around my neck and gave me a gentle squeeze. "Be careful of what you wish for." She released me. "Don't blame me, blame little sister here. She sprung me from the pen."

"Mercy," Iris began, exasperation sounding in her voice, "we had agreed—"

"I didn't mean to, I just . . . I just missed her."

"Well, perhaps it is for the best," Iris said, her shoulders relaxing. "But you, young lady"—she pointed at Maisie—"you are not to lift a finger against Josef, you hear me?"

"Yes, ma'am," Maisie replied, her tone reminding me of when Iris used to make us promise to come home before curfew.

Iris pointed at a chair and it slid out from beneath the table. "Sit," she commanded, and Maisie did as she was told without protest. "Good." Iris took a moment to look each of us over. I surmised she was trying to find the best way to make her case for a more rational course toward justice. "Listen, y'all. We are too close to this. We cannot be both victim and judge. I acknowledge our ordinary legal system is not capable of dealing with a creature like Josef. Still, I think we have to find a civilized way of dealing with him." A wrinkle formed between her eyes. "Perhaps we should turn him over to the anchors. Let them judge his actions."

"Iris," Adam said, causing his chair to squeak as he shifted in it, "I don't mean any disrespect, but I think you're only shifting the responsibility."

Iris's lips pursed, but she held her tongue.

"Besides," Oliver said, "we all know what will happen if they get their hands on him. They will execute him, and, I am sure, in a much less humane way than we might employ."

Iris licked her lips and nodded. "Perhaps if we could convince them to hold him as a prisoner of war."

"Yeah, right, sis. And if they do agree to that? You know they will end up trading him as soon as it is convenient for them to do so. Three weeks from now, you will probably wake to find Josef has been watching over you as you sleep."

I shuddered. That was not a pleasant thought.

"I'll take him," Maisie said, striking the rest of us dumb. It struck me as a mad idea, but her lovely face was calm and her blue eyes full of a clarity like I'd never before seen in them. "I'll take him to the dimension where they kept Gudrun. I know the way there."

"That isn't a bad idea," Oliver said.

"Of course, I'll stay there with him. Perhaps in time I can reach him—"

"Don't be absurd." Iris cut her off. "That is plain foolish talk. We are not going to allow you to sacrifice your life to that boy's rehabilitation."

Maisie folded her hands on the table. "He's been damaged by those who would end the line." Maisie's eyes moved from one of us to another. "I have been damaged by those who would preserve it."

"No, honey," Ellen said, leaning in toward Maisie. "You are nothing like Josef. Nothing at all."

"Nothing?" Maisie asked, but it was to me she addressed the question. "It's true Josef takes pleasure in killing, but I could end

Josef right now and not lose a moment's peace." She turned to Iris. "Am I really to live the rest of my life being locked in my room to prevent me from doing harm?" Then to Ellen. "I know you don't want to see me as being like Josef, but honestly, Aunt Ellen, to me he is the truest of mirrors. Perhaps I can help him. Perhaps I can help myself." She looked to Oliver. "Uncle Oliver, you understand, I know you do." Her comment struck me as being a shade cryptic, but I'd process that one later. "Josef may be my only true shot at redemption."

Hot tears burst from Oliver's eyes. "I understand, sweetie. I do."

"How could you agree to this?" Iris turned on her brother.

"Because I don't really care what we do with the boy. Kill him. Keep him. I do not care. But I do care about our Maisie here, and I just realized how inhumanely we have been treating her. She isn't a little girl we can warn not to run with scissors. She's a grown woman. A grown woman who has done horrible things. Things, thank God almighty, it is in her soul to regret." He paused and looked at Maisie. "That, my girl, is how you differ from Josef."

"He's right, Iris," Ellen said calmly. "We have been unable fully to embrace Maisie. We may not have served her with the death sentence, but we have locked her up without hope for parole." Ellen turned to Maisie. "I'm sorry. I do love you so very much. If you think doing this might bring you peace, help you find some form of resolution, then I too support you . . ." Her voice broke, and she choked back a sob. "Just promise me you won't stay away forever."

Maisie reached across the table to take Ellen's hand. "I'll try."

"What is happening here?" Iris said, fear and anger taking her over.

Oliver stood and circled behind Maisie. He placed his hand on her shoulders. "What's happening here is our little girl has grown up, and we've got to let her go."

"No," Iris said, her tone firm, resolute, unyielding. She blinked. "She may be grown, but she is still my baby." Iris looked to me for support. "You both are. I raised you. You're mine."

I drew a breath, fighting the emotions that threatened to overwhelm me. "And we always will be, but Maisie is right. We owe Maisie her freedom. She deserves a chance to become the person she would have been if the dispute over the line hadn't robbed her of the life she could have had." I turned to Maisie, and lost all control. "I know I've got to let you go, but I don't think my heart can take another loss right now. If you really need to do this, I won't stand in your way, but don't you dare say good-bye." I forced my chair back from the table and stood. I walked to the door, and put my hand on the handle. I couldn't look back or I would capture her, bind her to this house forever so she could never leave me. "And by God, you'd better come back to us or I will find you and drag you back . . . again."

"I'm counting on that," Maisie said.

"I love you," I said and yanked the door open.

"I love you too." Her words found me as I shut the door behind me.

TWENTY-SIX

I started walking in my fastest waddle toward the river. I had to put some space between myself and the realization that I had, once again, lost my sister. So many holes had formed in my heart, I could almost hear the wind whistling through it.

As a reflex, I went out into Savannah, my hometown, trying not to think how the city had been changed for me. So many parts of my city had come to seem polluted. I'd grown up playing in Oglethorpe Park. Now were I to walk its paths, I would either think of Gudrun, or feel the loss of Peter eating away at my heart. Looking across at the Candler Oak, I would sense if not see the remnants of the spell my grandfather had placed there to protect Savannah from the child-murdering demon Barron. Of course now, rather than feeling proud of Granddad, I would be left to wonder how he could have deserted his first family.

The good people of Savannah, the same I'd grown up with, befriended, loved, and tried to help whenever I could, they were rejecting me now my powers had come to me. The change in their attitude was not overt, but I still felt a chill in my heart as true friendship turned to mere politeness. All the same it hurt like hell to be rejected by the people of the city I loved, no matter how polite they were when building the walls between us. I knew the change wasn't their fault; regular folk just kept witches at an arm's length. Maybe this aversion on the part of the everyday Joe to those of us who had magic written in our very DNA had developed as a defense.

I realized there wasn't a single sidewalk in this city I hadn't walked a rut in. For the first time in my life, I began to see Savannah as the small town it was. A small town with no room for the outsider, even if that outsider had been born and raised here.

The only time I'd ever really been more than a stone's throw from it was when I visited Oliver in San Francisco after I'd graduated high school. After growing up in the low country, the hills amazed me. I loved the city and its vibrancy. The way it gravitated toward the new, despite its Victorian façade. Still, at that point, I couldn't imagine anywhere as home but Savannah. Now I wished I had traveled more. Gone to New York and Paris. But not even a year ago, it seemed like I had all the time in the world to see the world.

Was this how it had been for Ginny? Had the feeling I had right now been the same seed that grew into a harvest of bitterness in her heart? Had she felt trapped, regretful? Had the response of Savannah to her power caused her to come to feel like an unwanted guest at the party? I would not end up like she had, though. I had love in my life. I had someone to live for. Someone who in the end was far more important to me than I was even to myself. I may have lost my husband, but I still had my son, and I forced myself to hold on to the hope that nothing would take him away.

I would have to avoid passing directly in front of the Cotton Exchange. Now, the image of my mother's torso bound to Old Rex would be forever burned into my mind's eye. I could swing wide and head down East Broad past the Pirates' House. I ran inventory of recent trauma. No, the Pirates' House was still good. Nothing heartbreaking or terrifying had occurred there. Yet.

I could avoid the Exchange area entirely by cutting east down Bay. I stopped dead in my tracks. The green space in front of the exchange was called "Emmet Park." I couldn't believe I'd never before made the connection, but another realization piggybacked on that thought. I sighed and let my head fall forward. "You've been doing a good job hiding, but I know you're here. You might as well go on and show yourself."

The thin air before me opened like an envelope and out stepped my nearly seven-foot friend. "I've had to work hard," Emmet said, "to keep up with your own magical growth spurts. It appears you have surpassed my skills." He seemed both proud and disappointed in the same moment, never fearing even for a split second I'd lay into him. How many times had we had the talk about stalking?

Another day, a lifetime ago, I would have let him have it with both barrels. Today, I was glad to see his face. "Yes, your creepy habit no longer goes unnoticed." Even my sarcasm had lost its edge. Only when I took his arm did he seem in the least bit unsure of himself. "Walk me to the water?"

He looked down at me, his dark eyes the promise of a well-needed respite, his strong arm a promise of shelter. "Of course. It would be my pleasure."

I found myself leaning on his arm for support, taking more comfort, no, more pleasure from his strong and solid body than a married woman—for I still felt married—should. People would talk if they saw us. People would talk if they still even remembered Peter, that is. His Fae mother implied that as Peter reintegrated into his rightful world, he would be disentangled from our reality, every memory of his existence eventually erased from this world. How would it work, this forgetting? Would it roll back like the reverse of a pebble dropping into a pond, his memory receding first from those who knew him least, working its way back to the center, to those who loved him most? Would I be the last person on earth who remembered Peter Tierney had ever existed? Had Peter already forgotten me?

"We will work together to preserve his memory. For the boy."

I jolted to a stop. Emmet might just end up catching an earful today anyway.

"Too intrusive?" he asked.

I realized from his tone this was an actual question, not sarcasm. "Yes. Way too."

"I'm sorry." He began walking again, pulling me along. I didn't resist.

"How could you read me so easily?"

This time it was his turn to stop dead. He looked at me with wide eyes and an open mouth. "You don't realize you are broadcasting your thoughts?" He looked me up and down. "Your emotions are wafting off you. Even the stray dogs are crossing the street to stay out of your path."

"Shut up and walk."

He did as he was told, for about four and a half steps, then he started talking again. "Colin will know of his father. He will be proud of who Peter was. We will tell him Peter loved the two of you very much, but the pull of his natural world was too strong. We—"

"I'm not sure what all this 'we' is about, Emmet. There is no 'we.'"

He looked down at me, and this time his face betrayed an absolute conviction. "I, of course, will raise the child as my own. I will be a father to Colin."

"I don't remember asking you." I didn't know how to react, how to feel. I was touched by his devotion, angered by his sense of proprietorship, annoyed by his poor timing, shamed by how badly I wanted to throw myself into his arms, frustrated by having to choke back the urge to slap him cross-eyed.

He stopped again. I realized I was not going to be seeing the river today. "It wasn't necessary for you to ask me. I already love the child as my own, and you know I love you."

"Emmet," I said, his name carrying the sound of my exasperation, "I am not ready to even consider moving on from Peter. You have to remember, it isn't like I've lived years as a widow. I've only just lost my husband."

"I'm well aware of that," he said, and I was surprised to hear my vexation matched by his own. "But you have to remember I have waited for you my entire life." I started to speak, but he held his finger up to my lips. "You don't have to love me. I don't expect you to lie with me. I just want you to allow me to act as your support. To fill the void that has been created in your and Colin's life. I'll make an excellent father." He tapped his forehead with his finger. "I've got the experience of eight men and one Jewish mother filed away in here." He was referring, of course, to the nine witches, including Rivkah, who had created the golem from driveway dirt. When the line's power struck him and turned him into a real boy, he retained the memories of their life experiences.

I had come across the first stirrings as he rose from the earth. The sight of him had terrified me. Now he frightened me in a different way. I knew he was right. Colin couldn't hope for a better father, other than his own, that is. But I wasn't at all ready to entertain his plans. I pushed Emmet's hand away. "I know you care. I do. But you can't replace Peter."

"I don't want to replace Peter. I want to dedicate my life to preserving his memory. To raising his son. To cherishing the woman he too loved . . ."

"He's forgotten me." I began crying, and Emmet pulled me into his strong embrace. I let him. I let myself take comfort from him.

"He didn't forget you." Emmet stroked my hair. "Peter could never have forgotten you. His feelings, his memory, his history—everything was unwound. Peter not only lost you and Colin. He lost himself." Emmet placed a gentle kiss on the top of my head. "Don't blame him. Don't resent him. I know he would never have left you if he had even the slightest choice in the matter."

I drew in a breath, then sighed it out. I let his words soothe me, and I relaxed in his arms. I knew I could let myself go limp, but still I wouldn't fall, because Emmet held me. "Peter would kill you if he saw you holding me like this."

Emmet reached down and turned my face up to meet his. "No. Peter loved you. He truly loved you. I'm sure of that. Given the circumstances are what they are, your hotheaded fairy man would thank me."

"I would only be using you, Emmet." I tried to look away, but he wouldn't let me.

"Then use me."

"I care for you, I do . . ."

"You don't have to love me. I'm not asking you to feel one way or another for me. I am only asking you to lean on me. Let me help you stand until you find the strength to stand on your own again."

"What about when I do?" I searched his face for any sign of concern. I saw none. His black curls had grown back, and were threatening to fall over his eyes. "What if I don't need you then?"

"Oh, don't be ridiculous, Mercy," he said and pulled me down the sidewalk. "I'm a fabulous catch. You'll come to your senses soon enough."

I tugged on his arm, trying to slow our pace, but he didn't let me. "I don't want to hurt you, Emmet. I'm going through hell right now. I've lost so much." I realized he didn't even know yet about Maisie.

"I know," he said, and at first I thought his comment was a validation. "About Maisie that is." In spite of my appreciation for him, I reached up and slapped his shoulder. "Again, not my fault. I told you that you were broadcasting."

I realized maybe he was right, so I let it go. "Your strength and your support are so tempting, but you deserve a woman who can truly love you."

"Don't worry about what I 'deserve.' I am willing to gamble that someday you might just return my feelings."

"Or I might just end up putting you through hell."

"I've already gone to hell and back for you. I'm not afraid of a second trip. Ugh . . ." He brushed his chest where my head had been. "Enough of these tears. You've gotten me all wet." He winked at me and smiled, and even though it felt somehow adulterous, my heart responded, if only a little.

Emmet had once tried to convince me the line had created him for me. Could this be so? Had the line somehow known? Somehow anticipated my losing Peter and provided me with a soft place to land? Peter was gone. Forever. And all the tears in the world would not bring him back to us. The best I could hope for was to raise his son into a man he would have been proud of. The worry that Colin might never see the world tried to creep back up on me, but I refused it. I would put no energy into that fear, and every shred of my magic into making sure he would. I leaned my head into Emmet's shoulder. "I'll pay for the dry cleaning." For an instant I allowed myself to imagine the life Emmet wanted us to share, and the knot that had formed in my core loosened. Maybe he was right.

I felt a tingle race down my spine, but I realized instantly that it had nothing to do with Emmet. A witch, a powerful one, was nearing. The tingle increased in intensity until I felt it buzzing through me from head to toe. Emmet spun me into a protective embrace, leaving me incapable of seeing anything past his shoulders. I heard the sound of a car pulling up next to us, and struggled to loosen Emmet's grasp. It was like trying to pry open a vise. "Emmet," I said, and his name worked like a charm; his arms remained wrapped around me, but loosened their hold enough that I could turn.

A limousine, the shade of a storm cloud about to burst, came to a stop beside us. I hated limos. Nothing good ever came from riding in limos. The dark rear window hummed as it opened. As the onyx glass slid down, the sight of incredibly pale skin and impossibly fair hair came into view. Horrible blank eyes reigned over an expressionless face.

"Fridtjof Lund," I whispered.

TWENTY-SEVEN

Instantly recognizable, but still somehow different, less androgynous. That was it. His features had taken on a more masculine edge. A question shot its way up through my subconscious. "You are an anchor. How can you be here?" How could he be so far away from the point on earth where he was duty-bound to remain in order to anchor the line?

"Bilocation. I have been blessed with the ability to be in two places at once. My other half—or you might even call her my 'better half'—remains home."

His other half. Fridtjof was not the androgyne I had believed him to be. He, they, were some kind of symbiotic creature, male and female bound together, but as my eyes now testified, capable of division when necessary. I recovered quickly from the shock of seeing him here and in the flesh. He was going to have to try a lot harder than this to throw me after the turns my life had taken. I found myself more irritated than alarmed by his presence. Seriously, he could have at least called. "Okay, that takes care of the how." I patted Emmet's forearm until he clued in and let me go free. "Now let's move on to the why."

"I would assume that much is obvious. I'm here to partake of your world famous Liar's Tour." The blankness on his face gave way to a self-satisfied smile.

"Here's the condensed version: It's been lovely to see you."

Emmet chuckled behind me.

"Now, if it isn't clear to you that I am in no mood for your smartass responses, please let me assure you I am not." I felt a bead of sweat form on my forehead, and I wiped it away with my hand. "So tell me what you want, or keep on driving."

"Of course," he said, and the smoked glass of the window began to rise. For a moment, I honestly thought maybe he really would lift tail and run, but in the next moment the driver's door opened and a normal enough guy in a cheap dark suit hopped out. He reached for the handle of Fridtjof's door and swung it open, then stepped back. Fridtjof leaned out of the opening. "Please do get in."

I didn't take the shortest of moments to consider the invitation. My head was shaking before I could even register I had answered. "Uh-uh. No way." My voice finally caught up with the rest of me.

"Come along. You may bring your 'bodyguard' if you like."

"I said no. I meant no."

It was impossible to discern Fridtjof's emotions by examining his face. He could have been joyous, enraged, or maybe even just bored. His features appeared incapable of demonstrating anything other than smugness and contempt. I found myself casting an eye at the driver, trying to use his expressions as a barometer of Fridtjof's thoughts, until I realized I didn't care what Fridtjof was feeling. There was no way I was going anywhere near him, let alone with him. I turned and began to head home.

"I've been sent as delegate by your fellow anchors," he called out after me.

Okay, now we were "fellows." I stopped and turned back. "Then talk. Why did they send you?" Emmet insinuated himself between us, readying himself for, well, for just about anything, I guessed.

"We have agreed the unpleasantness between us is at least partially our fault."

"Partially?" My voice squeaked into a higher than normal register. "You tried to destroy my hometown."

"That is not entirely true. It was your mother—"

"Yeah, yeah, yeah. Stuff a sock in it." I'd already heard this from Beige. No need to sit through White's version of the same excuse. "What else you got?"

For a moment he seemed a bit thrown by the colloquialism. His head tilted and a line formed between his brows. His silence lasted just long enough for me to consider leaving him sitting there. He recovered just in time. "We have been withholding many truths from you. Truths about the line and its creation. Truths about the damage you and your family have caused to it." He gave his accusation sufficient time to register fully. "You may have saved your city from the hurricane's destruction, but that salvation came at a cost. Your activities have weakened the line."

His words had no sooner escaped his snowy lips than I felt an awareness burst all around me. "No. It isn't weaker. If anything, it's stronger than ever, just less in your control."

"Miss Taylor—"

"Mrs. Tierney," Emmet corrected him, earning himself more points than I had time to calculate.

"All right then, Mrs. Tierney, I had hoped you would accompany me willingly and that I wouldn't have to resort to threatening you . . ."

"You had better choose your next few words with extreme care," I said, reflexively pulling my hand back and feeling a ball of blue fire dance on my fingertips.

Fridtjof startled and slid back a bit, but he forced himself to recover. "You are leaving us with no choice. That you are such a slave to your passions you would even consider harming another anchor is proof enough."

I let the ball of fire dissolve. "Fine, spit it out."

"I hoped, we hoped, this could be a dispassionate meeting of the minds. That you would join me of your own accord and learn the error of the way in which you have been conducting yourself. However, I must warn you that if you refuse to accompany me, the other anchors are at the ready, prepared to perform a binding on you."

Emmet took a step toward the car. I used my magic to grab hold of him and stop him. I knew that otherwise Fridtjof might find himself split into three parts rather than two. "If I do agree to go with you?"

"Well, that would indeed be seen as a sign of good faith." I felt his sense of control return to him. His certainty hovered around him like a cloying cloud. "Come. There is something I must show you."

I turned to Emmet and he to me. "I have to go . . ."

"Not a chance will I leave you to go with this . . . chalky bastard . . . alone." He approached the car. "Slide it, frosty." He looked back over his shoulder, trying to appear confident and pleased with himself. He failed to cover up the concern in his dark eyes. Emmet had to duck to slide himself into the car, but soon I stood there alone, the expectant driver fixing me with a stare. A quick and silent prayer to anything out there that might be looking out for me, and I joined Emmet. The driver shut the door behind me.

The sound of the car door closing coincided with, if not triggered, a blinding incandescence, and rather than riding along the streets of Savannah, I found myself traveling in a way I'd never experienced before. I felt that my body sat completely still, and the world moved around me. Emmet's hand caught mine, his steely grip letting me know that no matter what, he had no intention of letting go. Images alternated with blackouts; each strobe of light revealed a new location, until an eruption of darkness washed the scene away.

The pace of the images relented as open fields spread out below us. The pictures grew finer in detail, alerting me that we were descending even though my senses swore to me I had remained stationary. Coming into focus was an area boxed in on three sides by a squared-off U made of trees. In the enclosure's center stood an unidentifiable structure. A grain silo? A water tower? No, neither. It cast too odd of a shadow to be either. The image gained in depth, and within the wink of an eye, we touched ground near a collection of enormous upright granite slabs. The edges of the colossal blocks remained rough, but their faces had been polished and inscribed in both modern and long-dead languages.

"The Guidestones," I said to myself. I'd never been here before, but I'd of course heard of them. Many called them "the American Stonehenge"; many others called them the work of the devil. As I registered the distance we had traveled, I fell into a panic. I was an anchor of the line. I knew I was to remain physically near the point where the line had selected me as such, but I had no idea how much leeway existed. Had I been brought here in an attempt to break my connection?

Fridtjof seemed to anticipate my anxious reaction. "Don't worry. You are still within the physical boundary you must maintain. At its limits, yes, but still within."

Emmet's hand remained tightly latched to mine. "Why the subterfuge of the automobile? Why not tell us you intended to transport us using magic?"

"I had to threaten your pretty friend to get her into an ordinary auto. Do you think I would have stood a chance getting her to come along through a less mundane form of transport?" He was right on that point. "The little teleportation trick you do," he said addressing me, "you've just experienced what it is like once you've mastered it." His pale face turned at an angle. "Or perhaps you believed this was a gift particular to you?" The question was an obvious jibe, intended to make me feel insecure in my own powers. It hit home. "No, this skill of yours is shared by all anchors. Its intended use is to make sure we can always return to our respective points of anchorage regardless of how far from home we might find ourselves."

"See," Emmet said to me. "I told you there was no need to click your heels." We looked at each other and burst out laughing. Fridtjof was less than pleased with our act of lèse-majesté, realizing Emmet had completely undermined his attempt to intimidate.

I focused on his face as sour and white as spoiled milk. "Why did you bring us here?"

"We wanted you to see this monument. To realize how close to your seat of power the enemies of the line have staked their claim." He motioned to the monument like it were a game show prize. "The men who commissioned these stones were enemies to the line." He took a few steps closer, leaving his back exposed to Emmet and me. He had evidently decided we were not a threat to his well-being. So far, he was right. So far. He turned back almost as if he had picked up on my thought. "Those who funded this monument dreamed of a 'New World Order' in which these suggestions would stand as absolute law, but there is nothing new in the hierarchy they would wish to impose on the earth. These 'guidelines' are based on the memory of the commandments that were handed down to us by the old ones. The old ones are the closest thing to God this world has ever witnessed." He craned his neck to take the stone in. "Of course, what you see here has been corrupted, sanitized, but judge for yourself. I believe you can get the gist."

I read the first guideline. "'Maintain humanity under 500,000,000 in perpetual balance with nature.' This isn't sanitized. It's a call for a global genocide."

"The enemies of the line, they would consider this a wise culling, not a genocide."

"Oh, I'm sure the seven billion surplus people will take great comfort in that."

"Indeed. Number two is golden too. 'Guide reproduction wisely," he read in a stentorian voice, "improving fitness and diversity.'" Fridtjof barked out an abrasive laugh. "Diversity indeed. Diversity within an incredibly limited spectrum. This is nothing more than the perennial call for the building of a 'master race.'"

"Eugenics is a crime against humanity." I took a few steps back. I wanted to go home. I wanted to get away from this odd man. I wanted to get away before he stated the obvious.

"You, Mercy, are the product of eugenics."

Well, too late to get away. He'd hit me in a very sore spot. "Yes, thank you very much. I am well aware of that."

"I too am a product of eugenics." His head tilted, and he seemed to be taking my full inventory. "Does that surprise you?" To my senses he appeared a freak, rather than the end product of a misguided breeding experiment aimed at achieving even the most twisted sense of perfection. "I am the idealized aim of these laws. My blood is so pure I have been left unable to breed with anyone other than my other half. Once I breed, I give birth and die." He turned back to the stones. "So perhaps you should stop feeling so sorry for yourself." He looked back over his shoulder at me, with an actual and bona fide smile on his ashen lips. "We know you have entertained Gudrun." He began walking away, circling the stone posts. He seemed to be giving me time to consider the implications of my having been caught fraternizing with the enemy. He finished the circuit then stopped directly before me. "We only want you to be cognizant of who she is"—his shoulders fell—"the degree of duplicity of which she is capable." He straightened up. "If she has managed to charm you, remember you are not the only anchor to have fallen for her lies. Ayako"—I heard regret in his voice as he said her name—"worked with her and your cousin Teague. Gudrun had convinced them both that they were acting in the line's best interest."

"No, she made no pretense of wanting to preserve the line." The emotion he betrayed when speaking of Ayako humanized Fridtjof to me. Had Ayako faced a binding, contrary to what Gudrun had claimed? Without considering the wisdom of doing so, I lowered my defenses. This man, person, I corrected myself, lost a friend. I could empathize with him over that loss. "She asked me to join with her to bring down the line."

Fridtjof nodded, lowering his jaw and fixing me with his blank gaze. "Yes, go on."

"The spell she cast to free herself. She said she could have used anyone's body to fix it, but she used Emily's."

The corners of Fridtjof's mouth pulled down, and his head jerked. "This spell you speak of, please explain."

"I don't know how it worked. Gudrun freed herself by invoking the demonic orders of the Tree of Life. She said I was special, and she sacrificed Emily to punish her for trying to harm me." Emmet's hand on my shoulder prompted caution. I fell silent for a moment. "That was all."

"I must warn you that Gudrun has lied to you. She had no need of invoking any of the sephirot's aspects to effectuate her return to this plane. She had tricked Teague into using a variant of a berserker spell to accept both her magic and her essence. Whatever use she had for your mother's corpse was outside her escape." He looked over my shoulder at Emmet. "Gudrun did speak the truth about one thing, though. You are special, and not only in the way your golem thinks of you as special." He lowered his blank gaze to meet mine. "You are special in that you are indeed a danger to the line. However, I do not believe it is your desire to do damage. None of us believe you want to risk ending the world as we know it."

I couldn't help smiling. "That's mighty big of you."

"Oh, now, Mercy. No need to take umbrage. I felt we had begun to develop an understanding of each other, you and I. Perhaps I was wrong, but then again, we have not given you much reason to trust us. We have kept you ignorant of things you have the right to know. Without this knowledge our actions must strike you as erratic at best, or more likely monstrous."

Yes, monstrous. Ding. Ding. We have a winner. Forbidding us to turn the hurricane Emily had aimed at Savannah back to sea. Expecting us to stand down and watch our home be destroyed as they had forced our cousins the Duvals to do when Katrina took New Orleans. Declaring war on us when we refused to capitulate. Binding my entire family, leaving them to drown, paralyzed and unconscious, beneath the incoming waves. Attempting to bind me, even though they knew that as an anchor, if I survived at all, I would be left to live out the rest of my life in a vegetative state. I was certain they never gave my child a second thought in this decision either. And afterward, when we had stopped them from wiping Savannah and its Taylors from the map, they turned their sights on my son.

I didn't even know how much I didn't know. The other anchors had even kept me ignorant of the line's origins. Had they done so out of caution, as Fridtjof seemed to imply, because they too shared Gudrun's opinion that I was the witch who would bring about its end? Or had they kept the story from me out of shame? They knew the ripples of carnage the line's creation had set loose across God only knew how many realities. The anchors had convinced themselves that the ends justified the means. Were they afraid I might somehow challenge this assumption and aggravate their heavy consciences? Perhaps the truth lay somewhere in between.

"We had hoped to keep you innocent, to protect you from the full onus of what you had been chosen for until you had time to adjust to being a witch. We acted solely out of concern for you, but you misread our intentions and acted wildly. I fear we can no longer afford the luxury of providing you with breathing space. There are too many forces trying to take advantage of your ignorance. An ignorance"—he rushed on lest I had time to take offense—"I and your fellow anchors have engendered. For your own good, but in truth for our own comfort as well. I cannot deny it, you have frightened us." This admission felt like the first bit of real truth I'd ever gotten out of the other anchors. "You are as yet still unaware of the stupendous power surging through you. You suppose you are a harmless flame, when you are in truth a nuclear blast. You know our grasp on the line has been loosened. I'm sure you sense that it has bent around you. Only once before has the line been shifted in this way."

"If the line seems to like me so much, why are y'all so afraid I'll cause it harm?"

Fridtjof raised his hand and pointed at me. "That is an excellent question, but before I address it, I must provide you with some context." He relaxed his hand and lowered his arm to his side. "We know you have learned of the fate of the Fae. We know how their story affects you personally. However, you must believe me when I say their world was doomed before they themselves had even been created. It had been doomed from the second the old ones discovered our planet. It is true that at one time our worlds were touching. No"—he pressed his hands together—"interlaced." He let his fingers slide together then tugged his hands to demonstrate the connection. "The proximity of our realities was not an accident. Witches, fairies, humans, we all owe our existence to the old ones and their experiments with breeding."

He looked at my waistline. "You of all people must realize that. How else could you have successfully mated with a Fae? We all come from the same source, just with slightly different balances of DNA. The Fae were engineered first, but they proved far too capricious, too willful. They would certainly have been destroyed outright had the old ones not found their appearance very pleasing. The Fae were spared the grunt work and found themselves set aside as concubines and entertainers.

Then came humans. Useful for heavy lifting, and per the remembrances left by the old ones, quite tasty when young. We witches came last, the product of unsanctioned matings between the two groups." The word "unsanctioned" spoke to me on two levels regarding control the old ones had held, or at least imagined they held, over the creatures of this world. The old ones felt themselves within their rights to determine our mating patterns, as if we were to them as cattle are to man. Still, the existence of witches showed the creatures of this world were a slippery group they couldn't completely control. Had this intermingling been the "original sin" that still colored so many people's perception of sex?

"Despite their early attempts to wipe witches out, our creation proved a happy coincidence for the old ones. Animal lust created the functional compromise between Fae and man for which they had been striving. Eventually witches were co-opted into the old ones' plans and were placed in functionary roles, overseers at the lowest of levels, monarchs at the highest. Our job was to keep the human population in line, in balance," he said, pointing up at the standing stone whose presence I'd nearly forgotten. "The Fae were slid slightly out of sync with the human reality, to prevent any further interbreeding between the two populations. The barrier between the worlds was largely impermeable, but not entirely impenetrable."

"Until the creation of the line nearly wiped the Fae out, then sent their reality drifting away from ours." I shifted my weight as much for comfort as for emphasis, widening my stance. I folded my arms over my chest. I was not going to let him simply gloss over our destruction of the Fae's world.

"The decision to act as we did was not made lightly, I assure you. No one feels the pain caused by the line's creation more deeply than we anchors. That's why we keep the dirty details behind its creation to ourselves. We bear the guilt so our friends and family can go about their lives, unfettered by the knowledge of the line's true costs." His face turned away from me. He looked toward the ground as if he were wishing he too could have been spared. "However, your ignorance is a luxury we can no longer afford. Tell me, what do you know of the creation of the line?"

TWENTY-EIGHT

Maisie had once suggested that deep down I knew the secret of the line's creation, but I'd never been able to pull the disjointed images into a coherent narrative.

"I've had glimpses. Dreams," I admitted to Fridtjof.

"Of course you have; you are an anchor. But these visions of yours are not dreams. They are memories, imprints that the line shared with you as it took you as its own." I could feel his taking my emotional pulse before he dared continue. "Your fellow anchors, in truth we have been working to limit you, suppressing your conscious ability to communicate with the line." He held his hand up as if to fend off outrage. I had none, as I had sensed it all along. "The line has been amassing its energy around you. We have been trying to act as a type of circuit breaker, to keep you from being overwhelmed by its surging power."

"Or to prevent her from gaining the power the line wishes her to have." Emmet's voice came from over my shoulder. I glanced back at him, but only for a moment. His expression was unyielding and wary. I consciously mirrored him.

"I assure you, should the full force of the line invest itself in your pretty Mercy, there would be no Mercy left to wield this prized magic." He lowered his face to my level. "Our ability to maintain a buffer between the line and your conscious mind is much more precise than with your dreaming mind. Your unconscious mind is much harder to pin down. We intend to continue dampening the line's access to you, for your own protection, of course." His phrasing struck me. They were less worried about my interacting with the line than they were about its interacting with me. "However, now is the time for disclosure. Tell me what you remember from your visions, and I will fill in the pieces for you."

I had no reason to believe he would tell me the truth. As a matter of fact, this whole offer of disclosure might just be a trick. Still, it seemed to be in my best interest to play along. I might learn as much from a poorly framed lie as from the actual truth. "I remember a man, or something that looks like a man at least. Only he has no features, his face is blank." I looked up to Fridtjof, seeking validation.

"Yes, go on."

"He has arms and legs, but he slithers on his stomach like a snake." I felt my grasp on this image fade, as if it were being shielded from further scrutiny. I felt my physical eyes zero in on a point in a nonexistent horizon as my mind tried to examine the odd man further. As I focused in on him, I saw the creature stop. It raised its head and turned it from side to side, a forked black tongue testing the wind. This was not my imagination, and this was no memory. The illusion of linear time had fallen away as I connected with the sight. This was happening right this moment in the eternal now. I yelped and jumped back.

Emmet caught me. "Enough," he said to Fridtjof. "Why are you playing games? Tell her what you want her to know then be gone."

"I am not playing games. She will not believe my words alone; she must experience this"—he pulled his hand into a loose fist and struck himself repeatedly on the stomach—"viscerally, in her gut, if she is ever to believe." His pale lids lowered, and he regarded me through narrowed eyes. "I could help you. I could help you focus, to remember what has been kept from you, but you would never believe I hadn't influenced your perception." I reckoned he was right on that one. "Forget the faceless one for now. What else do you remember?"

I let my mind drift back, try to grab hold of another of the vague impressions I carried. "There was a storm. A huge one. Lightning everywhere, but no . . ."

"But no thunder." Fridtjof sought to finish the thought for me.

"No," I said, then considered what he had said. "Well, yes. It's true. There was no thunder. There was no sound at all." Again the myth of time dissolved and I was left witness to an absolute silence falling all over the whole world. No sound of man, no sound of nature. Utter and total quiet. The thought terrified me. I could see multiple overlaying images, some nearly the same, others radically different, making me think of the twin cartoon images where you try to spot each subtle difference between the two. Only here the images overlapped and struck me as being beyond count, let alone comparison. The pictures quivered, then shook violently, each pulling an infinitesimal degree away from the scene at the center of my focus.

"This is no storm," I said aloud. I felt my heart pounding. I felt the need to run away, but the dimension where my awareness found itself began folding in on itself. The familiar three dimensions pressed against each other. "This is rape." I could find no other word that fit the sense of what unfolded before me. I was experiencing the rape not only of this planet where we stood, but of every iteration of this planet as it exists in every dimension. The magic was being drained from every contiguous realm. Our version of the world was awash, no, flooded, by the magic that descended on us. Then the silence gave way to a humming, gentle at first, but increasing in volume and pitch until I fell to my knees, pressing my hands to my ears in a futile attempt to block out the sound. The magic. It was aware, and it was screaming. "Stop it. Stop it." I added my own feeble voice to its heart-rending protest.

Monuments, ancient and many forgotten by the human race, came to life. Energy whipped around the dolmens of Stonehenge, Brodgar, Drombeg, and hundreds of similar sites I witnessed firing up with blinding blue light—*haint blue*, the precision pressed against my awareness then flitted away. My consciousness was caught up, and the globe of the earth flattened out before me, allowing me to observe every point in the same moment. "It's all a machine." I heard my own voice beneath the whinnying of the energy as it spooled around the circles. It washed into the circles, and drained away into their center, the bright-blue light disappearing from the face of the earth. Flashes of energy began to flare up at points along the plane. Pyramids and ziggurats, YaSen Garden, Nemrut, Argos, Ur, Monks Mound, the Valley of the Sun, Giza.

Logic told me that we knew for a fact these monuments had been built thousands of years apart. Still, these sites, spread across space and time, somehow functioned in unison, until all fell dark, save one. My awareness collapsed, and I found myself hovering near the Great Pyramid. A great rumbling took the earth, a quake so great I wondered if the pyramid could withstand it. Then the shaking stopped and the same blue light I'd witnessed before shot out through shafts on opposite sides of the pyramid. The beams of light enmeshed each other, extended outward like a web. A final brilliant flash, and the world around me returned to normal.

I was no longer on the Giza Plateau. I was in Georgia, draped over Emmet's arms as he knelt on the ground before the Georgia Guidestones. I was struck by the idea of how our little tableau must have resembled a poor man's Pietà.

"Creating the line required more magic than was at our command." Fridtjof spoke as if there had been no interruption to his lecture.

"They raped and pillaged," I said, trying to rise off Emmet's arm. He helped me find my footing. "They stole magic that never belonged to them. That should have never belonged to them." *They try and act like they did some noble thing for the rest of us. But all they did was take every last bit of the magic left in this world for themselves.* The memory of Jilo's words returned to me.

"We did not steal. We appropriated largely unharnessed resources in the interest of the greater good. Like the Colorado River was diverted to feed your city of Los Angeles, witches reached out to every realm they could touch and diverted magic from its natural course to weave the precious barrier that has protected this world for millennia."

Emmet stood next to me. "How was this even accomplished? How did the old ones not stop you? They must have witnessed your building, suspected you had some plan."

"They suspected nothing, as we were following their blueprint."

"Wait," I said, waving my hand at Fridtjof. "I don't understand. The old ones condoned the creation of the line?"

"The old ones condoned . . ." He paused. "No, commanded that the machine be built. They intended it to siphon the magic of this realm and relay it to them to help power their own works. That we managed to repurpose their device without their catching on is nothing short of a miracle." He drew a deep breath and let it go. "The old ones, they are not gods, they are empire builders, exporting the valuable resources of the planets they colonize back to their own realm."

"And if we had built their machine and not used it to create the line?"

"Then eventually this world would have been left dry and lifeless as the frozen desert of Cydonia." He nodded. "Yes, you have to look no further than our next-door neighbor to learn the future the old ones intended for our blue planet."

I felt a shiver run down my spine.

"I told you we followed a blueprint when building the machine. This machine has been replicated and continues to be replicated in every realm the old ones discover. I do believe what we have achieved here on earth, this may count as the first and only time the old ones' ambitions were ever checked. Should the line ever fall . . ."

For the first time, I truly understood the other anchors and the desperation that drove them. "But why would the witches from the rebel families ever consider bringing down the line? The old ones would destroy us all."

"No, not all of us. Only those of us who have remained loyal to the line's cause, and those the old ones consider cattle, those without magic. I am fairly certain the witches of the rebel families would be spared, if not rewarded, for their change of heart concerning the line." He tilted his head and gave it a slight shake. "Nothing like the joy of the prodigal son's returning to the fold, eh?"

"Still, the rebels would only live to see their world destroyed."

Fridtjof's shoulders relaxed. Not only had he sensed my coming around to his way of thinking, he had returned to the role of being my superior, my teacher. He felt comfortable around me as long as he remained in charge. "The old ones follow the same pattern: discovery, infiltration, invasion, breeding of hybrids that combine the DNA of the most adaptable local life form with their own. Oh, but they are as vain as they are rapacious. They visit the conquered planets, make holiday there, enjoy the worship of those they have conquered. Then when they grow bored with their new toy, they order the final stage of colonization: the building of the machine."

"But these places"—my mind flashed again on the ancient monuments—"they were built several centuries apart."

"And thousands of miles apart, but as your mind has little difficulty comprehending how the sites exist on different continents, the old ones have no problem understanding how they sit together temporally. The old ones exist outside the dimension we experience as linear time. Bound as most of us are by the flow of time, we aren't able to experience their machine as a functioning whole. From any given point in our timeline, one part of the machine is viewed as having existed in the past. Another in the future. The only moment when it is possible for us to experience their device as a functioning whole is when it is flipped on. The image your subconscious carries is of the moment when our planet was about to be destroyed. That moment transcends history; it exists in the past, in the future—"

"And in the now," I finished for him.

He nodded, seeming pleased by my understanding.

"But why would any witch cooperate with the building of the machine? They'd be committing suicide by helping."

"The inhabitants of the highest order, those who have been bred to contain the greatest concentration of the old ones' 'pure' blood, they build the machine, and as their home planets breathe their last gasps, the chosen ones leave behind the corpse of their mothers. They spread out through the universe like a virus, scouting new and suitable targets for exploitation. On earth this highest order is the witch, our having supplanted the Fae thanks to our functionary skills and the mercurial nature and general uncontrollability of the Fae."

"We were to build the machine, drain the earth of its life force, and go out to find other planets to destroy."

234

"Precisely, and the cycle was intended to go on forever, forward and backward through time, but here, on earth, we witches drew the line." He reached out for me, drawing my hands into his. "That, Mercy, is why we need you to demonstrate your loyalty. We need you to join us in protecting the line so it can continue to protect us all."

"I have never intended to do anything else." I weighed the pieces I had been presented. Incredible and contradictory tales, but no concrete evidence. I compared Gudrun's version of the story to that of this odd Swede. I had no idea how much of what either had shared was truth, and how much was lie. I suspected both had offered up no more truth than the bare-bones frame from which they suspended their stories. Fridtjof had without doubt white-washed history and offered me up a pious fiction. Still, my gut told me that Fridtjof's account was essentially true. Besides, I knew Gudrun was a monster by the company she kept.

With my hands cradled in his, Fridtjof bowed his head. "This is indeed good to hear. As you have expressed your commitment to preserving the line, we must discuss your mother."

"What about her?" I sensed all of this had only been the windup; now he was ready for the pitch. I freed my hands from his grasp.

We three turned at the sound of a car pulling off the road and coming to a stop on the gravel parking lot. A boy, maybe eight, maybe ten, climbed out of the backseat. He was a round little fellow, his horizontally striped yellow-and-blue shirt adding to the impression. Large, thick glasses. He came barreling toward us.

"Mitchell, I told you to wait until I could get your sister out." The voice of his harried mother chased after him.

The boy was entranced by the sight of the stones, but he stopped and walked sullenly back toward the car. "But Mom, they're right there."

"You will wait for me," his mother said, climbing out of the car and opening a back door, "or we will get right back in the car and go home." The boy folded his arms over his chest and stomped a foot; still, he didn't talk back. There was something so comical about the sulky expression he wore as his poor mother struggled with the buckles and straps of the child seat that I fell instantly in love with the boy.

"Finally," he said and sighed dramatically as his mother pulled a much younger child dressed all in pink out of the back of the car and onto her hip.

"The monument is closed for maintenance," Fridtjof called out to them.

"Oh," the mother said. "It's just we've driven here from Atlanta. Couldn't we just stay for a minute or so, get some pictures?" The boy was crestfallen, and within seconds on the verge of tears. I slugged Fridtjof on the shoulder and circled around him.

"Of course you can," I said, "and you can stay as long as you like." The woman flashed me a look that spoke of relief combined with gratitude. She saw me as another mother, willing to bend the rules to save another woman a two-hour return trip featuring a meltdown from a very disappointed child.

She handed her son a cell phone. "Well, go on then," she said to the boy, then smiled at me. Her son raced to the monument and began taking pictures. "Honestly, I have no idea how he even heard of this place," she said, bouncing the sweet and waking little girl on her hip. The child looked at me and smiled, then buried her face in her mother's shoulder. "This one's going through her shy phase, and that one"—she nodded at her son—"well, that one . . ." She shrugged signaling she had nothing more to say, but the love in her eyes spoke volumes. "Thank you so much. I promised him that if he got all As on his report card, we'd make the trip out here."

"No need for thanks." I glanced over at Fridtjof, who had slid on a pair of sunglasses. He still was unnaturally pale, but at least he had dealt with the most startling of his characteristics. I had no need to worry about the woman's reaction to Fridtjof, though. Although she kept one eye on her son, her other appreciative eye followed Emmet as he began circling the monument. "My," she said, wiggling her eyebrows and smiling as he began drawing nearer. Leaning in toward me, "Yours?" she asked in a whisper.

Emmet looked toward her. "I certainly am," he said as he stepped up to us. "I certainly am." His dark eyes bored into me. This moment told me more than any of his previous declarations. He would be persistent, patient, and most of all present. That he would be my husband and a father to my child were in his mind inevitabilities. Even though most of me rebelled against letting go of Peter, the tiniest part of my heart relaxed into the idea that Emmet was right.

"Isn't he just the sweetest thing?" she asked, shaking her head.

"Mom," the boy bellowed. "Take my picture."

"How about I take one of you all together," Emmet offered.

"You are so thoughtful." She flashed me a look that said, "You are so lucky." She called to her boy, "Okay, we'll take a few pictures, but we have to get out of these nice folks' way." She picked her way through the field toward the standing stones and Emmet followed. I watched as he played peekaboo with the little girl, who had obviously fallen just as hard for Emmet as her mother had.

"He is quite the charmer, your golem." Fridtjof spoke in a low enough voice that the others would not hear.

"He isn't just a golem, not anymore," I said, speaking in a near whisper. "He may have started out that way, but he's a man, a real human being now, and there is nothing anyone could say to convince me otherwise."

"I feel no compulsion to debate his humanity or lack thereof. We were concerned about him at first, but he has been deemed harmless."

"Why in heaven's name would you worry about Emmet?"

"Because of the prophecy made about the 'Babalon Working' and the fall of the line. We have reason to believe that before her death, Emily had attempted the great work. Perhaps her efforts were what led to her death."

"Babylon, like Mesopotamia Babylon?"

"No, Babalon with an 'a,' not a 'y.' It is an example of the blackest of magics, aimed at creating the 'Abomination,' a non-human spirit born into a human body."

"You all thought Emmet might be the result of this spell? But you allowed his creation."

"With all the changes happening, we had every right to feel concern. Even the best and most loyal of witches might be working with a covert agenda."

"Oh please," I said with a nod in Emmet's direction. "Look at him."

Emmet busied himself making faces at the little girl in an attempt to get her to smile for the photos. He snapped a few pictures on the woman's phone, then handed it back to the boy for his approval.

"What do we say?" the mother addressed her son.

"Thank you," the boy said, and it very nearly sounded sincere, but he was already off, running one last lap around the standing stones before his mother delivered the inevitable command to return to the car.

Fridtjof leaned in to my ear. "In the end we determined it was the line itself that bestowed your golem with his humanity, so his existence has been approved."

I wanted to ask Fridtjof just who the hell he was to approve or disapprove, but the mother returned, bouncing her daughter on her hip. The little one squealed in delight as Emmet waved a finger at her. "Thank you. No really." She took a deep breath and sighed. "If I had to drive all the way home without him seeing these things . . ." She paused. "What are they about anyway?"

I shrugged and lied. "We're just paid to maintain the place. Your guess is as good as mine."

She looked back over her shoulder at them. "I don't know. I'm glad we got to see them, but honestly, there's just something creepy about them, don't you think?"

"Yes, I do think."

She smiled at me, then at Emmet, only I noticed she blushed a little when looking his way. "Come on, Mitch," she called to her son, who had taken advantage of her lack of attention to begin a second circuit. He cut through the monument, and jogged along toward us. She reached out and patted him on the back. "Let's get going, big guy."

As they trotted off together to their car, I surmised Mitchell was satisfied with his visit. He jabbered on about a movie he was wanting to see, and his mother kept repeating the words "We'll see. We'll see." My heart ached to have this same exasperated conversation with my Colin.

The boy and mother both waved good-bye as they backed out onto the main road. Emmet and I waved back. Fridtjof behaved as if he had already forgotten they existed. "The Babalon Working . . ."

"Listen," I said. "You can tell the other anchors they have . . . the line has my support, but I'm ready to get home. I've enjoyed this little field trip immensely but my feet are swelling. I want to sit down, maybe have some tea—"

A table covered by a white tablecloth along with three comfortable chairs appeared before us. A large pot of tea and a three-tiered pastry stand sat on the table alongside cups, plates, and silver.

Fridtjof stood there contemplating his work. A crystal vase filled with daffodils shimmered into existence. "There, that's a nice touch, no?" He pulled out a chair for me. "About the Babalon Working," he continued. I looked at Emmet, who shrugged. "I brought you here to discuss just that."

"Here I believed," Emmet began, "I was no longer thought to be the world-eating spawn of the Great Whore."

"This has nothing to do with you, golem"—Fridtjof faced me—"and everything to do with your mother."

TWENTY-NINE

"I thought you didn't know what Gudrun's spell was attempting."

"I'm not speaking of Gudrun's spell." Fridtjof took a step back. "Whatever she was attempting, it has no relation to the Babalon Working."

"Okay, but seriously, I think you are confused. Emily attempted something she called the Babel spell. She tried to suck Emmet and me into it, but we handled her, right?" I looked to Emmet for validation.

"Yes," Emmet said, pouring tea into one of the delicate china cups and setting it on a saucer before me. "Or at least Jilo did."

"No, I'm not in the least bit confused. We are already aware of what happened through your mother's little Tillandsia project. Emily's Babel spell was intended to carry you beyond the line's protection. No doubt, it was a nasty piece of work, but it was a mere walk in the park compared to the great working. We know now that Emily's fascination with the Babalon Working goes back many years. She surrounded herself with books and artifacts and people, one in particular whom she disguised as a servant, that were related to the great work. I believe you have met her purported driver?"

"Parsons?" The image of the man's waxy gray face rose to mind. I washed it down with a quick sip of the hot black tea.

"Indeed. Fool of a man. Brilliant, very nearly capable of succeeding. He is a magic worker, but he is no witch. I personally am convinced that were he a witch, this planet would have been lost to the old ones long ago. As things stand, he nearly destroyed himself. Tell me"—he shifted gears without warning—"in your knowledge has Emily Taylor ever acted in the best interest of either you or your sister?"

I fought to keep my emotions from showing. Still, I was struck by the notion that perhaps the only time she had actually done right by us was when she faked her own death and left us in Iris's care. Iris had not been a perfect parent by any means, but I grew up knowing I was loved. Had Emily raised us, God only knows the person I might have grown into.

Fridtjof didn't seem interested in allowing me time for a full inventory. "No, I thought not." He leaned in toward me. "Emily knew your husband was a Fae changeling. She knew she could unravel your entire life simply by alerting Peter to that fact. So one is left to ask, why did she not?"

It was true. She had promised Peter would never learn from her about his true parentage. Had she been so sure his awareness would be otherwise triggered? Even if that were the case, she seemed to relish in bringing pain. Why would she not have rushed to do just that? "I really don't know why." I would have liked to believe it showed that deep down there remained a shred of decency in my mother, that maybe a subliminal part of her soul actually did love me. All the same, I knew Fridtjof was preparing to dash that hope.

"Your parents, and yes, we are now aware Erik was your father." He waited for me to respond, but I held my tongue and watched him through a cool eye. I had the suspicion our little bonding experience was coming to its official end. "We have investigated and determined that your parents had both dedicated themselves to ending the line. We are certain Erik's defection from his family's position was a ruse, though a convincingly played one." His pale eyelids closed partially over his blank eyes. "You have certainly heard of the prophecy about the combining of your bloodlines."

Yes, of course I had, but I bit my tongue. I would let him lay out his cards before me before I committed to anything.

"The prophecy stated that a union of the Weber line with the Taylors' could produce a child capable of bringing down the line," he added for my benefit, on the off chance this tidbit had somehow escaped me. "We never took it seriously, as there are similar predictions about many other supposedly dangerous combinations among the witch families. If the anchors had truly believed this to be an actual prophecy and not just an old witches' tale, your Ellen would never have been allowed to marry Erik."

"Why are we going through all this ancient history, especially if you hold no credence in the 'prophecy'?"

"Because we fear that your mother succeeded."

"How?" I asked. "If she had succeeded, why would she be dead and us playing tea party in a pasture?"

The lack of pupil and iris made it difficult to glean much information from his eyes. Fridtjof placed his hands on the table, and from the angle of his face, he appeared to be examining them. "Emily has been hiding your entire life, working in the background to achieve the end of destroying the line." His face tilted up to mine. "She could have chosen to return at any time, but she waited until you were pregnant."

It took a few seconds for me to realize where his train of thought was heading. What he implied seemed to be simply impossible. It was impossible he would even consider it. "No," I said, pushing back from the table. Emmet didn't seem to have made the connection yet, but he jumped up ready to defend me all the same.

"Mercy, you must realize, I get no pleasure from forcing you to acknowledge this. Think about it. I can smell the magic on you. The magic you and your family are using to keep your pregnancy viable." My hands fell to my stomach. "That is why Emily never told Peter about his parentage. She knew enough about Fae magic to realize that if he lost his footing in this dimension, if his existence here were erased before the baby could establish its own foothold in our reality, the baby would never be born."

I took a step back, sliding without intending to into Emmet's outstretched arm. He wrapped both arms around me, and I realized around Colin too. My senses were overwhelmed with Emmet's intention to protect us both.

"This thing growing in you—" Fridtjof stood and with a wave of his hand made the table and chairs disappear. "It isn't a child, it is the Abomination."

"You are wrong."

"Listen to me, Mercy," he said, folding his hands as if he were praying. "I know it is a horrible thing to hear."

"Shut up."

"You must realize what a blessing it is Peter returned to his world. You can save the line, you can save the entire world simply by letting go."

I looked over my shoulder at Emmet. His handsome face was twisted with rage. "We need to go," I told him, and prepared to slide us home.

"Can't you see how he loves you?" The question caused me to hesitate. "I can tell you love Emmet as well. Let yourself forget. Forget Peter, forget this thing that has taken root in your womb. Let it dissolve."

"I cannot forget my child," I said. "I *will* not forget my child."

"Your golem is fertile. You will have other children, you and your giant there. Beautiful children. So many. Simply let this one go."

"No," Emmet spoke for me. "If Mercy will allow me, I will indeed father children by her, but this one"—his large hand slid over mine—"will be our first. We will never let go."

"Then you leave us with no choice but to perform a binding on the girl," he said and raised his hand toward me. "Last chance, Mercy. Let the Abomination fade away. Understand this is your only choice."

"Only choice? You people are insane. Just how do you think one innocent child will destroy the world?"

Fridtjof blinked, and for a moment his features softened. "I'm sorry, but we don't believe your child is an innocent. The Babalon spell. Its aim is to bring a non-human soul into human form. We believe Emily succeeded in circumventing the line and bringing one of the old gods back into our world. That thing you're carrying is not a child. It's an embodiment of the force that will destroy us all." He lowered his head, as if he could no longer bear to see the agony he caused me. "All of your fellow anchors are awaiting my signal. When I begin the binding, all the others—all the others—will join in. We are unanimous. Once your magic is bound up in you, you will live the rest of your life as a vegetable, and you will also lose any ability to protect the monster inside you. It will never live to see the light of day."

"You are wrong! He isn't a demon. I won't let you harm him." I held my hands before me, ready to strike him with every ounce of power I could muster. My magic was so full of desperate anger it showed as obsidian sparks dancing on my fingers. A rumbling formed in the earth beneath my feet and rippled out. In my peripheral vision, I could see the Guidestones begin to sway.

Fridtjof's head leaned to the left, but he did not seem threatened by my show of strength. He held his hand up before me. "Then I truly am so sorry . . ."

I prepared myself, as I knew the next thing I heard would be the united voices of my fellow anchors condemning me to a living death. I closed my eyes and pulled Emmet's arms even more tightly around me.

Then Emmet laughed. My eyes flew open and I looked back at him. "Don't you see it, Mercy? You have nothing to fear from this white waste."

"What do you mean?" I asked, but Emmet did not answer.

Instead he addressed Fridtjof. "Go ahead. Bind her. Go on, we are waiting."

Fridtjof's hand dropped to his sides, and Emmet released me from his grasp. He stomped over to Fridtjof and lifted him off the ground with one hand. Emmet looked back at me. "They can't bind you, or they already would have." He threw Fridtjof to the ground, where he landed with a thud.

Relief gave way to rage. Red, angry fire flew unbidden from my fingertips and burned a path to Fridtjof, tracing a circle around him. He reached out to extinguish the flame, but it shot up into a solid curtain around him. "You would trick me into harming my child?" The voice I heard hardly sounded like my own. This, this had to be the final betrayal. That these people could be mad enough, driven enough by their fears, to attempt to trick me into murdering my own child. I wanted the fire to take Fridtjof, to burn him to ash and feed back through him into every single anchor who stood against me. I knew if I willed it, it would do just that, but reason told me the line still needed these impossible people. As long as this remained true, I would not act against them. I would not seek revenge.

I wouldn't have thought it possible, but Fridtjof's snowy complexion managed to blanch even further. His nostrils flared and his eyes were wide. Perspiration beaded above his upper lip. This man feared that in the next instant, he would see not only the end of his own life, but his entire line as well. Still, I sensed his greatest agony would be knowing that his other half would be left forever alone. "You have no idea how lucky you are," I said and dropped the circle of flames. I reached out with both hands and shot the bastard all the way back to Sweden.

I held out my hand toward Emmet. "We need to get home," I said.

"Of course." He took my hand in his.

I closed my eyes and focused on home, but a sudden burning agony filled my body, causing every nerve ending to feel as if it had caught fire. I would have collapsed had Emmet not moved quickly to scoop me up. I tried not to scream, but it felt like my insides were being pulled out. Along with the pain came a warm trickle. I smelled the coppery blood before I saw it, but more than the pain, more than the smell, it was the sight of my blood staining the material of my dress that told me the other anchors were actually trying to do it. They were trying to kill my baby.

THIRTY

I couldn't let myself panic. I had to keep my head. I knew my only hope was in making it home. Giving myself over to Ellen's care. She could heal me. She could help me fight. The pain nearly made me black out, but I was shocked by the sight of blood trickling down Emmet's forearm. It took a moment to realize that I had clenched him so hard my nails had pierced his skin. Another pang nearly carried me away in darkness, but Emmet took my face in one hand and forced me to meet his gaze.

"Fight. Don't let them do this."

"I'm trying," I cried. I was. I really was. I was fighting with my entire being to push the other anchors' magic from me. A brief respite gave me a second to wonder how they could be doing this to me. How the line could allow them to tap into its power and let them harm my child. I thought it had chosen me. I thought it wanted me to help it grow. How could it have deserted me, betrayed me? I buried my head in Emmet's shoulder and screamed.

"You must focus, Mercy. You must carry us back to Savannah. We have to reach your family." Emmet gave voice to the three facts my rational mind already knew to be true, but my rational mind had shrunk until it floated like a tiny island in a vast sea of fear and pain. "For Colin, Mercy, you must do this. He needs you. He needs his mother."

Something about that word—"mother"—struck me like a magical ward. It connected me to the birth travails of every woman, but it also connected me to every mother's strength. "I can find my way home," I panted between throbs. Their attack weakened my magic. "But it's taking almost everything I have to fend them off. I don't have the power to carry us both."

"Then go. Hurry. Take yourself home. I will follow as quickly as possible." He kissed the top of my head. "Know that I love you, Mercy."

I wanted to acknowledge his words, but I couldn't speak. I could barely breathe. I closed my eyes. I blocked out as much of the pain as I could, but still the scream I started before the monument's stones carried with me all the way back to Savannah.

When I opened my eyes, I was lying on the floor of my own room, only inches away from where the lifeblood had deserted Teague's body. *Blood calls to blood*, the incongruous thought landed between convulsions. My water broke and the convulsions gave way to contractions. "Ellen!" I screamed her name.

At first I thought magic was causing the room to flash in and out of existence before my eyes, but as Aunt Iris rushed into the room, I realized it was only that I was dying. Iris fell down to her knees beside me. Her frantic calls to Ellen married with my own wails.

"Dear God," Ellen said as she knelt near me, raising my torso up so she could wrap her arms around me. Relief. Cooling. The agony subsided.

"They are trying to kill my baby," I said, grasping hold of Iris's hand.

"Who is, darling? Tell me, I will make them stop."

I tried to speak, but they broke through Ellen's healing wall. "Anchors." The word was ripped out of me by another angry wave.

"The anchors are doing this?"

The room began to fade in degrees, bending back and growing darker around the edges. I noticed the sound of heavy, masculine footfalls on the stairs, coming down the hall.

"There is something wrong with Oliver." The sound of Adam's frightened voice as he burst into the room brought me back. I managed to turn my head so that he was at the center of my fading vision. "We were out in the garden," he continued without even seeming to notice the strangeness of the scene he'd just walked in on. "Just talking. He collapsed. And then this . . ." Adam stood there, shaking. In his arms he carried an elderly man. An elderly man who wore my uncle's clothes.

"I can't let go of her," Ellen said. My eyes drifted back just enough that I could see her beautiful face staring down at me. She looked so afraid. I wished I could comfort her. Another contraction hit, drowning out everything else in the world other than my own pain.

As the wave subsided, I heard a voice I felt I should recognize say, "Put me down. Put me next to Mercy." The voice was dry and cracked. It seemed to come from an ancient place.

A hand took mine. It was cold, withered. Still, there was something in his eyes. "Uncle Oliver?"

The old man nodded his head. "Yes, Gingersnap, it's me." Adam knelt next to him, holding him up. It seemed without Adam's support, Uncle Oliver would collapse.

"Was it the photo?"

"Photo?"

"The one you damaged. The one of you and Granddad?" The question cost me a lot. I had to pant to keep from passing out.

I was surprised by the sound of Oliver's reedy laughter. "No, sweetheart. It's nothing like that."

"Then what is it?" Iris demanded. Something in her tone seemed to say she had her hands busy enough with me, she didn't need any kind of nonsense from her little brother right now. I very nearly laughed, but such an act lay beyond me now.

"You tied your life force to the baby's, didn't you, Oli?" Ellen asked. I realized this link had been the cause of the gray hair I'd noticed earlier. He hadn't added his magic to the runic spell my aunts had drawn on my body—he had given his very life.

"Indeed I did," Oliver said, giving my hand a gentle squeeze. "Of course, I didn't count on the little fellow taking quite so much."

"You have to break off the connection," Ellen ordered. "The anchors, they are trying to take the baby. They will take you with it, if you don't cut the tie."

"And if I do cut the tie, they might just succeed." Oliver coughed, then wheezed.

Iris approached and loomed over us all. "Oliver. Break the connection. You must. If you let go, we might just be able to save you. Tell him, Mercy. Tell him."

I wanted to. For his sake. For Ellen's sake. But mostly for Iris's sake. She had virtually raised Oliver herself. In many ways, her little brother was less a brother and more of a son to her. She didn't want to lose her little boy. I understood that, but neither did I.

"Once upon a time," Oliver said, "I made an unforgiveable mistake. In anger, I made a mistake that took a child's life."

Adam's face convulsed in tears. "I forgive you. I forgive you," Adam repeated, then buried his face in Oliver's dwindling shoulder.

"Thank you," Oliver said, "but when I said 'unforgivable,' I meant I cannot forgive myself." His body trembled. "I know doing this does not make up for the life I took," he said, and I noticed the hand that held mine had begun to glow. The pain once again faded, and I could focus on his words. "I just hope somehow doing this gives my otherwise pointless life some meaning."

"Stop it right now," Iris commanded.

"Shush now, sis," Oliver said, then focused on me. "How about it, Gingersnap? Will you let me do this for Colin? And if not for Colin, then for me?"

Who knows? If my body hadn't been nearly ripped apart by pain, if I weren't so terrified for the life of my baby, maybe I wouldn't have allowed it. As it was, I nodded. "Thank you."

I no sooner said the words than the light that had built up around Oliver's cold and trembling hand shot into my own. Oliver's body slumped. Someday, when things were better, when Colin was sitting on my knee while I sang him lullabies, I knew my heart would break at the memory of the sight that was going on before my eyes in this moment. Adam clutched Oliver's frame, but within seconds, it began to dissipate, falling away into powdery dust. Adam tried to grasp at the disappearing residue, but the very act of clutching caused the fines to float away at an even faster rate.

Adam fell back on his elbows, his face betraying the onset of madness. Grief and horror filled his eyes, along with only the finest touch of blame. A wildness took over his features. He spun himself up from the floor, and ran out of the room, along the hall, and down the stairs. Even though I didn't register the sound of the door, I sensed he had left the house. A small part of me that could see past my own fear and pain worried I'd just watched a man lose his soul.

"Help me get her on the bed," Iris said. She had moved into crisis mode. She would find Adam. She would mourn Oliver. But her tone told me she had decided to deal with one tragedy at a time.

Ellen's response came in the form of a whispered prayer for serenity. Would my baby's fate be one of those things she might still change? Iris circled around to my feet, and I felt Iris and Ellen's combined magic levitate me and shift me over to the bed. Ever so gently they let me down on the coverlet.

"Did it work? Did Oli's sacrifice work?" Iris asked as Ellen laid her hands on me.

"I believe it has, but the baby is still coming," she said, then her voice fell as she whispered something to Iris.

"I see," was Iris's response to the unheard comment. She leaned over me and placed her hand on my cheek. "You be brave. Ellen's gonna see to it that you and that boy of yours will both make it through this. I'm going to go deal with the other anchors."

"Don't go." I reached out and grabbed her arm. "They will kill you."

Iris gently removed my hand from her arm and let it down gently. "No, darlin', they are gonna try." She turned to Ellen. "Take care of her. I am going to put an end to this. I will be back right after I make these sons of bitches pay." She placed her hand on my shoulder. "Aunt Iris is gonna fix this for you, honey. You just be a good girl and do what Ellen tells you."

Her eyes brimmed with tears, but she wiped them away with the back of her hand. She turned and hurried from the room. "You've got to stop her," I said.

"There is no stopping her. The other anchors, they've taken from the Taylors now. I don't care how much magic they have, Iris is going to take them all down. All of them."

"But the line. If Iris harms the anchors . . ." I realized Iris had decided to bind the other anchors, once and for all and all on her own. They would suffer the fate they'd willed for me. Living out their natural lives in a vegetative state until their bodies gave out. Then the line would move on to select their replacements. I was certain nothing like a mass binding of anchors had ever been attempted. How Iris thought she could achieve this was beyond my comprehension. I didn't have long to try to comprehend. Another wave of agony tore through me.

Ellen lifted my head up and slid another pillow beneath it. "Now, you listen to me," she said as she moved to the foot of the bed. "It's a very early delivery by normal human standards, but we both know he's got a lot of magic in him, from both you and his daddy. And the little guy is a fighter. I feel it."

"He's headstrong. Just like me," I said for my own comfort.

A small smile formed on my aunt's lips. "That's right, he is. And you know what? You get that stubbornness from me, and I am telling you that you and I are going to get this baby delivered before they can undo what good Oliver did for us." She pushed the skirt of my dress up. "You aren't fully dilated yet, so I need you to focus on helping me make that happen."

I heard steps coming down the hall. I took a deep breath, filled with relief that Iris had come to her senses. The steps stopped at the threshold of my room. The energy was wrong. It wasn't Iris. I sensed two there, instead of one. "Ellen," I whispered and pointed toward the door. She was so focused on me that she had noticed nothing, and looked distractedly up. She turned back to me. She had seen nothing. Was I delirious, or was I simply dying?

Two women, dressed all in black, floated over the threshold and into the room. I blinked, not wanting to believe my eyes.

"Hello, sweetheart," Emily said, then cackled. Her hair floated around her head as if she were swimming in water. Her skin was translucent. "Mama is home." She reached out to take Gudrun's hand. Together they floated to the side of my bed. Together they grasped me and carried me away into the darkening sky.

THIRTY-ONE

Their hands like sharp talons ripped me away from where I lay. I saw my body lying below me, with Ellen in attendance over it, over me, but still I felt the roughness of the witches' grasp. Gudrun cackled. "Whether in the body, or out of the body, I cannot tell: God knoweth; How that he was caught up into paradise, and heard unspeakable words, which it is not lawful for a man to utter." I knew these words, but how?

My form beneath me shrunk as we continued to ascend, encountering nothing to impede our rise. Wind buffeted us from all sides, and I could feel myself being pelted with drops of ice. "Am I dead? Is that why you've come?" I asked, but my question was only met with shrieks of laughter.

"Ask not for whom *die Glocke* peals," Gudrun said in her clipped Germanic accent. The two screamed with laughter, enjoying a private joke. They clasped their free hands together, completing a circle between us, and we began to spin faster and faster until the moment we fell.

We plummeted in free fall until the world rose up beneath us to catch us. They released me, and I tumbled to the earth, landing with a heavy thud. I seemed solid enough in that sense. At least I was solid as everything else around me, even though I couldn't venture a guess as to where they had carried me.

"Stand," Emily commanded. My eyes darted about, searching for any form of refuge, but I found myself on what appeared to be an endless grassy plain, beneath an eternal and uncurving starlit sky. "I said stand." She reached for me and jerked me to my feet. Was this what being dead felt like, invisible to those still living, incorporeal but burdened with the memory of your entire body like one enormous phantom limb?

An odd humming like the sound of a bass theremin caused me to turn. Directly behind me a bell-shaped object hovered, spinning slowly enough that I could see the rune-like engravings along its lower rim. I turned back to the dark witches. A thousand questions popped up in my mind. *Where are we? What is that thing?* "Why won't you just stay dead?" was the one that escaped my lips.

"Now, is that any way to speak to your mother?" Emily said and laughed, her laughter a cold metallic pealing that corrupted the night.

"I saw your body." I pointed at Gudrun. "She killed you. She used your body to seal a spell. She said she was punishing you."

Emily folded her arms across her chest. "Oh, my dear daughter, you are so incredibly gullible." Gudrun floated next to Emily and wrapped her arm protectively around her. "It was no punishment. It was a reward."

"Indeed, the process is unpleasant, but I believe you agree immortality merits a little agony, no?" Gudrun asked my mother.

"Indeed it does," Emily said and turned back to me. "Do you hear that, precious one? I am immortal. Truly immortal. And I owe it all to you and my foolish siblings."

"It takes not only much magic, but a special kind of magic to work the spell I completed for your mother. It takes soul magic."

"Gehenna . . ." I whispered the name.

"Yes, Gehenna," Emily said. "Your golem friend kept the door open just long enough for Gudrun to collect all the magic she needed."

"Then all that about Grandma, it was just a trick?"

"Oh, no, my dear mother was indeed trapped in Gehenna, but that is exactly where she deserved to be." Emily circled around me to face the humming object that still clung to the horizon. She glanced over her shoulder back at me. "It's a shame your golem managed to spring her. Don't get me wrong. She didn't deserve to be there for killing your grandfather. She deserved to be there because she took the coward's path and killed herself as well." She spun back around to me, rushing up angrily until she was immediately before me. "She should have been proud to kill that bastard, that corrupter of pure blood. He with his Negro wife and his half-breed children." She seemed to catch hold of herself, relaxing and sliding back a few feet. "I'm the one who told Mama, you know. It was your father who told me. Erik saved me. He showed me how to remove the stain of sharing blood with a lesser race."

"Lesser race?" I found my voice and screamed the words at her again. "Lesser race? You mean all of this has happened because you are a bigot?" Until that very second, I had believed this kind of blind hatred had been relegated to another century.

"Lower your voice," Gudrun commanded in a hiss. "Your mother, she is a purist. She has dedicated her existence to the return of the rightful order."

"There is no 'rightful order,'" I said and was suddenly overcome by a great sense of sadness. "There are only people, most of us decent and loving and not caring about anything other than those two qualities." If Colin and I somehow survived this, I would dedicate my life to raising him to understand viscerally just how wrong my mother had been, not only in action but in heart. Then my heart fell into the pit of my stomach. My hand clasped over my still bloodstained but now very loose dress. I gasped in the night air, as a sharp pain cut through my heart. I fell to my knees, then bowed over on the earth. They had succeeded. They had taken my child from me. *Oh, Colin, Mommy is so sorry she failed you. Mommy is so sorry.* An ever-expanding hole had been ripped through the center of my soul. "They killed my baby." I looked at my mother, incapable of believing I would not find at least a spark of humanity left in her. "They said my baby was an abomination." Emily stood as still as a marble statue, as cold and as unmoved.

"You poor, poor dear," Gudrun said in a singsong voice that sounded of anything other than sympathy. "So much betrayal. So much loss. So much pain." She knelt beside me and forced me back to my knees. "But it will all be over ever so soon," she cooed, and began stroking my hair in a caricature of caring.

I slapped her hand away with a satisfying smack, and pushed myself back, finding my feet. "You bitches have left me with nothing to lose."

"We can't take all the credit, dear. This was a group effort. You are the one, the one who is uniting all thirteen of the families. The line ends with you." They looked at each other and burst out in cackles all over again. "She still hasn't even begun to guess," Emily said, laughing so hard tears formed in her eyes and ran down her cheeks.

"Guessed what?" I felt so much anger at that moment, I might have killed her, killed Gudrun, and put an end to that hovering craft's annoying humming all in the same blast.

"That you never had anything to lose, dearie," Gudrun answered for her.

"What are you saying?"

"We"—Emily fought to regain composure—"we're telling you it is time for you to wake up. Time for you to remember." She paused as if she were waiting for an epiphany to strike, but none was forthcoming. "Your child was not the 'Abomination.' You are."

She began circling me in one direction, while Gudrun began to mirror her steps in the other direction. "Your father and I had such fun creating you. Our early days in Tillandsia were truly magical in so many ways."

I caught the image of a semitruck slamming into Erik's car, killing him instantly and flinging Paul from the vehicle. "Did you kill him?"

"I, no," Emily said. "Ayako did, but I knew it was coming."

"Ayako always was such a good little soldier," Gudrun said with a sneer on her lips. "All I had to do was convince her of the truth. That your father was a danger to the line."

"But why? If he was your ally?"

"Erik was losing faith in the cause. He had grown soft. He had lost sight of the end goal, and was enjoying his role as *père de famille* a bit too well. He wanted 'out,' as if he could simply walk away." She squinted at me, suddenly seeming irritated with having to explain her actions. She shrugged. "Besides, he had already served his purpose. He fathered you."

I turned to Emily. "You once told me you had loved him. Was that only another lie?"

"You have to understand," she said, her face smooth and free of any sign of regret. "You are my masterpiece. The line, it has to end with you. I didn't object because I wanted to make sure the prophecy was fulfilled, and that it would be fulfilled through you, my beautiful Abomination. If I could have squeezed your sister into that pileup, I would have, but Ginny had her claws dug too deeply into Maisie."

"Maisie is your daughter."

"Maisie was an unwanted byproduct of *your* creation, and you, my daughter, my Mercy"—she cast another amused glance over my shoulder at Gudrun—"you are merely a container, an envelope if you will, and it is time for that envelope to be opened."

The low hum of the bell-shaped craft began to race up the octaves. The sound prompted me to look over at it, and I saw it had begun to spin more quickly. "This 'bell,'" Gudrun said with an obvious pride, "is our greatest invention, our greatest weapon. It marries the highest of science with the greatest of magic to open up the dark and empty heart of the void you call God."

The machine continued gaining momentum until it became nearly impossible for the eye to track. It seemed to be pulling back from our dimension, an intense gravity building around it as it did so.

"It opens up the space where nothing exists, but where anything is possible. The inchoate can be made flesh, and all that has been made flesh can be returned to the nothingness from which it sprang."

I saw a tremendous flash of light; then in the next instant I was surrounded not by darkness, but by the utter lack of light. I felt myself trapped in the heart of an eternal and unfathomable emptiness. I knew I was now in the center of the void.

THIRTY-TWO

In the void, there are no cardinal points, no ups or downs, no forward or back. In the void, there are no illusions. No rationalizations. No comforting linear interpretations of cause and effect. In the void, it becomes clear there is no difference between the two. No difference between history and imagination. Both are lies in equal parts.

The greatest lie of my life had not been that my mother had died, or that no one knew who my father was. In a way, those things shone through as the brightest of all truths. My mother had died, on the inside, where it really mattered, and no one, no one, ever knew the man my father had been. No, the greatest lie I'd ever heard had been the ticking of Ginny's clock, the way it counted off the passing seconds so loudly, proclaiming itself the herald of time, the great god that ruled over us all. In the void, time has no meaning. Within the void it becomes clear that time is merely a side effect, not the great king it pretends to be.

In the void, I had no eyes, and I had no physical mind. Still, images of the illusion I called my life floated around my awareness. No, that implied they could possibly be separate from my awareness, and here, there was no separation. My awareness, and truly that was all I had left, acted upon itself to conjure images of Emily, memories of Erik. I had been born to monsters, but I, myself, was not a monster. She had called me the "Abomination." With those words she claimed I had no soul. Still, I felt that soul, that spark, felt I *was* that spark. I wanted to believe she was wrong about me, as she had been so horribly wrong about everything else.

As above, so below. Infiltrating Tillandsia, a harmless gentlemen's club, and turning it into a generator of dark magic, Erik and Emily had performed the ultimate act of sympathetic magic, but instead of clay, instead of cloth, they had used their own biology to create a poppet, a living doll capable of containing the essence of the line itself. The blood and the sex of Tillandsia proved to be the exact frequency necessary to capture a small piece of the line, and channel it into a human body. The body I'd thought of as mine. They had determined the best way to topple the line was to destroy it in its smallest expression, because through the laws of sympathetic magic, what can be destroyed on the molecular level will also be abolished in its greatest form.

Now, I found myself within the void, divorced from that body, but still aware of what was happening to it. It had all been such a glorious trick on Emily's part. The line had been created by the thirteen families, and it required all thirteen working together to destroy it, to destroy me. The ten families who had remained loyal to the line would never have knowingly agreed to unite with the three rebel families, but Emily had sowed the seed of fear in their hearts. They thought they were preventing me from harming the line. They had no idea I was the line.

THIRTY-THREE

The powerless ginger girl they had at first overlooked, then loathed, was the line incarnate. I found myself missing that girl. As the united witch families joined forces to destroy her, I felt the rebel families working to erase her. Here, in the void, I knew that was exactly what was happening. I was being twisted, erased, undone at the point of nothingness. The edges of my awareness grew fuzzier, dissipating into the absolute null of the void. I let my mind float, searching out the happier moments, although it seemed they were among the first to fade.

I was awash in horror. Ginny's corpse was spread out before me, or was it Teague's? The two murders blended together now. The fire at Magh Meall. Knowing I'd never see Peter's parents again. The kick in the gut as Peter leapt without so much as a wave through the portal into the world of the Fae. The realization that Maisie had once turned me over to be sacrificed. The sickening crack of my neck as Connor struck me, flinging me like a ragdoll against the wall of Ginny's house. The magical fire that consumed him. All things good began to escape me. I had family, family that loved me. There were two women. Sisters. They loved me very much, but I could not remember their names. Two men. They loved me. I knew that. They seemed like family to me, even though they certainly weren't brothers, but the same word pressed against my consciousness. Then that word was lost to me. I felt a shock and a sense of collapsing, condensing. There existed less of me and more of the nothingness in which I was an island. I could still see her, that girl, or was I simply imagining I did? She lay oh so very still, the red hair on her pillow a near match for the red blood that now clung to her thighs. I wished I could comfort her. I wished I could promise her things would be all right, but I sensed that she, like I, was fading. Another shuddering collapse and the vision failed.

No more images came. There was only darkness. Darkness and a single spark. With the sight of the spark, I regained the memory of color. I recognized it. The color blue. No, it was haint blue.

"Well, if you are just about good and ready to quit feeling sorry for yourself, we got some work to do."

My awareness, which had been so close to collapse, suddenly exploded, blowing wide open. I knew myself, I knew that color, and I knew her.

"Jilo." She had no form, she was just a shimmering, but still I recognized my friend.

"That's right, girl. It's your Jilo."

"Are you an angel?"

Laughter shook the darkness around me, the haint-blue light expanding into waves that reflected off themselves into infinity. "Well, the good Lord do work in mysterious ways. Maybe that what he has in mind, but if he do, then he got his work cut out for him." Another bout of laughter rippled around me. "Jilo's here for you. She's here, and she ain't gonna let nobody hurt her baby."

"I'm nobody's baby, I'm not even human."

"Bullshit." Her face coalesced before me. "It don't matter none if you human or you billy goat, you are Mercy, and you are my baby. I love you, girl. I have done ever since that evening I saw you leading your silly tour through Colonial Cemetery. You remember that evening, girl?" The memory of the night rose from the ashes to become real again. With that memory, I somehow became more *real* again too. "I saw you leading those paunchy crackers around, and there was something about you. Jilo, she thought to herself, 'You just walk away, Jilo. She just one of them crazy Taylors.' But Jilo's heart felt a tug at the sight of you. That's why Jilo put it in your silly head to come find her at her crossroads."

The urge to laugh hit me, creating shimmers of light in the void. "You did not."

"Oh, yes"—she put special emphasis on the word—"Jilo did. You just need to own up to the fact you would've been too scared to come if I hadn't set a conjure on you."

"Come to think of it, you're probably right."

"Hell, girl, ain't no probably about it." Jilo paused and seemed to be attempting to measure the endlessness around us. "Now, this here is one hell of a mess you've landed yourself in." Light and color faded as I again felt the hopelessness of my situation. "Oh good Lord, there she go again. Jilo said it a mess, she didn't say you can't get out of it."

"You don't understand," I said, wondering if my friend were just something my dying mind conjured to ease the fear of its last few minutes. "This is the void, the empty heart of God."

Jilo's cackles dissolved the darkness into a mad rainbow of color. Fandango lights shot forth and circled each other. For an instant I imagined I could see a horizon. "Shoot girl, this ain't the heart of God. This thing is counterfeit. It is a lie." Jilo let loose an angry harrumph. "Those fools, they think they can make themselves gods. They mix they science with magic and they come up with this 'bell' of theirs."

"But Emily—"

"But Emily nothing. Who you gonna listen to, that bitch or your real mama?" I didn't answer. There was no need. "All right. This thing we in. They found a way to mimic the true void, but you need to get it through that red head of yours that this ain't the true void. Ain't no man and ain't no witch either who gets to play in that sandbox."

"So what do I do?"

"What do you do?" I perceived a mental image of Jilo as she had been before her death, a birdlike old woman, hopping mad. "Ain't Jilo taught you nothing?" Somehow even her frustration with me came as a comfort. "What is the first thing, the very first thing, Jilo taught you about magic?"

I tried to focus, tried to remember the time we had spent together, her sharing with me everything she herself had learned through trial and error. It all seemed so distant in this place without time, without sensation.

"This void," Jilo said, "it is a powerful weapon, and those bitches have aimed this power at you."

The sensation of pain. A small stone bounced off my shoulder. Joy rushed through me. There was a stone, and I had a shoulder. "That's right, girl. You tell Jilo, who does that power belong to now?"

"The power is mine." A green and pleasant world flashed into existence around us. I stood before Jilo, who looked at me like she was going to burst with pride.

"And you are going to use it to kick some ass." She pulled me into her arms. Solid. Warm. Loving. Real. "First, they somebody who wants to say hello." Jilo released me, and waved her hand, calling someone forward.

She arrived first as a sensation, hesitant to show herself, afraid of my rejecting her. My heart nearly broke realizing the pain I had caused her. All that she had done for me.

"Ginny," I said, and the image of my great-aunt crystalized before me. She wasn't the bloodied corpse I'd last laid eyes on. More than a mere memory, a moment out of sync repeated itself. *Jilo smiled like a proud teacher. "That's right, my girl. You seeing the big picture now. Who would that old woman have accepted her death from? That's the question you need to be askin'."*

Now, I had the answer to that question. Wren had murdered Ginny, but she hadn't accepted her death from him. She had accepted it from the line. She had accepted it from me.

"I tried to do exactly as you asked me," Ginny said, looking at me with wonder in her eyes. Another flash from before. I remembered going to her, not as Mercy, but before Mercy, as the line. The line had warned her Emily and Erik had succeeded. They had completed the Babalon Working and captured a bit of the line itself. "It was so hard to treat that little girl like I did." Tears moistened Ginny's eyes.

"You did exactly like I asked you to." I held my arms wide and Ginny flung herself into them.

"I knew she didn't understand. I knew she was innocent, but you—"

"I told you to keep her separate, ignorant of magic." A harder truth hit me. "I asked you to take her magic, and use her sister as an anchor for what you could. To send the rest to a dimension where no one would notice it." I was the one. I had been the one to betray Maisie. To warp her by channeling power through her that no simple witch could experience without going mad. How strong Maisie must have been to resist as well as she had. Those times I waited in Ginny's hall, staring at the damned blank wall I had resented so, that was when Ginny had worked so tirelessly to balance the powers that threatened to tear me apart. I realized it had been a blessing in disguise that Ginny had found a way to channel some of that power through Jilo.

"Emily never intended for you to grow to an adult. They meant to end you as a baby." She shuddered at the thought. "If the other anchors had known who you really were, they would have taken you away from me. They would have sought some way to dissolve you as Mercy without bringing down the line. Failing that, they would have locked you away. Tried to contain you. They would have fumbled around until the line was destroyed as sure as if they were working for Emily themselves."

"As above, so below," I said. Anything the anchors tried to do would have filtered out through the line as a whole. Dissolve Mercy, end the line. Contain Mercy, trap the line. Either way, their actions would have been the end. They would never have let me be, and as soon as they started in, the rebel families would have piled on. They almost had me as a grown woman. As a small girl, I would have never stood a chance. "The anchors think of themselves as my masters, not as my partners." I had tried for millennia to free myself from their grasp.

"I had to protect you from them. I had to protect you from Emily." Ginny's body heaved with heavy sobs. "I had to let Ellen lose Paul. I couldn't risk the other anchors finding out about you." Ginny pushed back from my arms to look at me. "When that other boy got run over in front of her shop, he was hurt too badly. His injuries should have killed him. Ellen didn't have enough power to bring that boy back like she did. The anchors knew that. What they didn't know was she drew the magic from you."

I remembered watching as she laid her hands on the broken boy, wishing she could save him. Willing that she would. And save him she had. She had managed to pull him right back from the tunnel of light that had called him. Afterward, I had avoided Ellen for days, afraid of her awesome power. Now I knew I had been afraid of seeing my own reflection.

"I couldn't risk letting her draw power from you again. The other anchors were suspicious. We were being watched . . ." Her voice trailed off as she relived that dark day. "Oh, how my beautiful Ellen hated me after Paul's death. I saw it in her eyes every time she looked at me. The whole family hated me." Her eyes looked deep into my own. "Perhaps you most of all."

"I'm sorry. I'm sorry I had to ask you to give up your own life, your own happiness for this."

"No. I dedicated my life to a cause. A cause I believe in to the very depths of my soul." She released herself from my embrace. "There is no shame in that. It was an honor to act as your protector. To help you keep the demons who would destroy our world at bay." With those words, she faded from sight. I reached out, trying to bring her back.

"No, no, no, child," Jilo said and shook her head. "You let her go now. She's been waiting to see you this one last time, but that old girl has earned her peace." All animation left Jilo's tired face. "I think this old girl is about ready for a little peace herself. You think you can handle things on your own from here?"

"I don't know what—" I started to protest, but she grabbed my hand in hers.

"Of course you know what to do. This bell of theirs, it's counterfeit, but it's still powerful. They may not have created a sun, but they sure as hell strapped together a pack of atom bombs. Emily, she put you here thinking that its power combined with all those damned anchors trying to put an end to you would whisk the line away, totally undo you. She think this power hers. That she can use it to destroy."

"She's wrong, though, isn't she?"

"Damned right she wrong, my girl." Jilo pulled me into a tight embrace, her thin arms like bands of steel. I felt it. She never wanted to let me go, but she knew she had to. For her sake, and for mine too. She picked up on the intentions that had begun to form within me. This place. This void, artificial or no, would allow me to try my own hand at creation, or at least recasting the world that had been. Tiny surgical cuts to the timeline, a changed decision here, a different action there, perhaps I could set things right for those I loved. "Damn, girl. Don't get all carried away. You can't reach back and yank the apple out of Eve's mouth. You can't reach back any further than when Emily done conjured you into the world."

"Yes, I understand," I said.

"And you understand the other bit too, don't you?"

"Yes." I understood, even better than she did. The spell had been broken. No matter what else I might manage to achieve, the one fact I couldn't change was that Mercy Taylor had never really existed.

THIRTY-FOUR

Change a word here, a word there. We're not talking about rewriting the history of the world, just a judicious editing of events that are truly minor in the grand scheme of things. There may be a momentary sense of confusion, an uneasy déjà vu, but the chattering of seven billion minds will join in to drown out those odd but passing sensations. History might cough, but in a day or so, it will feel just fine.

- — -

A young woman lies on a bloodstained bed. The color of her hair is very nearly a match for the color of the life that has been bleeding out of her. Ellen holds the stillborn child, reaching into the deepest well of her magic, and when that seems to be failing, matches magic with prayer. "Come on little one," she whispers. "Come on." The baby is blue. It doesn't move. Perhaps the child had never truly been meant for this world. "Don't you do this to me. You breathe. Take a breath. One small breath for Ellen." The child gasps for air and cries. Ellen can't suppress the sound that peals from her, a groan that speaks of the deepest relief mixed with joy. She turns back toward the mother, reaching out with her magic to grab the escaping spark and hold on to it for dear life, but she realizes her aid has come too late. The spark is at first just out of grasp, then fading as it moves away at an exponentially increasing speed. Before Ellen can blink, it has moved beyond the veil. Ellen sits on the foot of the bed and clutches the orphan tightly to her chest.

Iris closes Emily's eyes. Iris blames herself. She should've taken better care of her little sister. Played a more active role in her life. Emily had seemed so lost since Mama and Daddy died. Then again, so has Iris. No time for self-pity now, though. She will find time to fall apart. Later. Now, Ellen sits crying and rocking a little girl who's just lost her mother. Iris goes to the foot of the bed and kneels before Ellen. A wave of anger strikes Iris out of the blue. Why had Emily been so stubbornly insistent about not telling them who the baby's father is? The child has the right to grow up with at least one of her parents. Then again, Iris has heard rumors her baby sister had been venturing into places better left alone. That club she'd been going to, what is it called? Tillandsia. Iris has heard stories about what went on at those gatherings. It may be that Emmy herself wasn't sure of the child's sire.

"The baby is out of danger now?" Iris asks her sister. Ellen trembles, won't or can't speak, but she begins nodding. "Then you've done all you can do. Let me have her, sweetie," Iris says to Ellen. "Let me take her and clean her up. Then I'll give her right back to you. I promise."

"Emmy wanted to name her Maisie," Ellen says.

"And so we shall." Iris has never really cottoned to the name Maisie. It strikes her as a somewhat unfortunate choice. Had Iris ever had a daughter, she would have named her Adeline, after her own mother. "Come to Auntie Iris, Maisie. I'll take good care of you." She places her first gentle touch on the newborn. "Oh," she says aloud, shocked by a psychic form of static electricity. *Well, this*, she thinks, *is something Erik and Ellen will have to work out between themselves.* She takes the baby from her sister's arms.

- — -

A young man, so hurt, so angry, stands at an open door. A heated exchange is occurring between him and a dark woman, beautiful, proud, too young to understand the danger of pushing a desperate lovesick fool a step too far.

"If you believe Adam really loves you, then prove it to me." Oliver pauses, the darkest of thoughts fighting its way to the surface. The one bit of magic he couldn't perform, that it came so easily to her made him physically ill. Grace would give birth to Adam's baby. No matter what, she would always have a hold on him. She stood there gloating, taunting. It would be oh so easy to make her undo it.

An unseen hand on his shoulder, a whisper to his heart. A reminder of what true love means. The words that have begun to form fall away, replaced with "You raise that baby right." His face turns red, and his body shakes. "You hear me? You fall one step short of being the most perfect mother this world has ever seen, and I will come for you. Believe me, I will. Now get the hell out of here and leave me the hell alone." Oliver slams the door in Grace's face.

- — -

A man raises his hand to strike his wife. Iris doesn't know why, but this time something snaps within her. "No, not this time," she says, raising her own hand and sending her husband flying against the wall. His eyes open wide with surprise. He struggles to stand, but finds he has been pinned in place.

Iris's sister has died, and she's been left to raise her girl. She had hoped she could count on Connor's stepping up and being a father to Maisie. God knows her real daddy isn't stepping up. He isn't even owning up. But no, Iris is not going to raise the girl in a house with a man who'd ever consider hitting his wife. She can't risk Maisie growing up believing on any level that this way of life is okay. If it had only been for her own sake, Iris isn't sure if she'd ever have found the strength, but it isn't just about her anymore. Connor squirms and tries to free himself, but defying all gravity, he begins to slide up the wall. His head bumps roughly against the ceiling.

"Pack a bag and get out of here." Iris lowers her hand, and the man who just stopped being her husband tumbles to the floor. "You got five minutes."

- — -

The rain falls so heavily it's nearly impossible to see the road. The semitruck ahead jackknifes. Not enough time for thought, let alone magic. The father dies on impact, but by some miracle, just the slightest amount of additional force holds the boy tight against the seat as the car flips and rolls for what seems to him like an eternity.

Ellen rushes to the hospital, nearly crashing en route herself. At the sight of Paul, she snatches him into her arms, rocking her son as she holds him tightly to her breast. Paul is traumatized by his father's death. He cries for Ellen as he endures X-rays and examinations, but in the end everyone is left to wonder at the accident that took the father, but left the son without a scratch.

- — -

A young woman lies on a bloodstained bed. The color of her hair is very nearly a match for the color of the sunshine flooding through the window. Ellen and Iris look at each other, and in that silent stare promise never to tell Maisie or her redheaded giant how close they'd come to losing both Maisie and their boy.

It had come with no warning. Maisie had gone from a perfectly normal pregnancy to crisis in a matter of minutes. Iris reckons sometimes it just happens that way. To look at them both now, mother and child, you would never guess they had ever been in the tiniest shred of danger.

"Go on," Iris says and smiles at Peter. "Go call your parents. They are going to want to see this carrottop boy of yours."

Peter is not budging. "You okay?" One hand holds tight to his wife's, the other lies carefully on his son's back.

"Yeah," Maisie says, and for the first time in her life, she feels she really means it. "I'm incredible. Aunt Iris is right. Claire will take a switch to you if she finds out you made her wait a second longer than she had to."

"Go on, we'll get everyone cleaned up and presentable." Iris gives her final command. She watches her sister leave the bedside and cross to look out the window. Maisie begins singing a lullaby, the same Iris remembers singing to her, about a place called Cill Airne, a place neither of them has ever seen.

Iris joins Ellen by the window. "I guess you can take a family out of Ireland, but you can't—" The look in her sister's eyes makes her words run dry. Ellen stares at the horizon, as if she can see something there Iris can't.

Ellen's eyes fill with tears. "I didn't fail her, not this time."

Iris shakes her head and pulls Ellen into her arms. "No, sweetheart, you didn't fail Maisie at all."

Ellen seems confused. "I don't mean Maisie."

Iris strokes Ellen's hair. "You mean Emily, don't you?"

Ellen considers the question. "Emily? No." She pushes back from Iris's embrace. "Honestly, I don't know who I mean. Something just seems a bit off."

"You've just worn yourself out. That's all," Iris says. "You go rest up a bit. I'll take care of things here."

Ellen hesitates. She wraps her arms around herself and tosses a nervous glance in Maisie's direction. "You sure?"

"I'm sure. Everything here is in good hands."

- — -

An arthritic hand hovers over the telephone receiver. Jilo has lifted it and returned it to its cradle ten times over. She's an old woman, and she knows her end is near. Jilo grimaces. She doesn't have time to pussyfoot around like this. She's held on to her sister's secret for years now, throwing all the hate she could find within herself against the Taylors. But then that fool Ginny went and got herself killed, and, well, somehow all the hate seems like too heavy of a burden to carry on her own.

She's been watching the younger Taylors. Oh, sure, they're snooty all right, but at the end of the day, they aren't really bad people. And Jilo feels it in her aching bones: she has arrived at the end of the day.

She feels moved for reasons she can't really understand to see to it that her sister's children and grandchildren spend a bit of time getting to know the cracker side of their kin. Right now, she can't remember why she ever felt otherwise. They might love each other, or they might wring each other's necks, but that is none of her nevermind. They deserve the chance, regardless of the outcome. She stares at the avocado-green phone with its square of gray buttons. Finally she summons her determination and dials the number scrawled in pencil on the back of a used envelope. The dialed number begins ringing, and she very nearly hangs up, but a voice on the other end says, "Hello?"

Jilo hesitates. She can't understand what is possessing her to do this, but doing this she is.

"Hello?" the voice on the other end says again.

"Hello. This is Jilo Wills. We have to talk."

THIRTY-FIVE

Forsyth Park was nearly filled to capacity, but Iris and Ellen had claimed a spot for the family picnic in the shade of what had become known to the Taylor-Tierney clan as "the climbing tree." Three blankets, six lawn chairs, and a touch of magic formed the boundary.

It would be a perfect Fourth. Mid-eighties, and for once a blessed streak of low humidity had claimed Savannah as its own. Ellen took off her sunglasses and placed them on top of her head. "I have to tell you, every time I look at that cooler, I think of Jilo."

Iris smiled. "Hers was red. This one is blue," she said, but seemed incapable of convincing herself. "No. I see what you mean. Who knows? Maybe it means somehow she is still here with us."

"And ready to play referee just in case this little family reunion goes awry," Ellen said and laughed. Then her expression softened, grew more serious. "Why do you think, after all those years of keeping Daddy's other children a secret, she broke down and told us?"

Iris pulled one of the chairs closer. "I don't know. She and Ginny squabbled so for decades, even though sometimes I swear those two were flip sides of the same coin. I think Ginny's death made her realize her own mortality. Maybe she just wanted to make some form of amends."

"Maybe she felt guilt for having cozied up to the demon that killed Ginny."

"Possibly, but I think it went deeper than that. Those two old girls shared a connection. I can't even hazard a guess what it was, but I think with Ginny gone, the dam Jilo had built broke. She chose to clean up her side of the street before she passed on herself."

"Are you nervous about meeting them?"

"Frankly, yes. If the rest of them are anything like Jessamine, well, then we've got our work cut out for us." Iris sighed. "A lot has changed since Ginny's passing."

It had been a little over two years since what witches had come to call the "Great Shift" occurred on the heels of Ginny's death. Somehow her demise had triggered an end of an era, no, the end of an epoch. The line still stood, that life on earth as we knew it continued was testimony enough to that fact, but the line had broken free from its anchors, seemingly of its own will. The historians of the line, witches like Iris herself, had only found one other similar shift such as this. The last was when the line was decoupled from the great monuments that had served as its original anchors, and was bound instead to the living anchors who had shouldered the burden of the line for millennia. That first shift had been debated, voted on, and carefully orchestrated. This change had occurred in a blink of an eye without a soul's having seen it coming.

"Everyone's magic is crazy now," Ellen said. "Witches who were once quite capable can now barely bend a spoon with both hands, and others who'd been perfectly average are accidently blowing doors off their cabinets."

"We are still in a period of adjustment, but in the end we will adjust." Iris felt something tickle her ear, and she swatted, thinking a bug had landed on her. "I wonder if the old rumor was true after all?"

"Which old rumor?" Ellen asked and laughed. "I've lost count."

Ellen was right. If Iris chose to apply herself, she could collect a canon of purported truths and old witches' tales concerning the line. Maybe with the Great Shift, she ought to do just that. Save the stories for posterity. "We've always been told that witches get our power from the line. The rumor is that the exact opposite is true. That the anchors used the line to control all magic and parcel it out in the way they saw fit. Maybe the line has rebalanced things, or even left us capable of what we naturally should be without the help or drag of others."

Everyone was indeed out of sorts, but the only ones who seemed to have suffered any real ill effect had been the former anchors themselves. Their magic had been cut from them, as cleanly as if the line itself had wielded the scalpel. Both the united and the rebel families had been affected. Even the great Gudrun had not escaped the fate. She had sent a distress cry to the other anchors to save her in the moments before the dimension to which she had been exiled folded in on itself and disappeared for what might well be forever.

"I don't know if I like the sound of that." Ellen poured a glass of lemonade and offered it to her sister. "Sounds a bit too much like what the rebel families wanted. You know, consolidate the power among the strong, crush the weak."

"Good heavens, Ellie," Iris said, taking the sweating plastic glass. "There is plenty of room between absolute magical communism and offering the world up as tribute to the rapacity of the old ones. I'm not saying I have any answers. I just think we witches have let the radicals do most of our thinking and all of the talking for us for far too long." Ellen poured herself a glass of lemonade. Her expression told Iris her sister was not convinced. "Now the volume has been turned down on the extremists, maybe those of us with common sense can begin to carry on a conversation. We may get nowhere, but it's been too long since we've tried talking.

Maybe the young ones from the rebel families don't want their home destroyed any more than we do."

"Why," Ellen asked, "do you think witches' connection to the line ended with Ginny?"

"I don't know." Iris fanned her imagined bug away once more. "Maybe the line thought she was somehow special. I fear in my heart of hearts we misjudged the woman."

"Tomorrow, I'll make up a nice bouquet, and we'll head over to Greenwich to visit her."

"Yes," Iris concurred. "Let's do that."

Ellen drew her knees up and wrapped her arms around them. Iris had to smile as something about the pose stripped decades away, leaving Ellen looking once again like a young girl. Still, Ellen's face clouded over with concern. "A lot of folk are frightened that even though the old ones remain banished, many lesser evils may filter through."

"Don't worry, sweetie. Even if it's true, I'm sure it's nothing we witches can't handle."

"But we aren't exactly accustomed to managing these infestations on our own."

"Then we will simply have to learn. I think for far too long we have forgotten the line is a security net, not a hammock. We are all going to have to toss in and do some work if we want to preserve our way of life." Iris noticed movement in her peripheral vision and ducked just in time to miss being hit by a football.

Ellen stood and placed one hand on her hip. "Paul Edwin Weber, you and Martell be careful with that darned thing."

"Sorry, Aunt Iris. Sorry, Mom," Paul called and waved at them.

"Really, Ellen, you still speak to Paul as if he were a little boy. He's getting married in two months."

"Ugh. Please, do not remind me of that."

"Ellen," Iris said, her tone a warning. "She's a lovely girl."

"That she may be, but—"

"Sorry, Mrs. Weber," Martell said, running over and scooping up the ball.

"Any news from Jessamine?" Iris asked.

"No, ma'am. She told me she was picking up the family at the airport at noon, and they are supposed to be here by twelve thirty. That's the last I've heard from her."

"By the way, how is your summer job with the police going?" Ellen asked. Iris knew her sister really did care about Martell, but she was sure the timing of the question had a lot more to do with avoiding the topic of Paul's impending nuptials.

"Really well, thank you. I even got to go on a ride-along with Adam. I mean Detective Cook."

"You are family, Martell," Ellen said. "It's okay for you to call him Adam."

"But not to his face," Iris said, rising from her chair. "Speak of the devil."

Adam trudged along, struggling under the weight of an enormous wicker basket. "Heads up," Martell called to Paul and threw him the football. He chased off toward Adam. "Here, let me help you with that," he said and relieved Adam of his burden. The older man regarded the younger with a mixture of gratitude and hurt pride.

Iris jumped in to save Martell from the consequences of his good intentions. "Martell was telling us how much he enjoyed going out with you on a ride-along."

Adam stopped and flashed her a look that said he knew what she was up to. "Yeah," he said, patting Martell on his back. "He's going to make a fine officer *after* he finishes his degree in criminal justice."

"All right, all right, I get the message loud and clear," Martell said and smiled at Adam. Martell idolized the detective. His expression gave that much away.

"Martell," Paul called and held the ball aloft. Martell ran off in Paul's direction, catching the ball as it came his way.

"So where is that handsome brother of ours?" Ellen asked. She was not about to discuss Paul's wedding plans today; that was pretty clear.

"Dear Lord, do not get me started. I feel like I am living in the *Twilight Zone.*" He snorted. "Ponder this if you will. My soon-to-be husband is going to arrive late today as he and my ex-wife are busy planning a party for Jordan."

"That's right," Iris said, grabbing Adam's hand and shaking his arm. "He finishes his internship soon!"

Adam smiled proudly. "My son, the doctor." His eyes narrowed and gleamed with mischief. "How about you, Ellen? Are we to have the pleasure of Tucker Perry's company today?"

"Why yes, we just might. He's got some deal cooking that he insisted couldn't wait, but he promised he'd try to make it." Ellen suddenly seemed to take offense. "Listen, I know you all don't like Tucker—"

"We all like Tucker fine," Iris said, "but you'd better warn him that if he lives up to his reputation and breaks your heart, I *will* turn him into a toad."

Ellen looked at her sister with a deadpan face. "If Tucker breaks my heart, I will turn him into a toad without your help, thank you."

"Note to self," Adam said. "Never piss off a Taylor."

"That is good counsel to keep, Detective," Iris said, feeling happy. No, she didn't have a special man in her life. Not even a scalawag like Tucker. But she wasn't alone, and she was a very happy woman. She said a silent prayer of thanks for the day she found the strength to send Connor packing. She'd heard he'd remarried. For the fourth time. This time a witch who lived outside Tulsa. Iris wished Connor all the happiness he deserved.

All thoughts of Connor vanished as she caught sight of a certain redheaded toddler stumbling along, one hand holding on to his mother, the other balled up and stuffed in his mouth. "Colin," Iris said and held her arms open. Maisie released him, and the boy carried on with faltering yet functional steps until he collapsed in his great-aunt's loving embrace. Peter followed behind, weighted down like a pack mule with his son's accoutrements. "Happy Fourth," he said, unburdening himself first of a highchair, then of a diaper bag.

"Happy Fourth, sweetie," Ellen said, then went up on her toes to place a kiss on his cheek.

"Mom and Dad will be here in a bit. They told me to warn you they can't stay long."

"We understand," Iris said and scooped little Colin up in her arms. "After Saint Paddy's and Christmas, this is the bar's biggest day."

"Listen, I hate to bring this up," Peter said as he and Maisie exchanged a nervous glance, "but will Emmet be here today?"

"We did invite him. We felt a duty to," Iris said, realizing the Great Shift did perhaps claim one last victim: the golem that had been created to attend the drawing of the lots that would determine Ginny's replacement. Something had occurred during the change that left him a living being. A man in his own right.

"Listen," Peter said. "I don't know why. Heck, I don't think Mom even knows for sure herself, but she just plain does not like that guy. If he does show up . . ."

"We'll make sure to keep them separated."

"I don't think we have anything to worry about," Ellen said, her attention suddenly becoming the sole possession of Colin. "No we don't. No we don't," she cooed at the boy, whose face lit up at her attention. "The last several weeks, Emmet's taken to spending most of his time at Bonaventure. I don't know what it is about the place that attracts him so, but I've followed him there a couple of times."

"Is he visiting the graves, or what?" Maisie asked.

"Not graves, just one particular one. He spends hours sitting next to the statue of Corinne Lawton. As far as I can tell, he goes there every day and . . ." Ellen hesitated, as if she were wondering if she should go on.

"And what?" Adam asked, his ears pricking up at the mention of an unsolved mystery.

"I don't know," she said. "I mean, it felt wrong for me to be there. Spying on him. I should never have said anything."

"But now you have," Iris prompted, "so spit it out."

Ellen shifted Colin to her hip and began to bounce him. "Emmet sits there talking to someone."

"That's kind of crazy," Peter said.

"No, what's crazy is I could have sworn I heard someone answer him." The group fell silent, each looking from one to the other until all eyes fell again on Ellen. "I don't know," she said again and shrugged.

Colin suddenly warbled out some very happy if indiscernible sounds. His face lit up, and he pointed at the climbing tree. "What are you looking at, little man?" Ellen took the hand he had pointed with in her own, giving it several rapid-fire kisses. He laughed. In the next instant, Colin's attention was captured by the sound of a bicycle's bell.

THIRTY-SIX

Next to the statue of Corinne Lawton is an empty seat, expressing her family's sentiment that Corinne's fate in the afterlife would depend on a conversation between her and God. Corinne had been born into one of Savannah's leading families, and spent many years as a patron of the arts. Long after the point when most women of her age had already married, Corinne fled to Italy, where she finally found her true love, an Italian painter. Upon learning of the impending nuptials, her family followed Corinne to Italy and forced her to return to Savannah. They found a "suitable" husband for her, and so her wedding was planned.

On the morning she was to marry the man her family had chosen, Corinne's body was found floating in the Savannah River, her wedding gown billowing up around her.

Her memorial is replete with imagery, not expressing her family's grief and regret as one might expect, but instead seeking to demonstrate how Corinne's death had been her own fault; they had done all they could to bring her back to a respectable life.

The rejected headdress she was to wear in her wedding lies at her feet, and her back is toward the cross and the archway that, for them, symbolized the gate of paradise. The outrageous audacity many people can demonstrate, believing themselves to be the arbiters of the will of the ineffable's secret heart.

I doubted if Emmet knew the significance of where he sat, or he might not have become so accustomed to plopping down there. Then again, knowing Emmet, he might have taken great delight in keeping God's seat warm. "So tell me," Emmet said as he joined Corinne, "what lies did you tell about this lovely lady?"

Truth was Corinne counted among the few of Savannah's historical figures whom I had not maligned in one way or another during my years leading the Liar's Tour. I had felt a kinship for the fallen bride, no, more than that, a sisterhood, that prevented me from making Corinne a target. Emmet reached up and placed his palm against the cool marble, caressing Corrine's cheek, then folded his hands in his lap and waited for me to answer.

"Corinne's story is sad enough as it is without tossing lies on top of it."

"I'd say that is true of the lives of most people." His face lost all animation, taking on its own stone-like and inscrutable expression. "Your family is having their annual picnic today, you know. The one you told me you enjoyed so."

Yes, I had loved the feel of the hot sun, the smell of the grass, the shade from the live oaks, the sips of champagne Oliver always sneaked me when Iris pretended not to be watching.

The enjoyment of these things was no longer possible for me, as even though Mercy Taylor's memories lived on in me, I was not Mercy Taylor. I was the line. Of course I had known the Taylors would gather today in Forsyth. The only Fourth the family had ever missed was the one following Ginny's death.

My desire to see the family had been so intense, it overwhelmed my better sense. I rationalized I deserved one last look, a chance to see them together and happy one last time. That Colin saw me and seemed to recognize me told me this was indeed the last time I'd dare give in to the temptation.

"I too have been invited." Emmet looked at Corinne. "Perhaps if you would consider being my date? No?" Emmet's lips tried to curve up into a smile, but the effort faded the second he turned back to me. "The others haven't picked up on the little tweaks you've made to the flow of time, but they have noticed you've shifted the boundaries of the line further out."

I nodded. It was true. I shifted the edge of protection out to include the realm of the Fae. I couldn't undo the horrors perpetuated against the Fae by the witches who created the line, but I could make sure that now the Fae enjoyed equal protection. Of course, my actions were not entirely noble. I had done what I did for Mercy's sake. Now Colin need never face losing his father, even if Peter did again learn of his parentage. There would be no more changelings causing heartbreak on both sides of the divide. There no longer was a divide. The realm of the Fae and of mankind might not be one, but now they were close enough.

I was about to answer Emmet, to explain why I had done as I had, when he threw his hands over his face. "How could you? How could you leave me and not take your memory with you?" Emmet said and began rocking back and forth. "Even Emily you have granted peace through true death." He looked upon Emily's demise as a boon. To me it had been the only option. The woman had used her magic to draw the line into human form. A form she nurtured in her own womb in anticipation of the day she could bring about my demise. She had declared war on me and all those I had loved. Had sending her once and for all to her grave been self-defense, a casualty of war, or murderous revenge? Maybe a bit of each. God would be my judge. Emmet shook his fist in the air.

"You grant her peace, but me you have deserted, leaving me with nothing but this pain, this sense of loss that will never fade."

"I haven't left you. Not really. And your pain will fade. All pain does in time."

He pulled back his hands from his eyes and looked at me. "You lie." He stood up and drew closer. He reached out for me, letting his hand pass cleanly through. "Why did you not steal my memory of you? You did it for the others. Why did you leave me the sole person to feel your absence? I am left with nothing but grief, and I cannot even share it with those who loved you." His fists clenched at his sides. "They don't even remember loving you. For them, you never existed."

That he still saw me in Mercy's form made acceptance harder for him. Over time I would have to change my image so he could find a way to let go. That change would not come easily, for either of us. I had spent millennia simply as the line, but the two decades I'd spent as Mercy Taylor felt more real to me than the thousands of years before Mercy. I had lost a friend; I had lost myself.

Heavy tears fell from his eyes, mixing themselves with the sandy soil at the base of the monument. "For everyone else, you spin pretty lies." For the first time, I heard anger in his voice. The lives I'd created for those Mercy loved were not lies, only alternative truths. Were it possible for their reality to be observed from the outside, the observer would perceive the still-healing cuts and grafts I had made. Sooner or later, though, all wounds would heal, and the history I had written for them, this chance for happiness I could afford them, would live on as the only story they had ever known. "For me, you leave nothing. Nothing but this void." He pounded his chest with his fist.

"Mercy never did exist. Not really."

"Mercy did exist." His voice boomed with a desperate rage. "You did exist." He trembled before me. "I know you existed, because I loved you."

I reached for him, but stayed my hand, realizing its impalpable touch might bring him even greater distress. His eyes flashed first with anger, then dimmed with an utter lack of hope. He wiped away his tears.

I had forced Emmet to share my sacrifice. I didn't have a choice. "The line must have its anchor. There wasn't a single pure heart among my former anchors, and yours was the purest heart I knew."

"And so"—his voice turned gravelly—"I am to be punished throughout eternity for my 'pure' heart." He kept his eyes averted, focusing on the sandy gray soil at the base of the monument.

I had thought myself past the ability to feel pain. I guess I was wrong. At the end, I trusted Emmet more than anyone else on earth; that was why I had chosen him as the final anchor. He would never age, never die, as long as the line existed. He had wanted eternity with me; this was the closest to that I could give him. I had chosen Emmet as my anchor, for he had more than proven himself as my rock. Anchor might not have been the role he had wanted, but it was the only part I had left for any man to play. Words alone would never allow him to understand, but his heart would someday come to realize that in his own unlucky way, he *had* gotten the girl.

For a moment I thought he had settled, but suddenly he lunged at me. "No. I will not accept this," he said, his face nearly wild, shining with newfound determination. "You ask me to understand. You ask me to accept." He came so close to me, I could feel his hot breath on me. It was the closest thing I had experienced to a true physical sensation since remembering my true nature. "My answer is no. I will not accept. You are not simply the line, and Mercy was not just a trick Emily played on the world. I will not accept that you, Mercy, never existed. You may be the line, but you are also Mercy. Mercy Taylor. And I will not accept that you, Mercy, are gone." He repeated the name like an invocation, as if mere repetition could bring her back. His passion was so great, so white hot, that for a moment I almost felt Mercy rise again in the physical world, but no, I knew that to be impossible.

He reached for me, tried to pull me into his embrace, but he tumbled forward as he passed right through me, his knees grinding into the gritty soil. He fell to his hands and knees, nearly howling from his sense of loss. I couldn't touch him. I couldn't comfort him. I hovered near him, willing, praying, that his heart would heal and heal quickly.

Emmet forced himself up and, stumbling backward, returned to Corinne's side. He sat some moments and quieted himself. When he could finally bring himself to look my way, his black eyes burned. "Somehow. Someday. I will find a way. I will bring you back. I will bring you back to this world. I will bring you back to your son. And I will bring you back to me."

He spoke of the impossible, but his devotion touched my consciousness deeply, reaching all the way down to the sacred place that had once been Mercy. Reaching all the way down to the part of me that still believed it might again be possible to *be* Mercy. In that instant, and only for that instant, she managed to push through. I offered her no resistance. Far from it, I welcomed her. For one last brief moment, Mercy Taylor lived again. She wanted so badly to comfort Emmet, to touch him and to let him feel her touch, that somehow and against all probability, she did. Anyone watching might have thought a breeze off the river had blown in to tousle his lengthening curls, but Emmet, Mercy, and I, we all knew better. It hadn't been the wind at all.

THIRTY-SEVEN

Two straight weeks of ninety-eight degrees and ninety-nine percent humidity. It was crazy-making weather, and the people of Savannah had begun to snap. Twelve assaults and three murders in forty-eight hours. Adam felt sure that the strain on the power grid that knocked out folks' air-conditioning had been a conspirator in at least one of the deaths.

"We're too soft, too spoiled," he said to a uniformed officer as they left the site of that crime. "We lose a little bit of comfort, and we go off our heads and start killing people." He felt a tad hypocritical as he cranked the patrol car's air up to high.

"Maybe, but damn," the officer replied, "it's like walking in dog's breath out there."

Adam experienced a slight jolt, a memory almost rising but then falling away, lost just beyond his ability to recall. Someone he once knew used to say that, but he would be damned if he could remember who. *Sucks getting old*, he thought to himself. He checked his watch. Three thirty. He had time to file his report and make it over to the Taylors' place in time. If Savannah's citizens could manage not to kill each other for a few more hours, he might just be able to enjoy Jordan's party.

Grace had originally wanted to hold the event at a fancy restaurant, but Jordan had stepped forward and said he wanted something much more simple. Adam's wallet had given a sigh of relief. Things had taken a truly odd twist, though, when Iris volunteered to host the get-together, and Grace had agreed. Adam knew happy endings were at least in theory possible, but he had never even let himself begin to hope that Grace's family and Oliver's people would not only declare a truce, but start making nice. Of course, it helped that, truth be told, they were all really one big family. Right now, it looked like they might end up as one big happy family, but Adam didn't feel it was safe to relax just yet. It was still early days, he reminded himself.

Precisely at five, he moved the marker next to his name to show he was off duty. Other municipalities had long since moved over to electronic sign-ins, but Adam appreciated the old name board. Savannah could be infuriatingly slow and resistant to change, but sometimes that reticence seemed like a good thing.

Outside the station, the sky had turned the color of polished steel. Rumbles from distant thunder suggested one hell of a boomer. An enormous streak of lightning ripped apart the sky. Adam's sense of direction told him that it must have hit somewhere in the no-man's-land off Randolph Street, near where Normandy Street petered out, north of the cemetery and west of the golf course. He braced himself for a massive clap of thunder, but none came. In fact the world seemed somehow hushed, lying silent in expectation. Another flash lit up the sky, and Adam would have sworn under oath that the bolt had hit in the exact same spot, but again no sound followed it. His skin tingled, and the hair on the back of his neck stood on end. He reached up and wiped the odd sensation away, then bounded across the parking lot to his own car, diving in before he might witness a third strike.

On a nice day, he would have walked. The Taylor house was well within walking distance of the station, but he didn't want to risk it in this weather. Yeah, it was the weather setting him on edge, not the deepening conviction that this silent lightning was somehow otherworldly in origin.

He pulled up to the house and parked in the street so the driveway would be clear for the other guests. He killed the ignition and applied the emergency brake. He scanned the horizon, and the look of the sky continued to disquiet him. It had turned darker, somehow shinier, like it had been carved from a huge chunk of hematite. Another flash. His internal barometer was telling him that the pressure building up out there had little if anything to do with the natural atmosphere. He got out of the car and was instantly buffeted by a tingling current that filled the air. Well, if this weirdness was due to magic, he was certainly at the right place to find out what was going on.

He took quick steps at first, but then his speed caused him to feel embarrassed and cowardly. He slowed his pace and circled around the house to the kitchen's entrance. He didn't bother to knock. He was past that point now; he was family.

He stepped over the threshold to find the usually inhabited room entirely empty. "Hello?" he called. Iris's best china and polished silver sat on the counter. In spite of the weirdness he felt while on the other side of the door, Adam smiled. It made Adam feel good that Iris was offering the best she had to honor his son. The Taylor women had been busy; the table was covered with various delectable-looking baked goods. He grabbed a cookie on his way past the table, and pushed through the swinging door into the hall.

"Oliver?" he called out. "Iris?" The entire house shook, rattled by the thunder that had until that moment held its peace. It was like the sound of the strikes he had witnessed had held off commenting until that very moment, when they could do so as one. Adam jumped and dropped his cookie. "Damn," he said and swiped the cookie off the floor. It wasn't like him to be so jittery.

The rage of the thunder had left him momentarily deaf to any sound other than the ringing of his own ears, but soon another sound, a furious cry, broke through. Adam made his way down the hall to the foot of the stairs. He heard voices coming from above, the loudest of which was baby Colin's. Another ear-piercing screech followed by the lower sounds of Iris's and Ellen's voices.

He shoved the cookie into his coat pocket and made his way upstairs. The nursery lay near the end of the long upper floor, toward the right. He followed the cacophony of the baby's cries. As he neared, he heard the sound of Ellen's attempts to console the little guy.

He came up to the door and stood in the threshold. Poor Maisie sat hunched over sobbing in the nursing chair. Iris knelt beside her trying to calm her as Ellen carried Colin around, patting his back and doing her best to console him.

"He teething?" Adam asked, causing the women to turn quickly toward him.

"No," Iris said, her hand still resting on Maisie's back. "We aren't sure quite what's wrong with him."

"He isn't sick," Ellen said, just before the child let out another shriek.

"Mama," Colin cried, and began trying to wrestle himself from Ellen's arms. She clutched him more tightly, but the boy wanted his freedom. She returned him to his crib, where he pulled himself up. He regarded Adam with a red face and wet angry eyes.

Adam entered and placed his hand on Colin's head. "What is it, little man?"

Maisie looked up, dark circles under her pained eyes. "He keeps calling for me, but every time I come near him, he starts screaming bloody murder. I don't know what to do."

Iris began rubbing large circles on her niece's back. "There, there. We will figure out what is wrong."

"Mama," Colin said and reached up to tug Adam's hand off his head.

"Do you think it may have something to do with this weather? I don't know if y'all have been outside, but there is something really weird in the air out there." As if it meant to punctuate his point, another flash of lightning lit up the window. Colin let loose with another wild shriek.

Ellen came and placed her hand on Adam's forearm. "It isn't the weather causing his distress," she said and paused for a clap of thunder. "It's his distress causing this weather."

"Okay," Adam heard himself saying. Every time he thought he had adjusted to all this witch stuff, every time he thought he had grown inured to the strangeness, the Taylors always managed to whip out one more little surprise. Adam's phone rang, and he startled. He felt a flush of anger rush through himself. He hated showing his nerves, especially in front of women he had vowed to protect. He looked at the caller ID; it was the station.

He answered it on the second ring. "Cook."

"Hey, Detective," the voice on the other end said. It was Miriam, one of his favorite uniformed officers. "I am so sorry to disturb you, I know you are off duty, and this is a big night for you and your boy—"

"What is it, Miriam?" he asked, feeling for all the world like he had just had a lifeline to normality tossed to him. He clutched on to it like a drowning man.

"Can you meet me over at the hospital? We picked up a young woman a few minutes ago. She was wandering around naked and confused."

"Drug-addled young people are hardly a novelty in Chatham County, Miriam."

"Of course, Detective, I know that. Only I don't think this girl is on anything. It's more like she has been in an accident or something."

He looked down at his watch. "No, my son's party starts in less than an hour. I can't make it right now." Something struck him as odd. The baby who had been screaming at the top of his lungs had now fallen silent, and was sitting in his crib paying what seemed like very close attention to his phone call. "Why are you calling me about this?"

"Well, when we picked her up over off Randolph—"

"I'm sorry, where?"

"Randolph," the officer repeated. "Not too far from the Baptist Center. When we picked her up, she asked for you."

"She asked for me?"

"Yes, sir," Miriam said; then Adam could hear the sound of the officer conferring with either a doctor or nurse at the emergency room.

"Who is she? What's her name?"

"She said her name is Mercy. She said you will know her."

"I'll be right there." Adam hung up the phone, never taking his eyes off Colin, who now sat before him cooing happily and clapping his hands.

"Mama," the child said and giggled.

"Something has come up," he said. Conflicting sets of memories began to fight it out in Adam's mind. Somehow, he did know this Mercy, but somehow he knew the world in which he had known her was a very different place from where he now stood. A sense of free fall, the sight of the ground rushing up beneath him gave way to a sense of being caught. *Mercy*, the name acted like a key, unlocking parts of him that had ceased to exist. He tore his eyes away from the baby and focused on the women. "Tell Jordan and Oliver I will be back as soon as possible." He knew Grace would be furious with him, but he couldn't worry about that right now. "This is an emergency. I've got to see to it," he said, backing up. The sky beyond the window caught his eye. In a mere instant it had changed from steel to cerulean. No, that's not the name he knew that color by. He knew it as "haint blue."

THIRTY-EIGHT

"So tell me, am I dead or not dead?" my cousin Paul asked, his complexion paling as he realized what my return could mean to him.

My aunts had been glued to my side from the moment Adam had walked me into the house. I sat now on the foot of Ellen's bed, wrapped in one of her light robes. Oliver had spun the chair of Ellen's makeup mirror around and stared at me in dumbfounded wonder.

I no longer had the nearly omniscient awareness of the line. I was no longer part of the line. I was just me. Mercy. Its secrets were no longer mine, and I was quickly forgetting the few bits of arcane knowledge I had brought back with me. I looked at my cousin, and searched his face for the boy I had known, the boy who had died. Two possibilities—alive or dead—balanced in the flux of what now passed for reality. My mind flashed back for a moment on Schrödinger's cat. Here was a wave I intended to collapse once and for all.

"If you were dead, I don't think you would be here to ask me that question." Somehow Colin had managed to extract me without undoing the changes the line had made on my behalf. At least it appeared so for now, although time might prove otherwise.

"Of course you're alive. We both are. We all are," Oliver said as he abandoned his chair to come and stand before me. He put his hand under my chin and drew my eyes up to meet his. He held me there some moments, staring deeply into my soul. Finally he shook the finger of his other hand in my face. "Gingersnap, don't you ever do that again."

"I don't think you have to worry about that," I said. He smiled and let go of me. I tried to return his smile but I couldn't. I had to see my son. I had to hold him. My eyes danced over to Ellen's alarm clock, and I confirmed another half hour had passed. Iris had promised me that Maisie would bring him up an hour ago. "What is keeping Maisie? And where is Peter?" I pushed myself up to my feet, but Ellen grasped my forearm, pulling me back down.

"They'll be here in just a bit. Oli, why don't you go see what is keeping them?"

A guilty and worried glance passed between her and Oliver. I tried to project my awareness out, to read their thoughts, but I got nothing. I tried to send out a psychic ping through the house to locate my son. Nothing. My hearing alerted me that the house had many visitors, but my magic failed to return me any knowledge beyond what my human senses could provide.

"Sure thing," Oliver said, another less genuine smile on his lips. He turned.

"Wait," I said. "What are you not telling me?"

Iris slid off the bed and knelt at my side near my feet. She looked up at me and took both my hands. "My darling girl, you cannot begin to comprehend how happy we are to have you with us. How grateful we are to whatever force brought you home . . ."

"It was Colin," I said. In one moment, my consciousness stretched out over the whole globe. I could see and access every point at once, regardless of the miles, regardless of whether the common sense of time said it lay forward or backward. I was the line and nothing more than the line. The construct that had been Mercy Taylor was merely a sleight of hand perpetrated by a heartless witch on an unsuspecting world. Still, the line remembered Mercy, and cherished her memory like a fond dream. But the line had awakened, and the dream was no more.

Then came the call. The inescapable magic of the first word spoken by a little witch who had not forgotten his true mother, no matter how much he loved the woman who had been left as a surrogate. "Mama." A one-word spell, so charged with my little boy's hybrid magic that it caused me to surface and break free from the consciousness in which I had been absorbed. I was alive again, and I was myself. Like one bubble rising and breaking off from another, I was again whole. I was myself. "Colin's magic brought me here. One minute I didn't even exist. The next I found myself standing at the heart of Jilo's crossroads."

"That's precisely it. It is so wonderful, so magical. But it happened in the blink of an eye. Two very separate paths reunited at the crossroads. One where you never happened, and the other where you lie at the core of our hearts. It's all so sudden. So terribly disconcerting."

Her cautious tone sent a chill down my spine. "Where is Maisie? Where is my son?"

Paul stepped over the threshold. "You should tell her—" he began, but a look from his mother stopped him cold.

"Tell me what?" I looked first to Paul to continue, but he lowered his head and left the room. "Tell me what?" I pulled my hands from Iris's grasp.

"Now, don't get yourself all worked up," Oliver said. "Maisie is just a little freaked out right now. Maisie has gone out with Colin, but don't worry, Peter is with them."

"She doesn't want me here," I said, deflated, worried that we were about to start the same sad story all over again.

"Of course she does," Ellen said, stroking my hair, "but Maisie is bound to feel conflicted. After all, you gave her your life, and now you're back."

Before I could respond, the sound of angry voices carried up the stairs. Most I did not recognize, but one foghorn baritone was unmistakable. "I know she is here. I feel it. I demand to see her." I bounded off the bed, pushing past Iris and pulling the flimsy material of Ellen's robe tightly around me. I ran down the hall, arriving at the head of the stairway just as Emmet found the foot of the stairs. He stood head and shoulders over those who were trying to block his access to the upper floor. I wanted to rush down the steps to him, but I stopped, uncertain as to what he would be feeling. Would his anger over what the line had done to him carry over to me? He was still linked as the anchor to the line, but I was no longer a part of the line. Now that I was back to being Mercy— just Mercy—who were we to each other?

"I should have realized," he said when he first laid eyes on me, "that the little one was the key." His eyes burned with both love and a passion I found hard to resist. Emmet pushed through those between us and held his hand out to me. I took a step toward him, and he toward me. We met in the middle.

He stared deeply into my eyes. I knew he wanted to touch me, but was afraid to, lest his hand pass clean through. I took his hand in mine. His chest heaved, and his eyes closed as his face smoothed with relief. He squeezed my hand gently and opened his eyes. "I know now is not the time for making decisions," he said, whisking me up into his arms so that my feet couldn't even touch the ground. He began carrying me down the stairs. "But when you get around to making those decisions, remember that I am the one who never left. I am the one who never forgot." Yes, I would remember these things, but once, in another life, I had made a vow, and it was not one I made lightly.

Emmet carried me to our rarely used living room and sat me on a loveseat there. He sat down next to me, his frame taking up most of the loveseat, but I didn't mind. I loved feeling him close to me. Confusion reigned as my newly extended family circled around us. All eyes were on me, and I watched as the sparks reignited in these eyes, as those who had known me recognized me, and those who hadn't stretched their awareness to make room.

A handsome young man with more than a passing resemblance to Adam caught my eye. "You must be Jordan."

"Yes, that's right," he said, but then seemed to find himself at a loss for words. His mother, Grace, so wonderfully alive, so not an angry spirit out for my uncle's blood, stood next to him, a cautious look in her eye.

"I'm sorry for hijacking your party," I said.

A smile broke out on Jordan's face. "No, girl, that is more than all right. I became a doctor. You came back from the dead or whatever. You win." He didn't have Paul's magic. He couldn't see that he himself had pulled a kind of Lazarus. I for one did not feel the need to alert him to that fact.

A child's squeal of delight caught my attention, and my eyes darted to the room's entrance. Peter's bright-red hair registered first, then the sight of my sister's tearstained face. I would address her pain. I would. But now all that mattered was the ginger-haired little boy squirming in her arms. Colin reached both arms out to me. "Mama."

"Let's give them a bit of privacy," I heard Oliver's voice command. Whether it was his magic or just good manners, everyone obeyed. Everyone except Emmet. I placed my hand on his arm and nodded.

He looked at me with narrowed eyes and a tight mouth, but he stood. "I will be in the garden, waiting."

"While you're there," Oliver said, "maybe you could do something about patching that pothole you left in the driveway." Emmet pulled his shoulders back and glared at Oliver. Oliver threw his hands back in a gesture of surrender. "Just kidding. Just kidding. Grow a sense of humor, Sandman. Trying to diffuse a tense moment. That's all."

Emmet turned back and winked at me, then followed Oliver from the room.

Colin began fussing, straining with more force in Maisie's arms, reaching out toward me. Maisie took a few reluctant steps toward me, looking for all the world as if she were heading to her own execution. Her head was held low. She wouldn't make eye contact with me. I patted the seat Emmet had vacated, and she joined me. Colin escaped her grasp and pulled himself into my arms. I clutched him tightly to me, closing my eyes and breathing him in. I willed everything else in the world to go away, at least for an instant, so that I could take this experience in, engrave its memory on my soul. For this moment, he was mine and mine alone. Colin cooed happily, placing slobbery kisses on my cheek. Then it was time to open my eyes and learn how to share.

Peter hovered over us, standing nearly at attention. I smiled at him, and his eyes warmed. "God, it's good to see you." His eyes slid from me to Maisie and then back to me. "Especially together." He raised his eyebrows and sighed. "What the hell happened? How did we get here?" I studied his face, wondering what, if anything, he remembered of his journey to the Fae.

"More importantly," I said, tightening one arm around Colin and reaching out to him with the other, "where do we go from here?" He hesitated, casting a worried glance at Maisie, but took my hand. "I love you so much, Peter. I do." He acknowledged my words with a bob of his head followed by tears that rolled down his cheeks. He let go of my hand and wiped away his tears. "I'm not trying to cut you out. Believe me. But I need a bit of time alone with my sister. Can you give us that?"

"Yeah," he said, although I knew he was tapping into his deepest resource of strength to say so. "I'll wait for you outside," he said, then seemed to remember Emmet had claimed the garden as his own. "On the side porch." I noticed his eyes had been on Maisie when he said this. It was Maisie he would be waiting for, and maybe that was right. He turned and exited through the house's front door.

We sat together without speaking, searching for words, waiting for our feelings to settle enough to allow us to say them.

"I feel like I am Colin's mother," Maisie said after a long and uncomfortable silence. I knew Ellen was right. Maisie was bound to be conflicted in her emotions. She finally raised her eyes to meet mine. I could read in them that she was genuinely happy to the root of her soul to have her sister back, but she was worried about the costs. "I feel like I am Peter's wife."

"That's because you are both those things."

"But you are too." She wrapped her arms around herself.

I placed a lingering kiss on the top of Colin's head, and then shifted him over toward her. "Here," I said, fighting the urge to hold tightly on to my boy.

She reached out for him, and he did not resist. His bright eyes, one green, one blue, filled with laughter. Laughter and knowing. Maisie pulled him into a desperate grasp and cried till she could cry no more.

"I don't know how," I said, stroking her hair, "but we will work this all out. There is room in Colin's life for more than one mother."

"And in Peter's life?"

The way Peter's eyes had remained fixed on Maisie as he spoke led me to think his heart had already made its choice. Still, I decided not to respond right off. It would take a while for things to settle, for us to figure everything out. Peter and Maisie and I, and yes, Emmet too, we would need to have some very honest conversations to decide how we fit now within each other's lives. But we could start with what we had in common: our shared love for Colin.

In time we would figure everything out. We would find a way to adjust as the two warring timelines, the two sets of memories, settled and made peace with each other. All that mattered now was that we were together. Everything else would eventually fall into place. All I really cared about today was spending time with the most important man in my life, my son.

EPILOGUE

September brought blue skies and bearable temperatures. It also brought a special delivery in a large cardboard box. I ventured into our garage, where my battered old bike, perhaps my first true friend, leaned against the wall waiting for me. I oiled the chain and wheeled it out into the drive, where the box was still sitting. Just for the heck of it, I pointed my finger at the box and willed it to open. I was delighted when it remained sealed and sitting exactly where it was.

When I was returned to this reality, I had been separated from magic. Perhaps that was the price of my return ticket. I was completely and utterly powerless, no longer a magical being. I had come back to this world as an ordinary person, and I couldn't have been more happy about that.

I went back to the garage and dug out a box cutter and a wrench. The sharp blade cut through the packaging to reveal the neon-orange trailer I had purchased for my boy. It clashed with the pink bike even worse than Jilo's chair had clashed with her cooler, but we were certain to be visible. I wheeled the trailer around to the back tire of my bike and after a cursory glance at the instructions attempted to connect the two. Then, realizing I had done it all wrong, I went back and read the instructions. Everything by hand now. No more magic, and that made me feel so good I very nearly broke down and cried with relief.

But I didn't cry. Instead I bundled up the cardboard and put it in with the rest of the recycling. I hopped on my bike and did a quick circle around the block to make sure everything worked right, then returned to the drive. I went inside to wash the oil from my hands, then made my way upstairs to the nursery where Colin sat happily waiting for me. He clapped his hands and laughed as I came through the door.

"We are all set," I said, reaching into the playpen to lift up my boy. I kissed his cheek, then the top of his head. I pressed my nose against him, breathing him in. Cherishing his realness. My realness.

"Okay, little man," I said and planted another kiss on his forehead. "Mama hopes you are ready, 'cause she is going to take you on a tour and tell you some black and wicked lies about the people of our dear home." He squealed happily in response. "Now, you might ask why your mama would make up lies about a city with so many interesting true stories to tell." I gave his round tummy a gentle poke. "Go on, ask . . ."

Acknowledgments

I would like to thank my spouse, Rich Weissman, and my wonderful stepdaughters, Rebecca and Madeline, for their continued loving support and encouragement, my agent Susan Finesman of Fine Literary, and the amazing team at 47North, especially Jason Kirk and Nicci Jordan Hubert who stepped in to edit the conclusion of the trilogy and ended up walking me through at least nineteen nervous breakdowns. Thanks also to my literary midwife, Kristen Weber, who's been with me since word one. A very special thank you to David Pomerico for signing me for the series, and to Angela Polidoro for her work on the first two Witching Savannah books. Finally, no list of acknowledgements would be complete without a heartfelt thank you to my furry co-authors, Duke and Sugar.

ABOUT THE AUTHOR

© 2013 Levy Moroshan

J.D. Horn was raised in rural Tennessee and has carried a bit of its red clay with him while traveling the world, from Hollywood to Paris to Tokyo. He studied comparative literature as an undergrad, focusing on French and Russian in particular. He also holds an MBA in international business and worked as a financial analyst before becoming a novelist. Along with his spouse, Rich, and his furry co-authors, Duke and Sugar, he divides his time between Portland, Oregon, and San Francisco, California.